And This
Shall Be for
Music

And This Shall Be for Music

Susan Moore Jordan

Shaggy Dog Productions, LLC

This is a work of fiction. All incidents and dialogue, and all characters (with the exception of Aimee Mullins and the late Paul Kellogg), are products of the author's imagination and are not to be construed as real. Where real-life historical figures appear, the situations, incidents, and dialogues concerning those persons are fictional and are not intended to depict actual events, with one exception, or to change the entirely fictional nature of the work. In all other respects, any resemblance to actual persons, living or dead, is entirely coincidental.

Aimee Mullins, American athlete, actress, and motivational speaker, continues to be an inspiration.

The speech given by Paul Kellogg at the opening of the New York City Opera season on September 16, 2001, appears as it was reported.

ISBN: 978-1-950625-22-2

Published by Shaggy Dog Productions, LLC

Library of Congress Control Number: 2022917989

Cover design and art by Wesley Goulart

Books by Susan Moore Jordan

The *Carousel* Trilogy:
How I Grew Up
Eli's Heart
You Are My Song

Jamie's Children

The Cameron Saga:
Memories of Jake
Man with No Yesterdays

And This Shall Be for Music

"More Fog, Please"
(non-fiction)

Augusta McKee Mysteries:
The Case of the Slain Soprano
The Case of the Disappearing Director
The Case of the Toxic Tenor
The Case of the Purloined Professor
The Case of the Chrysanthemum Murders
The Case of the Unearthed Evidence
The Case of the 'Carousel' Killer
The Case of the Bogus Beatle

Table of Contents

PART ONE

Chapter 1 13

Chapter 2 19

Chapter 3 39

Chapter 4 55

Chapter 5 71

Chapter 6 83

Chapter 7 97

Chapter 8 111

Chapter 9 125

Chapter 10 141

Chapter 11 157

Chapter 12 163

Chapter 13 181

Chapter 14 195

Chapter 15 213

Chapter 16 227

PART TWO

Chapter 17 243

Chapter 18 259

Chapter 19 275

Chapter 20 289

Chapter 21 305

Chapter 22 321

Chapter 23 335

Chapter 24 351

Chapter 25 365

Chapter 26 381

Chapter 27 397

Chapter 28 409

Chapter 29 425

Chapter 30 441

Chapter 31 457

Chapter 32 471

Acknowledgments 485

Videography..489

Recurring Characters 490

About the Author 491

For the Music Makers
and the Healers

Music can heal and inspire, calm and incite.
It can lighten the dark corners of the mind
and soothe the pain of a wounded spirit
or a broken heart.
It is the most powerful force in the universe,
and how we share it can make a difference
in the lives of many.

PART ONE

Music is enough for a lifetime,
but a lifetime is not enough for music.

—Sergei Rachmaninoff

Susan Moore Jordan

Chapter 1

March 1996

There's something wrong with the soundtrack in my dream. Merritt and I are singing the Don José-Micaëla duet from Carmen and David is at the piano, and all three of us are nailing this thing. Only it's not a recital, it's the Conservatory production, so we're in costume, and David is in the orchestra pit making his piano sound like a full orchestra. But one note in that orchestra doesn't sound right. It's out of tune…it keeps ringing and ringing….

The ringing telephone dragged me out of my lovely dream. I heard the answering machine pick up, all three of us talking: "You've reached David, Lindsey, and Merritt. Leave a message." The caller hung up and I turned over, trying to find my way back into my dream.

But the phone started ringing again, and I sat bolt upright. *Something's wrong.* I glanced at my watch: after midnight, twelve-thirty a.m. I raced to the phone, picked it up, and heard Leah Rosenthal's voice. She didn't even wait for me to say hello.

"Lindsey, sweetheart, there's been a terrible accident."

"What?" It came out like a croak.

"I'm here at Good Samaritan Hospital with Merritt's mom and dad, and we need you to come right away. Merritt's being taken in for surgery."

Leah's voice sounded odd, strained. *Oh God. David.*

My knees started to give way. I could hardly breathe and I pressed my back against the wall to keep from falling.

"Leah, where's David?" I heard the panic in my voice.

A pause. "Just get here as quickly as you can. We need you here."

"Leah, what's happened? *Where is David?* You have to tell me." *No. I don't want to hear this. I know what you're going to say.*

She said softly, "David was…David's left us, Lindsey. My beautiful son is gone."

I slid down the wall, clutching the phone. "Oh, my God, Leah," I whispered, unable to get much sound out. "I'm so…so, *so*, sorry."

"I know." Her voice a whisper, and I could tell she was about to break down. But she paused a moment, sounding stronger when she added, "The Nobles need us, sweetheart. You need to be here."

"Yes. I'll get a cab and...." My voice trailed off. "I'll get there as quickly as I can."

I found it hard to think. I threw on jeans and a sweater, called a cab while I pulled a brush through my tangled hair. *It's chilly for late March.* I pulled on a coat and grabbed my purse, ran outside, and the cab arrived in minutes.

"Good Samaritan Hospital, please."

"Emergency entrance?" I wondered how many times he'd had this kind of fare.

"Yes, I guess. Yes, emergency entrance."

Good Sam was close to the University of Cincinnati, and during the short ride my thoughts were about my boys. Automobile accident, obviously. *But Merritt's such a careful driver. Maybe hit by a drunk? God, this is so awful.* My mind jumped to my senior recital, only weeks away. David was my

14

pianist. *Well, not anymore. And I guess I can scratch singing the duet with Merritt.*

Lindsey Cameron, you are a terrible person. How can you be thinking about this when David is dead and Merritt…God knows what is going on with him. It has to be bad, though.

I reached into my wallet with numb fingers for bills to pay the cab driver—and saw the photo, David and Merritt smiling at me. A picture I snapped two weeks earlier at their commitment ceremony. *My beautiful boys, looking so happy, and now…*I choked back the tears. *Hold it together, Lindsey.*

Leah was waiting for me when I walked in. "We have to take an elevator to the fourth floor," she said.

I just stared at her. *She seems so…composed.* "Do you know what happened? How badly was Merritt hurt?"

"Merritt's condition is critical," she replied, answering the second part of my question first. "We'll know more after the surgery." We stopped at a bank of elevators. "We don't know much, but the police told us it was some kind of freak accident. They'd parked and just gotten out of Merritt's car. They were hit by a pickup truck that jumped the curb for some reason."

How can she be so calm? It hasn't really hit her yet. Her son…she's never going to see him again. David is…was…the light of her life.

A tone sounded, the "up" arrow flashed and the elevator doors slid open, stirring the air, more felt than heard. *It's so quiet here in the middle of the night.*

"One thing I'm grateful for: David apparently died instantly." Leah put out a hand and leaned against the wall of the elevator. I saw her eyes fill with tears and I reached for her. We hung onto each other for a long moment, then she stepped back and wiped her eyes. "We have to be strong for Grace and Howard."

I nodded, questions racing through my head. *Where's Arthur? Out of town again? Where is David...David's body? How in the world can you be here, and be so...together?*

Eerily, it almost appeared as if she had heard me. "Arthur is in Detroit. He'll be back by noon tomorrow. David...David's body is being prepared for burial, but...I'll need to come to your house. I want him buried in his tuxedo, he would like that."

I nodded again. I knew Reform Jews had the option of selecting clothing other than a shroud for burial because David explained it not long ago. I couldn't remember how it came up, but recalling it sent a chill through me.

Leah and I walked into the surgical waiting room, and I saw Merritt's parents sitting together, clutching each other, anguish etched on their faces. I ran to them and the three of us hugged.

Grace gave me a tremulous smile. "I'm glad you're here, Lindsey. It means a lot."

"Where else would I be?" It sounded like a line from a B movie, but I meant it. I almost broke down when the dream I was yanked from came to my mind again...and I saw Merritt vividly, heard his beautiful voice in my head. Grace and Howard returned to the sofa and Leah and I sat on a loveseat facing them.

I hate hospital waiting rooms. I haven't been in many, but they all seem the same. The lights are too bright. The smells are too medicinal, but I guess that comes with the territory. They all have the same quasi-comfortable furniture and tables with six-month-old magazines tastefully arranged on them. The same large potted plants that are probably artificial, a couple of vases with flowers in them that look too perfect to be real.

None of us spoke. What was there to say? I shivered and pulled my coat tighter, trying to get warm. Something else about a hospital waiting room: they are always cold. I glanced at the wall clock: two a.m. *How long has it been since Leah called me?* I couldn't remember.

The Nobles must be going through hell.

I flipped through a magazine, not even seeing what was on the pages, and glanced at the clock again. Two-fifteen. I wanted to get up and walk around, but decided it would be insensitive. Leah sat quietly. Grace and Howard held hands, their eyes closed. *I know they're praying for Merritt.* I closed my eyes and had a vivid picture in my mind of Merritt's engaging smile as he sang to me at our rehearsal. Mere hours ago…and I said a prayer of my own. *Please, God, let him live.*

Another fifteen minutes passed. I recalled seeing a coffee machine just outside the elevator and asked, in a voice that sounded tiny and shaky, "Can I get anyone coffee?"

Howard and Grace shook their heads no but Leah replied, "I'd like some, Lindsey. Black, please. Thank you."

Fumbling in the bottom of my purse for change, I grabbed a handful. My hands started shaking when I stood at the machine, and it took me three tries to insert coins for Leah's coffee. The rest of them spilled to the floor, and I went down on my knees to retrieve them.

That's when I lost it. I started sobbing uncontrollably, my tears falling on my hands, on the coins, on the floor. I wanted to stretch out right there and wail. Instead, I forced myself to stand and walk into the ladies' room, dampened a paper towel and pressed it against my face. The sobs came again and I had to lean against the vanity to steady myself.

I want to call my parents. I need them here. Call in the morning, Lindsey. What can they do tonight? I wiped my face and remembered Leah's coffee. It was still sitting there in the machine, so I collected it and took it to her. She accepted it and when I sat down, she put an arm around me and I leaned against

17

her. *Her son just died in a horrible accident and she's comforting me.*

Three a.m. A doctor in scrubs wearing a somber look on his face came in and all four of us came to full attention. My heart started pounding in my ears. But he went to a group of people in another corner of the room and we relaxed a bit. Leah let out a little sigh and I looked at her more closely, seeing the strain and sorrow etched on her face.

David is dead. I tried to grasp it. *David is dead.* It felt like a kick in my gut. Beautiful, gifted, kind, funny, gentle, passionate David, a pianist with a brilliant future. If any of the three of us could make it in the music world, Merritt and I were always sure it would be David.

And now he's gone. Just like that. In the proverbial blink of an eye.

Merritt may survive this crash…but will he be strong enough to survive losing David?

Chapter 2

The good news: Merritt would survive.

The bad news: his right leg had to be amputated below the knee. He had three broken ribs. The severity of his head injury was still a question mark and would be for at least another day or two because he was now in a medically-induced coma.

When Lindsey finally left Good Samaritan Hospital after six in the morning, Leah Rosenthal went to the house with her to collect David's tuxedo. The burial would be at seven that evening…within the twenty-four-hour period observed by Jews. It would be preceded by a brief service at Rockdale Temple.

Lindsey hesitated before going upstairs to David's room. Going into the room would make it too real. *David is never coming back here.*

"I'll get it, Lindsey," Leah offered. Lindsey waited downstairs, trying to focus, trying to process what had just happened.

Waiting made her aware of how empty the house felt. How quiet it was. She offered to go to the funeral home with Leah who told her, "No, you look exhausted. Try to get some rest and I'll see you this evening." As Leah left, they exchanged a sad but somehow comforting hug.

Lindsey didn't call her parents until almost eight, lifting a handset that felt far too heavy, dialing with numb fingers.

Andrew answered the phone. When she heard her father's voice, a voice she knew and loved so well, Lindsey immediately ached for his presence. Fighting to control herself, she choked out, "Daddy...something awful...David is dead...Merritt was badly hurt...." She began sobbing, unable to continue.

"Oh, my God, Lindsey, what happened? Please try to calm down, sweetheart, and talk to me. Do you need us to fly out there?"

She gulped back the tears and tried to stop shaking. "Yes. I need you and Mom to come to Cincinnati." The words spilled out. "There was a terrible auto accident last night and David was killed."

It pained Lindsey to hear the words coming out of her mouth, but she forced herself to continue. "Merritt had to have surgery and he's...he had a leg amputated below the knee and he had a head injury and...he's going to be in the hospital for...I don't know how long."

"We'll get there as soon as we can, Linds. Were you hurt?"

"No, I wasn't with them." She shook her head, even though she knew her father couldn't see her. "They just...they just went to a movie and were going to stop for a drink on their way home. I didn't go because I was tired after my rehearsal with David. Leah Rosenthal called me from Good Sam to tell me...."

"Where are you now?"

"I'm at home, by myself. Leah was here...to get David's tuxedo...." Overwhelmed, Lindsey clutched the phone and again began to sob as she leaned against the wall.

"I'm sorry I'm not there right this minute, Lindsey, so I could hold you tight. You know I'm holding you in my heart." It was something he always said. *Holding you in my heart.*

Lindsey managed to control the tears as she felt her father's love, even at this distance.

"I don't know what to do, Daddy." Lindsey swallowed hard.

"Do you think it would help you to listen to music? That's what I always do when I'm dealing with something that feels overwhelming," Andrew said.

"Yes, I know. You always listen to the Brahms Requiem."

"I find it comforting. I'm sure you have a recording. Why not try that? Just sit and listen to it, and think about what it's saying to you, sweetheart." He paused for a moment. "I'll put it on here, too. Even though we're many miles apart, in that way we can feel we're together."

My sweet father. How caring he is. "Yes, Daddy. I'll do that." *He's giving me a goal, something to focus on instead of this grief that I can't even comprehend.*

"Mom or I will call you as soon as we have plane reservations. I love you, Lindsey."

"I love you too, Dad. Please hug Mom for me."

Still weeping, Lindsey searched through the CD collection, barely able to see. She found the CD of Brahms' *German Requiem*, managed to get it onto the player, and curled up in the big armchair they bought when they first moved into the house. *'Perfect for listening to music,' David had said.* The thought brought a fresh burst of tears.

Listening to the Brahms—her father's favorite piece of music—calmed and comforted her. Such an affirmation of God's love, of the continuation of life. It had been introduced to her in that way as a child, and it was how she always thought of it.

Lindsey's mother called back within a half-hour; they were able to get an early flight from the Philadelphia Airport and should be at her house by one, in time to attend David's funeral. Something to hold onto. But the best news was that M.J. would be with them. A student at the University of Pennsylvania, Maxwell Jacob Cameron had a light class schedule for a couple of days and was sure he could make up the work. Lindsey's whole family would be with her when she most needed them.

She returned to the big armchair as she listened to the rest of the Brahms Requiem, and tried not to feel so empty, so terribly sad. *I wish it was twenty-four hours ago and I was looking forward to rehearsing with David for my recital, and that the phone call never happened, and my boys would be coming out of their room soon, and we'd be in the kitchen fixing breakfast...but the phone call did happen. David will never be in this house again.*

With a sigh, Lindsey closed her eyes, listening to the comforting music and thinking back to happier times, to when she first met David Rosenthal and Merritt Noble.

***

In September of 1992, her freshman year at the Cincinnati Conservatory, Lindsey's parents, along with her brother M.J., drove her from their home in West Chester, Pennsylvania, to the campus. Lindsey had asked if she could have a private dorm room, and her parents had agreed. Lindsey tended to be very "choosy"—M.J.'s word—about who her friends were, and a private room would avoid a possible conflict.

Her father, Andrew Cameron, had earned recognition as a major talent in the art world, with paintings on display in museums internationally. Lindsey's mother, Mary, a pianist, had given her daughter piano lessons and encouraged her in her musical development. M.J., two years younger than Lindsey, managed to keep his sister from being too impressed with herself. And while she complained about his usually humorous but very pointed remarks, secretly Lindsey knew those comments helped her maintain some humility.

Unlike Lindsey, who admitted she could be standoffish, M.J. liked everybody and was well-liked in return. She appreciated having him there her first day. After he and her parents helped her set up her dormitory room and checked out the campus, Lindsey's family left early the next morning.

M.J. pulled his sister aside before he got into the car. "Be nice. Remember, you're not the star of this campus and you're going to meet a lot of people who have at least as much talent as you do. Maybe more."

"I know that," Lindsey said, a little miffed.

"I'm not sure you do. Way too many people back home have told you far too often how great you are." He grinned. "And you are, I won't deny that. Try to relax, will you? You aren't going to sing at the Met Opera by the end of this year."

"I know that, too," Lindsey laughed. "I have years and years of hard work ahead of me. I'm going to miss you, little brother."

"I'll write. And I'll call. Try to enjoy college, at least some of the time. Promise me."

"I promise. And of course, I'll be nice to people. I'm always nice. My parents raised me right."

That evening she met many of her classmates at the Freshman Mixer. Her first impressions of most were less than favorable, but she liked David Rosenthal and Merritt Noble immediately. They were both from Cincinnati and took turns entertaining her with stories about the high schools they had attended. Both were in advanced music programs in city schools and they'd crossed paths over the years at a number of festivals and performances. Lindsey also learned she and

Merritt were in the same studio at the Conservatory, under the tutelage of the highly respected Claudia Prince.

During the next week, Lindsey saw both young men in three of her classes, among them the top section of Music Theory. Lindsey well knew that Music Theory was a *thing* in any college music degree program. *It's what separates the serious, dedicated musicians from the dilettantes. If you can't get through two years of Music Theory, you can't graduate...end of your dream. That always surprises non-musicians, who often have the absurd idea a Bachelor of Music isn't a legit degree.*

On the fourth day of classes, Lindsey spotted David seated by himself at a table when she went to the cafeteria for lunch, and decided to join him.

He glanced up when she placed her tray on the table. "Hi, David. We met at the mixer, and it seems we have some classes together," she said. "I'm Lindsey Cameron."

"I know who you are." Lindsey liked the grin David gave her, sweet and a little self-effacing. "The lady with the gorgeous soprano voice. When it's your turn to sight read, I don't even bother pretending to watch the notes...I'm caught up in wishing you were singing 'Caro nome' or maybe some French art song."

Pleased, Lindsey laughed along with him.

"Well, I've heard that you're an exceptional pianist. Famous all over Cincinnati. Child prodigy type." She sprinkled dressing sparingly on her salad.

David blushed and took a bite of his hamburger. As he chewed, he commented, "Um, that's hardly going to get me a major recording contract."

I like this young man. He makes me laugh. I think we'll be friends.

Almost immediately, Merritt joined them. David's eyes shone when he looked at Merritt. *Definitely more than just tenor-worship*, Lindsey thought. *A full-out crush.*

"Lindsey Cameron, I'd like to sing with you," Merritt said, without any preamble. "With that voice, you have to be a vocal performance major."

"You should hear Merritt, Lindsey," David said, never taking his eyes off Merritt as he spoke. "I've been helping him with a couple of Strauss songs."

"It surprised me when you guys told me you've known each other for a couple of years, since you didn't go to the same high school."

"The music community is pretty tight in Cincinnati," David explained. "Even at the high school level. I saw Merritt perform at Walnut Hills High School last year when he played Charlie Dalrymple in *Brigadoon*. He was great."

"Is that what you want? Musical theater?" Lindsey asked Merritt.

"Actually, I hope to sing opera. Is that your dream as well, lovely Lindsey?" Merritt continued, "Singing at the Met by the time you're thirty?"

"Twenty-eight," Lindsey replied. "Why wait until I'm thirty? I always say if you're going to dream, dream *big*."

***

The first time Lindsey heard Merritt sing she was sitting outside her teacher's voice studio, listening to a fine tenor voice through the door. The song was a favorite of hers, Rachmaninoff's "In the Silence of Night." He sounded great until he reached for the high A near the end. It sounded slightly forced and weak, and it should have been the most exciting note in the song.

Could that be Merritt Noble? she wondered. Professor Prince stopped him and Lindsey tried to guess what she might be saying to him. *'Don't push from your throat. Let your breath do all the work. Focus the sound higher, lift your soft palate more.'* At least that's what I would have suggested.

After hearing Professor Prince's instructions, Merritt tried again and this time it was stunning, and he laughed with delight. His teacher joined in the laughter and Lindsey smiled. *I think I'm where I belong.*

The door opened and Merritt emerged. Flushed and energized by the breakthrough he'd just experienced, he grinned at her. "Fancy meeting you here."

"Funny, I was thinking the same thing. I was pretty sure I was hearing Merritt Noble."

"We're in a great studio, Lindsey. Claudia Prince is absolutely the best."

"I heard that last A you sang. Thrilling. Pretty much perfect."

"It felt great. Just a few things she pointed out to me…." He shook his head as though he could hardly believe what he'd just done. "Well, I'm holding you up. Hope your first lesson is as wonderful as mine was."

Lindsey wasn't sure what to expect at that first lesson with Professor Prince. A petite woman with auburn hair and friendly eyes, her exuberance and trim figure belied the age of 65 listed on her bio.

After taking Lindsey through some vocal warm-ups, Claudia Prince studied the sheets of paper in her hand. "You have an extensive repertoire, Lindsey, which is impressive. You've been studying voice since you were thirteen?"

"Well, actually, a little longer than that. My teacher in Philadelphia worked with me a few times before my thirteenth birthday. She's been very careful with my voice; she believes a young voice must be allowed to develop at its own pace. My voice seems to have opened up earlier than some sopranos. High notes were never a problem."

"You auditioned as a coloratura soprano, as I recall. I think one piece we heard was Douglas Moore's lovely song from *The Ballad of Baby Doe*." She motioned to her studio accompanist to move to the piano. "Will you sing some of that for me again?"

Lindsey liked "The Willow Song" and its challenges. The poignant ballad, while not strictly a coloratura aria, included an octave jump to a sustained high D. Professor Prince listened thoughtfully and dismissed the pianist when Lindsey finished, saying "We'll see you at Lindsey's next lesson, Marilyn. Thank you."

Claudia Prince sat at the piano while Lindsey stood, waiting to see what would come next.

"I'm glad you performed this song. High notes are obviously no problem for you and you navigate them well." She leaned an elbow on the piano top and laced her fingers together.

"Here's what I hear. I hear a promise of a richer sound in your voice. I believe you can sing more dramatic music than you've studied to this point, and I believe you're a lyric coloratura. Maybe a potential *leggiero* soprano, with the warmth of sound to navigate such roles as Juliette in *Roméo et Juliette* and perhaps even Violetta in *La Traviata* one day."

Lindsey had never expected to hear this. She wanted to jump up and down with delight. "Really? You think that's a possibility?"

"I'm not guaranteeing anything," Claudia laughed. "But I want to work on your middle and lower register first. We'll see how it goes. We can also work on 'Sempre libera,' but you know that one aria is only a small part of the role. And remember, I said this is a possibility for the future."

She smiled at her new student. "Don't get ahead of yourself, Lindsey. We're going to start with some Mozart—the *Exultate, jubilate*. Willis Music has it in stock, I'm sure."

"Actually, I have it. I've worked some on the 'Alleluia' section." Lindsey had always been told she was strictly a coloratura, with a light, silvery, flexible voice, able to navigate high notes with ease. Now, Professor Prince suggested that as her voice matured, she would keep the flexibility and the high notes, but her voice would have a richer, slightly darker sound.

The music Professor Prince mentioned, especially Violetta's, was the music Lindsey had always longed to sing but thought she never would, except for her own entertainment.

She floated from the studio. Despite what Professor Prince had said, she *had* to get to a practice room and at least look at "Sempre libera."

At Lindsey's next lesson, she found Merritt waiting in the hall when she came out of the studio. His lesson preceded hers, and she wondered, *What on earth is he doing here?*

"I hung around because I wanted to hear you sing something substantive," he said. "Mozart's 'Alleluia' is a terrific piece for you. You're as amazing as I knew you would be."

These were nice words from a fellow student Lindsey admired. "I don't know about that, but thanks. High praise coming from a first-class tenor."

"Well, not first-class yet...but I sure want to try to get there." They exchanged smiles; two voice students with a common goal.

"David and I thought we'd try this place off campus for lunch," Merritt said. "Wanna come with?"

"Sure, I'd like that." They strolled to the café, talking about operas they loved, roles they hoped to sing. David was already there, waiting a little impatiently.

"Oh, good." He smiled when he saw Lindsey. "I hoped you'd come." From that moment, they became a threesome. Some members of their class referred to them as "The Big Three," others found them annoying. For better or worse, though, they had bonded.

***

Cincinnati is a sprawling city and includes suburbs to the north, east, and west. The Ohio River forms its southern boundary, but small cities in Northern Kentucky also are considered suburbs. Many people crossed the river daily for work. Claudia Prince lived in Covington, Kentucky, and often hosted gatherings of her students and her studio pianists at her apartment.

David lived in the northern suburb of Amberley Village and had attended the School for Creative and Performing Arts. Merritt lived in Hyde Park, an older suburb on the eastern side of the city, and attended Walnut Hills High School. Both schools required admission exams; David also had to audition to be accepted at SCPA.

Considered something of a prodigy, David had performed with the Cincinnati Symphony on a Young People's Concert when he was sixteen and a junior in high school. The pianists in the entire school and not just the freshman class were impressed with what he had played at that young age— Rachmaninoff's Second Piano Concerto, a demanding work for a virtuoso pianist, let alone a kid. Slight of build, with large, luminous dark eyes, David looked younger than his eighteen years.

Many of the girls, upperclassmen as well as freshmen, had their eye on Merritt. Tall and athletically built, with wavy dark hair and hazel eyes, he exuded confidence and sex appeal. Lindsey was well aware he didn't respond to their sultry looks and batted eyelashes, and she suspected she knew why. Merritt confirmed it one day at lunch when he casually commented, "I want to sing with you, Lindsey, but I don't want to sleep with you. Even though you are a gorgeous blonde, blue-eyed babe who reminds everyone of Botticelli's 'Venus.'" He grinned when he said it, and she laughed.

"I kind of figured that, Merritt. I want to sing with you, too, but I'm not looking to sleep with anybody right now." The three of them laughed together, but Lindsey noticed David's blush. *Yes, I know you have a crush on Merritt. I wonder if anything will come of that.*

Both boys lived at home and commuted that first semester, but Merritt found a room to rent off-campus for the second semester, which opened the door for his friendship with David to move in a different direction.

Near the end of the spring semester, the three of them met one morning for breakfast. Lindsey gazed at the two young men as David cleared his throat and said tentatively, "Uh…Lindsey…we…uh…."

"You don't have to say a word. It's all over both your faces."

Merritt said, "We don't want this to change anything between us, I mean, you know, among the three of us."

Lindsey took a bite of her Belgian waffle. "Why would it? You're still the same guys. I like that you're together."

They both smiled, and David exhaled audibly. She put her fork down as she added, "I just don't want anybody to get hurt."

Merritt jumped in. "That isn't going to happen. I promise you. We love each other."

David blushed and said softly, "You just can't imagine how happy I am."

No, I can't, I haven't experienced that yet, Lindsey thought as she continued to eat. *I know Merritt is your first. Your first romance. Your first lover. Above all else, I don't want David to get hurt.*

Merritt may have sensed her concern because he turned to Lindsey when David left the table to get more coffee. "I really love him, Lindsey. This is real, and it's for life. I want us to be together forever. I've never felt this way about anyone."

"I hope you're being honest with me." She gazed directly at Merritt. "David is one of the best people I've ever met. I could never forgive you if you hurt him."

"That won't happen," Merritt assured her.

"Come on, Merritt. You're a tenor. A group not known for being faithful. According to some people, a whole different kind of human—remember *Men, Women, and Tenors* by Frances Alda?"

"Yeah, I've heard about that book." He gazed directly into her eyes. "This is different. David gets me, Linds. Being a tenor can be a bitch. I'm grateful for this voice, and I love to sing, but when you're a tenor people have different expectations. They listen critically to every freakin' note you sing, especially every high note. Sometimes it gets to me. David knows exactly when to praise and when to criticize. He's totally honest with me."

"The other part of that tenor mystique…a lot of people think you're stuck on yourself," she commented. "You have to know about the gossip."

"Yes, I do. On the other hand, how can you perform if you don't have confidence? How much is too much? David…well, we practice a lot together. He's making me a better musician. He also lets me know if I'm getting cocky. And I can take it from him because it's David."

Lindsey saw first-hand that David could read Merritt the riot act when he needed to be taken down a notch, and comfort him tenderly when Merritt's nerves were on edge and he was ready to throw in the towel. David had become his anchor.

It wasn't all smooth sailing, especially when they ventured off the university campus. Lindsey was shocked when she stopped at Merritt's apartment one Saturday afternoon. Merritt had a bruise on his forehead and cut over his lip…and more concerning, David's left hand sported a bandage.

"What on earth happened?" She embraced them both.

"Oh, we had a little dust-up at a gym we were thinking about joining," David said.

Lindsey carefully took his bandaged hand in both of hers. "A little 'dust-up'? This doesn't look so little to me."

"It's not broken. They X-rayed it in the ER," Merritt said calmly.

"Will one of you please tell me exactly what happened?" Lindsey demanded.

Both of them had been using the university gym periodically but sometimes found it difficult to get to the equipment they wanted, so had thought they'd join a private gym. They decided to try one they'd been told about in the Over-the-Rhine section of town.

"You two in Over-the-Rhine?" Hands on hips, Lindsey stared at each of them. "You knew some people in that area wouldn't be too welcoming of gays, right? What on earth were you thinking?"

"I guess we weren't," Merritt admitted. "Things have been pretty cool in Cincinnati recently since the AIDS epidemic is dying down."

"A couple of young guys got mouthy," David said.

"Define 'mouthy,'" Lindsey said, hands on hips.

"Oh, what you'd expect. I'm used to it, but they were really looking to harass Merritt. They wanted to know why a good-looking faggot couldn't do better than the ugly Kike fairy he was with."

"Well, what they didn't know is that David may look frail, but he's got Rachmaninoff Third Piano Concerto muscles…chest, shoulders, arms. And a mean left hook."

"I decked him, Linds," David boasted, grinning broadly. "Guy went down hard."

"I had to go after the other one, of course," Merritt continued. "This and this..." he indicated his lip and forehead… "these are nothing compared to what he got."

"A black eye for sure, and maybe a broken tooth," David said. "They took off." Both boys laughed.

"Why didn't you call the police?"

"What would have been the point? It was just another street fight. We were pretty damn lucky, for sure." Merritt grew serious. "That might have been a problem. David threw the first punch. They looked like teenagers, maybe still in high school. I was relieved when they ran off, and we quick jumped in the car and I drove to Good Sam."

David's hand healed quickly, and Lindsey made them promise they would stay far away from that part of town for the rest of their lives. *They definitely were lucky*, she thought. *That could have had a very bad ending.*

Lindsey liked that "my boys" were together and were a devoted and loving couple. Merritt's parents and his sister Kathleen were happy for their boy and welcomed David as one of their family. Leah Rosenthal had long been aware David was gay, and it pleased her that he'd found someone who loved him.

Arthur Rosenthal was another story. Though he was proud of his son and his ability as a pianist, when David tried to explain his relationship with Merritt, his father refused to hear

33

it. He felt sure this was a "phase" and David would come to his senses. That created problems for David, who loved and admired his father.

David told Lindsey that on the rare occasions Merritt was invited to the Rosenthal home, Arthur barely tolerated his presence. Leah tried to talk to him but Art's disappointment in David was apparent. David had let him…and God…down. Arthur might be a Reform Jew, but he was a staunch traditionalist. He wanted a grandson. He loved his son, he told Leah, and he simply couldn't understand this choice David had made. They were not completely estranged, but a strain existed between father and son.

***

Lindsey and Merritt performed together that spring on Claudia Prince's class recital, a scene from *La Traviata*, and David played piano for them. Until Professor Prince had pronounced it a future possibility, Violetta was a role Lindsey never expected to perform, and she loved singing the poignant aria "Addio, del passato." She and Merritt sang the third act duet, and Merritt sang Alfredo's second act aria, "De miei bollenti spiriti." Lindsey couldn't wait to be in Opera Workshop as a sophomore. She could see herself soon in a production on that stage.

In the fall Lindsey and Merritt were cast opposite each other in an opera workshop production, a scene from *L'Elisir d'amore*. Also that fall, the two friends were hired by the Episcopal Church of the Redeemer in Hyde Park as soloists and section leaders. Many churches in Cincinnati had followed this practice for some time, giving Conservatory students a source of income with what they called "God gigs." While both had

34

received scholarships, they were pleased to be able to use this income to help pay for their living expenses.

They found another professional opportunity when Rockdale Temple hired them to sing for special services. A prestigious, historic temple and one of the first Reform temples in the country, Rockdale was also the Rosenthals' temple. David's father attended the Rosh Hashanah services and heard Merritt perform one of his favorite songs, the dramatic and moving *Avinu malkeinu*, magnificently. At nineteen, Merritt's remarkable talent was already apparent. To everyone's surprise, Arthur walked up to his son's lover and complimented him, thanking him for his music with a warm handshake. David almost cried and Merritt was greatly relieved. The cloud had lifted just a little.

***

David and Merritt became very protective of "our girl." Any guy who showed any interest in Lindsey had to pass inspection with her men before they would permit her to date him.

Merritt: "Lindsey, I'm not sure about this guy Gary. I know he wants to ask you to go out with him. How well do you know him, aside from the fact that he plays pretty decent oboe and seems okay?"

Lindsey: "I just want to find out if being an oboist makes him a good kisser." They both stared at her.

David: "*What*? Why would you think that? And when did you go around comparing how some guy...guys...kiss...kisses you? You never told us you were doing that."

Lindsey started laughing and they looked a little sheepish. "He's nice, and I'd like to go out with him. I've hardly dated since I arrived at this school. I don't want to be a nun or I'd have joined a convent. I think we'll have a good time. He just

35

wants to take me to dinner and a symphony concert. You two are worse than having my brother here."

"We just want to keep tabs on you. Who knows when you might take a notion to break out of your shell and act a little wild?" Merritt's eyes brightened. "We should live together. The three of us. That way we can really look out for Lindsey." David nodded his agreement.

"Who's going to look out for you two?" she replied, a little annoyed. "And why does Lindsey need looking out for, anyway? I'm a big girl."

***

But it felt right, Lindsey mused as she waited for her parents to arrive. *We were family, the Three Musketeers.* The idea of finding a house to share appealed to them, and they agreed to start looking that spring so they could be moved in by the time school started in the fall.

She and Merritt sang together often with David as their pianist. He played for all their recitals, and for any programs they were invited to sing for women's clubs and civic events. *We were the golden trio, the kids with bright futures, the students envied by other music performance majors. Even the grad students hated us. Well, the singers hated Merritt and me. Nobody hated David.*

She sighed and looked again at her watch—eleven-thirty a.m.

And now David is dead. Not David! He was the best of who we were…reminding us life isn't fair, having a career in music was a complete crap shoot, we would be lucky if we didn't lose our voices somehow. One of his mantras. "I dearly love both of you, but sometimes you can be such pains in the ass. For God's sake, you can't build a career solely on the basis of

36

having some success at the Conservatory as undergraduates. It's a big world out there, ladies. Stop being so stuck on yourselves.

"Live each day as it comes. Be grateful for your good fortune, and dammit, be nicer to people." David didn't just preach it. He lived it.

Chapter 3

Andrew Cameron phoned Lindsey from the Greater Cincinnati Airport at about noon to let her know their plane had arrived on time and they should be at her house by one.

She had managed to drag herself from an armchair to answer the phone, surprised that she had fallen asleep there and how stiff and tired she felt. She glanced around the downstairs, at the kitchen and living-dining room. *Not too untidy, it's okay.* The last thing she felt like doing was any kind of cleaning.

She pulled her mind away from the thought of going to David's and Merritt's rooms. *I guess I should eat something, though.* That idea was equally unappealing.

Lindsey stood in a hot shower for close to half an hour and felt a little better. She threw on clean jeans and a button-down shirt, slipped her feet into flat-heeled shoes, and applied a touch of lipstick and blush, gazing at herself critically in the mirror. *I look pretty awful, and I don't care.* She went back into the kitchen, put a few things away, stared into the refrigerator again. Nothing looked good to her.

The doorbell had never sounded so welcoming to her, and her family engulfed her with embraces. She clung to them as a feeling of relief swept over her. *They'll make it right. They'll fix it. They always have.*

They sat together in the living room as Lindsey told them exactly what had happened the night before. "We didn't hear about Merritt until after…I think four a.m. That's when his doctor, I guess the surgeon who…amputated his leg…told us they put him in a medically-induced coma." A deep sigh. "Dear God in heaven. He'll be destroyed when he learns David was killed. We were told they don't plan on taking him off the sedative until tomorrow morning sometime."

M.J, seated beside Lindsey on the sofa, squeezed her shoulders. "He's going to be facing a difficult time, Linds. Something I'm sure he never imagined."

"I didn't either," she said softly. "How could this happen?" She glanced at her parents. "I'm so glad you're all here. You can't even begin to know how much I need you."

"Oh, I think we can, sweetheart," her mother said gently. "Do you want us to stay here at the house with you, or should we all find hotel rooms together and get you out of here?"

"Why not let me stay with Lindsey, Mom, and you and Dad go to a hotel?" M. J. suggested. "I'm sure you would be more comfortable, and I'll be here with our girl." He observed his sister closely. "Lindsey needs to rest, and she probably would do that better right here."

Lindsey nodded. "I'd like that."

"Sounds like a plan," Andrew responded, and he went to the phone to start making calls. They listened as he first called Good Samaritan Hospital to find out about Merritt's condition, but apparently wasn't successful in learning anything. Andrew then called the Vernon Manor, only about a mile away, and reserved a room. They had rented a car at the airport.

Lindsey promised to call if she heard anything more about Merritt, and when she learned the arrangements for David's funeral from Leah.

M.J. gazed at his sister after their parents left. "I have a feeling you haven't had a thing to eat today."

"I haven't," she admitted.

"I'll bet I could tempt you with something." He grinned and ruffled her hair. "Let me fix you one of my specialties...remember my omelets?"

"I do. I'll try to eat if you fix something."

M.J. worked magic with a frying pan and eggs and whatever he found in the refrigerator, and the aroma was enticing. He watched closely as Lindsey took a first bite.

"Oh, this is wonderful. Thank you."

M.J. sat with his sister to be sure she continued to eat. "What a business, Lindsey. You realize you're in shock."

"Yes, I kind of figured that. Why did this have to happen, M.J.? Everything was so great. Life was pretty much perfect."

"Sadly, this kind of awful, tragic event happens all the time, sis. And it can happen to anyone."

She stopped mid-bite. "You know, I remember your saying something like that to me once before."

"Did I? I don't remember. But it's a hard truth. I probably heard it from Dad."

Lindsey felt slightly better after eating. She offered to clean the kitchen but M.J. shooed her away. "You need to get some rest. David's funeral is going to be tough, Linds. Go lie down."

"I don't know if I can sleep."

"Maybe not. But stretch out and try to relax." He glanced at the CD collection. "How about some Fauré? I know you love that one."

"Yes, I do. It's there." She embraced her brother, appreciating the feeling of being wrapped warmly in his strong arms. "I'll try to sleep."

She relaxed in her darkened room as she listened to the ethereal sounds of the Fauré *Requiem*, but sleep eluded her. Lindsey's mind drifted back to the time two years ago when she and her boys moved into this house. *We all brought our*

41

*favorite CDs...I think this was one of mine. We loved our house.
David's mom found it for us.*

***

Leah Rosenthal had found the house on McMicken Avenue for
her son and his friends, and they moved in the August before
their junior year. An older, comfortable house built in the
nineteen-twenties in a mixed neighborhood of old houses and
newer apartment buildings, close to the University.

Two bedrooms upstairs, and a combination living-dining
room, a kitchen, and a third room downstairs which would
serve as Lindsey's bedroom. Luckily, two full baths as well,
which was unusual. Delighted, they pronounced it perfect.

The Three Musketeers had a great time making the place
their own. The house was fully furnished, even with pots and
pans and some dishes and tableware. They purchased linens
and a few other small items, and all three brought their favorite
CDs to enjoy, thanks to David providing a CD player and stand
for the living room. They found an overstuffed armchair at the
Goodwill Store which David proclaimed "perfect" for music-
listening. Once they had the house in order, they stood in the
living-dining room and realized something was missing.

"Pictures! We need some artwork." David wandered
around. "I have some prints at home that will look nice here."

"How about this: framed pages of music? They add a lot
to a space." Merritt pressed a hand against an empty wall.
"Some Rachmaninoff right here, what do you say?" They
happily agreed.

Lindsey disappeared into her bedroom and emerged with
two enlarged photos, one of her and Merritt in costume for
L'Elisir d'amore and another of the three of them, a publicity

shot before a recital for the Women's Club. "How about we frame these?"

They piled into Merritt's car, zipping first up to Amberley to pick up a large parchment of measures of music by Rachmaninoff and some small prints of Cincinnati scenes. Then a stop at a frame shop near the University where they pooled their resources and then went "home" to add the finishing touches to their new dwelling.

Merritt and Lindsey drove to Skyline Chili and brought home Three-Way for their first dinner in the new house. David produced a bottle of champagne. "My mother thought we should toast ourselves for our first meal."

Lindsey, her mouth full of Cincinnati's special version of chili, mumbled, "She probably meant we should cook. Sorry, Leah."

"She didn't say a word about cooking," David piled more oyster crackers on his chili. Skyline Chili was more like a stew with Greek seasonings, served over spaghetti and topped with enormous mounds of shredded cheese, and served with oyster crackers on the side. Lindsey doubted anything could possibly be more delicious.

"Champagne and Skyline," Merritt yodeled, lifting his glass. "To our junior year."

***

A few days after they moved in, David said, "We could use a piano in this house. We're not in an apartment building so we could practice whenever we want." The Rosenthals bought them a sweet little Baldwin piano that David found and fell in love with. The three of them were thrilled to have it there, it meant they wouldn't have to compete with other students for practice rooms at school. They set up a schedule and attempted to adhere to it, but that wasn't always easy to do.

Lindsey: "I just need a few minutes to work on my audition piece. And David, will you please play through it with me?"

David: "Well, this is supposed to be my practice time…but sure, I'll do that. I love hearing you sing this, anyway."

Merritt: "When you two are finished, David, can you play through my audition song? I need to sing it one more time before we go to auditions."

David: "Um, okay. You both owe me time, though."

That was typical David, generous to a fault. Lindsey found her rehearsal times with him were often about much more than the music they worked on together. He would compliment Lindsey on her expressive singing of a particular line in a song, and then turn that into a sweet comment about something he loved about her as his friend.

"You're turning me into a better person, David," she quipped.

"You're a good person, Lindsey. You can be a little prickly sometimes, but you have a kind heart. And that's a good thing." His eyes twinkled as he spoke, making her laugh.

Merritt and Lindsey continued their "God gigs" at Redeemer and Rockdale, and David, from the second semester of his freshman year, had been on the Conservatory's accompanying staff. He actually earned more than either of his housemates, but Lindsey and Merritt insisted all household expenses be split equally among the three of them. David added to his share of expenses with generous gifts, usually in the form of gift certificates to Willis Music and to Shillito's or Pogues' Department Stores for music and formal clothing, both expenses his housemates couldn't avoid as aspiring singers.

Lindsey and Merritt received an invitation to perform in October with the Cincinnati Symphony Orchestra. That fall concert, a special concert to showcase talent from the Conservatory, was considered an honor by the students invited to perform. Lindsey and Merritt were asked to sing the Don José-Micaëla duet from *Carmen* and each of them would also sing an aria from the opera.

Some of the upperclassmen and grad students were annoyed that they had been passed over for this concert. No one actually knew exactly how the student performers were selected or who made those choices. The Nobles had friends on the CSO Board of Directors, so there was gossip. Lindsey and Merritt heard the gossip and chose to ignore it. They knew that the dean of the Conservatory had some say in the choices as well.

David waxed philosophical. "Sad but true, there is some politics in everything, children. Even in something as sacrosanct as classical music. The point is, you are both exceptional singers and performers, far above your status as third-year undergrads. It's nice to have that recognized."

The Cameron family planned to fly to Cincinnati for the concert. Not just Lindsey's parents and her brother M.J., but her uncle would fly down from Montreal.

"Your dad's brother?" David asked. They were in the midst of cleaning up after a meal. Lindsey, in a rare burst of enthusiasm, had provided the food by actually cooking, creating a casserole of chicken, rice, cheese, and broccoli, which the guys proclaimed "not half bad."

"His younger brother. And…how do I explain this? Once upon a time, he was Jacob Cameron—Jake. Now his name is Jean Couvreur. He's been living in Canada for many years and is an executive at CBC Montreal. He's head of the classical music division, and produces their live performance broadcasts and sometimes still does on-air interviews with musicians."

"What's the name change all about?" Merritt demanded as he put dishes away.

"There's a good reason for it. My Uncle Jean was in Special Forces during the Vietnam War, and when a helicopter he was in crashed, he suffered a traumatic brain injury."

Lindsey finished wrapping the leftover casserole and placed it in the refrigerator. "He completely lost all memory of who he had been. He could remember a lot of things about the world and how things work, but those personal memories—they're called 'episodic' or 'autobiographical' memories—were gone. And many of them he's never recovered."

"Good God, Lindsey. That sounds awful. I can't even imagine." David stopped sweeping the kitchen floor and sat down abruptly. "Losing yourself completely. He must have gone through hell."

"He's at the CBC and does stuff with classical music and musicians?" Merritt, now also seated, asked. "Was he a musician before? I mean before he lost his memory?"

"No, actually, he was a jock in high school. Captain of the football team. And quarterback. And captain and catcher for the baseball team. I've seen lots of pictures."

"So, his interest in music didn't happen until after he lost his memory?" David leaned forward eagerly. "That must be some story. Have you ever talked to him about it?"

"Well…no, I haven't." Lindsey was a little surprised herself. *Why haven't I ever asked Uncle Jean about this?*

David frowned but didn't comment, and Lindsey continued hastily, "It's kind of a complicated story, but he disappeared for a time, eventually ending up in Canada where some people helped him find a new identity and start a new life. He's been there for about twenty years now, and along with his fabulous job, he has an absolutely gorgeous wife and three beautiful kids."

Complicated is putting it mildly, she thought. *But these guys don't need to know all the details.*

Merritt eyed her speculatively. "I think there's a lot more to this story, Linds. But it's apparent your family is now on good terms with your uncle, and that's what's important."

Lindsey smiled at him gratefully. "It is. He and my dad have always been close." *Well, not quite true. Jake stayed away and they didn't have contact for well over fifteen years. Despite that, they never stopped loving each other.*

The morning of their rehearsal with the orchestra, Lindsey stood staring at her reflection in the bathroom mirror. *This is really happening.* A performance with a major American orchestra. *You've got this, Lindsey,* she told herself. *Enjoy every minute.*

"Let's go, Linds," Merritt called to her. He let out a low whistle when he saw her. "Man, you look fantastic, soprano. The people in the orchestra will appreciate you before you sing a note." She had chosen a dress in powder blue topped by a fingertip-length white jacket, complimenting her fair-haired, blue-eyed looks.

"You look pretty great yourself, tenor," She responded. "Oh, Merritt, are you as excited as I am? Soloing with the CSO. It's a milestone."

Lindsey had been on the stage of Cincinnati's magnificent Music Hall before, but as a member of a chorus. Stepping onto that stage as a soloist gave her a feeling of reverence. Merritt murmured in her ear: "It feels like some great singers left an echo of themselves on this stage." Lindsey turned and gave him a brilliant smile at the thought of the performers over the years who preceded them. *He's right, we're following in some impressive footsteps.*

Looking out onto the ornate white and gold décor of the auditorium with its rows and rows of crimson seats, and up at the majestic crystal chandelier which graced the hall, gave Lindsey a new sense of excitement. She turned to Merritt, her eyes shining, and saw he was sharing the moment with her. *It's like a dream*, she thought.

Her family flew into Cincinnati the next morning for the afternoon concert. After arriving at Music Hall, they were escorted to box seats by a member of the CSO staff. Mary later commented to her daughter, "We were treated like royalty. That was lovely."

After the concert, which was received with prolonged applause and numerous curtain calls, the families enjoyed a private buffet dinner at the Netherland Hilton Hotel, where the Cameron group were all staying.

David and his parents were included, of course, and the room was filled with laughter and happy chatter. Lindsey made sure she sat next to her uncle during dinner.

"I can't begin to tell you how happy I am that you're here," she told him. "I loved seeing you stand after I sang Micaëla's aria."

My handsome uncle, who looks so much like my handsome dad. Same dark hair and expressive brown eyes. Jean Couvreur definitely had something of the air of a cosmopolitan man of the world about him, while her father, a successful artist, was gentle, less sophisticated.

"You both sang remarkably, Lindsey. You've shown considerable improvement since you started studying with Claudia Prince. I hear a warmer, more expressive sound."

"We've been working to achieve that. And you know what she does?" Lindsey leaned toward him eagerly. "She insists that we translate everything we sing, word for word. Then she requires that we write a summary and express in our own words what the song means, what we're trying to convey to the listener."

Jake—she always thought of him as Jake, though she called him "Uncle Jean"—gave her a warm smile. "That's excellent. It's what I heard when you sang."

"Uncle Jean...sometime I'd like to hear about how you ended up in the classical music division of CBC Montreal. I know this isn't the right place or time, but soon."

Another smile. "I'd be happy to share that with you. How opera came to be my favorite art form." He chuckled.

I wonder why I've never asked him before, Lindsey thought. She caught her brother staring at her with one eyebrow lifted. *Oh, I know what he would say: 'You're so wrapped up in yourself, Lindsey. You don't think nearly enough about other people.'*

M.J. approached her as they left the private dining room. "You were great, Lindsey. I mean that. I heard things in your singing I've never heard before."

Somewhat surprised by the praise, she turned to gaze at him. "Thank you for saying that. I'm learning how hard this is going to be, M.J. There are a lot of talented singers in this world. In this country. The competition is fierce...even more so if you're a soprano."

"No doubt that's true, but you really impressed me today."

Basking in her brother's unexpected but welcome approval, Lindsey hugged him. "You can't even imagine how much it means to hear you say that."

He grinned at her as he tucked a lock of hair behind her ear. "So, big sis, have you found a boyfriend yet?"

"I've told you before, I'm not looking for one," she laughed. "That's a complication I'm not interested in at present. Besides, I have two terrific men in my life who keep me entertained."

"No doubt. But they don't keep you warm."

"I have lots of blankets and quilts that take care of that. I sleep well, thank you."

She made light of this with M.J., but there were times she did miss having someone in her life. She saw that Merritt and David had something truly wonderful. The loving looks, tender touches, lingering embraces, subdued laughter…*yes, these men are deeply in love with each other, of that there is no doubt.*

Other than the considerable time she spent with David and Merritt, Lindsey socialized at times in a group or at a party. She knew she tended to be aloof—thanks to David's humorous but sometimes pointed comments—and she was making more of an effort to be friendly with her schoolmates. While she had been involved in activities in high school, Lindsey tended to be her own person. She knew what she wanted to do with her life, and that was her focus. Her peers in high school had accepted that.

Auditions for the spring opera, *Carmen,* took place not long after that October CSO concert. Singing the duet with the symphony caused Merritt to joke it was a sure sign that he and Lindsey would be cast in lead roles.

"Don't be so cocky," David cautioned him. "There are some new graduate and transfer students at this school now. You could be beaten out for those roles."

He shook his head as he stared at both of them. "You worry me. You're both so damned sure you're headed for operatic stardom. You could very well be headed for a major fall."

"On the contrary, David, I told my brother after the concert that I'm just becoming aware of how tough this is going to be," Lindsey said. "I mean this path we're following—or trying to follow—to a career in opera. I know we're not shoo-ins for these roles."

"Seconded," Merritt said. "But would I ever love to sing Don José."

The auditions proved David to be correct about there being some exceptional talent now attending the Conservatory, and Lindsey and Merritt began having doubts about being cast in leading roles. At dinner after the auditions, the two singers stared gloomily at their LaRosa's takeout food and admitted they probably had been overly confident, Lindsey's protestations notwithstanding.

"You're right, David," she said. "We've been a little ridiculous. We're in one music school in this huge country, where there are numerous fine music conservatories. What's the competition going to be like when we come face to face with a lot more of these excellent singers?"

"You know, that quintet in the second act is pretty terrific stuff," Merritt said thoughtfully, gazing at a forkful of lasagna. "I could deal with being cast as Remendado. It's actually a darned good role."

Silence for a moment as Lindsey contemplated her glass of wine.

"I'd be happy with Frasquita," she said. "It's a great supporting role."

"Well, good," David told them. "Now you're beginning to get it. It's rough out there, girls."

"We were cast last year in the leads in that opera workshop scene from *Elixir* partly because those roles required lighter and more flexible voices. We knew that," Merritt conceded.

"Maybe so, but it sure went to your heads," David replied. "Anyway, children…why do we sing?"

"We sing for the music because we love it," the two of them answered in unison, parroting what David had told them hundreds of times.

51

"Yes, we do," David slapped his hands down on the table and beamed at them, "And…?"

"And because we want to share it with our listeners," Lindsey said, while Merritt said at the same time, "Because we're privileged to be able to sing this music which is a gift from the universe."

David applauded as all three laughed.

"Don't forget, you have another year of undergrad study after this one," David reminded them. "We all need to start thinking beyond that to grad school. You're not going to grab your diploma and have a Met contract waiting for you. Or even a contract with a small opera house in this country or in Europe. Lots of hard work ahead."

Merritt grinned. "It's not work if it's your passion. And you both know it's mine."

When the *Carmen* cast list was posted, sure enough Merritt's name appeared opposite Remendado and Lindsey's opposite Frasquita. Both were also to understudy the tenor and soprano leads, with other singers assigned to understudy their roles.

"That's a lot of work. We have to learn two roles and there's probably no chance we'll get to perform the leads," Lindsey whined.

Merritt looked her straight in the face. "Knock it off. You ought to learn the role of Micaëla. Who knows when in your upcoming career you might suddenly be invited to perform it? Singers get sick and have to cancel. Listen, lady. Learn every damn role you can." He shook his head. "I swear, Lindsey, sometimes you can be such a princess."

Lindsey had to giggle. "Merritt Noble, you sound just like David."

Carmen was a learning experience Lindsey came to appreciate. She attended every rehearsal, whether her name appeared on the schedule or not. She mastered two roles at the same time, and she and Merritt were able to perform the roles of Don José and Micaëla at the first dress rehearsal. She found she enjoyed being Frasquita far more than she anticipated. She even developed a nice friendship with the sophomore girl, Amy Chang, who understudied Frasquita.

The experience gave her a renewed appreciation for the importance of every person on stage in an opera. *It's not just the stars who bring it to life.*

And David was right. We sing for the music. The music is paramount.

David didn't just preach it, he lived it. It was never about him, even though he had extraordinary virtuosic skills and the ability to make the lyrical sections of any piece shimmer with emotion. It was always...ALWAYS...about the music, about what the composer has gifted us with.

But now David is gone. I'll never see him again, never hear him offering me words of wisdom again...never experience what he shared so freely with such love.

.

Chapter 4

May 1995

Near the end of their junior year, Merritt came home filled with excitement. "You know the Summer Opera has *Turandot* on their schedule for July, Linds. I just found out a couple of things. One, that they're hiring extra choristers for the big chorus they need for the opera." He ran a hand through his hair, barely able to contain himself. "And this is the best. Jamie Logan is performing Calaf, the Unknown Prince. I can't wait to see it."

Lindsey had learned early on that Merritt was a huge fan of Jamie Logan, one of the premier tenors in all of Opera World. The recordings of operas Merritt owned were mostly those which featured Logan. He'd seen Logan perform at the Cincinnati Summer Opera some ten years earlier in the title role in *The Tales of Hoffmann*, the opera which was to be the spring production at the Conservatory.

They were both super excited about auditioning for *Hoffmann*. Merritt wanted the lead role even more than he had hoped for Don José in *Carmen*. And Lindsey hoped for a role as one of Hoffmann's three loves. She knew Giulietta was out because it required a more dramatic voice and was often performed by a mezzo. That left Olympia, a role she had the high notes to sing, and Antonia, Hoffmann's doomed love—

the role Lindsey wanted. Merritt and Lindsey planned to spend a lot of time over the summer studying the opera.

Lindsey ended up spending the entire summer in Cincinnati. She and Merritt auditioned for the extra chorister positions for *Turandot* and were both hired. After seeing operas every summer at Cincinnati's iconic Music Hall, they would actually be on stage there, rubbing elbows with some of the stars of Opera World. For Merritt, standing on the same stage as his idol would be a dream come true.

"You told me you met Jamie Logan one time," Merritt said at dinner one night.

"I did more than that. I sang for him," Lindsey responded smugly.

"Get out!"

"I never told you about that? I was sure I had." *I must have told him that story.*

"Well, I never heard it," David chimed in. "So tell it again."

"Well, it seems there's kind of a connection between my family and Mr. Logan's family, and so my dad contacted him and asked if he'd be willing to hear the music I was considering for my college auditions and give me some suggestions."

"That would require a pretty strong connection," David mused.

"I don't really know the particulars," Lindsey said. "Friends of friends, I think."

"Okay, go on." Merritt urged.

"Mr. Logan and his family live in Montclair, New Jersey. We made a weekend of it; stayed in New York City, went to some events…in fact, Dad had a gallery show, and that was the main reason we were there. The Logans were kind enough to invite us to dinner."

"You broke bread with the man?" Merritt exclaimed.

"It's amazing, Merritt. He eats just like any mere mortal does. Cuts his meat with a knife, picks up a piece on his fork...." Lindsey teased.

"Oh, stop," Merritt laughed.

"So afterward, I sang three arias for him. These were pieces my teacher in Philadelphia had suggested I might use for college auditions the following year. I was even then considering the Conservatory as my first choice, and he thought it a good one. He liked the *Baby Doe* aria the best and thought I should concentrate on that, along with at least four art songs."

"And he said...?" Merritt prompted.

"He was very encouraging. He said I'd had an excellent teacher who hadn't pushed me, he thought she'd made good choices. He liked my voice and said I was quite musical. All nice things to hear from a man who is at the top of his profession."

"Who played for you?" David asked.

"Mrs. Logan—Meredith. She plays well, she has a Master's degree in music. But did you know she's the head of the Department of Psychology at Montclair State University? Obviously, a brilliant woman. And really nice."

Lindsey put her fork down. "You know, I just remembered something he said to me that you'll both appreciate. You especially, David."

"Something about music, I'm guessing." David leaned forward eagerly.

"Yes, exactly. I want to be sure I get this right. He talked about why we sing."

David slapped the table triumphantly. "Ha!"

"I know he said this: 'Sing because you love to sing.' Then he talked about the wonderful music we have available to us, thanks to great composers. Oh, and then he said this: 'Sing to share your love of music...' no, wait. 'Sing to share the love of music you have in your soul.' And then something about singing because it makes us happy."

"I can't believe you didn't write it down," David stared at Lindsey.

"Well, obviously, I didn't need to." Lindsey returned the stare.

"Interesting. He never said sing because you want to be a famous and adored soprano, worshipped by all in Opera World," David said tartly.

"I don't do that," Lindsey protested. "That was mean."

"You're right, it was. Consider it withdrawn," David said sheepishly.

"No, don't withdraw it. I need those reminders about ego, and you're the best person to do the reminding because I know you love me anyway." They grinned at each other and clinked glasses.

Merritt totally ignored this exchange. "Will you introduce me to him first chance you get? We'll be at rehearsals together."

"Of course, I will. If he remembers me," Lindsey cautioned. "That was four years ago, after all. But I guess I could remind him I'm Andrew Cameron's daughter."

"I don't think you'll have to," Merritt said. "From what I've heard about him, he's a pretty terrific person."

***

Members of the *Turandot* chorus were requested to arrive at their first rehearsal with their music learned. Lindsey and Merritt had to set *Hoffmann* aside, and spent many evenings working on *Turandot*. They had both listened to the opera numerous times and found the music fairly easy to learn and even to memorize. A full week of chorus rehearsals was

58

scheduled and then a week and a half of staging rehearsals were to follow for the entire cast.

"You know, I'll never forget the first time I saw this opera," Lindsey told her housemates. "The first act just blew me away. Almost non-stop chorus from the beginning until halfway through the act. And so many changes in mood. I was enthralled. And how great to be actually singing this incredible score."

Much to Lindsey's astonishment, at the first rehearsal combining soloists and chorus, Jamie Logan sought her out.

"I saw your name on the cast list," he smiled as he extended a hand. "So, you did end up here. You chose an excellent school."

You saw my name on the cast list? You are a good guy, to take the time to read through that long list of chorus people. "Thank you! It's so nice to see you again. I've been very happy here, and I have a great teacher. I'm working with Claudia Prince." She became aware of Merritt hovering nearby with a hopeful look on his face.

"Mr. Logan, I'd like to introduce you to one of my housemates, who happens to be probably your greatest fan. Would that be okay?"

"Of course, Lindsey. I'd be happy to meet your friend."

Lindsey would never forget the look on Merritt's face when Jamie Logan gave him a warm handshake. "Actually, I've heard about you, Merritt, and you as well, Lindsey. Claudia and I had dinner the other night and she was singing your praises."

Merritt, usually quite self-assured, was so star-struck he could barely express his thanks. And he and Lindsey were thrilled that Professor Prince had spoken so highly of them. They both walked on air for the duration of the rehearsal.

Turandot was Puccini's final opera and in many ways his most complex musical work. Set in ancient, mythical China, it's a complicated opera, and staging rehearsals were sometimes lengthy and intense. Merritt seemed to be floating through them, standing in the wings whenever possible to watch and listen to Jamie Logan. Another surprise to Lindsey: how much she enjoyed being part of the ensemble. She'd always enjoyed singing the big choral works she loved, and she found being in this group, on stage in costume, equally rewarding. *Another lesson learned*, she told herself. *It is all about the music, really. Mr. Logan and David have it right.*

Lindsey and Merritt dragged David along for the after party at Mecklenburg's Beer Garden following the final performance. They had a few moments to talk with Jamie Logan, who had been approachable and pleasant throughout their time with him.

"Mr. Logan, I saw you in *The Tales of Hoffmann* ten years ago, when you performed it here," Merritt told him. "I think that was when I first decided I wanted to sing opera. I'll never forget that performance. I'll never forget *your* performance. You sure lit up the stage. And you sure inspired this guy as a young kid to pray he'd be a tenor when his voice changed."

Jamie laughed. "I take it you'd been singing before that, Merritt. Maybe in your school chorus?"

"Yes, that, and a children's chorus sponsored by the Symphony. We actually did a couple of performances. The one I remember best was Vaughan Williams' *Hodie*. Lots of rehearsals. Lots of music."

"I'm sure for a young child that seemed a lot to learn," Jamie chuckled. "And one of these days, you may be singing those great tenor solos and ensembles in that magnificent piece."

"Wouldn't that be something?" Merritt beamed. "It's been an honor to be on stage with you, Mr. Logan. Just watching and listening, I've learned a lot."

"Thank you, Merritt. I appreciate hearing that more than you know." He turned to Lindsey. "Please give my best to your family. I hope to see them again sometime."

David drove them home, Merritt uncharacteristically quiet.

"Penny for your thoughts, tenor," Lindsey said.

"I meant what I said to him. Just being on that stage, so close to him, was an education in so many ways. He never, ever forced the sound. Everything on the breath. And he doesn't even have to think about it, so he's totally immersed in the character. And man, can the guy *act*. He's considered the best for good reason."

"A lesson for you both, I'd say," David replied. "Meanwhile…here in Cincinnati…a different fantasy world awaits you both. Back to work on *Hoffmann*, children."

***

They discussed the story and the characters endlessly, sometimes late into the evening.

"You know, Hoffmann is a dreamer, I think that's obvious," Merritt said. "He meets Olympia and falls madly in love with her. He meets Giulietta and falls madly in love with *her*. The two women are total opposites."

"Olympia isn't a woman. She's a life-sized doll. For some reason, Hoffmann can't see that, but everybody else can," David observed.

"Hoffmann sees what he wants to see," Lindsey commented. "He comes closest to reality with Antonia, but even there…he can't see how ill she is. He's bound to lose her to death at some point, and he tries to ignore that."

"But I think she returns his love," Merritt said. "She's the only one of the three who does. But because she dies…it means none of his loves could be meaningful. I mean none could be a lasting love."

David worked with them as they learned the arias and ensembles. The more they learned, the more they came to love this unusual piece of music. Lindsey thought it tragic that Offenbach never knew how immensely successful his masterpiece proved to be. He died before the full score was completed and was still at work on the orchestration at the time of his death. A family friend helped Offenbach's eighteen-year-old son finish the score.

During the years she studied with Claudia Prince, Lindsey's silvery lyric coloratura had darkened and grown. Professor Prince was confident she could perform Antonia in *The Tales of Hoffmann* and they worked together on the music. Lindsey also prepared Olympia's aria, knowing many people on the Conservatory staff still thought of her as a coloratura, rather than a *leggiero* soprano.

The audition notice for the opera was posted early in the fall, and Lindsey began to get nervous. She wondered aloud if she were offered Olympia if she would accept the role. Antonia was *her role*. She had to sing it. David sat her down one evening.

"I know you want this more than you've ever wanted anything in your life. But the fact is, Lindsey, you have no control over how this opera will be cast. It concerns me that if you blow off a chance to do Olympia, you'll get a reputation as a prima donna. You don't need that, and you don't want it. If you're asked to sing Olympia's aria, of course you'll have to do your best with it, which is pretty damn good. You're one of the few sopranos on campus who can navigate the high notes. That could be a determining factor."

"Olympia is such fluff." Lindsey frowned and leaned her chin on a fist.

"She's a human-sized doll. The singer has to do quite an acting job to pull that off. It's a damn good role, whether you want it or not." He leaned toward her and gazed at her earnestly. "If this is what you want to do, perform in opera, you have to learn to accept what you're offered and make it great. You sure did that with Frasquita in *Carmen*—when you were on stage I couldn't take my eyes off you. It's what every opera singer has to do, at least in the beginning stages of their career. If you can't accept that, you don't belong in the business."

"I know you're right, David. Everything you're saying is true." She sighed. "It's just…well, I *know* Antonia, inside and out. I understand her. I know I could do this role justice."

"This won't be the only chance you'll have to sing this opera if you stick with this." A firm but gentle hand on her shoulder. "Whatever happens, I want to hear you accepted it graciously."

"I promise I'll do that. I'll even congratulate the girl who gets the role I really wanted."

"There's more. If you get the role…think of it as incredible luck. Be grateful. That's even more important than being gracious."

The casting call listed Giulietta and Antonia's Mother as mezzo-sopranos, as well as the trouser role of Nicklausse, Hoffman's sidekick. For Olympia and Antonia, they indicated "soprano." *Maybe I will have a shot*, Lindsey thought.

Merritt won the role of Hoffmann, beating out the tenor who had sung Don José the year before.

Lindsey saw another soprano cast as Olympia. *I'm not going to get either of them, after all.* She started to turn away, but instead, forced herself to continue to read down the list:

Antonia .... Lindsey Cameron

She gasped in surprise when she read the result, her hand to her mouth. *I don't believe it. I honestly thought I'd never get to do this role. Maybe it's a mistake.*

She looked again. No, there it was in black and white. She had been cast as Antonia.

The Three Musketeers treated themselves to dinner that night at La Normandie Grille in downtown Cincinnati, spending ridiculous amounts of money on food. The décor was quite French, and the waiters were attentive and just shy of obsequious. It was an elegant place to dine, second only to its sister restaurant, The Maisonette, a five-star establishment next door in the same building. They had agreed they didn't feel they could afford quite that much elegance.

It surprised Lindsey to see that Merritt seemed pensive. "I thought you'd be beside yourself that you landed this role," she commented, breaking her dinner roll under the watchful eye of a server. *Why do they hover like that? I guess it's part of the ambiance.*

"Well, I'm thrilled, but I'm also a little…apprehensive. It's a huge role." Merritt drained his water glass and it was refilled by another server the instant he set it down. Merritt smiled and mouthed "thank you." The waiter half-lifted an eyebrow as if Merritt had committed a major faux pas.

"You knew that. We worked on this music all summer. Every act is different because each of Hoffmann's loves is so different. That's what makes it such a remarkable opera," Lindsey observed.

64

David stared at her. "I'm glad to see Merritt's aware of the responsibility he's tackling with this role. It shows some maturity. Some growth as an artist."

"While I, on the other hand, only have to deal with one personality." She tipped her head as she returned David's look. "Antonia, the sweet one."

"Well," David replied with a twinkle in his eye, "You'll have to work a little to achieve that. Nobody ever accused Lindsey Cameron of being saccharine."

"Just chill out, you two," Merritt grumbled. "Lindsey can be sweet. She's going to be terrific in this role."

Lindsey watched as one of the servers artfully drizzled dressing on her salad before she tasted it. She nodded her approval, reminding herself not to thank him.

"I get to die on stage. That's the best part. And do you know, Offenbach has it in the score: 'Antonia dies on a trill.' Now, that's going to take a little doing."

She smiled sweetly at David who laughed, Merritt joining him.

Champagne was served, and David offered the toast. "To my best friends. May they light up the stage in the spring with their performances, and continue upward in their quest for operatic success."

***

The second semester flew by like a musical dream. Rehearsals for *Hoffmann*, frequently with David present as their rehearsal accompanist. An audition for grad school at the Curtis Institute of Music in Philadelphia, and another at the Peabody Conservatory in Baltimore, both of which she felt good about. She was sure she'd be accepted by both and have a decision to make, but Curtis seemed to her the best choice.

The cast for *The Tales of Hoffmann* bonded, all of them excited to perform in what they considered an unusual opportunity. Merritt did indeed have a challenging task. There needed to be subtle differences in the character of Hoffmann during each section, and there was a lot of music in the prologue, the three acts, and the epilogue. Each act was based on a short story by the real Ernst Theodor Amadeus Hoffmann, a German author of fantasy and Gothic horror who lived in the late eighteenth and early nineteenth centuries.

Lindsey found a rare friend in Amy Chang, the lovely Chinese-American girl who played Olympia and had understudied Frasquita the preceding year. Petite and delicate, she made an ideal Olympia and sang the role perfectly.

Esteban Ruiz, the Puerto Rican bass-baritone cast as the villain, tried to get Lindsey into his bed, but to no avail. She thought him a fine performer and a great-looking man—he was twenty-eight—but he didn't particularly impress her as a person.

"What are you waiting for, the love of your life?" he commented sarcastically after determining she actually was not interested.

"Maybe I am, and you are definitely not him." Lindsey turned to walk away, then glanced back at him. "Too bad. You're probably a great lover. Or at least think you are."

When she told David and Merritt about this conversation they hooted with laughter, Merritt slapping her on the back as he said, "That's our girl."

After an intense eight weeks of rehearsal, finally the weekend of performances arrived: two performances, Friday and Sunday, to give the cast a day between to rest their voices. Both shows were sold out.

Merritt performed brilliantly and received high praise from the critics. Lindsey felt good about her performance as

Antonia. During her act, the villain, Dr. Miracle, kills Antonia by enticing her to sing even though she's been warned singing will result in her death. The tension between Lindsey and Esteban increased the drama on stage. The critics noticed and were particularly complimentary of the "Antonia" act and of Lindsey's performance.

Lindsey floated through that weekend. Everyone in her family came: her parents, M.J., her grandparents, even Jean Couvreur and his wife and three children, Toinette, Marie, and André. She had her own cheering section. Friday night, there was no performance, but instead a dinner party at the Hyde Park Country Club, courtesy of the Nobles. Merritt's grandparents, cousins, and two sets of uncles and aunts, some of whom Lindsey had met, were there, and the Rosenthals, along with David's grandparents.

Lindsey looked around the large room with its buffet table groaning with a wide variety of food, and the smaller tables with contented family members chatting and enjoying the repast. *Maybe fifty people here? A lot, that's for sure.*

She took her dessert to a table where her aunt Noémi, a strikingly lovely woman with large, dark eyes and curly dark hair, sat with her grandparents and M.J. "I've wanted to talk to you for a while," Lindsey said, tasting the crème brûlée. *Oh, so, so good.*

"You must be thrilled, Lindsey. What a fine production and your performance was a highlight. Not just for your family, but the audience showed you such appreciation." Noémi laid a hand on her niece's arm and squeezed it gently.

"It's been an experience I'll never forget. I've wanted to ask you this for some time. I know you had a career as a ballerina for several years, but then chose to teach instead in the company's school when you started your family."

"Yes, that's exactly what I did."

"Uncle Jean said you were a remarkable dancer. Do you…do you ever miss performing?"

Noémi laughed softly. "What do you think?"

"I think you and Uncle Jean are blissfully happy. But performing…wasn't that a part of who you were?"

"Our lives, and our needs and wants, can change, Lindsey. I was happy performing. But I love your uncle more than I have ever loved anyone. He never asked me to stop dancing, and he never pressed me to have children."

Noémi glanced across the room to see her husband talking animatedly with the Rosenthals. "I fell in love with Jean the moment I saw him. He never said it, but because of his history, I sensed he had a strong desire to be a father, to make a family. But it was my choice. I love teaching. I adore my children, even though sometimes they can be...how do you say it? A handful." Another laugh. "I wouldn't change the life I have now. I have happy memories of the time I spent on stage."

"And Marie is quite a little dancer, I understand."

"She's almost eleven, and she is definitely gifted. What Marie does with that is strictly her choice. When I was twelve, I became part of the junior company at our ballet—Les Grands Ballets Canadiens."

Noémi took a sip of tea. "You seem to be heading toward a promising career in opera at this point in your life. Are you having second thoughts? Is that why you asked about my choice?"

"No second thoughts; I'm committed to a life performing in opera. I was just curious as to how a successful ballerina could walk away from a flourishing career." She finished her dessert. "I hope I haven't overstepped."

Another gentle laugh. "You have not overstepped at all. I was happy to answer your questions."

Lindsey rose early on Monday morning to see her family off. They'd again stayed at the Netherland Hilton, and David drove her downtown to tell them goodbye. She felt a sudden sense of wistfulness as she watched them head out, though she couldn't understand why. Graduation wasn't far off and she expected to see all of them again in May.

Busy weeks followed; she had to prepare her recital and complete her course work. She was accepted at both Peabody and Curtis and elected to attend Curtis. She liked the idea of being close to home, and Curtis was quite prestigious.

Lindsey helped arrange for a commitment ceremony for Merritt and David, held at the Nobles' home in Hyde Park, a beautiful, special day for her boys and those who loved them. Even Arthur attended, he had accepted Merritt as his son's partner. A truly happy moment.

The trajectory I was on seemed straight ahead and upward. For all three of us.

It crashed in an instant with that horrible phone call from Leah.

Chapter 5

Lindsey heard the phone ring and M.J. answer it as she lay quietly, recalling where she was and what had happened. Thinking of David and her many good memories of their time together had calmed her for the moment, and she joined M.J. just as he hung up the phone.

"That was Leah Rosenthal, confirming David's service is to be at seven. She asked if we could be at Rockdale Temple by six-forty-five. I need to call Mom and Dad and let them know."

Lindsey nodded. In the kitchen, she poured herself a glass of cold water, which she drained and refilled as she listened to M.J.'s side of the phone conversation, making plans for their parents to pick up food for dinner before they came back to Lindsey's.

David's funeral. It should have happened many, many years from now. But here it is, and here we are.

Her brother took the empty glass she clutched and set it on the counter. "Can I fix you some tea or something?"

"Yes, that would be nice." She waved a hand toward the canisters lining the adjoining counter. "Peppermint, please."

They sat together at the table. "I can't thank you enough for taking care of me, M.J. I'm a mess." Lindsey blew across the mug. "Just having you here with me has helped more than you know."

"This is tough, Linds. I know what a good friend David was to you. It's going to take some time to deal with his death."

"Yes…but there are some other things I must think about." Lindsey sighed deeply. "My senior recital is scheduled for April 12. There's no way it can happen now. And it's too close to graduation for me to find another pianist. Besides, I couldn't possibly sing the program I had planned with someone else. David and I spent so much time exploring the music together." Lindsey clutched her mug, her throat tightening.

M.J. gazed at her. "You don't need to think about this right now."

"I think I have to. I guess one option is to perform my recital during the summer session. That way I could still graduate." She swallowed hard. "I can't even conceive of walking for graduation without David and Merritt."

Another sigh. "Who knows what will happen with Merritt? There's no way he can finish this semester." Her voice caught. "I can't bear to think how he'll react when he finds out about David."

M.J. pressed a warm hand on Lindsey's shoulder. "Why don't we just take one thing at a time, sis? David's funeral is in a few hours. What are you going to wear? Just think about that for now."

"I have a couple of black dresses. Standard singer wardrobe," she tried a smile that didn't work quite right and felt a tear trail down one cheek. Lindsey brushed it away. "I've never cried so much in my life."

"Tears are good, Lindsey. Cry all you need to. What just happened is unbelievable."

"Yes, but…look at Leah. She's amazing. She's been a rock. Staying at the hospital all night with Merritt's parents. Calling me to ask me to come to Good Samaritan. I had to pry out of her what had happened to David. And then she had to make all the arrangements for his funeral because his father is…was…out of town. How does she do it?"

"Just guessing, but maybe life experience and a deep personal faith." M.J. stared into his mug. "Planning the funeral gave her a purpose. Of course, she's grieving. She does sound like a strong woman."

Lindsey gazed at her brother. "I always thought of myself as a strong person. But…I don't know, now." She leaned both elbows on the table and rested her forehead against her hands.

I can't stay in this house, she thought. *I can't afford it by myself. And all this stuff…David's and Merritt's…somebody has to pack everything up. But if I don't live here, where can I go?*

Lindsey's stomach tightened. She couldn't recall when she had felt so lost. Bewildered, she glanced again at M.J. "You're right, though. If I try to think too far ahead, I just get confused. And scared."

M.J. stood behind his sister and rubbed her shoulders. "The people who love you will be right here to help with everything. I have to get back in a few days, but Mom and Dad plan to stay as long as you need them here."

The knot in her stomach eased a bit, and Lindsey felt herself relax slightly.

M.J. responded to the tap on the door and ushered in Andrew and Mary Cameron arriving with dinner for the four of them. Wonderful aromas emanated from the bags they carried into the kitchen. "The Vernon Manor hospitality knows no bounds," Andrew said. "They provided us a complete take-out of something that smells incredible."

Mary embraced her daughter, gazing at her with concern. "Did you get some rest?"

"Some. M.J. kept the music going, and that helped a lot." Lindsey returned her mother's hug. "I'll set the table."

73

"No, you go sit with your father. M.J. and I will do kitchen duty."

Lindsey noticed her parents were dressed for David's funeral. "Let me get you an apron, at least, Mom."

"I'll find one. Go sit with your dad." Another quick hug.

Seated on the sofa, Andrew wrapped his arms around Lindsey and pulled her close. *My sweet Daddy. I always loved to have him hold me on his lap or pull me close like this.* A subtle fragrance she associated with him, something woodsy and pleasant. She leaned against him, a little girl again for a moment.

"Have you eaten anything?" he asked.

"M.J. made me an omelet. I ate most of it. He's a great cook. A lot better than I am."

Andrew chuckled softly. "I take it you listened to the Brahms this morning. What did the family disc jockey play for you while you were resting?"

"Fauré. And then some Ravel instrumental music I've learned to love. Do you know his 'Pavane for a Dead Princess'? I don't think I remember that from my childhood. Merritt introduced me to it."

Merritt has to be told David is dead. I don't want to think about that. I don't want to be there when that happens. It will destroy him. She pressed her face against her father's shoulder.

Andrew hugged Lindsey even more closely, and she leaned back to look at him. *He has the kindest face, the gentlest eyes.* "What would we do without music, Daddy?"

"Life wouldn't be the same, sweetheart. It's an essential part of who we are, that's for sure."

She sighed and snuggled against him as she had so many times as a child. "Someone told me recently that I had an enchanted childhood, and I absolutely did. It was because I had a magical father and mother."

"Food's ready," Mary said, interrupting them. "Come and eat something, Lindsey, and then you need to change."

It had been nice to escape briefly into her past, into music, but Lindsey was brought back to full consciousness of what lay ahead. *I have to dress for David's funeral.* As appealing as the food was, she managed only a few bites and then excused herself to shower.

Mary stood in her daughter's bedroom, looking through the closet when Lindsey emerged from the bathroom. "I see two black dresses...which one?" She held up hangers, one in each hand.

Lindsey pointed to the one with the higher neckline and allowed her mother to help her dress, fix her hair, and even put a touch of blush on each cheek. The tender ministrations that had been part of her life for more than twenty years comforted Lindsey. "Thank you, Mommy."

The phone rang and Andrew answered, spoke to the caller briefly, then covered the mouthpiece. "Lindsey, it's Rabbi Ephron. He'd like to speak with you."

What could he want? Somewhat apprehensive, Lindsey took the phone. "Yes, Rabbi?"

"Lindsey, David's family would like to have you join the mourners at the service tonight. We all know you were like brother and sister. David would want that."

Lindsey's eyes stung and her voice quivered. "I'm honored, Rabbi." She knew this was the select group of people closest to the deceased. "I really...I really need to be with my family, though."

"That's understandable, and they can be part of the group as well. I'm in the process of writing David's eulogy, and I want to ask you, as his dear friend, if there's anything in particular you think I should include. What first comes to your mind when you think of him?"

75

Lindsey had to wait for a moment before she could reply. "Rabbi Ephron, David was one of the best people I've ever known in my life."

"Yes, he certainly was. But why do you say that?"

"He was unfailingly honest with his friends, with Merritt and me. He helped me to see those things about myself that he admired, and those things he thought needed changing." She took a deep breath. "But he always did it with love. I can't even begin...I can't even begin to tell you...how much I miss him already."

"Thank you, Lindsey. Leah will appreciate all of this."

Lindsey replaced the phone gently and turned to her family. "They want us to be among the mourners at the service." She glanced at each of them. "I thought we'd just be attending, not participating."

"Are you okay with this?" Andrew asked.

Lindsey shook her head. "I don't know how I feel. Of course, I agreed, since David's mother made the request. I'm more grateful than ever that you are all here."

They were quiet on the half-hour drive to Amberley Village. Mary held her daughter's hands as they sat together in the back seat. Lindsey, lost in her thoughts, appreciated her family respecting her silence.

***

This is David's funeral.

Lindsey's father and mother kept her between them, and M.J. stood directly behind her. As mourners, they were taken into a small room before the service. Prayers were chanted, and each person was given a small piece of black ribbon to pin on their clothing. Lindsey's hands began to shake, and Mary gently took the cloth and pinned it to her daughter's shoulder.

Lindsey knew what the ribbons were for. *David told me when he attended a funeral and still had the ribbon on when he came home. "In Orthodox congregations, garments are torn as an expression of grief. In Conservative and Reform congregations, strips of cloth or ribbons are used symbolically." He had worn it for seven days. "It's our tradition," he said. How tragically ironic that I was now doing this for him.*

"*Adonai natan, Adonai lakach, yehishem Adonai m'vorach*—God has given, God has taken away, blessed be the name of God." The beautiful Hebrew words sung in Rabbi Ephron's warm baritone voice opened the floodgates, and Andrew pressed his handkerchief into Lindsey's hand. Rabbi Ephron gazed at her with concern.

She covered her face with her father's handkerchief to stifle her sobs. *Now I understand why they rend their garments. I want to do something—tear at my hair, scratch my face, anything to relieve this awful wave of grief.*

Lindsey managed to compose herself when their group was ushered into the front rows of the sanctuary, where the other attendees were waiting. Once inside the temple, she experienced a strong sense of awe, a sense of the majesty of Yahweh. Ahead of them stood the ornate cabinet housing the Ark of the Covenant where the Torah—the sacred scrolls— were kept. Lindsey lifted her eyes to the large skylight in the shape of the Star of David, opening the sanctuary to the heavens.

Directly in front of her, she saw the plain wooden casket, closed. She shut her eyes for a few moments and had a vivid image of David within the coffin, dressed in his tuxedo, his face peaceful, his curly hair carefully brushed. She swayed, but M.J.'s strong hands on her shoulders steadied her.

The service began with readings from the Psalms, followed by Rabbi Ephron's heartfelt and beautiful eulogy. He talked about David's immense talent, of his family's love and pride, of the brilliant future that now would not be realized. He talked about how it remains a mystery why these things happen and can challenge our faith. He spoke of focusing on the gifts David bestowed on all during his time here, and included what Lindsey had told him about David's honesty and love for his friends.

"David Eli Rosenthal was a bright comet that crossed our sky for a moment in time, spreading light and love through his music and compassion. He will never be forgotten. He will always be loved and honored. His parents tell me they are planning to establish a scholarship in his honor at the Conservatory for an exemplary piano student. The recipients will continue David's traditions of musical excellence, a legacy which means his gifts will continue to be in our lives."

A final prayer consigned David to being "sheltered beneath the wings of God's presence." *That's a beautiful image, I will remember those words always*, Lindsey thought as the mourners were ushered into the private room while the casket was removed. She glanced at the attendees and saw Howard Noble and Merritt's sister Kathleen. *Grace must be at the hospital.*

The Cameron family joined the funeral procession and in silence drove to the cemetery for the graveside service. Of everything she remembered later about the funeral, what came next was the most vivid.

Her legs felt wobbly as she walked to the grave, grateful to have her father on one side, M.J. on the other. She dreaded this—leaving David, knowing the casket would be covered with earth. More prayers graveside and the casket was lowered into the grave, each mourner invited to throw a shovelful of earth on the casket.

The shovel was presented to Lindsey but her hands were shaking so badly she couldn't grasp it. Andrew put his arms around her and supported her arms so she could hold it. He helped her lift a small shovelful of earth and toss it into the grave. She was the last one. She stood for long moments staring at the casket, imagining David within it lying in his final resting place.

Beneath the shelter of God's wings.

***

The Rosenthals had asked not to have the attendees and mourners go to their house after the service but would open their home for shivah—the formal mourning period—the following day. Leah had not had time to prepare for hospitality. Lindsey and her family would not have been there in any event. Lindsey didn't feel she could handle being around people after burying the young man she loved like a brother.

As much as she hadn't wanted to talk on the way to the funeral, Lindsey couldn't seem to stop talking on the ride home. "Wasn't that beautiful, that last prayer in the service? About David being in the shelter of God's wings. I'll always remember that. Leah said David was killed instantly. So, he didn't suffer. He didn't have to deal with any pain. That's how I tried to picture him. I saw him lots of times asleep on the sofa. That's how I think he looked in the coffin." She paused. "Except I'm sure his hair was brushed. He always had such messy hair. Merritt and I were forever after him to get it cut. To have it cut shorter. I think he liked it longer and more curly."

They arrived back at her house and M.J. found an unopened bottle of merlot in the kitchen. "How about a glass of wine, folks?"

Andrew gazed at his daughter. "Sounds good to me. How about it, sweetheart?"

"Sure. There's some cheese in the fridge. And I have crackers." Lindsey began to pull out items as she talked. "Merritt bought the wine. We were going to watch a movie on TV this weekend and...." She stopped abruptly, staring at her family. "Tonight." Her voice faltered. "We wanted to do that tonight."

Andrew put his arms around her and she pressed her face against his shoulder. "I can't do this. I just can't."

Her father walked her to the sofa and helped her sit down. "You don't have to, Lindsey. Go ahead and cry. Scream. Whatever you need."

"It hurts so much." A sobbing breath. "This can't really be happening." She clenched her hands together. "We just buried David. And we don't even know how Merritt will be when he wakes up. I'll have to be at the hospital when that happens. Somebody will have to tell him about David." Lindsey covered her face with her hands. "*Please* tell me I won't have to do that."

Lindsey was unaware of the concerned glances shared among her family members. Mary sat next to her daughter and gently guided her hands away from her face. "I think one of his doctors will do that, Lindsey. And we'll be right there with you."

M.J. knelt at her feet, pressing a wine glass into Lindsey's hand. "Drink this. Just sip it. We're all right here, and we'll be here to help you through this."

A few sips of the merlot, and she sighed, relaxing a little. "Hysteria. I guess that's where I was just now, wasn't it? I was getting hysterical."

They were silent for a moment until Lindsey took a deep breath and waved a hand around the room. "I can't stay here. First of all, I can't afford the rent on my own. Merritt won't be able to come back here. I don't know what's going to happen with him. Dear God, he lost a leg. And we don't know about his head injury yet."

"You don't have to make any decisions tonight, Lindsey," M.J. went to his sister and wrapped his arms around her. "Remember what I suggested earlier…one thing at a time."

"Yes, I know what you said." She leaned against him. "I'm trying to do that, but it's so hard. All these thoughts just keep racing around my brain."

M.J. guided Lindsey back to the sofa as Andrew stood and went to the CD player, looking through the CDs. "This might help." In moments the quiet opening chords of the Verdi *Requiem* filled the room.

Lindsey sighed and rested her head against the back of the sofa. "We all loved this recording so much. We would listen to it together and let the music take us someplace else. How did you know that, Dad?"

With her family close, Lindsey allowed Verdi's magnificent music to soothe her grieving spirit. She lost herself in the hushed opening sounds of the chorus and orchestra, followed by the strong descending melody in the low string instruments and the beautiful tenor voice of Jamie Logan soaring above all.

Emotionally drained by the intense experiences of less than twenty-four hours, Lindsey gave in to her exhaustion, drifting into blessed, oblivious sleep.

Chapter 6

It was her senior recital, and Lindsey and David were performing the Schumann song cycle *Frauenliebe und Leben*. When she sang the third song in the cycle, "Er, der Herrlichste von allen," Lindsey sang it for David. As they learned the music together, she had told him she thought the song described him perfectly—*the noblest of all*—and recalled his blush when she said it.

"Oh, come on, Lindsey. The song is meant for the singer's true love."

"Well, in a lot of ways, that's what you are to me. Not a lover, of course, but my dearest friend, the best person I know, who I love with all my heart." As she sang it at the rehearsal, she glanced at him from time to time and saw him grinning from ear to ear.

But then the mood changed when she began the final song, "Nun hast du mir den erste Schmertz getan." She sang the first line, "Now for the first time you have caused me pain," and David seemed to fade from his place at the piano. She stood alone on a dark stage, feeling lost and disconsolate.

Lindsey pulled herself from the dream which was not much different from the reality she awoke to. *David is gone. Yet he seemed so real, we were so happy performing.* She had no memory of getting into bed. The last thing she recalled was listening to the Verdi *Requiem* with her family.

She smelled coffee, threw on a robe, and wandered into the kitchen to see M.J. at the table, reading a newspaper. He smiled at her as he stood. "Feeling a little better?"

"Actually, I am. I dreamed about David. Most of it was a happy dream, but then it became terribly sad and I woke up." She sat at the table and M.J. placed a mug of coffee in front of her. "I don't even remember going to bed."

"Mom and Dad tucked you in before they left. They'll be back at any minute with something for breakfast."

Lindsey stirred cream and sugar into her coffee and took a sip. "Today is going to be awful. Even worse than yesterday. I wish it was tomorrow and it had already happened."

M.J. observed her closely. "You can't avoid this, Lindsey. Merritt will need you there when he learns what happened."

"Yes, I keep telling myself that. Please don't tell me to 'be strong.' I'm not a strong person, M.J., you know that. I'm hanging on by my fingernails at this point."

She glanced around the room. "I have to figure out what happens next. I told you, I can't stay here."

"I can sure understand that," M.J. said.

"So where do I go?" Lindsey stared off into space, speaking her thoughts aloud. "I guess I'll have no choice but to stay in Cincinnati for a while, at least until we can figure out what we're going to do, Merritt and I." She sighed. "We just think somebody dies…but then what? Everything just goes on like it used to? It's complicated, isn't it?"

M.J. leaned toward her. "You mentioned yesterday performing your recital this summer rather than trying to scramble to put another program together in just a few weeks. If you did that, you could probably graduate at the end of the summer session. What about your coursework? Could you stay here to finish up your classes?"

"I'm not sure. I don't know if those classes will be offered this summer. Another thing...I could stay in Cincinnati and see what I could do for Merritt, then go back to school in the fall and do all of it. My recital, finish the course work." She linked her fingers together, pressing them against her chin. "But then what about grad school? I've been accepted at Peabody and at Curtis. I'd pretty much decided on Curtis. But I can't start grad school in the fall if I'm still here as an undergrad."

A tap at the door, and once again Mary and Andrew Cameron came in with bags, this time containing groceries. They each hugged their son and daughter and began putting items on the counter as M.J. removed the frying pan from a cabinet.

"Pastries from the Vernon Manor?" he asked.

"Yes. They have a nice menu," Mary replied. "We thought scrambled eggs and bacon." She gazed at her daughter with concern. "I hope you can eat a little more than you did yesterday."

"I think I can. M.J. and I have been talking about my...." She paused.

"No, go on," Mary prompted, handing M.J. a stick of butter. "I'd like to hear it."

"Well, I guess about my immediate future. It's confusing." She shook her head. "No, it's bewildering. I don't know what to do."

All of the Camerons pitched in to get breakfast on the table, M.J. manning the frying pan to scramble eggs, Andrew found a cooking sheet for the bacon and prepared to put it in the oven. Mary arranged pastries on a platter and Lindsey set the table.

This is so nice. Just like being at home. The thought struck her suddenly, *I want to go home. At least for a while, so I can figure things out. But what about Merritt?*

85

They sat down to eat, and Lindsey took an appreciative bite of her apricot pastry. "This is so good. This is all good. I mean, everything about this moment." Her family members glanced at each other.

"Oh, don't look like that. But there is something I want to say to you." She put her fork down. "Here's something I believe I should do." She glanced at each of them, taking in a deep breath. "I think I should withdraw from school for the rest of this semester."

No one responded.

"Think about it. I can't possibly give my senior recital between now and early May. I have to find another pianist to work with. And I can't...." She took another deep breath to steady her voice. "I can't sing the program David and I spent so much time on. There is no way I could sing that music with someone else."

"That's understandable," Andrew said. "But what about your classes?"

"I believe my professors would give me an 'incomplete' and help me find a way to finish the work later...maybe over the summer. Daddy, I don't think I can bear being on campus right now. I wonder if I wouldn't just...spend all my time missing David and Merritt. They're all I can think about."

"Merritt's going to need your help, Lindsey," Mary reminded her. "I don't think there's any question of that." She gazed around the table again. "That poor boy. We don't know yet what he's going to be facing."

"What'd you have in mind, sis?" M.J. asked. "You said you can't live in this house. Somebody has to oversee getting all the stuff moved somewhere, though."

"I'm sure the Nobles and the Rosenthals would help with that," Andrew said. "I would think Merritt's belongings will all be taken back to his parents' house."

"Poor Arthur couldn't deal with anything right now," Mary mused. "I didn't think he was going to make it through the funeral service last night."

Lindsey had just picked up her fork to resume eating but stopped. "Why do you say that?"

"Mr. Rosenthal could hardly stand up, he was in so much pain," M.J. told her.

Lindsey clenched her hands together. "Oh, no. Why wasn't I aware of that? I should have known…I should have seen it."

"You were dealing with a lot, Lindsey," Andrew said.

Mary added. "Lindsey, you were having such a hard time yourself. How could you have seen anything else?" She sighed. "How awful, to lose an only child."

"And here I am trying to figure out what to do about school like I'm the only one this tragedy happened to." Lindsey tossed her napkin on the table. "What's wrong with me? Am I some kind of…unfeeling bitch?" Her voice became shrill as she felt bile rise in her throat.

"No, you're not," Andrew said firmly. He reached across the table and squeezed her hand. "You're making perfect sense. You do have to decide what to do about a lot of things right now. And that's exactly why we're here, to help you in any way we can."

Lindsey gratefully returned the squeeze, her thoughts focusing on the young man in the hospital. "I saw Merritt's father and his sister Kathleen at the service last night. I guess Grace must have stayed at the hospital."

"You didn't see Merritt Saturday night, did you?" M.J. asked.

"Well, technically, it was Sunday morning when I was at the hospital. The accident happened late Saturday night around…before midnight, I think." Lindsey pushed her plate back. "I got to the hospital before one and we waited until around four before Merritt's surgeon came and spoke to Howard and Grace."

She stared at her uneaten breakfast. "They were the only ones who were allowed into his room in the ICU. Leah and I waited until they came out. They had a hard time talking about…how he seemed to them." A shuddering breath. "I never saw David. I haven't seen Merritt. I don't know if that's a bad thing or a good thing."

"Why did they sedate him so heavily…I mean, to the point of putting him in a coma?" Mary asked.

"He was unconscious when he was taken to the hospital. He had a head injury and they weren't sure how bad it was. His leg…was so shattered they had to amputate it immediately to save his life." Lindsey closed her eyes. "I don't think there was a skull fracture, though." Her eyes flew open. "I can't believe I'm sitting here calmly telling you any of this."

Mary went to her daughter and embraced her. "Not so calmly, honey. You don't realize how agitated you are." She gazed at Lindsey with concern. "I really wish you'd eat something."

"Well, I wish the Nobles would call and let me know what's going on with Merritt." She turned to her father. "You're awfully quiet, Daddy. It's because of Merritt's head injury, isn't it? It's making you remember what happened to your brother."

"It's a very different situation, sweetheart. Medicine has made giant strides since Jake was injured in Vietnam. But yes, I understand how uncertain a brain injury can be."

Lindsey took a sip of coffee. "I want to see Merritt, and at the same time, I dread it. Am I an awful person?" She picked up her fork and tried unsuccessfully to take another bite of eggs. "I'm sorry, Mom. I just…I'm not hungry."

"Sitting here and speculating about Merritt's condition doesn't seem at all productive to me," M.J. pronounced. "Let's get back to Lindsey and what she needs to do."

Mary and Andrew nodded their agreement and M.J. continued, "Lindsey, maybe you should make a list. Can you get some paper and a pencil?" She slowly stood and went into her room, returning with a pad and pencil and sitting at the table to write.

"Okay, number one: contact the Conservatory and tell them...I won't be back this semester. Number two: contact my professors about giving me an 'incomplete' for the present until I figure out when I can get back to school. Number three...." She stopped, pencil poised in the air, unable to continue.

"I can't finish this until I know what's going to happen with Merritt." She stood as she choked out the words, throwing pad and pencil on the floor in frustration.

Andrew guided his daughter to the sofa, pulling her down beside him. "Lindsey, I wish with all my heart none of this had happened. But it did."

"I'm a train wreck, Daddy." Lindsey's voice shook. "I thought if I ever had something awful happen, I'd be stronger. I'm not at all. I just want to go to sleep and wake up and find out this has all been an awful nightmare."

The sound of a solo piano filled the room as M.J. put on a CD of Chopin etudes. "Maybe this will help," he said, kneeling beside the sofa. "You said David would play Chopin for you when you were troubled."

Mary softly kissed her daughter on the forehead, then retrieved the pencil and pad from the floor and studied Lindsey's short list. "If you're sure about this, honey, I can call the Conservatory. Or go over there if you think that would be better, and see about making these arrangements."

"I am sure. I can't go back to school to finish the semester. I just can't."

"I'll go with you, Mom," M.J. offered. Lindsey was only dimly aware of the two of them leaving the house as she closed her eyes, allowing the music to soothe her.

Not speaking, Andrew continued to hold her close as she relaxed. After several minutes, Lindsey sighed and pulled back to look at him.

"When Uncle Jean disappeared, how did you ever handle that?"

Her father gazed at her. "Not well at all. I can appreciate what you're going through because I had a similar response when faced with a crisis. Only I tried to pretend everything would be all right, and I ended up in the hospital because of that. Don't internalize what you're feeling, Lindsey. Cry, scream, yell, hit things, but don't hold those feelings in. They'll find a way to bite you."

Lindsey rested against her father's shoulder, thinking about what he'd just said. "I want to see Merritt, but…I'm also dreading it. I just don't know what to expect."

Andrew squeezed her shoulders, offering comfort as he had her entire life. "I'm guessing about this. For one thing, he may be confused and disoriented when he first regains consciousness; that's what happened to Jake. Merritt may not remember what happened, or he may have only a vague memory."

Lindsey gave a shuddering sigh. "Finding out he's lost a leg. Merritt, who is always complimented for how beautifully he moves on stage. That's going to be so hard."

"Yes, for Merritt it's losing a limb. For my brother Jake, it was losing himself."

Lindsey considered this. "I still don't know how he…how anyone could learn to live with that."

90

She remained silent for a moment. "Merritt...on top of losing his leg, worst of all he'll have to be told about David— and he just committed himself to David for life." She shivered. "I don't know how he's going to cope with any of this."

"Life can present us with situations that seem impossible, Lindsey. Maybe it would be helpful for you to talk to Jake at some point."

Father and daughter sat quietly listening to music. M.J. had loaded more than one CD. Wrapped in her father's warm arms, Lindsey found herself drifting off when the next CD proved to be music by Rachmaninoff—the tone poem "The Isle of the Dead" and an instrumental version of his "Vocalise."

When the music ended, Andrew made a pot of coffee and brought Lindsey a mug, which she accepted gratefully. Mary and M.J. returned as they were finishing their coffee.

"Mission accomplished," Mary announced. "I was fortunate enough to catch the dean who agreed immediately to your request and said he would contact your professors about your course work. Of course, he offered his condolences and said the students were shocked and saddened by the news. None of them had heard anything until this morning."

M.J., nearest the phone when it rang, fielded the call. Lindsey scarcely noticed what he was saying as she asked Mary a few questions about her meeting with the dean.

Her brother interrupted. "That was Grace Noble. Some good news: Merritt's head injury isn't as serious as they had feared. No swelling, and confirmation he had a relatively mild concussion but no skull fracture. So his doctor has been reducing the sedatives he's on. He may be conscious by around four this afternoon."

Lindsey's heart plummeted through the floor. "I guess that means we should be at the hospital a little before that?" A sharp intake of breath.

I can't take much more of this…this emotional rollercoaster.

***

They arrived at Good Sam a little after three-thirty and were told to go to the ICU waiting room and the Nobles would be informed. The ICU waiting room was almost a carbon copy of the surgical waiting room, and again Lindsey began shivering, aware it was more anxiety than cold.

What could I possibly say to Merritt that might help him? 'It's going to be okay.' No, it will never, ever be okay. 'You'll get through this.' And then how am I supposed to tell him how that could possibly happen?

When the nurse came through the door and headed for their group, Lindsey felt every muscle in her body freeze.

"Lindsey Cameron?"

"Yes, I'm Lindsey Cameron."

"Come with me, please."

All the Camerons stood. "Sorry, you can't all come with her. The patient is in a small room."

"Can I please have at least one member of my family with me*?" I hate how tiny and scared my voice sounds. Probably because I feel tiny and scared.*

The nurse considered Lindsey's request and relented slightly. "Well…only one, dear. I suppose that would be all right."

"Daddy?" Lindsey clutched his arm, holding it tightly as they moved through the waiting room, down the hall, and stopped outside the door to Merritt's room.

"Please stay near the door when we go inside," whispered the nurse. "Your friend's parents are at his bedside, and they'll let you know when you're needed."

92

Lindsey and Andrew stepped inside. Whirring machines, a strong light, Merritt lying still on a hospital bed with tubes and wires attached to his body. His left leg covered by a sheet and a blanket.

She pressed her hand to her mouth to keep from gasping at the proof positive half his right leg was no longer there. *Dear God in heaven.*

The doctor at Merritt's bedside, shining a light into his eyes, moved to one side so Grace and Howard could move closer and touch their broken son.

Merritt's voice, a soft croak. "Mom? Dad?"

"Right here, son," Howard kept his voice low and gentle. "We're right here."

Then a pause so long Lindsey wondered if Merritt had drifted off.

"I don't understand. Why am I...this is a hospital? Isn't it?"

"You...were in an accident, Merritt." Grace's voice sounded strained and scratchy. *Of course. She hasn't slept at all.*

"An accident?" Merritt asked.

Lindsey pressed her back against the wall, gripping Andrew's arm for dear life. He covered her hand with his free hand and squeezed.

"You don't remember?" Grace again.

"No...I...David and I went to see a movie." He paused. *"Romeo and Juliet."*

Another pause. "I guess...I guess that's the last thing I remember." He tried to change his position. "What's wrong with my leg?"

Oh God oh God oh God.

"Do you remember you and David stopping for a drink on your way home?" Howard asked, his voice fraying at the seams. "You had left the car and then a pickup truck hit you…both." He stopped, unable to continue.

Mercifully, the surgeon came to Howard's rescue.

"This won't be easy to hear, Merritt. Your right leg was very badly damaged below the knee."

"Oh." A pause as Merritt struggled to process this. "Is that why it hurts so much?"

Phantom pain. I've heard of that. Just go ahead and tell him.

"We had no choice but to amputate your lower leg," the doctor finally said. "What you're feeling is called phantom pain. I know this is difficult to hear, son. But you will be able to use a prosthesis successfully."

Merritt's voice caught in his throat as he struggled to respond. "You…had to…cut off…part of…my leg?"

Why isn't he yelling or screaming? …I know why. He's too weak. He's sedated and in shock. This isn't really registering yet.

And then it hit him—a sobbing intake of breath. "What about David? Is he okay?"

No response, and more forcefully, "Is David okay? Somebody tell me!"

Neither Grace nor Howard could handle this, so the surgeon finally said, "I'm very sorry, Merritt."

"You're *sorry*? What the hell…where is David?"

"Your friend didn't make it." He spoke quietly, with compassion.

So now Merritt knows everything.

Another long pause.

Then something Lindsey would remember forever, watching her friend struggle to lift his arm to cover his eyes, his shoulders shaking with soundless sobs, the rest of the room dead still.

Grace motioned for Lindsey to come to the bed, and with Andrew at her back, she managed to walk there on legs made of wood.

"Merritt, Lindsey is here," Grace said softly.

Silence.

A sigh from the depths of Merritt's soul, then a gurgled sob. "I wish…why David and not her?" His voice splintered as he spoke.

The words cut through Lindsey like a knife with a blade made of ice. She turned and stumbled from the room, her father right behind.

Once in the hall, Lindsey crumpled to the floor, sobbing uncontrollably.

Andrew knelt beside her, attempting to offer comfort. "He didn't mean that, Lindsey."

"He wishes I were dead," she wailed.

"That was his pain and grief talking. He didn't mean it."

Lindsey clutched Andrew as he helped her struggle to her feet. "I can't do this. I have to get out of here. I can't stay here. I want to go home."

"You can do this. Merritt needs you."

"No, Merritt needs David. You heard him. He wishes I were dead. Please, Daddy, take me home!"

Susan Moore Jordan

Chapter 7

Andrew guided Lindsey into the ICU waiting room, a protective arm around her. Mary and M.J. stood and went quickly to them, startled by Lindsey's demeanor. She fought to control herself as sobs threatened to break out again.

"What on earth happened?" Mary asked as she embraced her daughter.

"We need to leave. Merritt needs a lot more help than Lindsey can offer him right now." Andrew collected Lindsey's coat and helped her with it. "I'll explain more when we get back to the house."

Howard Noble met them in the hall. "I'm so sorry, Lindsey. Merritt didn't know what he was saying."

Lindsey rested a hand on Howard's arm. "I know he needs something I can't give him right now, Mr. Noble." Her voice quivered as she spoke.

"There's a psychiatrist with him now." Howard Noble looked helplessly at Andrew. "I don't know what to say."

"You don't have to say anything, Howard." Andrew squeezed Howard's shoulder. "I think both our children are completely overwhelmed at the moment. This is just too much for them."

M.J. and Mary, one on each side of Lindsey, walked her from the room as the two men continued their conversation.

"I think Lindsey needs to get out of here, Mom," M.J. said in a low voice. "I mean she needs for us to take her home."

"You mean back to West Chester?" Mary pressed a hand to her throat.

"I think so. Dad can tell us more, but it's pretty obvious something bad happened."

Andrew caught up with them. "We exchanged phone numbers," he said. "Howard and I will stay in touch with each other."

Lindsey was barely aware of the flurry of activity around her that afternoon. The rental car was exchanged for a van, and suitcases and boxes were filled with as many of Lindsey's belongings as they would hold. She assisted with the packing, automatically folding clothing, and sorting through music and CDs.

She vaguely heard bits and snatches of phone conversations between her father and Leah Rosenthal. "We think it's best...." "Merritt is going to need a lot of help emotionally and mentally, as well as physically...." "Lindsey needs to have some time...." "We're taking as much with us as we can...."

She overheard a whispered conversation between her parents, Mary expressing dismay at her daughter's emotional distress. "I wish I had something to give her. Some medication. I've never seen Lindsey like this."

"Let's just get her home where she's away from this awful situation. She needs time and distance so she can begin to process it," Andrew told his wife.

"Andrew...what did Merritt say to her?"

Andrew noticed his daughter glancing in their direction. "Something hurtful, and I doubt he even knew he said it."

M.J. distracted Lindsey by sorting through CDs. "I'm not sure which are yours."

"It doesn't matter much. We have a lot of these at home," she said. But she stopped and selected one. "This was David's but I want to borrow it. I don't think Leah would mind." She picked up a CD of the Rachmaninoff third piano concerto.

Lindsey stared at the CD in her hand. "David had been working on this over the past year—he intended to audition for the Van Cliburn Piano Competition next year in Texas, and it was to be his concerto if he made it to the finals. He loved this work so much. His favorite piece of music. The three of us listened to it many times."

No one spoke and Lindsey added, "I can bring it with me when I come back to see Merritt."

A look of relief came over her parents' faces at the mention of coming back to Cincinnati. Hands on hips, Lindsey tipped up her chin. "I'm not running away forever. I'm really not. I want to come back at some point and learn a new recital and finish the coursework for my degree. And I know at some point Merritt and I need to talk. But right now, I can't stay here. I just can't."

After carefully stripping Lindsey's bed and stacking the folded linens on it, Mary vacuumed the downstairs. M.J. made sure pots, pans, and dishes were all put away. Andrew kept his arms around Lindsey as she checked to see if she'd missed anything.

He stopped and pointed to the framed, enlarged photo on the wall of Lindsey, Merritt, and David. "Do you think it would be okay if I borrow this for a while?"

"Of course. It actually belongs to me." She gazed at him. "You want to paint David, don't you? For the Rosenthals." She hugged him hard. "You would do something wonderful like that, Daddy. Thank you."

Lindsey resumed her perusal of the house. "Looks like we got everything we can take with us."

"Leah told me she's coming over later this week to begin to organize everything so it can be stored at the Rosenthals' house," Andrew told them. "She said we shouldn't worry about anything, and she'll stay in touch with us about what she's done." He glanced at Lindsey again. "And she'll let us know how Merritt is doing."

"Can I please have a minute by myself?" Lindsey stood near the piano. Her family exchanged glances. "Please. Just a moment before I leave here."

"We'll be right outside," M.J. told her. "Yell if you need us."

Lindsey watched them leave, then moved slowly around the living-dining room, collecting memories of special moments. She touched the page of Rachmaninoff's music hanging on the wall near the piano, remembering when they had hung it. *(Merritt, teasing David: "Why Rachmaninoff?" David: "Because he's taller than you.")* She sat for a moment in the armchair, recalling David seated at the piano, explaining the third piano concerto to her as he worked on it. *(David: "Listen to what he does here. How he takes this simple melodic theme and develops it into something dazzling.")* She touched the dining table as she recalled sitting there singing with Merritt as they learned duets together. *(Merritt: "I have to be careful not to overpower you here. You can stomp on my foot if you need to."* At which Lindsey became convulsed with laughter.)

Standing by the sofa, she envisioned the three of them as they spent special time together doing what they loved most, immersing themselves in music—Lindsey relaxed in the middle, her head resting against the back of the sofa; David sprawled on her right, stretching his legs out and resting his head on her shoulder, his left hand loosely holding her right hand; Merritt lounging on the other side of her, his head in her lap, holding her left hand, legs draped over the sofa arm—the three of them connected to each other. They always turned the lights down and the CD player up, letting the music flow through them. *And now that will never, ever happen again.*

M.J. opened the door slightly, and when he saw his sister's face, went to her and held her tight.

"This shouldn't be happening. None of this. This is so hard." Lindsey leaned against a wall as her brother flipped off the lights. M.J. gently led her from the house, closed the door behind them, and helped her into the van.

The drive would take them just over eight hours. They left at about ten and thought they might make it home by sunrise at the latest, and M.J. and Andrew agreed to drive in two-hour shifts. Lindsey dozed in the back seat, scarcely aware when they stopped to eat. Mary and Andrew went for food as M.J. watched over his sister. Lindsey sat up long enough to drink a chocolate malt, then went back to sleep.

She stirred occasionally when they went through a town, but once they reached the Pennsylvania Turnpike Lindsey fell into a deep sleep, not even waking when they stopped briefly to switch drivers, and she had to be awakened when they reached the Cameron house in West Chester.

Lindsey stopped in the kitchen to get herself a glass of water, which she drained, before heading upstairs to her room. She took off her clothes and pulled a soft cotton flannel nightgown from her closet, shrugged into it, and fell into her bed, where she slept soundly until late afternoon.

***

Music coming from downstairs, the Fauré *Requiem. Dad's started on David's portrait.* Lindsey glanced at the clock and saw it was past three in the afternoon. She rose, stretched, threw on jeans and a sweatshirt, and, pulling on a pair of warm woolen socks, wandered downstairs.

Mary stood in the kitchen, peering into the refrigerator. She smiled at Lindsey. "You look better. I guess that was what you needed...a nice long sleep."

"I definitely feel better. It's so good to be home. I feel more like myself. Not so lost and confused." She poured herself a tall glass of water. "Why am I so thirsty?"

"Lindsey, you hardly ate or drank anything for a couple of days. You're dehydrated. What sounds good for dinner? I have chicken and pork chops."

"Pork chops sound great. And maybe baked potatoes? I'll help."

"No, let me spoil you a little." Mary pulled items from the refrigerator. "I know your dad would like to see that you're up and about."

Lindsey drank another half glass of water. "I suspect he's painting David's portrait. I want him to use David's music. Is all my stuff upstairs? I brought home a CD Dad needs to use...and I think I want to hear it."

She found the CD quickly but stopped before taking it downstairs to her father. *Can I listen to this? I know it will make me cry, Rachmaninoff is so emotional. How sad David never had a chance to play it in performance.* She recalled David telling her so much about this concerto—referred to often by aspiring pianists as the "Rach Three"—as he worked on it. He loved Rachmaninoff above all composers, and this concerto more than any other of the Russian's works.

"He was the soul of Russia, Linds. We hear so much of what he'd heard all his life. Some melodies that echo folk tunes or liturgical chants. The unique sounds of Russian church bells. All those gorgeous melodies he wrote had their genesis in how much he loved his country's music. It broke his heart when he had to leave Russia and come to the U.S."

David had warmed to his subject. "And man, could he play. You know about his enormous hands. It's thought he might have had Marfan's Syndrome...he was unusually tall."

"Yes, I know he was six feet six and had hands to match. You're one of the few people I know of who can even attempt this concerto, most piano students are terrified by it. It's incredibly difficult, yet you make it sound easy."

"Well, I'm a long way from having it up to performance level," David laughed. "I'll keep working on it, though. It was a thrill to perform the second concerto. If I get to perform this one, it'll be like standing on top of Mt. Everest."

Lindsey went to the window, looking out on the yard she had played in as a child, helped tend as a teenager. *I helped Mom and Grammy Toni plant those flower beds. And tended them every spring.* One of her grandmother's greatest joys, flowers.

Definitely another wonderful thing about my childhood, having my dad's parents living so close by, Lindsey thought. *I did have a charmed childhood. Doting grandparents, parents who idolized me and gave me everything I needed. A brother who is already a compassionate man who helps me however he can.*

Grammy will completely understand what I'm going through, Lindsey thought. When Toni was a young mother, her family had been violently attacked, and both her parents were shot and killed, leaving Toni and her two sisters orphaned. Little Andrew and Jacob were eight and six years old when it happened, and they witnessed the horror. *It happened many years ago in another era, an era when people were advised to "put it out of your mind." As if that is even a remote possibility,* Lindsey thought with a sigh.

She glanced around her room, still decorated in white, gold, and blue. A soft, cornflower blue rug on the floor, faux French colonial white-and-gold furniture, a white duvet on the bed, powder blue drapes at the window. Striped wallpaper, narrow strips of white and pale blue. As feminine and romantic a room as she could imagine, and she loved it. She was glad they had brought her home to this house, to this room, where she could just be Daddy's little girl again—for a while at least.

The Rosenthals had visited the Camerons the previous summer on their way to New York when David wanted to tour Juilliard. They stayed at a hotel nearby and were the Camerons' guests for dinner.

Before the meal, David asked Lindsey if he could see her room. A little startled, she said, "Sure, why not? It's just a room. Pretty 'girly,' but I like it."

"So, this is where you grew up." David leaned against the wall, his arms crossed, grinning. "You were right, it's definitely girly. But it's right for you, Linds." He moved around the room, touching the stuffed animals on the bed, picking up a black and white panda.

"I wish I'd known you when you were a little kid." He laughed as he tossed the bear to her. "On the other hand…I'll bet you haven't changed much. I'm sure you liked to have your way, even then."

Lindsey joined in the laugh. "My parents tell me I was always a very determined child," she giggled.

The memory faded, but Lindsey continued to smile even as she brushed away a tear. *My sweet David. You gave me so many wonderful memories. I'll miss you for the rest of my life.*

She joined her father in his studio, CD in hand, and watched him as he prepared the canvas. Lindsey saw that Andrew had a board on a second easel with some photos pinned to it, and moving closer realized that were pictures of David from that visit last summer. One of David sitting at her mother's piano. Another of herself and David at the piano as he played for her.

Andrew turned to her. "I'm glad I have these. I thought maybe David at the piano?"

"That would be perfect. I'd totally forgotten Mom took these pictures last summer. What was I singing, do you remember?"

"I do remember. Rachmaninoff's 'Vocalise.' I thought it was a polished performance by two young, gifted musicians."

Lindsey sighed as she relaxed into a chair. "We were going to do that one on my recital. That and two more Rachmaninoff songs—'The Island' and 'In the Silence of the Night.'" Her voice cracked on the second title as a line from the song ran through her mind: *With your beloved name, I wake the silent night.*

She took a long, shuddering breath. "It hurts too much, Daddy. I just can't believe David is really gone. I'll never see him again."

Andrew brought her a box of tissues. "Cry, Lindsey. Cry all you need to. I know it hurts. David was your best friend."

She handed him the CD. "This is David's music, Dad. It's everything he loved. Powerful. Passionate. And sometimes ethereal and—well, celestial. Otherworldly. Right straight from the realms of heaven."

"Are you sure you want to listen to this? It may not be easy."

"I know it won't. Not at first. And I'll probably cry through the entire piece. But you know something? It will bring David back to me for a while."

***

Just as she anticipated, Lindsey wept as she listened to "David's music" with her father, sharing with him some of the interesting details David had pointed out to her…the opening theme that some people thought sounded similar to a liturgical chant, the difficulty of the long solo piano cadenza in the first movement, the beauty of the melody in the second movement. Most of all, the almost unplayable section for the pianist near the end of the concerto, followed by an expansive and expressive statement by the full orchestra, which Lindsey found breathtaking.

I'll always love the Rach Three, and I'll always think of David when I hear it. Lounging comfortably in a chaise in her father's studio gave her a sense of peace. She couldn't remember when she had not spent time in this room. From her earliest childhood, her dad had wanted her nearby when he was painting. Later, M.J. had joined her, and they were told that when they were babies the floor was covered in warm blankets and they could crawl about at will, toys scattered around for them. Andrew kept a supply of baby blankets and quilts on a chest, and if his children fell asleep their father would cover them to keep them warm. *Who does that, besides my angelic father?*

When we were toddlers, we had tables and art and craft supplies in the studio, and Dad would take time to talk to us and teach us how to hold a brush, how to mold clay…whatever we wanted. Truly, a magical childhood, where I spent many hours immersed in art and music.

Her grandparents, Toni and Max Cameron, brought dinner with them to Andrew and Mary's house that evening, and wrapped Lindsey in a comforting, loving embrace, staying close to her all through dinner. The family circle was complete.

Later, Lindsey went along when Grandy Max drove M.J. to the train station for his return to U. Penn in Philadelphia.

"I'm glad we brought you home," M.J. said as she waited with him in the station while Max looked for a parking space. "You appear to be dealing with David's death a little better. Next step will be to start thinking about Merritt, but you know that."

Lindsey nodded, struggling to keep her emotions in check. "Dad's calling Mr. Noble tonight," she said. "I hope Merritt is…coping. No, that's stupid. He can't possibly be. I guess I hope they're keeping him sedated for now, until he's stronger. Is that a dumb thing to wish?"

M.J. gazed at his sister. "Not at all, and it's probably exactly what they're doing. He's still in a lot of physical pain, along with the heartbreak he's trying to deal with." He hugged her. "One thing. Don't wait too long to go back. He may not know it yet, but I'm sure you're the best person to help Merritt through this."

"Because we both loved David so much." Her voice quivered and she pressed her face against M.J.'s chest. "I'll miss David for the rest of my life. Merritt will miss him even more."

Max and Lindsey had a quiet return drive to the Andrew Cameron house, where Andrew waited with news of Merritt.

"He's resting comfortably, whatever that means," he told them. "Howard says they're keeping him sedated and Merritt's surgeon has a whole team—including a psychiatrist and psychologist—on standby, ready to do everything they can to help him through this."

"My poor boy," Lindsey murmured. "How will he ever recover from this loss?"

Her father searched her face. "It's good to hear you say that. Does that mean you're getting over your anger at Merritt?" Andrew asked her.

"I've never been angry, Dad. I was shocked and hurt by what he said, but I kind of understand why he said it."

Lying in her comfortable, warm bed, Lindsey's thoughts turned again to "my boys." *David loved Merritt so much. He was so happy. They were planning their future; they had decided to go to grad school together and were hoping for Juilliard—David had already been accepted, and Merritt had high hopes. They would have done anything for each other.*

I have to go back soon. Maybe in a few days. I have to be there. But how can I get Merritt to even talk to me?

***

Lindsey spent the next two days wrapping herself in the comforts of home and family. Helping Grammy Toni clean flower beds. Cooking with her mother. Sitting at the piano in their living room, playing through song accompaniments. She spent many hours in Andrew's studio, watching him work while they listened to music: the Brahms Requiem, Verdi's Requiem. A lot of Vaughan Williams, including "The Lark Ascending" which Lindsey played three times. Chopin preludes and etudes. And finally, once again the Rachmaninoff Third Concerto.

"Did I ever tell you David heard this performed in Pittsburgh when he was fourteen? André Previn and the Pittsburgh Symphony with Horácio Gutierrez. David already loved the piece, but hearing it live was a transcendent experience for him—so challenging to play, so beautiful. He said that performance stayed with him for weeks, and from that time playing it became his goal."

Andrew put down his brushes and sat on the floor with Lindsey as they listened again. This time, the emotion she experienced was evoked by Rachmaninoff's sublime music and not her grief for David. As the majestic finale ended, her father hugged her close.

"I think I'm about ready to go back to Cincinnati and see Merritt, Daddy."

"That's good to know, sweetheart."

A light tap on her door the next morning woke Lindsey and dragged her from yet another dream about David.

"I've been sent to fetch you to breakfast, niece." Her uncle's voice.

She leaped from the bed and quickly donned a robe, throwing the door open. "Uncle Jean!" Lindsey threw her arms around him, and he gathered her close. "Nobody told me you were coming. When did you get here?"

"About an hour ago. I came in on a red-eye. You should be flattered, I hate flying during those hours."

"I am so, so, *so* glad to see you," she brushed tears from her cheeks, simultaneously laughing and crying.

"Your dad said maybe I could be of some help to you, Lindsey. So I got here as quickly as I could."

She saw the love and concern on his face. "Do I have the most wonderful family in the world, or what?"

They went downstairs—Jake with an arm around Lindsey's shoulders, her arm around his waist—and joined Mary and Andrew for breakfast.

Family chatter during breakfast, Jake catching them up on news about his children. "Toinette is definitely your niece, Andy. Another first prize in the school art show, this one for a landscape. Our house on a winter night, a marvelous depiction of Old Montreal. Not bad for a thirteen-year-old. I think you'd love it."

"She's definitely a gifted artist, Jean. Other than her teachers at school, has she had any instruction yet?"

"We thought next year when she starts high school, we'd look into that. Our Museum of Fine Arts has programs for young people." He took a swig of coffee. "And Marie continues to excel at ballet. It's definitely her gift and her passion."

"What about my namesake?" grinned Andrew.

"Ah, André, the nine-year-old bedeviler of older sisters," Jean returned the grin. "As a matter of fact, he's discovered soccer. Absolutely loves it. I guess he is definitely my kid."

"Have you remembered more about your high school days?" Mary leaned forward eagerly.

"Yes, I have, as a matter of fact. Not vivid memories, but I have flashes about some high school football and baseball games. And that I was kind of impressed with myself, sorry to say." A raised eyebrow. "Noémi says she loves me anyway."

"You were a kid, Jake…Jean. The hometown hero. You were being scouted by some colleges—Penn State for one, beginning with your junior year. It's no wonder some of that went to your head," Andrew punched his brother in the arm. "That's good news, though. More recovered memories."

"My psychologist thinks so. But he's cautioned me that some memories…including memories of my time in Vietnam…may never come back." Jake draped an arm over the back of Lindsey's chair. "That's not why I'm here, though. I'm here to help Lindsey if I can."

"It means more to me than you can ever imagine, Uncle Jean. Let me shower and dress and I'll meet you in the living room." Lindsey ran upstairs with a lighter heart.

I think if anyone can help me figure out what I can do for Merritt, it will be my uncle. People helped him through a terrible ordeal.

Chapter 8

"I just…I don't know how to help him." Lindsey sighed and wiped her eyes again with the handkerchief Jake had just handed her. "He's in such pain."

She curled into the corner of the sofa, hugging herself as she remembered Merritt's despair. *He didn't want me there, and I literally ran from his hospital room.*

"I understand that, *ma fille*. But I honestly believe you are the person Merritt needs most right now." Lindsey had to smile when her bilingual uncle used a French term of endearment with her…a term she'd often heard him use with Toinette and Marie. *My girl.*

Jake stretched an arm across the back of the sofa. "You told me it helped you to listen to the Rachmaninoff concerto David loved so much."

"I think it would help Merritt, too. But how do I convince him to listen to it? It wasn't easy for me to hear, but I was so grateful I did." She paused, hearing the music echo in her mind. "I felt closer to David. More at peace."

Jake studied his niece closely. "You know, when I was at Walter Reed Hospital after I'd lost my memory in the helicopter crash in Vietnam, I had a very wise nurse who introduced me to another patient. A man who had lost his sight. And the use of one hand."

He glanced into the distance for a moment, and Lindsey swallowed hard, waiting for the rest. *So many men were damaged by that war.*

"His name was Lieutenant Matt Geiger, and he had been a pianist for the Philadelphia Opera Company."

"Oh, dear God." Lindsey covered her mouth with a hand as she shivered. "How awful for him."

"Matt's reaction was different, at least when I met him. He couldn't hear enough music. He had a portable record player in his room and a collection of recordings, and he listened almost constantly." Jake smiled gently. "Matt's favorite was opera."

"And he played his recordings for you?"

Jake nodded, resting a gentle hand on Lindsey's shoulder. "Yes, he did. I guess I had heard some of it before, but I didn't remember that. I vividly recall standing outside Matt's room listening to the love duet from *Madama Butterfly*. Hearing it at that highly vulnerable time in my life stirred something in me. I was hungry to hear more. Anything to get me out of my head. And Matt liked sharing it and talking to me about it. Looking back—I think it helped both of us."

Lindsey slid closer to her uncle. *He's been through so much. I know it was a long time ago, but still, it was pretty awful,* she thought.

"Then your grandfather bought me a small portable radio so I could hear the Met Opera broadcasts on Saturdays," Jake continued. "And after I went back to West Chester with my family—our family—your mother introduced me to more music. Sacred vocal music, mostly, like the Brahms Requiem."

Lindsey nodded. "Dad's favorite piece."

"It sure is, and now it's also one of mine. Over the next months, different people played a lot of music for me. Mostly classical, and I learned a lot." He paused. "I know I told you about George Smallwood—the Choctaw I served with in Vietnam—and the cleansing ceremony he performed on me."

She nodded. "Yes, I remember. You were in Washington State, in the Cascades, trying to decide what to do next with your life."

"Yes, and in a very real way, my healing began with Matt Geiger introducing me to opera, and George completed it."

"Was there music?" Lindsey asked. "I mean, during the ceremony?"

"As a matter of fact, there was. George chanted during the ceremony…but I would swear I heard other voices. Many other voices."

Lindsey leaned back, staring at him. "That must have been an incredible experience."

"One I will never forget," Jake replied. "So, there I was, at a point where I had to make a decision about what to do with my life."

Jake again looked off into the distance as he recalled that time. "Not long after George's cleansing ceremony, I went camping in the woods in the Cascades. Your dad had given me a Walkman and I had a whole collection of tapes. I chose Ravel's 'Pavane for a Dead Princess,' and as I listened, I understood who Jake Cameron needed to be."

He leaned toward Lindsey. "A man whose love for music and how it made him feel had changed him. I knew I could never again be Jake Cameron, the warrior. I realized this new Jake would have music as the focus of his life—of my life. I didn't know how that would happen, but I knew it was what I needed. And at that moment I decided to go to Canada and become a whole new person."

"And you did just that." Lindsey hugged her uncle briefly. "Oh, Uncle Jean, I don't know that I ever truly understood how difficult your life became after you were injured."

"Every life has moments of light and darkness." Jake smiled as he gently took Lindsey's hand. "We learn from the dark moments and cherish the light even more because of them."

He gazed into her eyes. "*Ma fille*, Merritt needs somebody to convince him he has to deal with his terrible loss and help him figure out how to do that. Remembering David through the music that spoke to him might be the best way to help Merritt now. And I think you should be the person who makes that happen."

She wadded the damp handkerchief in both hands. "I'm ashamed that I've been so worried about myself. About what I'm going to do next about my degree and grad school and all that inconsequential stuff when my friend Merritt is facing the crisis of his life."

Lindsey tugged on Jake's handkerchief and began tying a knot in it.

"Don't be too hard on yourself, Lindsey. What you're attempting to do with your life requires that you look out for yourself. Becoming a professional performer is challenging."

"Maybe." A shaky sigh as Lindsey shot her uncle a regretful smile. "Still, let's not forget how I behaved the first time I met you. I was rude and disrespectful. I didn't think at all about what you'd been through."

"I understood why you were so angry with me. You knew how much my absence hurt your father. You had watched him suffer for years." Jake waved a dismissive hand. "But that's ancient history. We both need to think about what you can do for Merritt."

Lindsey gazed into the distance. "I don't think he'll even want to see me."

Jake took Lindsey by her shoulders and gazed into her eyes. He had to clear his throat before he spoke. "Listen, kiddo.

Merritt needs help—your help. He needs you as nobody has ever needed you before."

Jake stood and pulled Lindsey to her feet. "I'd suggest you get back to Cincinnati as soon as possible. You must let Merritt know you didn't desert him. You just had to have some time to understand what had happened."

"Do you think he'll accept that? I just…ran from the room. His dad understood, though."

"The only way to find out is for you to see him. Do you want to try for a flight today?"

"I'll have to talk to my parents first, I think."

Over coffee at the kitchen table, Jake allowed Lindsey to be the person to present her plan to her parents. "It helps me to think there's something I can do. A way to maybe make things better for Merritt."

"Someone should go with you," Andrew said. He gazed at his brother for a moment. "Is there any possibility you might have a few more days?"

Jake lifted an eyebrow. "Don't you think you or Mary should go?"

"I think your experience dealing with amnesia and your total loss of memory might be extremely valuable for Merritt to learn about," Andrew replied. "Because of that, you—more than any of us—have a greater sense of his traumatic loss."

"If Lindsey wants, I can definitely arrange to take a few more days," Jake replied.

Andrew turned to Lindsey. "What do you think, sweetheart?"

Lindsey considered the discussion. *Mom and Dad have to be angry with Merritt because of what he said to me. Dad especially, because he actually heard it. And I would love to have some time with my Uncle Jean.*

"I think Uncle Jean would be a great help. To me, and to Merritt."

"I'd be honored to do this for Lindsey and her friend," Jake interjected. "We'll call you often. Lindsey says you've begun a portrait of David for the Rosenthals," he nodded at Andrew. "Why not finish it and bring it to Cincinnati after you've completed it?"

Mary reached for her husband's hand. "I believe that's a good plan, Andy. Leah and Arthur will love the painting. It would be nice to get it to them soon."

That settled, Lindsey looked from one parent to the other. "Have you heard anything more from anyone in Cincinnati? Mr. or Mrs. Noble, or Leah?"

Andrew stirred his coffee. "Leah Rosenthal called earlier, while you and your Uncle Jean were talking. She'd been to the hospital to try to see Merritt. He doesn't want to see anyone, but she talked to Grace Noble."

"How is he?" Lindsey felt herself grow tense as she waited for the answer.

"Not good. Physically, he's improving, mainly because he's young and strong. But he hasn't yet been willing to talk to the mental health professionals on his medical team. He does speak to Grace but doesn't say much. He won't talk about his leg. Oh, he's receiving physical therapy but he's not making much of an effort, so his progress has been slow. Mainly he keeps saying that he wishes he had died in the accident with David."

"Oh, how awful." Lindsey twisted her hands together. "But it doesn't surprise me he might say that." She gazed at the three adults. "You don't suppose…he can't be…."

Jake laid a soothing hand on her arm. "No, I don't believe that means he's suicidal. He's in a world of pain after losing the person he loves." He looked down. "David's death was such a shock and is so new, it seems to me Merritt's just expressing his grief. If he continues to say such things, though, it would be something that has to be addressed. It's good there are professionals at the hospital who can help."

"They can't be any help if he refuses to talk to them," Mary said. She glanced at Andrew, who nodded. "You need to know this, Lindsey. Merritt asked where you are, and why you're not there with him."

"What was he told?" Lindsey nervously played with her spoon. "I should be there. I shouldn't have run away."

"I don't agree," Mary said. "You were in no state to be of any help to him at all. It was important for you to come home for a few days." She took a quick sip of coffee.

"Grace told Leah what Merritt said that caused you to think he didn't want you there," Andrew explained. "But she said Grace couldn't tell him that…she didn't have the heart."

"So do you know what he was told?" Jake asked.

"That Lindsey needed to be with her family for a while," Andrew replied. "He seemed to accept that."

Lindsey stood, tipping her chin up. "You're right, Mom. I had to…well, to get my head together, I guess. But right now, I have to get back to Merritt and find a way to make him listen to me."

A deep breath. "I know Merritt. I know what's going on in his head. David is dead. He's lost a leg. He's thinking he'll never have either of the things he wanted most…a life with the man he loves or a career." She thought for a moment.

"One thing that's difficult for people who aren't performers to understand is how much *ego* is required. Not ego in the way most people think of it, as someone being egotistical, conceited. We need to have a strong sense of self-esteem to step onto a stage and believe people will like what we do. Right now, Merritt sees himself as…broken. Not a whole person.

Definitely not able to perform as a tenor, who people judge harshly to begin with. We may know that he can be fitted for a prosthetic leg and relearn how to move, how to be on stage again…but his shattered ego will get in the way of him believing it."

Jake lifted an eyebrow. "And no one understands that better than another performer."

Lindsey headed for the kitchen door, speaking over her shoulder, "I'm going upstairs to pack. Please call the airport and get us on a plane as soon as possible."

A chorus from the three adults in the kitchen. "Yes, ma'am!"

Lindsey smiled as she started up the steps, hearing her uncle say, "Well, now I get exactly what you meant when you told me Lindsey is nothing if not determined."

***

Andrew found a flight leaving that evening and put them on standby. He drove them to the airport and waited with them, relieved to learn cancellations meant Jake and Lindsey were able to be on the flight. They'd made tentative reservations at the Vernon Manor and Andrew told them he'd call the hotel to confirm they would be using the suite Mary had suggested.

They checked into the historic old hotel which stood near the original site of the Cincinnati Conservatory. Since it was too late for them to try to see Merritt, they rose for an early breakfast and headed to Good Samaritan Hospital where Howard stood waiting in the lobby.

"You remember my uncle, Jean Couvreur," Lindsey said by way of re-introduction.

The men shook hands. "Yes, we met during a much happier occasion recently, seeing you and Merritt perform in *The Tales of Hoffmann*," Howard said.

He led them to Merritt's room as he said, "It's good you're here, Lindsey."

"I'm glad I'm here, too, Mr. Noble. Though I don't imagine Merritt will greet me with open arms. I'm sure he feels I abandoned him."

They stepped off the elevator and headed down a hallway. "I think my son is confused and brokenhearted, Lindsey. He needs you, even if he pretends he doesn't. I know how close you've been for the past four years." Howard's voice shook slightly as he spoke, and Lindsey noted that he looked exhausted. *Poor man, his hair seems grayer than I remember. He's gray all over.*

When he tapped lightly on the door, Grace opened it and stepped into the hall. "I think we should leave you and Merritt alone," she whispered. "We'll be in the waiting room. Try not to be too shocked at his appearance, Lindsey. It's surprising what can happen in only a week."

Lindsey stepped into the dimly-lit room, heavy curtains blocking the sun's rays. It was almost too warm, and Lindsey removed her coat as she moved quietly to the bed.

Merritt, unshaven, his wavy hair a tangled mop, his eyes sunken, slowly looked up at her. The half leg on one side of the bed caused a pang in her heart. Only one machine remained, monitoring his heartbeat. Lindsey stood beside him for a long moment and rested a hand on his arm.

He roughly shook it off, closing his eyes and turning his head away as he growled, "Get the hell out."

"I'm so sorry, Merritt. I should have been with you through all of this." She spoke in a low voice, but clearly and firmly. *No backing down now. We're going to get through this.*

119

"I said get out."

"I'm not going anywhere. I need to talk to you. You need to listen to what I have to say."

His head snapped back and his eyes flew open as he glared at her. *He really hates me,* she thought, startled by the vehemence of his reaction. She took an involuntary step back.

"What you have to say? That's a joke. Lovely Lindsey is going to make it all better with her words of wisdom." He spat the words at her. "I don't think so."

Lindsey took a quick breath to settle her nerves. "I know you're angry."

"That doesn't even begin to describe what I'm feeling about you. I wish you'd never been born."

That hurt. *I have to be careful what I say.* "If our positions were reversed...."

"Well, they're not," he interrupted. "I'm here and you're standing there on two legs. I resent the hell out of that." He lifted an arm and covered his eyes.

"I can't begin to understand how you feel about losing a leg." *Keep calm, Lindsey. Don't fight with him.*

A snort of laughter. "Merritt Noble, the One-Legged Tenor, will now attempt to sing the role of Pagliacci...another clown."

This is worse than I even imagined. "But I can understand how you feel about losing David."

"Oh, really? Then I guess the two of you must have been getting it on behind my back."

"You know that isn't true." *He doesn't mean any of this. How can I reach him?*

His eyes flew open again, this time revealing hurt and pain. "I needed you days ago, Lindsey. And you weren't here."

"I know that. I'm sorry." She bit back the urge to tell him why she had stayed away.

"Just get out." He turned his head away. "I never want to lay eyes on you again."

Defeated and overwhelmed by the feeling of total rejection, Lindsey retreated to the hall, to her uncle's warm embrace. She managed to repeat what she could as he listened carefully, comforting her.

"What do I do now, Uncle Jean? I really, really tried."

"Not quite hard enough, *ma fille*. This will be the toughest thing you've ever done. You have to get back in there and beg his forgiveness. I think that's the only thing left for you to do. And I think he'll accept your apology and forgive you."

"He's turned me away twice now." Lindsey's voice cracked on the word *twice*.

Jake took her shoulders gently and gazed into her eyes. "He doesn't know that. He doesn't remember what he said that caused you to leave the first time you saw him after the accident. Do you really want to tell him what he said?"

She drew a long, shuddering breath. "No. Not now. Maybe someday."

"This will be even harder. If you have to, go down on your knees when you apologize. I think that will soften him."

"Are you serious?"

"I've never been more serious in my life. And you have to mean it. He'll know if you're acting."

Lindsey glanced at Merritt's parents, who had joined them. Grace Noble had her face buried against her husband's shoulder, her entire body shaking with soundless sobs. The look of anguish on Howard's face was unbearable. Lindsey could almost hear Jake saying, *Do this for his parents as much as for him.*

She took a deep breath. *David, if you're close by, help me help our friend.* Thinking of the young man she and Merritt both loved so much gave her a moment of calm resolve, and

Lindsey re-entered the room, took more deep breaths to steady her nerves, and again went to Merritt's bedside. She went down on her knees near his head, collecting her thoughts. He closed his eyes and turned his head away from her.

"Merritt, I love you. Please forgive me for abandoning you the way I did. I was terribly confused and upset and had just buried David the night before, and I simply couldn't deal with seeing you like this. I ran away. It was so wrong. I'm begging you to forgive me, so we can comfort each other." Her voice broke when she spoke David's name and she pressed her head against the side rails of his bed.

Long moments—an eternity—passed in silence, until Lindsey felt a gentle hand on her head.

Merritt's voice, heavy with tears. "I'm sorry, too, Linds. I'd give anything if we'd stayed home Saturday night. I keep wishing it was Saturday again, and after the movie, we just got in the car and drove home. I can't believe what happened. I'm so sorry it happened. And I'm sorry for the awful stuff I just said to you."

Lindsey pulled herself up and stretched out on the bed next to Merritt, and they held each other close, sharing the grief that overwhelmed them. The sobs gradually subsided, but they remained in an embrace.

"I don't know what to do," Merritt's voice cracked. "I don't know how I can live without David."

Lindsey sat up and smoothed his hair back from his face. Glancing around the room she saw a rolling table with a basin and linens on it, and she moistened a face cloth. Sitting beside Merritt, she bathed his face and hands as if he were a child.

"It's hard to believe he's really gone," she said softly. "The funeral was so sad, but it was comforting. Rabbi Ephron said exactly the right things. And one of the prayers I'll never forget—it ended by committing David to the shelter of God's wings. Isn't that beautiful? I can see him there."

Another shuddering sigh. "I wish I'd been there. My dad and my sister went."

"I know. I saw them there. It was tragic…but it was consoling, too. David would have liked it." She stopped. "No, David liked it. I'm sure he was there. I could feel him."

"Lie down beside me again. Please." *Like a hurt child.*

"May I tell your mom and dad to come back into the room? And my Uncle Jean is here with me."

"In just a bit. I want to ask you something first."

Lindsey lay quietly, her arms around Merritt.

"Where do you think he is right now?"

"David? He's right here…" she touched Merritt's heart…"and here." She touched her own heart, then linked her fingers with Merritt's.

"He's everywhere. The whole universe is open to him now." *How did I know to say that?* A flutter in her chest.

"I know there will be times when we feel him close…because I already have."

Susan Moore Jordan

Chapter 9

Lindsey leaned up on an elbow, gazing at Merritt's face. *He seems calmer. I'm so glad I'm here, we both needed this—to be together.* In this position, she became more aware of the stump of his right leg bearing witness to the severity of the wounds he suffered in the accident. The flutter in her heart made her catch a quick breath.

"Something else the rabbi said at the funeral when he gave the eulogy. Wait, I want to remember exactly how he phrased it." She stroked Merritt's arm as she tried to recall the precise words.

"He said…David was a bright comet that crossed our sky for a moment in time, spreading light and love through his music and compassion."

"It's true," Merritt murmured. "But his time with us was too short." The last two words came out as a hiccupy sob.

Lindsey blotted his face with a tissue. "I know, baby, I know. And Rabbi Ephron added that David would never be forgotten, but always be loved and honored. I don't know if anyone told you, but the Rosenthals are establishing a scholarship in David's honor."

"Mrs. Rosenthal came to the hospital…I think yesterday? I should see her."

"We both need to do that. I left so quickly that I never got to their house to sit *shiva* with them. Just think what they've lost. Their only child."

"God. I've only been thinking about myself," Merritt stared at Lindsey. "What a royal prick I've been."

His words hurt her heart. Lindsey gently put her arms around him.

"No, you haven't," she said firmly. "What's happened to all of us is…something we couldn't ever have imagined. But we can help each other." *I can't even think of a word that expresses what you're dealing with, my sweet boy.*

Merritt sighed and relaxed, his head on her shoulder. "I'm…David would tell us we can't just quit."

"Yes, he would. Despite everything, we have to find a way to go on living. Even though right now that seems like climbing the highest mountain in the world." *Climbing. Not the best choice of words, Lindsey. Will Merritt ever be able to climb a mountain again?*

A tap on the door, followed by a nurse entering with a tray of medication. "I had a hard time gaining entrance to this room, Merritt. Three guardians at the gate."

She smiled at Lindsey. "I think you're the best medicine Merritt has had yet. It's good that you're here."

Lindsey sat up slowly, not wanting to jar Merritt, aware of his fragility. "I probably shouldn't be on the bed, should I?"

"I have to take Merritt's vitals and change the dressing on his wound before I bathe him." The nurse's name tag read *Carolyn*. "I'll tell your parents to come in."

Lindsey carefully moved off the bed to a chair in a corner. *What an idiot I am. This man just had his leg amputated and I really think I can help him?*

Carolyn returned to the bed and checked Merritt's temperature and pulse. "Looking good," she commented as she made notes on the chart hung at the end of the bed.

Lindsey whispered, "I hope I didn't do any harm by lying next to him. We just…he wanted me to hug him."

126

Carolyn smiled and replied in a soft voice, "I'm sure you didn't. His incision is healing fine. And I noticed how carefully you moved."

"This is all...." Lindsey gestured helplessly, searching for words.

"...a lot to deal with," Carolyn finished for her. "I know. You've certainly improved his spirits. I meant what I said about it being a good thing you're here."

Grace and Howard Noble approached the bed, supporting each other. "You're looking better, son," Grace said, touching Merritt's face.

Lindsey watched this exchange, seeing the relief on the faces of both parents. She glanced toward the door, where her uncle leaned against the wall. He smiled slightly and gave her an approving nod. She joined him as the Nobles conferred with Carolyn.

"Looks like you done good, *ma fille*," Jake said quietly.

"I didn't actually do anything except apologize, Uncle Jean," Lindsey murmured. "You were right, it was what he needed to hear."

Jake gazed more closely at his niece. "Something else?"

Lindsey clutched his arm. "Lying right next to him, I was so aware of Merritt's right leg...not being there...."

"Steady, Lindsey. You're doing great. Just keep giving him what he needs."

Carolyn, basin in hand, approached them. "I'm going to bathe him now and once again try to persuade him to let me give him a shave," she explained. "And then his surgeon is coming in shortly. I hate to interrupt what is obviously an important visit, but can you give us about an hour?"

"Of course, we can," Jake replied. "How's the cafeteria?"

"It's good. Full breakfast menu, pastries, fruit...whatever you might like. Thank you for being so accommodating."

Howard joined them. "My treat," he said. "Grace is going to stay and help Carolyn. Merritt seems to like that."

The cafeteria proved to be better than Lindsey expected, bright and airy, with an abundant selection of breakfast foods. The staff was beginning to change the cases to lunch items, so they quickly made selections and found a table near a window.

Howard leaned toward Lindsey as he sipped coffee. "I can't believe the change in Merritt, just from that short time you were with him, but I'm not surprised. I knew being with you was what he needed more than anything."

Lindsey felt her chin quiver and blinked back tears. "I should have been here from the beginning."

"No, I think this worked out as it was supposed to," Howard replied. "He was still in a lot of pain those first few days, and extremely confused. I doubt he'd have responded to you as he has today."

"You see a marked difference in him, I take it." Jake broke a croissant in half and buttered it.

"For the first time, I see hope in his eyes instead of despair," Howard said softly. "I think he'll start cooperating more with his physical therapist."

"He hasn't been doing that?" Jake asked.

"Well, barely. His therapist is a capable and caring guy who is working hard to engage Merritt more in his treatment. He told us he thought Merritt would soon be able to use a temporary prosthetic if he'd make more of an effort. That might happen now."

Lindsey pressed a hand to her mouth. "I want so much to help him."

"You're off to a good start," Howard told her. "What did you say to him?"

"Mainly, I talked about David. And we hugged each other and cried."

Howard had to look away for a moment. "He hasn't done that, not since he first learned that David had died."

Lindsey pressed both hands to her mouth, unable to comment. Jake placed a warm hand on her shoulder as he said to Howard, "Then it's definitely good that Lindsey is here."

***

Returning to Merritt's hospital room, they found Carolyn had not only taken care of changing his bed and hospital gown, but he'd allowed her to shave him and Grace was toweling his hair dry and brushing it.

Lindsey stood at the foot of the bed, searching for the right words. *He's so fragile, but I love that he's clean-shaven and let his mom wash his hair. I need to say something.*

"Now you're my beautiful tenor. Thank you."

The ghost of a smile. "I didn't want to scare you off. You always hated it when I didn't shave for a couple of days."

Carolyn gathered up towels and washcloths. "I'm having some food sent up. Lindsey, Merritt would like you to stay with him if you can. Ethan, his physical therapist, will be here around one. You should meet him."

Grace relinquished the chair next to the bed. "Sit here, Lindsey."

"Are you sure?" *Should I do this? Maybe Grace should stay, But I would like to meet Ethan.*

"Yes, I am. Howard and I need to run home for a while. Jean, you're welcome to come with us."

Lindsey glanced at her uncle, who nodded as she tried to send him a mental message: *I'll be fine.*

Apparently, it was received. "Thanks, but I have some things I can do at the hotel." Jake followed the Nobles from the room.

Lindsey eased into the chair, taking one of Merritt's hands with both of hers. *He's so pale. He was horribly injured...physically and emotionally. I'll let him talk if he wants to. Or we can just sit and be together, this is good.*

His breathing became soft and even, and she began to think he had drifted off to sleep.

"I'm told I'm a good candidate for a prosthesis." His words were slightly slurred.

That wasn't easy for him to say, Lindsey thought. "I'm told you have a terrific physical therapist."

"Yeah, I guess. He's okay. We don't need to talk about that right now."

"Whatever you want."

Merritt grew quiet again. "How long can you stay?"

"You mean in Cincinnati? As long as you want me to. I came back to be with you."

"I wish I'd been at David's funeral. It helped you a lot, didn't it?"

Here's my opening. "It did. Something else that helped— after I got home, I listened to the Rach Three with my dad. I talked about the sections David found especially sublime."

She saw a muscle work in Merritt's jaw. "I don't know that I could do that. David and I listened to it often. We even...." he sighed and closed his eyes.

"Why wouldn't you? It's filled with passion."

Tears slid from beneath Merritt's lashes. "Will I ever be able to think of him without crying?"

"Not any time soon, but I believe eventually we will." *I need to get this thought into his head.* "I understand how you feel about the concerto. When Dad and I listened to it the day after I got home, I cried all the way through it. But I felt better afterward...as though David was close. Then we listened to it

130

again the next day, and it was truly wonderful to let Rachmaninoff's heavenly music just wash over me."

She drew a breath. "I have the recording at the hotel. I also brought a portable CD player. Do you think you and I could listen to it?"

He gazed at her steadily. "I'd like to try. Maybe not today, though. Let me think about it."

"Of course. When you feel ready."

A tap at the door and an aide entered with Merritt's lunch. The aide adjusted the hospital bed so Merritt could sit up to eat. After deftly placing a pillow behind his back, she rolled the tray table into place across his lap. Vegetable soup, a roll, applesauce, a slice of angel food cake. A small container of vanilla ice cream. Milk to drink.

"Want some help?" Lindsey offered.

"This actually looks pretty good. You know something? I'm kind of hungry, how about you butter that roll for me?"

Lindsey broke the roll, buttered it, and watched him eat. It thrilled her that her boy polished off every bite of his lunch.

***

Promptly at one, Ethan arrived as promised. *Good Lord. Nobody told me this man was an Adonis.* She guessed over six feet tall, athletically built, short-cropped sandy hair and calm blue-gray eyes. A strong jaw and photogenic features. A quick glance at his left hand: *No wedding ring.*

He nodded to her. "Miss Cameron. I heard you were here."

Why is it news? She stood, extending a hand. "Lindsey, please." Firm, decisive handshake. "May I call you Ethan?"

An infectious grin, "It's a lot easier than Jagodzinski."

Lindsey smiled. "Polish?" she guessed.

"Proud Polack here. Merritt guessed correctly when he first heard it, too. Must be something about singers and strange languages."

"Would you like for me to leave?"

"I'm fine with you staying if it's okay with my patient."

My patient. I like that.

"It sure is. I'd like her to see what we're doing," Merritt agreed.

Glancing at Merritt, Lindsey was pleased to see more color in his face. A different demeanor from his aspect when she'd first arrived. *The food must have helped.*

Ethan stepped into the hall briefly and returned with a portable wheelchair. "Today's the day we get this done."

Lindsey stood against the wall as she watched Ethan. Gentle but sure, he spent quite a bit of time checking Merritt's physical condition, his muscle reflexes, and strength.

He conversed with his patient all the time, discussing, of all things, classical music. Opera. *The Tales of Hoffmann.* Startled, Lindsey realized from their conversation that Ethan had seen them perform only weeks earlier.

He discussed the amputation matter-of-factly and spoke about a temporary prosthetic leg. He talked about Merritt's future, and Merritt didn't contradict him. *No snarky remarks about a one-legged tenor.*

When Merritt responded positively, Lindsey didn't miss the expression on Ethan's face. *This is a change*, she thought. *Merritt's been resisting this kind of talk.*

Eventually, Ethan had Merritt push the stump against a pillow, pressing hard. He nodded approvingly, then had Merritt sit up and maneuver closer to the edge of the bed. Lindsey held her breath, fearful Merritt might fall.

Ethan knelt on the floor and carefully explained the mechanics of operating the chair, Lindsey as rapt a listener as Merritt.

"Once we get you on this, the sky's the limit. You'll be racing down the hall in no time."

Merritt's laugh was music to Lindsey's ears. "I highly doubt that."

"Ready to give this a try?"

With great care, Ethan assisted Merritt with the bed-to-chair transfer, vigilant for any difficulty he might have, ready to catch a fall or a slip. "Take your time. Don't rush."

He guided Merritt's hands as he helped him find the proper handholds to make the transfer as easily as possible, placing them on the back and arms of the chair, showing him how to shift positions. Lindsey didn't realize she was holding her breath until Merritt was sitting in the chair.

She wanted to yell bravo and applaud, but managed only a squeaky "That's wonderful."

Ethan stepped back, folded his arms, grinned broadly, and commented, "Well done!"

They reversed the procedure, getting Merritt from the chair back to the bed. Then Merritt moved to the wheelchair again with minimal help. Ethan handed his patient tissues to mop the sweat from his face.

"Tomorrow, I think you'll be able to do this by yourself. And we can start to talk about sending you home."

A look of near panic on Merritt's face. "I'm not ready to go home yet, Ethan. You said we have a lot of work to do."

Ethan placed a strong hand on Merritt's shoulder as he said, "We do. I'll come to your house and bring one of our staff members with me. That therapist will see you at least three days a week. Every day at first."

"I'd rather it be you."

"East Side Orthopedic Clinic has an excellent staff, Merritt. You'll be happy with whoever I assign your case to. And I'll be stopping by from time to time. After a few weeks, you'll need to come to the clinic frequently to use our equipment, and I'm nearly always there."

"Oh. Okay." Merritt visibly relaxed, playing with the wheels of the chair.

"Want to take it for a spin?" Ethan stepped to one side. "Lindsey can push you. Using it on your own takes some practice."

Merritt considered it. "I'm kind of tired." He glanced at Lindsey. "It's been kind of an…emotional day."

"Then get some rest." Ethan lifted his patient back into his bed, brought him a glass of water with a straw, and tucked covers around him. "Do you mind if I borrow your friend for a few minutes? I'd like to get to know her."

"Sure, that's fine." Merritt gazed at Lindsey. "My best friend. My dearest friend in the world," he said softly.

Lindsey bent and kissed his forehead. "Why don't you get some sleep? I have some things I need to do at the hotel. I'll be back later this afternoon."

Merritt's eyes widened. "Promise?"

"I promise." She kissed him again and left the room with Ethan.

They moved down the hall to the waiting area before Ethan spoke.

"Do you have any idea what a difference it's made to have you here?" He stood facing her, arms folded across his chest.

Lindsey was unsure how to reply to the question. He didn't sound any too friendly; she sensed an undertone of *Where the hell have you been when my patient needed you?*

"I'm beginning to realize that. And I know you must be wondering why I wasn't here sooner."

Ethan glanced at the floor for a moment. "It might have been helpful if you had been. Merritt hasn't been completely uncooperative. But his negative mental state has affected his treatment." A pause. "He really wanted to get into that chair today. He was a different guy."

"It's complicated," Lindsey began. *That sounds so lame.* "I love Merritt, and we both loved David. When this happened…." She glanced around nervously to be sure there was no one nearby. "Do you mind if I sit down?"

Ethan gestured toward a chair and sat opposite her, where he seemed thankfully less intimidating. Lindsey wasn't sure how much to tell him.

"I'm not a doctor, Lindsey, but I want to assure you anything you tell me will be confidential," Ethan spoke more quietly. "My sole concern is Merritt. He can have a good recovery, physically. He's an ideal candidate for a prosthesis. He's young and strong, drinks very little, and has never smoked. He's in excellent health…or he was. It's been a concern that he's eaten so little. Carolyn tells me he polished off his lunch today. First time."

"How much do you know about the accident?"

"Freakish accident when these two young men were walking down a sidewalk. Merritt's partner David was killed instantly. Merritt had to be told that right after he learned he had lost a leg. I have some sense of how difficult this must be for him. I would think you understand better than I."

"Did you know they had been together for almost four years and had just celebrated their love with a commitment ceremony?" Lindsey struggled to keep her emotions in check.

"No, I wasn't aware of that," Ethan said slowly. "Um. It just gets worse and worse. But I am aware you were in Cincinnati and left abruptly after David's funeral."

Lindsey gazed at Ethan for a long moment. "I need to know you will never tell this to your patient. I've decided he must never hear it."

Ethan raised his right hand. "You have my word."

"I came to the hospital the day after David's funeral when we knew Merritt was being brought out of the coma. I was in the hospital room when he received the..." she gestured helplessly... "I don't even know what to call it. Two bolts of lightning hit my sweet boy, one after another. He was reeling."

Lindsey bit her lip, her chin quivering. "Mrs. Noble told Merritt I was there. And he said...."

Ethan didn't rush her, just waited quietly.

"He said—'why David and not her?'" The tears spilled over. Ethan gently patted her shoulder with a strong hand.

"Good God. You took that as a rejection."

"I know he didn't mean it, but...for a moment...he wished I were...." She swallowed hard. "How would you have taken it?"

He was quiet. "Probably exactly the same way." He leaned back and waited for her to staunch the tears and wipe her face.

"Am I going to cry forever?"

"No. But for months to come, times like this will hit you when you least expect it." He sighed. "Well, the important thing is, you're here now. How long are you going to stay?"

"As long as Merritt needs me."

"Don't say that unless you mean it. It will be months. It'll be at least six months—maybe as long as nine—before he can be fitted for a permanent prosthesis because the stump has to heal completely. He'll have a temporary leg soon, to help him learn to balance all over again. But when he gets the permanent leg, he'll be able to take off."

"Walking?"

"Walking. Running. Dancing. Back on the stage, where he doesn't think right now he'll ever be again. I know a little about singing and realize how important the lower body is for an opera singer. He'll learn to compensate."

Lindsey managed a smile. "That's wonderful to hear."

Ethan leaned forward. "You're from Pennsylvania, right? Near Philadelphia?"

She nodded.

"There's a remarkable young woman from Allentown your friend needs to hear about. Aimee Mullins. She's the same age as you and Merritt. A congenital birth defect meant she had both lower legs amputated when she was a year old."

Lindsey stared at him. "Good Lord."

Ethan smiled again. "Her parents were told she'd be in a wheelchair all her life. Boy, did she ever prove them wrong. She was walking I think by the time she was three. Right now, she's in college and is a sprinter on her school's track team. I mean the collegiate track team, not one for physically challenged students. And she's going to the Paralympics in Atlanta."

"That's incredible. You haven't told Merritt about her?"

"He hasn't been ready to hear it. I think now he will be."

"You said you will bring a staff member to the Nobles' once he gets home to continue his therapy. How does that work? The hospital makes those arrangements?"

"East Side Orthopedics doesn't work for the hospital. We're a private clinic and rehab facility of which I'm part owner. The Nobles asked for our services after we were recommended to them."

"Well, I'm happy to know you'll be in charge of his treatment. I saw how great you are with him."

Another warm smile as he continued, "I love what I do. And I genuinely like Merritt. I want to see him perform again before too long. And I hope to be at his Met debut in a few years."

Lindsey impulsively leaned forward and put her arms around Ethan. "So do I. I think we can get him there."

He returned the hug. "I like the sound of that. Merritt needs a team that will get him back to living. I think you're a valuable part of this team, Lindsey."

***

Glancing into Merritt's room, Lindsey was pleased to see him sleeping peacefully. She knew now exactly what she needed to do. Grace Noble and Leah Rosenthal were headed toward her, deep in conversation, when she stepped back into the hall.

Lindsey put a finger to her lips as she walked toward them. The three women moved to the waiting area where they could sit down.

"It's so good to see you." She embraced Leah and held her for a long moment. "I'm so sorry we didn't make it to your house before we left."

"I had a good talk with your father when I called yesterday," Leah replied. "He explained about your return, and Grace and I agreed to meet here. I'm hoping to see Merritt."

"He wants to see you. Right now, he's sleeping peacefully and I think he needs rest. He's had quite a day." She smiled at Grace. "He ate every bit of his lunch, then had a successful physical therapy session with a terrific man named Ethan."

"Oh, that's wonderful!" Grace exclaimed. "Having you here has made all the difference. I hope you're planning to stay."

"As long as Merritt wants me to. My Uncle Jean will have to get back to Montreal in a few days, though, so I'll need to find somewhere else to stay."

"Both you and your uncle are welcome to stay with Arthur and me," Leah said.

"We live closer to the hospital, Lindsey, and we have room for both of you as well." The two women smiled at each other.

"Listen to us," Leah commented. "Grace has a point about distance, I think, but maybe you could come and stay with me for a day or two."

Lindsey observed both women: Grace trim and stylishly dressed, with chestnut brown hair which needed the attention of a hairdresser for understandable reasons. Leah, her gray hair pulled into a bun, more matronly but also dressed fashionably. They had become close friends over the past four years, and now had a bond that would tie them together forever.

"Thank you both, and that sounds like a perfect solution. I think I'd like to be close to the hospital, but I'd love to spend some time with Mrs. Rosenthal, too."

She looked from one woman to the other. "Can one of you please drive me to the Vernon Manor? I need to let my uncle know about my plans."

Grace volunteered to drive her, telling Leah she'd be back.

After taking the elevator to their suite, Lindsey told Jake what had happened at the hospital. "I know you need to get back to Montreal, Uncle Jean, and I'm going to be okay. Mom and Dad will probably drive over with David's portrait for the Rosenthals soon. I'll call and ask Mom to bring me more clothes. Some summer dresses. Oh, and some of my music. I'm going to stay as long as I'm needed. Talking to Merritt's physical therapist helped me make some decisions."

"Are you considering going to summer school?" Jake asked.

"I've decided not to. What I'm aiming for is Merritt going back to school with me in the fall."

"That's ambitious, Lindsey," Jake cautioned. "You were advised he probably won't be using a prosthetic leg that quickly."

Seated in their suite's velvet Victorian love seat, Lindsey kicked off her shoes and tucked her feet under her. "He might be, though he might not be able to do a lot of walking. But until then, he can be in a wheelchair. I saw the kind of chair he's learning to use. It's lightweight and portable and can be put into the trunk of a car. I'm sure I could handle one. I can stay with the Nobles and drive us back and forth. And we'll be in the same three classes. I can do this."

"You've been doing a lot of thinking," Jake smiled at her. "There's that 'Lindsey being determined' thing again that your dad told me about."

"You know what, Uncle Jean? It really helps me to have a plan. I believe this has been in the back of my mind since you agreed to come to Cincinnati with me. If I could only get Merritt to talk to me. I don't believe I had thought beyond that."

She glanced into the distance. "Well, I did get him to talk to me, thanks to your advice. And look what's happened since that conversation."

"Yes, seeing you has undoubtedly made a change in Merritt. But bear in mind he has a long journey ahead, and there may be relapses and unexpected pitfalls," Jake advised.

Lindsey tipped up her chin. "Whatever happens, I intend to be right here with him."

Chapter 10

Jake booked a flight to Montreal for early the following morning. He and Lindsey made plans to meet the Nobles for an early dinner at the Good Samaritan Hospital cafeteria so he could see Merritt that evening.

"Cincinnati does have some excellent restaurants, Uncle Jean," Lindsey commented as they left the Vernon Manor. "It's too bad you've had nearly all your meals at Good Sam's cafeteria."

"I didn't come here to explore the city's gastronomic delights, *ma belle*. Another time, maybe." He glanced at her. "You certainly had a full day. No chance to listen to music, I don't imagine."

"Not yet. We did talk about it, and Merritt said he'd think about it. One thing I realized is that his hospital room isn't an ideal place for what I hope hearing the concerto will accomplish. I told you Ethan mentioned Merritt should be going home soon. A much better place for us to have that experience. We'll be able to have uninterrupted privacy."

Grace and Howard Noble appeared drained to Lindsey, and it concerned her. *Well, it's been a long day for everybody.* "I think I'll run up and let Merritt know I'm here if that's okay."

"I think he'd like that, but he's pretty tired. He may perk up after he has dinner," Grace told her.

"Maybe I should ask for a tray so I can eat with him? Could I do that?"

141

"Probably. Carolyn is off duty, but Marlene is equally nice. I'd suggest you go to the nurses' station and talk to her before you go to his room," Grace said. "Tell him we'll be up after we've eaten."

Lindsey entered the room quietly. Merritt seemed to be asleep, so she stood by the door, uncertain as to whether she should disturb him.

"I'm not asleep, Linds." His voice sounded drowsy. "I'm glad you're here"

She went to him, taking his hand and leaning on the bed. "You had a long day, Merritt."

He opened his eyes and gave her a brief smile. "Yes, for sure. I'm kind of tired. But some good things happened." A sigh and a shiver. "Nothing has changed, though. Not really."

He means David is still dead and he didn't grow a new leg. His world is forever changed.

"I think I understand. But for what it's worth, I'm not going anywhere. I'm going to be right here, beside you, for as long as you want me to."

Another smile and this one reached his eyes. "I thought you were having dinner with my folks downstairs."

"I got pushy and came up here so I could eat with you," she told him, eliciting another smile.

"Marlene was really nice about ordering a tray for me. You have wonderful nurses. And your physical therapist is just plain terrific."

"Ethan the slave driver? Yeah, he's okay." He covered the yawn with his hand. "I can't believe how tired I am tonight."

"I won't stay long, Merritt. Uncle Jean wants to see you after he finishes dinner. He's leaving for Montreal in the morning."

"Mom says you're coming to stay with us. I like that. Just as long as you and my sister don't gang up on me."

142

"If we do, it will be to smother you with love."

"How do you do that, anyway? Smother somebody with love?"

An aide arrived with their trays. Lindsey had requested a meal identical to Merritt's. *Not too bad.* Omelet with home fries, the potatoes finely diced. What appeared to be thin-sliced, sauteed vegetables. A fruit cup, consisting of thin slices of peaches, pears, and some berries mixed in. Two cornbread muffins that looked delicious. A slice of cheesecake. Milk again. *Protein. They want him to have plenty of protein.*

"You didn't answer my question. And, hey, why'd you order the same meal as mine?"

Good question. Why exactly did I do that? Because I want to try to feel what you're feeling, Merritt.

"Oh, I just told Marlene I'll have whatever Merritt's having."

Merritt's intense hazel gaze startled her. "Liar. Are you trying to get inside my head, Linds?"

"Is that a bad thing?" she asked softly.

He glanced down for a moment. "Maybe not." A pause. "It's exactly what David would do."

She reached for his hand, sensing something more than his touch, something she couldn't explain. Again, Merritt gave her a genuine smile. Though neither of them spoke of it, Lindsey felt they had shared a moment of awareness of David's love.

***

Jake and the Nobles arrived in Merritt's room just as his and Lindsey's trays were being taken away. Lindsey gave up her chair and stood behind her uncle so he could sit close to Merritt.

"*C'est bon de te revoir*, Monsieur Couvreur," Merritt said.

Jake was delighted. "*Je ne savais pas que tu parlais français.*"

"*Un peu seulement.* That's almost my entire vocabulary, but I think it's a beautiful language and I'd love to learn more. Anyway, I think I messed up. I should have used *vous* instead of *tu.*"

"Why? I used *tu.* We're family, Merritt."

Perfect, Uncle Jean. He needed to hear that. Lindsey smiled at both of them.

"You and Lindsey must come to Montreal. My children will have you talking like a true Québécois in no time."

Jake observed Merritt closely. "I know you've had a long and stressful day, Merritt, but I wanted to have a few minutes to talk with you before I leave Cincinnati."

"Thank you. And thanks so much for bringing Lindsey to stay with me. It means a lot."

"I think I have some sense of what you're going through right now because of what happened to me," Jake pressed Merritt's arm. "I know Lindsey has told you about my memory loss, a near-complete loss of who I had been except for a very few childhood memories. It wasn't the physical loss of a limb, and certainly not accompanied by losing the person you loved and expected to spend your life with."

"No, but you lost *yourself.* I can't imagine what that must have been like."

"It was an arduous journey." Jake sat back and steepled his fingers. "In my case, physical as well as emotional. I'd just like to suggest a few things that might be helpful to you if you don't mind hearing them."

Merritt nodded, and Jake leaned forward. "First of all, don't hesitate to reach out to people. I had a difficult time doing that for many months…even years. People want to help and will do everything they possibly can. Lindsey tells me your physical therapist wants to get you back on stage as soon as possible. It must seem daunting right now, but advances are being made constantly to make life better for even double amputees."

"It's hard for me to even think about that right now. I'm having a hard time looking ahead when I know…I'll never see David again." He smothered a sob. "I'm sorry."

Jake squeezed Merritt's arm. "Never apologize for expressing what you're feeling right now. You've had two great losses you have to attempt to deal with at the same time. Let yourself feel what you're feeling. Don't hold it in, that's the worst thing you can do."

"Losing David is the worst." Merritt struggled to go on. "He would help me deal with the other thing…with losing my leg."

Lindsey wiped her eyes with her hand.

"I'm sure he would. About David…Lindsey has told me a lot about him. What a remarkable young man. Prodigiously talented and loving, with a strong sense of self and apparently an ability to help the people he loved to see themselves more clearly. I know I don't have to remind you that the years you spent with him made you a better person."

"They were the happiest time of my life."

Jake nodded. "But think about this…those years with you may very well have been the happiest time of David's life as well. You gave him something beautiful he might not have had otherwise."

Merritt's shoulders shook as he sobbed openly, and Jake leaned forward and embraced him.

"This may sound trite right now. But file it away for future reference. At some point, you'll be able to think, 'Don't be sad because it's over. Be happy that it happened.'"

Jake reached for Lindsey and pulled her close, comforting the two young people as best he could. Lindsey saw her uncle was close to tears himself.

Jake cleared his throat hard. "I'm sorry I have to leave." His voice shook slightly. "But either of you can call me at any time. Lindsey has both my home and office numbers."

Merritt had been clutching a box of tissues, and he offered them to his friends. A group nose-blowing had the men chuckling and Lindsey giggling.

It's true, tears and laughter are so close to each other, she thought.

"My uncle's as big a softy as my dad, Merritt," Lindsey remarked. "You know, you have three families now. Yours, the Rosenthals, and mine."

"I'll give you a minute, Lindsey," Jake said as he stood. "We should get back to the hotel, and this young man needs a good night's sleep."

As if on cue, Marlene came into the room with a syringe. "Sorry to evict you, folks, but…" she gestured with the needle, "…doctor's orders."

"We were on our way out," Jake said. "Can you give Merritt and Lindsey a couple of minutes?"

"Sure, I can." Marlene winked at Jake as they left the room together.

"Was your nurse coming on to my uncle?"

Another chuckle. "Probably. Your family are all lookers, Linds." He sighed, but it was a good sigh, one born of physical fatigue and not sorrow. "What he said about me giving David years of happiness…I'll remember that."

"I'll be back tomorrow, but I'm not sure when. Your dad is coming to the hotel in the morning to help me move all my stuff to your house. I'll try to be here by lunchtime."

She kissed him softly, twice. As she left the room Lindsey smiled at syringe-wielding Marlene. It had been a good day.

***

A lot of activity took place at the Noble house. Lindsey watched as the downstairs study became a new bedroom for Merritt—making space for a hospital bed, widening the door between the study and the downstairs bath, and adding a shower. Merritt's occupational therapist, who would be working with Merritt once he got home, had walked through the house with Grace and Howard.

"You need to make sure everything Merritt might need is easily accessible when he's in a wheelchair, including items he might need to get to if no one else is home," she told them. "Also, be very careful there are no small items anywhere he might trip over when he's using his prosthesis."

Howard showed her the downstairs bathroom. "Luckily, this bathroom is big enough, but we're adding a shower. We think the original owner had planned on a full bath and then changed his mind, so we won't need to knock out a wall. Our contractor has actually done this kind of work before, which is a big help."

The therapist nodded approvingly. "Be sure you add sufficient safety railings as well. A non-slip floor in the shower is essential. I'd recommend a floor cabinet rather than one above the sink." She pointed out items in the kitchen that might need to be moved to a lower level. The transformation took place fairly quickly, due to their sympathetic contractor's efforts.

Lindsey hung the clothes she had with her in the closet in what had been Merritt's bedroom and placed items in the chest. *This feels so strange. As if I'm intruding.* The house, an

American Foursquare, stood at the end of a cul-de-sac. A spacious yard surrounded it, with trees and flower beds, a patio, and a detached garage, much like her own home in West Chester. The Nobles' house had undergone considerable remodeling over the years, and had all the latest amenities, even though it had been built in the nineteen-twenties.

Grace stuck her head in the door. "Need any help?"

"No, I think I have this covered. Do you have an ETA for Merritt coming home?" Lindsey asked.

"Maybe by Friday, certainly early next week if not then. Soon. I'll be so glad to have him home."

Maybe less than a week. "Yes, Ethan said once he was comfortable with his wheelchair he could come home."

"We'll have a family session sometime this week with Merritt's medical team to give us the information we need to care for him here," Grace said. "And Ethan's staff member will be here daily at first to continue his PT. Later, it will probably be two or three days a week. Howard and I have already learned how to give him injections if he should need pain medication." She pushed her hair back from her forehead, her eyes shining in anticipation. "You should learn to do that as well, Lindsey. Kathleen's just too squeamish."

His mother will be so happy to have him home. Good Sam is an excellent hospital, but it's still only a place to visit.

"What about the temporary prosthesis Ethan mentioned? When will he have a chance to try that?" Lindsey asked.

"Probably very soon…maybe tomorrow. They'd like to get him up on his feet. Well, foot. Well…you know what I mean."

"How does that work? He won't be able to put his weight on it…the prosthetic leg…will he?"

"He'll use a walker at first, I think. Or maybe crutches. Whatever works best for Merritt. And eventually, a special cane which has four tips in a square instead of one. For better stability. Ethan told us it may be nine months before he can be fitted for a permanent prosthesis."

Lindsey nodded. "Ethan told me he sees no reason Merritt can't return to his chosen career."

"The only thing that will hold him back is Merritt's reluctance right now to even consider it. That's why you being here is so important." Grace gazed earnestly into Lindsey's eyes. "You have to convince him to start singing again. We can't do that. I don't think even Claudia Prince could. I know you can."

"That's a tall order, Grace." Lindsey sighed "But that's my goal, too. I'll do everything I possibly can."

***

Lindsey soon settled into a routine for the remainder of Merritt's hospital stay. Help around the house in various ways first thing in the morning. Be at the hospital by ten-thirty or eleven to spend some time with Merritt before lunch. Eat lunch with him, then stay through his physical therapy session, then back to the house to practice singing, and return to the hospital at dinner.

She met his surgeon, his primary physician, and his psychologist, a charming woman named Dr. Elizabeth Evans. During a conversation, Lindsey learned Dr. Evans knew a Cameron family friend and fellow mental health specialist, Penelope Abramson.

"How do you know Dr. Penny?" Dr. Evans asked.

"She treated my dad for the PTSD he suffered from his time in Vietnam," Lindsey told her. "She's since become a family friend. I think she's one reason my brother M.J. is pursuing psychology at the University of Pennsylvania."

Merritt began responding to Dr. Evans, much to everyone's relief. "She's cool, Linds. She just lets me ramble, and sometimes she'll ask a question that helps me think through some stuff."

"That sounds perfect, Merritt."

He still didn't want to talk about singing again. Lindsey tried, she even sat beside his bed and softly sang the opening phrase to a duet from *La Traviata* they had performed numerous times, hoping he would join in.

Parigi, o caro, noi lasceremo,
la vita uniti trascorreremo.

Merritt smiled wistfully, closed his eyes, and turned his head away.

Lindsey and Ethan went down to the cafeteria for a snack after a PT session and she discussed this with him. "It's as if he's decided that part of his life is over. It isn't. You and I know it isn't. I don't know what he tells Dr. Evans, and of course, I can't talk to her about this."

"Give him more time, Lindsey. Isn't it possible one reason it's hard for him to sing is that David always played for him?" Ethan unwrapped his granola bar. "You've told me he was also your pianist when you performed together, and he often played for opera production rehearsals."

"That's true." She took a sip from her bottle of Evian water. "You know what I want to do? When we get him home, I want to see if I can get him to listen to music with me. What we call David's music—the Rachmaninoff third piano concerto."

"He hasn't listened to any music at all, has he?"

"No. When I ran away…." Ethan started to protest, but she stopped him with a raised hand. "No, that's exactly what I did.

150

My family took me home. And one of the first things I did was listen to that concerto." She paused for a breath. "I kind of felt like I had to listen to it."

Another deep breath. "It honestly made me feel better. I felt I had a connection with David. And I listened again the next day, and it was, well…liberating. It was this sublime piece of music that all three of us listened to together."

"Did David ever perform it in public?"

She shook her head. "Not that concerto. He had performed Rachmaninoff's second concerto with the Cincinnati Symphony at the age of just sixteen. Performing the Rach Three was a dream—it's so difficult—and he practiced it often. When I walked into our house, I could hear it even when he wasn't practicing or we didn't have the CD on. I know that sounds strange, but music can be like that."

"I'd suspect the music wasn't in the house, but in your head." Ethan grinned at her.

Lindsey laughed. "I'm sure you're right. I honestly think it would help Merritt to listen to it. I have the CD at his house and even brought a portable player from home. I've suggested it to him already but I know I shouldn't push him. I think it would be better to wait until he's at home, don't you?"

Ethan broke off a piece of the granola bar. "Yes, I do. I think what you want to do requires more privacy than you'll get here. I'd guess the concerto would be at least thirty minutes."

"Forty-three," Lindsey replied, taking a spoonful of peaches.

"But who's counting? You do know this piece, don't you?" Ethan chuckled. "May I make a suggestion? When Merritt agrees to listen to it, get him to relax. Massage his shoulders, maybe. Have low lighting in the room, and encourage him to stretch out. Ask him to share his feelings with you while the two of you listen."

Intrigued, Lindsey commented, "You sound as if you've had such an experience."

"I've heard about it. There's a music therapy technique called Guided Imagery and Music, and it's similar to that. Although the therapist doesn't physically touch the patient, she does get him to relax and talk to her about what he experiences as he listens to selections of classical music."

"I haven't heard of that. It sounds perfect, though. I'll see what happens. Merritt will be home in a few days."

***

It took Merritt a couple of days to relax once he arrived home. At first, he seemed tense, but with the efforts of his family—which now included Lindsey—he became more comfortable, moving with ease around the first floor of the house not only in the wheelchair but attempting to use the temporary prosthesis Ethan had given him two days before he left the hospital.

"You will have four steps from the sidewalk to the front porch," he told Merritt. "Hang on to your dad if you need to. We'll learn to use the prosthesis just for going up and down steps for now. I'd like to see you moving easily on your feet."

"My feet? I only have one foot. I can't feel the other one. It's a fake."

"It will begin to feel more natural once you're moving. No, you'll never be able to wiggle your toes, but other muscles on your right side will begin to respond."

Ethan brought Molly O'Malley to the house the day after Merritt came home. Lindsey was with Merritt when they arrived and Ethan invited her to stay for the PT session.

152

A tall, healthy, bouncy blonde, Molly had a great smile and while Merritt seemed uncertain about this new person at first, he began to respond to her sure touch and positive attitude. Ethan stayed through the session, observing and making suggestions at times. *Another excellent member of Merritt's team*, thought Lindsey. *I like her, and I think Merritt will, too.*

Merritt worked hard and became more adept at using the prosthesis. Within a few days, he settled into being back home. He had moments of melancholy and depression, but his family did all they could to keep him positive.

The day they were informed the driver of the truck that hit Merritt and David had been arrested wasn't easy for any of them. Lindsey could tell from Merritt's expression that the news had taken him right back to the moment he awoke in the hospital to learn he'd lost his leg and his love.

"I hope they're going to throw the book at him," Grace said, her voice cracking.

Howard had been present at the driver's arraignment. "He's being charged with Leaving the Scene of an Accident, Aggravated Vehicular Assault, and Aggravated Vehicular Homicide. Sounds like he's going to do a lot of time in jail to me."

"Who was he, Dad?" asked Kathleen. "Old? Young? A real sleaze?"

"Sorry to say, he was young. I think early twenties."

Merritt put up a hand. "I don't want to know anything about him." Lindsey heard the anger in his voice. "I know what he did. I know better than anyone what he did."

They all fell silent.

"I don't ever want to hear anything more about this. And I never want to talk to anyone."

"Well...if there's a trial...," Howard said.

"I mean it, Dad. How could I testify, anyway? I never knew what hit me."

No more was said, but Lindsey continued to wonder about the man who had taken one life and destroyed another.

Before Merritt came home Lindsey had been using the piano in the living room for an hour or more every afternoon to sing. She didn't have music with her but found Merritt's vocal collections that all singers use, and since Merritt was a tenor, they were in the right key for her as well.

Once Merritt returned home, that ended. When Lindsey would start to sing, he'd retreat to his room, shut the door firmly, and turn up the TV. She went to the campus a couple of times in hopes of finding an available practice room but had no luck.

This was beginning to be a problem, Lindsey needed to sing, whether Merritt wanted to hear music or not. *Time to get past this.* She knew his sister Kathleen planned to spend the weekend with friends and quietly took Grace aside.

"I really need some time alone with Merritt," she explained. "His refusal to sing or even to listen to music has to be addressed, and I think I know what will help. Could you and Howard go to the movies or something Friday or Saturday?"

Grace looked somewhat dumbfounded. "Well…yes…but I don't understand. Why do you need us out of the house?"

"I need to try to persuade Merritt to listen to a piece that meant a lot to David. I'm sure it will be very emotional for him and it would be easier if it was just me. Merritt tries to please both of you…I understand completely, I feel the same about my parents. He knows how much it upsets you to see him grieving, and that is bound to happen."

"Why would you want to put him through that, Lindsey?" Grace's gaze was troubled.

"Because I put myself through it, Grace, when I went home. Yes, it hurt, but it was worth the pain because it brought David closer and helped me begin to heal. And I truly believe it will do the same for Merritt."

Once everyone else left on Saturday, Lindsey turned up the volume on the CD player and the opening sounds of the concerto filled the living room. Visibly agitated, Merritt moved his wheelchair toward the CD. "Turn the damned thing off!"

Lindsey blocked his way. "Not tonight," she said calmly. "Tonight, we listen to David's music."

"I mean it, Lindsey. Get the hell out of my way."

She knelt beside the wheelchair and looked directly into his eyes. "Please, Merritt. You can't keep music out of your life. It's who you are."

He gripped the arms of the chair, avoiding her gaze.

"You're doing so well physically. But you won't heal completely until you open yourself up to music again. You know that."

"I don't know anything anymore."

Lindsey heard the crack in his voice. *Maybe I'm getting through to him after all.*

She put a hand on his arm. "It's our life, Merritt. You'll never be whole until you do this. And this is the perfect piece. I told you how much it helped me. It can do the same for you."

Resting an elbow on the arm of the chair, he leaned his chin against his fist. "I think I'm...scared. I know this will tear me up inside."

"It did that to me, but I needed to hear it." She touched his face. "I won't force you, baby. I have an idea how much you're hurting."

A sigh from the depths of his soul. "I don't know why I keep putting this off. I do want to listen to it."

Lindsey kissed his cheek, stood, and wheeled his chair close to the roomy, comfortable sofa. "Come and stretch out here, and let's listen to it together."

Remembering Ethan's suggestion, she turned the lights down, brought a quilt from Merritt's room, and covered him lightly. Going to the CD player, she adjusted the volume slightly and began the piece a second time.

Lindsey lay next to Merritt, holding him close, his head on her shoulder and his eyes shut tight as Rachmaninoff's sublime music filled the room.

Chapter 11

As we listened to the opening notes of the concerto, I felt Merritt grow tense. I held him close, rubbing his shoulders. He took a few deep breaths, shivered, and swallowed hard.

"Don't hold it in, baby. Let it out. Nobody can hear you except me."

"*I can't....*"

I have no idea where my next words came from. "Yes, you can. You have to. Scream, yell, stop denying the awful pain you're feeling."

And he did. Sounds the like of which I'd never heard before. Merritt turned his face away from me and released that horrible pain and grief in prolonged *wails* from the very depth of his being. I held him even tighter.

"*Oh God oh God oh God oh God....*" His whole body shook.

I was frightened for him, wondering if he could endure this. But after a few moments, the wailing began to subside, though he still trembled with sobs.

"It's okay. It's good. Let it out." I said over and over.

The sobbing slowed, and he took a long shuddering breath. Then another. I'd hardly been able to hear the music, but now it became more audible. I kept rubbing his shoulders and he pressed his face against my shoulder.

"I'm sorry, Linds...I'm so sorry...."

"No, baby, you needed to do that. Cry all you want." My voice quivered as I wept with him.

Gradually, we both grew quieter, and Merritt began to relax, really relax, against me.

A last shuddering sigh. "Can we turn it off for a minute?"

"Of course." The first movement came to an end, I disentangled myself from him and went to the CD player and turned it off.

"God," Merritt said.

"I need water," I told him. "Can I get you some?"

"Please." His voice sounded rough. I hoped he hadn't damaged his vocal cords.

I helped him sit up and handed him the water, and we sat together quietly, leaning against each other. I wondered if I had made an awful mistake insisting that he listen to this music with me, but he seemed calmer.

"I think…I think this is why I haven't been able to sing. I would have broken down like I just did. I guess I knew that." Another shuddering breath.

"Do you need anything?" I knew he had a prescription for a mild sedative and wondered if Grace had filled it. "Those pills you were prescribed.…"

"No. Just give me a few minutes." He gave me the ghost of a smile. "And keep hanging onto me, will you?"

"Willingly." I hugged him close again.

"Hope I didn't scare you."

"Of course not." *Liar.* I'd been terrified, dismayed that I might have done him harm.

"Still…I'm sure you got more than you bargained for." A faint chuckle, followed by a hiccup.

"Well…kind of. But I think you badly needed to get that out. I don't think I realized just how much awful pain you've been in."

A deep sigh. "I guess I have." A pause, and he finished the water and handed me the glass. "I want to listen to this music. To my David's music. Can we start it over, from the beginning?"

***

From the first notes, I had this sense of being transported somewhere else. I always felt this with Rachmaninoff—the anticipation of embarking on a journey to a magical place where all things were possible.

"That first theme," I said. "So different from Rachmaninoff's usual big melodies, yet so perfect. Simple and so, so Russian. It takes me right out of myself."

"I feel exactly the same way about this piece. Kind of ethereal, isn't it? I know we're going someplace which is…well, far beyond ordinary life, for sure."

Good, he was talking. I decided to remain quiet in the hope he'd continue expressing himself to me. The piano began to play rapid runs, accompanying the orchestra.

"Now this is wonderfully…I guess turbulent. And *so* passionate. It just lifts me even more."

More orchestral passages, sweeping strings. "This part takes me straight to the heavens," Merritt said. "A place where everything is possible. Stunning."

The second theme started, the pianist introducing it. A sweeping Rachmaninoff melody, more typical of his style, the embodiment of romance.

"God, listen to that. Where did Rachmaninoff find this? Straight from the best the universe has to offer." I glanced at him and saw the smile I'd heard in his voice.

Strong chords from the piano, then more intricate, delicate painting with sound.

"It's all so perfect. If only life were that way."

The first theme returned, and Merritt sighed and closed his eyes, still smiling. For a time, we both lay quietly, holding each other, letting Rachmaninoff's glorious music wash over us, lift us up and carry us away.

"This is almost unbearably intense," Merritt murmured. He was right, a prolonged climax of sound. Both our hearts were beating faster.

"That flute...it sounds like a glimpse of...I don't know...."

The music grew quieter, and then the pianist began the lengthy, almost unplayable cadenza. Both of us had David in our minds and hearts, and Merritt said as much. "I can just hear him playing this, can't you? He looked so frail, but he was so strong. He couldn't have played this if he hadn't had the power as well as the delicacy."

We held each other and cried again...but these were healing tears. I know Merritt felt David's presence as strongly as I did.

The cadenza ended gently with the orchestra re-entering, a solo flute painting yet another graceful sketch in sound. More solo piano, this time lyrical and achingly expressive, Rachmaninoff at his most passionate.

"God. That is so gorgeous. I want to go and live there and have this beauty always surrounding me." Merritt sighed, a sigh of satisfaction and not pain.

The opening theme returned a third time. Low brass and winds supporting it, a slow build to a burst of brilliance from the piano. An exchange between orchestra and piano, and the movement drew to a serene close.

The quietly rhapsodic second movement began with more melodies in different sections of the orchestra.

"That's just awesome. A vision of what life can be. God, Lindsey, what would life be if we didn't have music? Why did I ever think I could live without hearing this?"

We listened together to more hauntingly beautiful passages for the piano, again thinking of David, of how exquisitely he played this section, with such depth, such emotion.

"You know, I feel sorry for people who have never heard this," Merritt said. "It's like being in another world for a while. I feel such joy. Such hope."

He listened quietly through the next sections, but his breathing quickened from time to time. The piano and orchestra again built to a climax, and Merritt let out a long breath.

"That's it, isn't it? We experience every emotion—*every* emotion there is—listening to this music."

He paused. "No, not every emotion. Every good emotion. Love. Joy. Hope. Passion. Peace."

He was right: they were all there, one after another, wrapping us in every good thing in heaven, wherever that might be. At the moment, I felt that's where we were.

With no pause, the piano abruptly moved into the final movement, with brilliant bursts of sound. Full orchestra, complete excitement.

"Do it, Rach!" Merritt yelled, his eyes shining, making me laugh. "This is sheer joy, Lindsey. Sheer joy!"

A burst of sound again from the piano. We both knew this was another part of the piece that was nearly unplayable by most pianists.

"David really tore this up, didn't he? God, he was *so* good! I don't know how he did it."

Orchestra and piano trading pieces of melody. More intricate playing from the pianist, the orchestra accompanying. Then a quiet, surprisingly delicate section.

161

Now the music again started to build to almost unbearable tension, but Rachmaninoff backed away rather than resolving it and kept the tension going. Then a more serene moment.

"This. It's like…afterglow." Merritt gave me a sidelong glance, and I laughed.

Another peaceful moment, where our hearts grew calmer. Followed by yet more brilliance from the piano, accompanied by subdued, sustained orchestral playing.

A return to the opening themes for this movement, quickening our heartbeats again.

"He just wrings you out completely, doesn't he? But it's so great. So wonderful to live this."

That's exactly what we were doing—what I always did when I heard this piece.

Rachmaninoff continued his interplay of orchestra and piano, painting musical images with all the forces at his disposal, the tension building almost unbearably. By the time the pianist and orchestra brought the work to a close with the final crashing chords, Merritt and I were clinging to each other, laughing and crying.

"Play it again," he demanded, his eyes shining.

So I did.

Chapter 12

The strong, dissonant opening chords of Puccini's opera *Turandot* awakened Lindsey the next morning. Sunlight streamed through the window and a glance at the clock showed her it was almost ten.

Still enjoying the music she loved, she quickly threw on shorts and a sleeveless shirt. She ran into the bathroom, pulled a comb through her hair, tied it back, splashed water on her face, and brushed her teeth, all the while listening to the unmistakable voice of the great Jamie Logan soaring above the chorus in his role as Calaf, the Unknown Prince.

Merritt, showered, shaved, and in crisp, clean shirt and shorts, sat in his wheelchair by the stereo, opera score open on his lap. He glanced up and grinned at her as if it were the most natural thing in the world that he was listening to opera. In the past it had been, but not for many weeks.

"Why didn't you wake me up?" she asked, a little disoriented, as she heard the bloodthirsty chorus demanding the life of Turandot's latest victim.

"I think I just did," Merritt laughed. *Music to my ears. Merritt has the best laugh.*

"Well, yes, you sure did. I can't deny that."

He waved toward the kitchen. "Fruit, scones, coffee, juice…Mom and Dad are outside. Kathy won't be back until tomorrow night. I figured I could blast this as loud as I wanted."

The choir had reached the lovely, quiet hymn to the moon. Lindsey called from the kitchen, "Didn't we have a blast singing in this opera last summer?"

She rejoined Merritt, balancing her plate on her knees as she sat in a chair near him.

"We sure did. Being on the same stage with Jamie Logan was an experience I'll never forget."

They listened together as the choir of children, singing like angels, escorted the doomed prince onto the stage. Once again, the townspeople changed their tune, pleading with the haughty Princess Turandot to spare her latest victim. Merritt grinned broadly at her as Logan's voice once again ascended above the crowd, followed by that group repeating the word, "Pièta!"

"Well, that part was easy to memorize," he laughed.

I can't believe the change, Lindsey thought. *Could this be real? Do I have my Merritt back?*

Merritt turned the sound down and moved his chair closer to her. "Lindsey…what you did for me last night…."

She blinked back tears, happy tears. "I can't tell you how thrilled I am to see you sitting here listening to *Turandot*. It's the most wonderful thing that's happened in a while."

"I wanted to hear it first thing when I woke up. Rachmaninoff to Puccini…kind of makes sense, doesn't it?"

"It does to me."

She finished her scone and licked her fingers. "Forgot to grab a napkin."

Merritt took her hand in both of his. "I need to say this to you. I'll never be able to thank you enough for allowing me to…express my feelings and to play David's music for me and let me feel everything I needed to feel."

She pressed a palm to his face. "It was something we both needed."

"I know I'll always miss David. And there'll be lots of times when I'll be sad, thinking about him. But in a way…it's kind of hard to explain…I think I let him go. I mean I accepted that he's no longer here, that I'll never again…." He sighed. "Linds, you helped me see that he will always be here in my heart. In my memory and in the music."

Lindsey placed both hands behind Merritt's neck as she leaned her forehead against his. "I feel the same way, baby. Though I know my missing him can't compare with yours. You two had so much."

"I'm beginning to understand what your uncle said to me, about being happy for the time we had together…listening to *Turandot*, I can remember how David helped us learn this music and how much he loved it. That's a good memory, and that will get me through."

"It will," Lindsey said softly.

"I have to turn up the volume…we're almost to Calaf's first big aria."

And I hope someday soon you'll try singing that again, Lindsey thought. "Please do. Logan sings this so wonderfully."

They listened together to the end of the act, when Calaf strikes the gong three times while singing the Princess's name three times on a high A, sustaining the last note for an impossibly long time.

"Man. Can that guy *sing*." Merritt turned off the stereo and removed the CD, replacing it in its case.

"So can you," Lindsey said, quietly. "Merritt, you need to sing again."

He nodded. "I will. Not today. My voice feels a little rough."

"I understand. And I don't think I would start with an aria from this opera."

165

That drew a smile. "No, I guess not. But will you play for me? We can do vocal exercises and maybe a couple of Italian songs from the 'Italian Hits' book." He referenced a standard book of vocal collections, *24 Italian Songs and Arias of the Seventeenth and Eighteenth Centuries,* used by voice students for generations.

Grace and Howard came inside, Grace with her arms full of flowers. They beamed at Lindsey, who joined Grace.

"Can I help you with those?"

"Yes, I'd like that." Grace closed the door to the kitchen as they heard father and son conversing.

"Lindsey, God bless you. I don't know what happened, because you were both asleep when we got home, but Merritt got up before anybody, showered, shaved, dressed, and was in the kitchen putting coffee on when I came downstairs. I just couldn't believe it."

Lindsey sighed. "It was rough, Grace. But it was wonderful. Merritt said he realized that without music..." a catch in her voice... "he realized that music is his life."

Grace put her arms around Lindsey and hugged her close. "It can't have been easy. His eyes are still red. There must have been many tears."

"And there will no doubt be many more. He's lost so much. But my dearest friend is stronger than he realizes, and one of the bravest people I know. He'll get through this."

"With your help." Grace brought a vase from the pantry and began arranging the flowers.

Howard returned to the kitchen. "Merritt's asking for Skyline Chili, ladies. How does that sound for an early lunch?"

"Sounds wonderful," Lindsey replied. "Would you like me to come with you?"

"No, that's okay, honey. Stay here with Merritt. I've got this." Whistling, he went out into the pleasant, sunny day.

Lindsey glanced through the kitchen window. *It's gorgeous outside. When did it turn into full spring? I've lost track of time.* Just before she left the kitchen to rejoin Merritt, she glanced at the wall calendar. April 13. The date nagged at her, for some reason.

Merritt had moved onto the sofa and patted the seat next to him. "Sit here, Linds." As she did, the realization struck her. *April 12 was supposed to be my senior recital. I should have been singing last night, all that music David and I worked so hard on.* It must have shown on her face because Merritt stared at her in surprise. "What is it?"

"It's…nothing. What would you like to do? Listen to more music?" Lindsey heard the shake in her voice as she sank down onto the sofa abruptly.

"Lindsey?"

"Oh, Merritt…I just realized…yesterday was supposed to be my senior recital." The dam burst as she leaned against him. "I'm sorry. I'm so sorry."

"Let it out, sweetheart," he held her close, rocking her like a child. "Cry all you want. Some wise person told me that recently."

Lindsey had to laugh through her tears. "It's just…we worked so hard on the music. David was so incredible, he knew every word of every song. He could have sung the damn recital."

Merritt kissed her softly on the forehead. "He always did that. That was David being David, and we always knew he'd back us up no matter what. Any memory slip. He'd fix it."

Another paroxysm of tears. "This is so hard."

"Yes, it is." He continued to hold her close. "I've been so wrapped up in myself. You've lost something…someone as well."

Lindsey grew quieter and put her arms around Merritt. "You know what? I'm sure glad we have each other."

"I am too."

***

With Lindsey at the piano, the following day Merritt took another step forward by beginning to sing again. Everyone at the Conservatory looked for ways to support Merritt, and Claudia Prince had sent over the music for his vocal exercises. Lindsey led him through a warm-up session, beginning in his mid-range and vocalizing first downward and then moving up the scale. She didn't have him tackle high notes, just had him continue to sing in the middle register for several minutes.

He stopped her at one point. "I've never gone so long without singing at all, not even when I was sick," he commented. "Seems strange, doesn't it?" He took a long drink from the bottle of water Grace had provided.

"Wasn't it Jascha Heifetz who once said something like, 'If I go for a day without practicing, I know it, two days and the critics know it, three days and the public knows it'?" Lindsey remarked. "Honestly, you don't sound half bad."

"Well, that must mean I don't sound half good," Merritt quipped. "What I'd really like to do is sing 'Parigi, o cara,' with you, but that's way too ambitious. You would definitely show me up. Okay, let's do an Italian song. A lot more fun than vocal exercises."

"Maybe no high notes yet. How about 'Vergin, tutto amor'? That's pretty."

"How about 'Vittoria, vittoria'? A little more challenging musically. And it doesn't go too high."

Lindsey was pleased with what she heard. It had been weeks, and Merritt had physically, mentally, and emotionally

168

gone through the most difficult time of his life. He negotiated the song successfully and she told him so.

"You're going to be back before you know it," she encouraged him.

"I'm kind of surprised that singing in a seated position isn't as much of a problem as I thought it might be." Merritt drained the water bottle.

"There was no damage to your intercostal muscles or your abs, and I know using those muscles is part of the exercises Molly has you doing," Lindsey reminded him. "You know who Marjorie Lawrence was, don't you?"

"Famous Australian soprano who had polio and was paralyzed from the waist down. I know what you're saying, she had to learn to breathe all over again, but she eventually got back on stage. She could only sing roles where she could sit and didn't have to move, but she sang opera again."

He grinned at her. "Even so, now I'm eager to learn to stand more securely. I need that lower body support for all the high C's I intend to sing."

Lindsey hugged him, and they clung to each other for a minute, tears closer to the surface than either of them cared to admit.

Merritt murmured, "We're going to get through this, Linds." She nodded. "You okay with losing your recital? That was tough."

"I will be." She sat back and flipped through the Italian songbook again. "One more?"

"Yes, but I want to sing a Schubert song," Merritt pointed to the nearby bookshelves where he kept his music.

"I already have it," Lindsey reached across the rack to some music she had stacked on the piano and selected a book. "Something from one of the song cycles?"

"No, I want to sing 'An die Musik,'" Merritt said softly. *Schubert's exquisite, heartfelt, simple tribute to his art.* Lindsey's eyes met Merritt's, and she felt their stronger than ever connection.

"Perfect."

Merritt sang softly in German:

You lovely art, how often in a desolate hour
When I am overwhelmed by life's unrest,
Have you set alight my heart to the warmth of love,
And lifted me to a better world,

Often a sigh, escaping from your harp—
That sweet, celestial chord from you,
Has shown me a heaven of happier times.
You lovely art, for this I thank you.

***

Ethan came by himself the next day for a physical therapy session with Merritt and arrived just as Lindsey and Merritt were singing a duet from *La Traviata*. Absorbed in the delight of singing together again, they weren't aware he had entered the room until he applauded heartily after the duet.

"Bravo. Or maybe I should say 'bravi.' What a treat to hear you two."

"No Molly today?" Merritt asked.

"No, just me. She called in sick this morning." Ethan chuckled. "Despite our best efforts, even health care professionals sometimes catch something."

He noted Merritt was wearing his temporary prosthetic leg. "Are you standing more?"

"Trying to. Keeping it on is easier than having to fumble for it. That's okay, isn't it?"

"Yes, it is. Using it will help your stump form to its final shape. However, there's a difference between getting used to using a temporary prosthetic leg and the intense rehab you'll undergo when you get your permanent prosthesis. Use this one more for balance than weight bearing."

"I have to admit I still feel like I'd rather hang onto something—or somebody—than try to walk by myself, even with crutches or a cane. I'm afraid of falling."

"Understandable. Are you still having phantom sensations—the pain, the itching and throbbing?"

"Once in a while. Especially at night. I'd sure like for those to stop, it's...strange."

"Unfortunately, it may be quite a while before they stop completely. Your mind takes however much time it needs to adjust to the fact the leg is no longer there."

"I get that." He paused and sighed. "I miss my leg."

"Of course, you do. You're still in the grieving stage for it. This is a process, Merritt. We don't rush it because we want to get it right."

Lindsey closed the music and stood. "I guess I should leave you gentlemen alone."

There is no way I can help with his physical healing, she thought. *Merritt has so much work ahead of him. Much as I love him, I can't ever understand what he's going through. Nobody can, really, unless it's another amputee.*

Lindsey wandered outside to help Grace with weeding and trimming a flower bed. Grace smiled as Lindsey knelt beside her on the ground, and handed her a pair of gloves.

"Did you get chased out?"

"Not really. But when they were talking before Ethan started his session, I realized...I felt so helpless, Grace. I

171

observed his PT sessions several times at the hospital because Ethan invited me to stay. But there's not a thing I can do to help him with what's happened…having a leg amputated." She dug into the ground and removed a particularly stubborn weed.

"I know exactly what you mean. I so wish I could do more for him. But it takes experienced people with expertise in this particular area of medicine."

"You've taken on quite a bit," Lindsey told Grace. "Cleaning and bandaging his wound and checking carefully for any problems. Massaging his stump."

"Kathleen is a real help, and I like doing it. It reminds me of caring for him as a baby, but I'd never tell him that." They chuckled together. "He's healthy and strong, he's healing quite well. And I know Ethan checks his stump every time he's here."

She paused. "Isn't it surprising how easily I say that? 'His stump.' Something you never, ever think you might have to help your child deal with."

Lindsey pitched another clump of weeds into a bucket Grace had provided. "Sometimes all this feels like a bad dream. But it isn't. It's our actual reality now."

Grace smoothed the bare soil and tamped it down. "It's like a patch of the worst weeds imaginable, and we have to find some way to wrestle with it and then smooth things over as best we can. Life goes on."

Weeding completed, Lindsey carried the bucket to the compost heap at the back of the yard, appreciating the spring day. *The Ohio River Valley at its best, pleasant and not humid. Summers could be brutal at times, but spring and fall were mostly ideal*, Lindsey thought. *Philosophers and writers love to liken life to the seasons.*

She was washing her hands in the utility sink in the pantry when Ethan came looking for her. "Walk me to my car, will you? I'd like to talk to you."

"How did our boy do today?"

"He's making good progress. He mentioned to me that the two of you had listened to the Rachmaninoff concerto Friday night. I see a definite difference in his whole demeanor. It's obvious it helped him."

Lindsey followed Ethan to his car. "I have to thank you for the suggestions you made. It was…I've never experienced anything like it."

"Want to talk about it?"

"I do," she said eagerly. "Ethan, Merritt was able to let go…really let go…of the awful emotional pain he's been in. It scared me a little at first, even though I knew it needed to happen."

"You anticipated that."

"I did, but not…not like what happened with him. I've read about it…people *keening* because of their intense grief. I was afraid for him…afraid I'd made a mistake by insisting he listen to music with me that I knew would affect him so deeply."

"Um. Go on." He leaned against the car, ankles and arms crossed.

"And we both cried and held onto each other, and…well, I decided to turn off the recording after the first movement. We talked for a bit, and then he said he wanted to listen to…he said, 'my David's music.' So I started it over."

She took a quick breath, recalling the moment. "I said a couple of things to him about how this music affected me, and then he started talking, and he shared his feelings as he listened. It just…spilled out of him."

She paused again. "Here's what he said that made me so elated. He said, something like, 'How did I ever think I could live without music?' It thrilled me to hear that. And then the next morning, he said to me he believed he would be able to let David go." Another breath. "It seemed to me that was important."

Ethan nodded. "I would agree. You did a good thing, Lindsey."

"No, Ethan. The music did it. I was just there to witness how much hearing that piece helped my dear friend."

"You guided him into experiencing it more deeply. More precisely. Finding a way to begin to get out of the awful hole he's been in."

"Is that what I did?"

Ethan stepped away from the car and fished the keys from his pocket. "Do you recall me telling you that what I suggested is similar to a specific technique used by some music therapists?"

"Yes, I remember...I think you said guided something...oh, yes. Guided Imagery and Music."

"I know a music therapist who is learning to use that technique with some of her patients. She's excited by the results. Would you like to meet her and learn more about it?"

Lindsey considered it. "Not right now, but thanks for the offer. Right now, I've got to figure out how in the world I'm going to put together and sing a senior recital...without David."

***

Lindsey's parents were due to arrive in a few days to bring Andrew's completed and framed portrait of David and to attend the unveiling of David's headstone. M.J. would be with them and they had reservations once again at the Vernon Manor Hotel. They planned to stay only over the weekend.

"I asked them to bring me some summer clothes and my music." Lindsey, seated at the piano, flipped through the tenor aria book.

"Linds—maybe you should go to West Chester with them for a while," Merritt stood next to her, balancing himself with his four-pronged cane. "Bring that stuff when you come back."

She stared at him. "What on earth prompted that?"

He maneuvered himself onto the piano bench and put an arm around her. "I think you need to spend some time at home," he said, gazing at her. "You look tired, and you've lost weight. Your family seems to be the best tonic for you when you're stressed."

"I'm okay," she assured him, touched by his concern.

"No, you're not. You've been taking such good care of me that you haven't taken care of Lindsey. I'm doing a lot better. Go home for a while."

"I don't want you to stop singing."

"I have no intention of doing that. Kathleen can play for me. She'd like that, you can leave her in charge until you get back." He hugged her close as she sighed and relaxed against him.

Maybe he's right, Lindsey thought. *He's doing so much better. I am tired. And it might be good for the Nobles to have Merritt all to themselves for a few weeks. Kathleen especially. How sweet and generous of him to suggest this.*

She wiped her eyes and smiled at him. "You are the sweetest boy in the world," she murmured. "I think you're right. I know Kathleen will be a great vocal coach."

The unveiling of the headstone and a gathering at the Rosenthal's to present David's portrait to his parents would be

Merritt's first outing since the accident, and Lindsey knew he was nervous about it.

Ethan talked to them after Molly left, suggesting it would be best if he stayed in his wheelchair for these events. "And actually, when you start back to school in the fall, I'd recommend continuing to use it. You'll have long walks from the parking lot into the building and through the halls, and people rushing past you could throw you off balance. Once you have your permanent prosthetic, within a few months you should be much more secure."

"Who said anything about me going back to school this fall? Or ever?" Merritt demanded, glaring at Lindsey, who was momentarily stunned by his vehemence as she exchanged glances with Ethan.

"I did," she responded firmly. "You need to complete your degree as much as I do. We'll be in the same classes, and there's no reason at all I can't help you get around." She sounded determined as only Lindsey could. "I'll bet I can almost lift this chair with one hand."

"Say I manage to complete my Bachelor of Music degree. Then what?" Merritt stared gloomily into space.

"You get busy on your Master's Degree," Lindsey said calmly. "Stay here and continue to study with Claudia. She's a great teacher. Keep working with Ethan and Molly, and after you get your permanent leg, concentrate on mastering moving with ease. Ethan and I see no reason you can't stand on a stage and sing opera again."

"You two have it all figured out, do you?" Merritt stared hard at each of them. "How easy it's all going to be. Was anyone going to tell Merritt about these plans?"

"I have to agree with Lindsey," Ethan commented. "If you continue to progress as you have to this point, there is absolutely nothing stopping you. Unless you choose to decide you can't do it. Which would be a damned shame." He paused. "But of course, it's your choice."

Merritt didn't reply, and Lindsey and Ethan exchanged glances again. *At least he's considering it*, Lindsey thought to herself. She started to speak but Ethan shook his head no.

After a few moments of silence, Merritt stood abruptly, almost falling, Ethan immediately sprang to steady him, and Merritt shook him off.

"Back up to that part about Lindsey picking up this chair with one hand." He rolled it toward her. "I have to see that."

Lindsey, never one to back down from a dare, folded the chair, took a deep breath, planted her feet firmly, spat on each hand, flexed her muscles—which caused even Merritt to smile—gripped the back of the chair with her left hand, and with considerable effort lifted it two inches off the floor for about twenty seconds.

"Holy shit," Merritt chortled. He grabbed Lindsey and hugged her. "Okay, you win." To Ethan he said, "I want you to promise me I'll be able to win an argument with this sassy broad someday."

"Anything is possible," Ethan laughed. "We just saw proof of that."

***

When Lindsey's parents arrived in Cincinnati, M.J. picked up his sister and brought her to the hotel to stay with them. Mary Cameron and Grace Noble had planned the schedule for this visit: it would be a gathering in which Merritt's condition had to be their first consideration. They agreed the visit to the cemetery and then to the Rosenthals would be more than enough excitement for Merritt, so avoided any kind of combined family gathering prior to that.

The next day, the Camerons met the Rosenthals in the cemetery office before going to David's grave. Rabbi Ephron gave Lindsey a warm hug. "It's good to see you, Lindsey. I understand you've been a great help to Merritt during this difficult time."

"Today won't be easy, Rabbi," Lindsey said. "It will be very sad for him to be at David's grave."

"Yes, I know. It's a brief, informal ceremony—we use Psalm 23 and the Kaddish, and I'll say a few words to thank the people who have come to honor the young man we all loved. The memorial stone is exquisite."

Lindsey stood near the grave as she watched the Noble family approach, Howard pushing his son's wheelchair, Grace and Kathleen with their arms linked. Merritt was pale and Lindsey's heart ached for him. Her father sensed her distress and put an arm around her.

There were about fifty people present, all by invitation. The rabbi thanked them for joining the family as they unveiled their monument to their beloved son, and began the recitation of the Psalm. Lindsey felt her throat close, and she couldn't speak.

Merritt had begun to cry and she longed to comfort him. Kathleen knelt beside his chair, pressing her face against his arm. Grace patted his shoulder. *That's as it should be*, Lindsey thought. Three families joined in grief, each comforting their child…except the family whose child lay in the ground. She felt her own tears running down her cheeks.

The Kaddish came next, and the cover was removed from the marker. Lindsey trembled when she saw the beautiful granite stone, the shape representing a wing. *Under the shelter of God's wings*, she thought, and hoped Merritt remembered she had told him about that prayer. The assembled group stood in silence for several minutes, and Rabbi Ephron ended the brief gathering by saying, "On behalf of Arthur and Leah, I extend thanks for your presence on this occasion. David will be forever in our hearts."

The Nobles left the cemetery first out of consideration for Merritt, this time Kathleen carefully pushing the wheelchair. Lindsey and her family lingered briefly. She touched the memorial, again thinking of David sheltered by God's wings.

A smaller gathering at the house: Rabbi Ephron and close friends of the family joined the Nobles and Camerons. Kathleen helped Leah set out some light refreshments.

With no ceremony, Andrew carefully placed the portrait on an easel Arthur had provided, and made sure it was in good light before he removed the soft cloth which covered it.

The people who loved David gazed at the painting in awe. Under Andrew's skilled hand, canvas and acrylic paint glowed with life. Andrew had painted David from the waist up, seated at the piano. He looked toward them as he smiled, the hand nearest them on the keyboard ready to play, the other turning a page of music. He looked as if he'd been practicing and someone spoke to him, and he had turned to respond.

A moment in David Rosenthal's life captured forever.

Susan Moore Jordan

Chapter 13

Lindsey helped Kathleen serve refreshments to the other guests, noting Arthur Rosenthal deep in conversation with Andrew Cameron. Merritt sat gazing at the portrait of David, and she couldn't read his expression. She was filling a plate with almond cookies, rugelach, and small slices of apple cake to share with Merritt when she saw her dad lean down to speak to him. Whatever her father said elicited a smile and a hug, and Merritt continued to smile when she approached and handed him the plate.

"That's a lot of goodies for one person," he observed.

Lindsey dragged a footstool closer to his chair. "That's because we're going to share," she responded, relieving him of the plate and balancing it on her knees.

Kathleen, carrying a tray of drinks, stopped to speak to Lindsey. "Your father is an amazing artist, Lindsey. I'll bet he's painted you a lot."

"Yes, he has, since I was an infant. And yes, he's definitely talented. Sometimes I wonder if I'm really his daughter. I've never been much of an artist." She selected demitasse glasses of red wine for herself and Merritt. "M.J., on the other hand, is pretty good at it."

Kathleen's face lit up at M.J.'s name. "Oh, really? That's cool." She spotted M.J. and headed toward him.

"Did you do that on purpose?" Merritt asked with a wry grin. "Are you playing yenta, Lindsey?"

"Well, she's only two years younger than he is. And I know the University of Pennsylvania is a school she's considering, though she's uncertain about her major course of study. Maybe M.J. can interest her in psychology."

Lindsey closely observed her friend. "What did my dad say to you that made you look so pleased just now?"

"He told me he's working on another painting of David. This one's for me."

"I love that." She smiled at him and was treated to an equally warm smile. "I didn't know."

"I think he wanted to be the one to let me know about it. He says he'll bring it when you come back to Cincinnati."

"About that...."

Merritt put a finger to her lips. "I know exactly what you're going to say, and the answer is absolutely not."

Lindsey took a sip of wine and bit into one of Leah's almond cookies. "You were having a hard time at the cemetery, Merritt. I did wonder if it might be better if I put off my trip home for a while."

"I don't believe I had a hard time, Linds. Of course, I was sad, we all were. But you know what? It helped me to be there, to see where David's resting. And seeing the memorial stone...it's, well, kind of inspirational. It reminded me of what you told me about one of the prayers at the funeral—David being in the shelter of God's wings. I love that. The headstone is perfect."

"It is, isn't it? I had the same thought."

"I understand now why people like to visit the graves of people they love. I'll do that. I want to go back and just be there." They sat together quietly for a few moments.

"So don't for one minute consider not going home with your family." Merritt picked up another cookie. "We talked about this. There will be many times when I think of David and shed tears. You told me it's a good thing. I want to spend some time with the Rosenthals, too. Mr. Rosenthal talked to me before you guys got here."

Merritt glanced away, tears gathering in his eyes. "He said he needs me to be his son now."

Lindsey swallowed hard to get the lump out of her throat. "Oh, Merritt."

"So, you see, I have my family, David's parents, my medical team—Molly and Ethan and Dr. Evans—who'll be taking good care of me. You don't have to do it all by yourself." He placed his empty wine glass on the nearby end table.

"I just don't want you to in any way think I'm abandoning you again."

"It was my idea for you to spend some time at home, wasn't it?" He grew silent. "I know why you went home right after David's funeral, Lindsey."

She stared at him, not able to speak.

"I remembered what I said to you. I'll regret that the rest of my life, but I know you realized I wasn't thinking at all. And I already know you forgive me."

Lindsey leaned her head on Merritt's shoulder as he wrapped an arm around her, trying to balance the plate of cookies on her knees. Grace witnessed this exchange and grabbed the plate in time to avoid a small calamity, causing all three of them to chuckle.

Goodnights were said, and Lindsey hugged Merritt for a long time. "Call me. Or I'll call you."

"Every day. I promise. Listen to lots of music. Watch your dad finish the portrait he's painting for me. Enjoy the sunshine. Rest." He gently pinched her upper arm. "And for heaven's sake, woman, put some meat back on these bones, will you?"

Quiet laughter between them, and another long embrace.

***

Lindsey spent her first week at home doing as little as possible, following Merritt's instructions. Sleeping late and taking a daily nap. Lying under an umbrella in the yard, enjoying the lovely spring weather and balmy breezes. Watching Andrew work on his new portrait of David: a smaller canvas, David's head and shoulders, an expression on his face she'd seen often when he looked at Merritt. *The expression of a man in love.*

She listened to music. More Rachmaninoff: the second piano concerto, the one most people loved best; the Second Symphony; some of his orchestral tone poems. A lot of Ravel's instrumental music including "Pavane for a Dead Princess."

Mary and M.J. prepared food they knew she liked, and Lindsey cleaned her plate at every meal. She spoke daily with Merritt.

"I'm drinking a lot of chocolate malts. It surprised me to learn I'd lost twenty pounds, so you were right."

"Getting enough rest?"

"I've been sleeping in every day and taking a nap in the afternoon. Is that enough?'

He chuckled. "Glad to know you're following my suggestions."

"Is that what they were? They sounded more like orders to me. I'm also singing every day. Are you?"

"Does the sun rise? Kathleen is as tough as you were." They both laughed. "It feels good, though. I've been through every aria I ever studied with Claudia. Speaking of who...whom...she offered to come to the house and give me lessons."

"That doesn't surprise me one bit. You always were her favorite. I hope you said yes."

"I sure did. I want to try the *Turandot* arias. They may be a bit much to perform right now, but I can learn them."

The May days flowed together and it became warmer, more humid, but still pleasant. The Camerons decided to take a weekend at Cape May, and M.J. came over from Philadelphia to join them.

"Hey, Linds, I just found out the Philadelphia Orchestra is performing your favorite piece of music at the Mann Center the second week of June. If you're still going to be here, want me to see if I can get tickets?"

"Who's the pianist?"

"Jean-Yves Thibaudet."

"Oh, then, yes, yes, yes! I'd love to hear him play that in person. His recording is just incredible. David thought it was the best. He said Thibaudet plays the third movement at least as fast as Rachmaninoff did."

Lindsey realized something had shifted. She'd spoken David's name casually, a happy memory. And no tears threatened. She thought more about that after they returned from the shore when she visited her grandmother Toni to help her pick flowers.

"I'm finding I can think about David without shedding tears, Grammy Toni. I mean, I'll always miss him, but the realization that he's gone doesn't hurt quite as much."

"That's a good thing, Lindsey. Though don't be surprised if you have moments when you still need to grieve."

Lindsey carried the blooms inside where the two women cleaned and trimmed the stems, preparing to arrange them in two vases. "When your parents died, is that what you experienced?"

"Well…yes, in a way," Toni put her garden shears down for a moment. "It was such an awful shock. But I had two little boys to care for, and I had to think of them first. Andrew and Jacob were only eight and six."

"When people die so unexpectedly and so young…that has to be the worst."

"Yes, I think it is. You regret things you never said to them, things you never did with them that you'd put off until 'later.' Only then it's too late. 'Later' never comes." Toni placed bunches of flowers in each vase, artfully arranging them.

The Camerons decided to make a weekend of their visit to the Mann Center, staying in a downtown hotel in Philadelphia, doing some clothes shopping for Mary and Lindsey, visiting the Art Museum on Friday, and the Zoo on Saturday before the concert.

The visit to the Art Museum included some time in the contemporary gallery where they appreciatively viewed three of Andrew's paintings—one of the Vietnam War and two neo-impressionistic landscapes, the style of painting with which Andrew had achieved his greatest success. Andrew and Mary sat on a bench while Lindsey and M.J., pretending to study the labels next to the paintings, eavesdropped on people making comments about their father's work.

M.J. nudged his sister. "Mom and Dad are making out again."

She glanced at her parents to see Andrew, one arm around Mary, holding her close, his lips on her forehead as she leaned against him, her eyes closed.

"Oh, man," M.J. muttered with a grin, "get a room, folks."

They joked about it, but both of Andrew's children felt fortunate that their parents were still so deeply in love after all these years. *I hope someday I'll find someone to have a bond with like that,* Lindsey thought.

The concert proved to be everything they had hoped for. Thibaudet delivered as expected, and watching him, Lindsey was reminded of David—their styles were quite similar. A flutter of pain in her heart as it struck her again that David would never perform this work he loved so much.

***

Cincinnati in July can be brutally hot and humid, and Lindsey was grateful for the central air-conditioning in the Nobles' house. She'd never been a big fan of summer weather and knew Merritt wasn't either. She had returned during a heatwave, and they spent most of their time inside, drinking copious amounts of water and lemonade.

It pleased Lindsey to see how well Merritt was doing—definitely stronger, more comfortable with his temporary prosthesis. Ethan advised Merritt to limit the time he used it, explaining he wouldn't, and shouldn't, begin to feel completely comfortable until he had his permanent leg.

Merritt sometimes stood when he sang, trying to find a way to achieve the support on his right side that was there on his left. Lindsey thought he sounded wonderful, singing high notes with ease, his voice more mature than she remembered. Singing with more depth of expression.

School would begin in about six weeks, at the end of August, and Lindsey talked to Claudia Prince about a pianist for her recital. "I need to start selecting music and set a date," she said. "I'm not...I just can't perform any of the songs David and I worked on together. I know attempting to sing those would just be…I couldn't handle it."

"I understand completely. There's a new grad student in my studio who is minoring in voice, and majoring in composition. She's also an excellent pianist and is continuing lessons with her local teacher. She might be ideal. Why don't I set up a meeting between you two?"

"Yes, I'd like that. A new grad student from Cincinnati…I guess she did her undergrad work elsewhere?"

"She's an interesting young woman. I'll let her fill you in, but she went to McGill University for her bachelor of music degree."

Lindsey met with Zivah Margolis and liked her immediately. Claudia gave them the use of her studio for an hour, and Lindsey sang through several arias and art songs she thought she might include. Zivah, tall, thin, with dark hair pulled severely back from her face and wearing oversized glasses, sightread every piece except one which she had played before, and she proved to be an adept and sensitive collaborative pianist.

The severity of Zivah's looks belied her wicked sense of humor and irreverent, no-nonsense approach to life. "With Zivah, what you see is what you get," Lindsey told Merritt after that first practice session. "I really like that in people."

"David was like that," Merritt said wistfully. "God, I miss him, Linds."

"I know, baby. When I attended that concert and watched Thibaudet play…I could just see David playing that concerto." She sighed. "My grandmother would say that some things just aren't meant to be."

"I'd like to hear it again," Merritt said. "Could we?" The two of them snuggled on the sofa and allowed Rachmaninoff to work his magic on them yet another time before they said their goodnights.

Lindsey woke abruptly and sat bolt upright. *Something's wrong.* A glance at her wristwatch showed her it was two a.m. She lay quietly, listening for any strange sounds, but heard nothing. Still, she grabbed the light robe from the foot of her bed and went downstairs as silently as she could, continuing to listen.

Faint sounds from Merritt's bedroom. A light shining under the door. Fearfully, she slowly opened it. Lindsey's heart sank when she saw him lying on his back on the floor, dressed only in boxer shorts but wearing his prosthetic leg, his breathing rapid and shallow.

She gasped aloud. "Oh, God, Merritt. Let me help you."

Merritt put up a hand, took a slow, deep breath, and said calmly but firmly, "No, don't touch me. Stay where you are. And keep it down, will you? I don't want to wake up my parents or Kathleen."

"But you need help." She began twisting her hands, not knowing what to do.

"I fell. It can happen, I always knew that." His breathing slower and steadier, he continued, "Ethan recently supervised Molly working with me on this. I know exactly what to do, and the worst thing you could do is try to pull me up or move me around."

"What do you want me to do?"

"Stay right there for now. I got up to pee and put my leg on, but then I zigged when I should have zagged. I'm just catching my breath for a minute. I know I'm not hurt...the first thing I did was get into this position and assess myself. Nothing hurts. I'll bet you don't see any blood, either." He looked up and winked at her.

Merciful heavens, he's so calm. Making jokes. Who are you and what have you done with Merritt?

A nervous giggle. "No blood, Merritt."

"Let me take some deep breaths. I can handle this."

Lindsey did as instructed but had to fight against the urge to yell for Grace and Howard. Or maybe phone for an ambulance.

One last deep, slow breath, and Merritt lifted himself into a sitting position. He checked his prosthesis thoroughly. *He's making sure it isn't broken or twisted*, Lindsey thought. Merritt then turned to his left and lifted the prosthesis across his left leg. The muscular strength he had developed in his arms, shoulders, and chest became apparent as he maneuvered. *Good grief, I had no idea how ripped he's become. All these months working with weights, I guess.*

Moving slowly and carefully, Merritt rolled over onto his hands and knees. Lindsey looked on in admiration as he crawled to the bed and grasped the bars on the hospital bed. Keeping his left foot under him, he extended his right leg out as he pushed up into a standing position.

Lindsey let out a breath at the same time Merritt did. "Okay, now you can help. Bring my chair over here and place it right behind my butt so I can ease myself down onto it."

The sound of the wheelchair awakened the rest of the household, and Lindsey heard Grace, Howard, and Kathleen racing downstairs.

"I'm okay," Merritt called out. "I just had a little fall. But I'm fine."

Grace stopped herself and her husband and daughter from going to Merritt. "This is what you've been working on," she said, trying and failing to sound casual.

"Yes, it is." He gave all of them a crooked grin. "I did it."

Lindsey, standing behind the chair, noticed the perspiration across his back. *That took tremendous effort. And he was so calm. He's superb.* Grace ran into the bathroom and returned holding a towel, draping it over Merritt's shoulders.

"Are you sure you're okay?" Howard asked anxiously.

"Pretty much, but I think I should go to Good Sam and get checked out just to be sure I didn't do any damage to my stump. Would you hand me a shirt, Mom?"

"Is it okay for me to drive you?" Howard asked.

Merritt is totally in charge of this. He's magnificent. He's going to be fine. Lindsey was thrilled at this display of courage and determination. *How far he's come.*

"I think you should phone for an ambulance. Please tell them your son is a below-the-knee amputee who just took a fall, and he thinks he's probably all right but needs to be seen to be sure. That way they won't send an ambulance with a siren screaming out here. It's not a dire emergency."

Howard waited with Merritt for the ambulance while the two girls and Grace ran upstairs, threw on clothes, and drove to Good Sam, passing an ambulance with flashing lights but no siren headed for their house. Lindsey ran inside as soon as they arrived at the hospital and phoned Ethan, who showed up minutes after Merritt's ambulance got there and he had been taken into an examination room with his family.

Rushing into the hospital, Ethan approached Lindsey as soon as he spotted her. His demeanor surprised her—the usually calm and collected Ethan appeared agitated and somewhat unkempt. *Well, well, well, this is interesting. I wonder if Ethan's concern is for Merritt as his patient or maybe something more?*

"I'm sure he's fine," she soothed. "But, oh, Ethan, I wish you'd seen him. He was so—he didn't get flustered at all. He

191

just focused on doing what he needed to do. You taught him well."

A quick breath and the veil was drawn over his face…again the consummate professional physiotherapist.

"He's been working on this. Falls can happen, and it was important for him to understand they don't need to be a source of fear. They're manageable. It's good to know how he responded."

You sound like Mr. Cool now, Lindsey thought. *But I know what I saw.*

Ethan was allowed to enter Merritt's examination room, but Lindsey was neither a medical professional nor a family member. She found a seat in the crowded waiting area and glanced around. *So many people here in the middle of the night.* A flashback to March, when she had been one of those anxious people coming in looking for a loved one who had been brought to this emergency room for immediate medical attention.

She watched the staff members as they dealt with frantic people who needed their help. They projected an air of calm and caring, exactly what was needed.

All these professionals, so dedicated to helping others. Caring for people sometimes in unimaginable circumstances. This has to be the most demanding place in the hospital for the staff members.

Another ambulance arrived, this one with sirens blaring. Members of the staff raced the rolling stretcher through the unit as the ambulance driver ran behind it, something in his hands over the victim's head, a tube extending to an arm.

Maybe a blood transfusion? The victim of a gunshot wound?

Lindsey thought back to all the times she had been here at Good Sam when Merritt was first admitted until the day he was sent home. Until March, she had seldom been in a hospital except to visit a few friends who'd been injured or had minor surgery. Her own health had always been excellent, and her doctor visits routine. She had never given much thought to the doctors and nurses she'd come in contact with, other than they had undergone rigorous and lengthy training…and they were nice and she liked them.

A family was ushered through the unit, sobbing uncontrollably. Lindsey's throat constricted. *Someone they love just died.* The medical staff members accompanying them displayed such compassionate care. *How do they do it? Constantly deal with life and death crises?*

A smiling Ethan spotted Lindsey and beckoned her to come into Merritt's room.

"You were right, he's fine. A couple of bruises. He can go home in the car." Inside the room, more smiles, a sense of calm.

Merritt, sitting up on the examining table, blew her a kiss. "I told you I got this."

"Yes, you did, and you are absolutely magnificent."

"Hey, all I did was crawl over to the bed and stand up. No big deal." Smiles all around from the staff gathered near their patient.

A happy ending for them, something they must live for.

"Thank you. We're so fortunate this hospital has such great people to care for us. Thank all of you, so much, from the bottom of my heart." Lindsey said, meaning every word.

"Merritt's friend speaks for all of us," Howard added.

The physician who Lindsey guessed must have examined Merritt nodded to her.

"Just doing our job."

Heroes, all of you, she thought.

Susan Moore Jordan

Chapter 14

"This is terrific, Lindsey. Why haven't you ever performed it before?" Zivah Margolis smiled at Lindsey from the piano bench, the sounds of "Sempre libera" from *La Traviata* still echoing in Claudia's studio.

"It's definitely a stretch, but Claudia agreed I could use it after we went through it yesterday. Violetta is my dream role." Lindsey leaned against the piano and smiled at her pianist. "I'm hoping to convince Merritt to sing Alfredo's offstage solos from the wings," she added.

"That would be great," Zivah commented. "Want to grab something to drink?"

The two women had been working on Lindsey's recital music for over an hour. Lindsey had selected the music for most of her recital, making sure she fulfilled the requirements for an undergraduate program. She'd substituted songs by Fauré rather than those by Duparc that she and David had rehearsed, and reluctantly put away the music to the Schumann song cycle she had so looked forward to performing, using pieces by Schubert instead.

The aria from Verdi's *La Traviata* replaced "Un bel di" from Puccini's *Madama Butterfly*, which was probably even more of a stretch because Lindsey doubted Cio-Cio-San was a role she would ever perform. But because it was an opera David particularly loved, she had planned to sing it. She still needed to make another selection for an oratorio aria and to replace the Rachmaninoff songs, for which she had used English translations to fulfill that language requirement.

"Yes, let's. Something tall and cold. An ice cream soda?"

"That sounds good," Zivah agreed. "How about we meet at that ice cream place on Vine Street?"

"Why don't we pick something up at Graeter's on Reading Road and drive to Eden Park? It's a beautiful day, and I love sitting at the Overlook. We can take my car and I'll bring you back before I go home." Home being, of course, the Noble house.

Lindsey had learned that Zivah, while a resident of Cincinnati, was actually French Canadian by birth. Her father was offered an important position with Procter and Gamble when Zivah was a toddler, so her family relocated and had been in Cincinnati ever since.

Settled on a bench in the Outlook at Eden Park, the women gazed across the river and sipped their ice cream sodas.

"Do you miss Montreal?" Lindsey asked. "Any special reason you came back to Cincinnati for graduate school? I understand McGill is excellent."

"We go back to Montreal at least once a year, so I was kind of bilingual but not fluent." Zivah swished her straw through the soda. "When I thought about college, I decided to apply to McGill and perfect my French, then come back home for graduate school before applying to the Sorbonne."

"Montreal is a fabulous city. My uncle lives there, and I've visited several times. I've picked up a little Québécois. But is being fluent in French Canadian actually going to be that helpful in Paris?"

"At present, McGill has an intensive study in both forms of French. That appealed to the nerd in me," Zivah laughed. "Your uncle lives there?"

196

"Yes, he's Director of CBC-Two in Montreal. Jean Couvreur."

"Your uncle is Jean Couvreur?" Zivah arched an eyebrow. "I've actually met him. He and my dad's brother Abe are good friends. Wow, Lindsey, your uncle is famous. He's also well-known as a champion of First Nations; they even made him an honorary Abenaki."

"Our family is very proud of him." Lindsey took a spoonful of mint chocolate chip ice cream, letting it melt on her tongue. *So good.*

"I'll be sure to let my Uncle Abe know you and I are performing together in the fall. Do you have a date?"

"I haven't attempted to schedule one yet, but I want to perform it before Thanksgiving. I thought I'd wait until I've selected music for my last two groups—the oratorio aria and English songs. I'd like to find something out of the ordinary for the English group."

Lindsey found time a few days later to go to a music retail store and browse through the sale tables. One item caught her eye: a CD by British tenor Robert Tear singing poems of A.A. Milne set to music by a composer Lindsey hadn't heard of, Harold Fraser-Simpson. Intrigued, she bought the CD and asked one of the clerks if they possibly had the printed music for this collection. A search came up empty but he told her he'd see if another of the stores might have it.

Merritt listened to the CD with her as they sat together on the sofa. "Well, I guess they're cute," was his comment.

"Don't be so dismissive. Some of them are quite charming. I would only need to perform four or five, and they're certainly different from the rest of my program. The contrast might be interesting for my audience, don't you think?"

"I think Robert Tear sounds veddy, veddy British," Merritt smirked.

"Snob." She punched him lightly.

Merritt laughed and rubbed his arm. "No, he's very good. It's a pretty voice. Tear was kind of up against it while he was singing because his rival Peter Pears was so popular in British music circles at that time. Tear's career as an opera singer consisted mainly of character roles, I believe."

"Well, I'm going to see if I can find the sheet music." Lindsey turned toward him, her arms linked on the back of the sofa. "I love A.A. Milne. My parents used to read the Pooh books to me and my brother. Every time Mom got to the 'Horrible Heffalump' story she would start laughing so hard she cried. I never understood why until I tried reading it to my little nephew André and I did exactly the same thing. He stared at me as if I'd lost my mind, and that just made me laugh harder."

"My mother did that, too," Merritt chuckled. "Maybe Milne actually wrote for the child in the adult? You're probably right, Linds. These will be an interesting change of pace in your program. It's also good they won't be as vocally demanding. You have enough of that on your plate."

Lindsey managed to find a book of the songs in the Hamilton County Public Library and was given permission to make copies. There were more than twenty songs with lyrics from the Pooh books and other of Milne's writings. Lindsey and Zivah selected five they both agreed would work for her recital.

She hadn't asked Merritt yet if he'd be willing to sing offstage during her recital, the few phrases the character Alfredo sings while the courtesan Violetta is performing her tour-de-force aria, "Sempre libera."

He seemed to be doing well, singing all the time, progressing in his work with Molly, but she wondered if it

198

would be too much for him. *Ethan would be the best judge of Merritt's readiness*, she thought.

The next time Ethan stopped by a PT session to see how Molly and Merritt were doing, Lindsey walked him to his car afterward, asking why he had said it was better for Merritt not to stand and move too much on his temporary prosthesis.

"Because that's what it is, a temporary prosthetic leg. It doesn't fit perfectly and sometimes if amputees depend on it too much, when they get their permanent leg, they have to re-learn, in a way. Their gait can be off. Once his stump has completed forming, his permanent prosthetic will be carefully measured and fitted to it. That's when the real work will begin for him."

"But I hope he can have it and learn to use it well enough to walk at graduation. That's something I really want to happen. I can arrange to walk with him. It would mean a lot."

Ethan gazed at her thoughtfully. "Yes, I can see that. I can't promise anything, Lindsey. It can take as long as nine months for the stump to be ready for a permanent prosthesis."

Lindsey looked away, a little disappointed. "That would be December. We graduate on the twelfth of December." She sighed.

"He could still walk using his temporary leg," Ethan suggested. "And remember, that's the 'worst case' scenario. It's possible he can have it fitted as early as October. I'm impressed with Merritt's progress, but my biggest concern is always his well-being, that he has a steady recovery without major setbacks."

"I know that, Ethan. You are...I mean, your care is the best thing that could possibly have happened to Merritt after the accident."

He started to open the car door but turned to her instead. "Lindsey, I've wanted to thank you for your understanding…and your discretion."

Lindsey gazed at him. "There's been no need to say anything. Molly is Merritt's physical therapist, not you, which is no doubt wise."

"You see how well he's doing. There are rules in my profession, and I adhere to them."

"I appreciate that. I hope you continue to oversee his treatment. He trusts you." She rested a hand on his arm. "And honestly, if the circumstances were different—and someday they will be—I believe you would be great together."

"What I want is to see Merritt get through this next year and learn a new way of living. He'll be an amputee for the rest of his life. That's not easy for anyone to accept."

Lindsey shivered slightly. "It really hit me when I found him on the floor after he'd fallen. Just because he needed to make a trip to the bathroom. We take so much for granted, you know? We just get up out of bed without giving it any thought at all. Merritt can never, ever do that again."

"You are beginning to get it, aren't you?" A warm hand on her shoulder. "Merritt is adjusting, and I honestly believe he can get back on stage. I know you want that as well."

Lindsey took Ethan's free hand in both of hers. "I want it so much I would give up my career if it would ensure Merritt having his."

"I believe you mean that." He gazed at her.

"Well, he's always had a better shot at it than I have," she smiled wryly. "He's a tenor. I'm already his biggest fan." She considered what she had just said and added, "Well, one of them, anyway. He impressed you when you saw him onstage in *Hoffmann*, didn't he?"

He leaned against the car and sighed. "More than that. He blew me away."

Lindsey saw the flush on his face. "Oh, so that's how it was? You're already such an important part of his life, Ethan. I've always been told patience is a virtue." She pretended to pull a zipper across her mouth. "And my lips are sealed, I promise you."

Ethan gathered her in his arms for a bear hug. "Lindsey Cameron, I don't think you have any idea what a remarkable woman you are. I love you, lady."

She hugged him hard. "It's mutual. I love you, too. I'll never be able to thank you for everything you're doing for Merritt."

She abruptly pulled away and frowned at him. "Oh, and by the way, you probably didn't notice there was anyone else in *The Tales of Hoffmann*—you were so mesmerized by Merritt— but it happens I also was in that production," she said, pretending to pout.

Ethan laughed out loud. "Of course, I noticed you, the tragic Antonia. Your singing was glorious and you are drop-dead gorgeous...but Merritt is just more my type." He pulled her back into their hug.

***

Lindsey selected five of the songs from the Tear recording and went through them with Zivah, who lifted an eyebrow. "So. you really want to use these? I guess they're somewhat charming. I'm not sure if the voice faculty will accept them as recital material, though."

However, taking into consideration the difficulty level of Lindsey's other choices, the faculty approved them. The addition of the aria "Hear Ye, Israel," from Mendelssohn's *Elijah* completed Lindsey's program.

"Good grief, Lindsey, 'Sempre libera' and 'Hear Ye, Israel' On one program? Pretty heavy stuff," Merritt commented, looking over her written notes.

"I doubt seriously I'll ever sing 'Hear Ye, Israel' in a performance of the oratorio. You're right, it's dramatic. But I'm okay with doing it for my recital, and Claudia agreed it would work if I don't try to sound like Leontyne Price and I can keep the emotion of the piece under control."

The week before classes started Lindsey invited her new pianist to the Nobles' to rehearse her recital. Merritt and Zivah hit it off immediately; he remembered meeting her at David's Cincinnati Symphony performance of Rachmaninoff's second concerto. The two of them kibbitzed during the rehearsal more than once, and Lindsey was delighted to see Merritt interacting easily with a person who would soon be a fellow grad student. He had applied for the graduate program and signed up for one class for the spring semester.

Lindsey handed Zivah the full score to *La Traviata* for the aria, and she flipped through the pages. "Well…what do we do about this part where Alfredo comes in and interrupts the aria near the beginning? Just skip over that?" she asked innocently.

"Oh, that's right, I didn't mark it," Lindsey said. "Too bad I don't have a tenor to sing it. I think it enhances the aria considerably."

Both women turned slowly and stared at Merritt, who burst out laughing. "Don't you know the meaning of the word 'subtle,' Linds?" He grew serious. "Actually…if the circumstances were different, I'd love to sing this with you."

"You could be in the wings, Merritt. I can't even begin to tell you how happy that would make me."

202

Merritt hesitated, and Lindsey held her breath. *Please, Merritt.* He'd been seated on the sofa with his cane at hand, and he stood and walked to the piano.

"Well...I'll sing through it for now. I'll take the high note in falsetto, though." He held up a hand. "I'm not making any promises. We'll see."

He sang the section, and despite what he had said, sang the high C full voice. Lindsey could hardly contain herself, and when he finished the solo, Zivah stopped playing.

"If that's your falsetto high C, Merritt, I don't think I want to be in the room when you sing it full voice." She glanced around the room. "I'm surprised I don't see any shattered glass anywhere."

Lindsey hugged him. "Please, Merritt. You sound absolutely incredible. What a treat to hear you. It would be such a thrill if you'd perform this with me."

"I guess...if you're okay with me singing from the wings."

"Of course, whatever you want. Alfredo is supposed to be offstage." *Oh, I have another idea, my beautiful tenor. But I'll wait a bit before I suggest it.*

***

"I'm not sure about this," Merritt said the day before classes were to resume. "I want to get back to school...and I don't. I didn't realize I'd have such a...an emotional reaction to this."

"I understand." Lindsey sat next to him on the sofa. "I know when I first went to Claudia's studio in July, driving to the campus and walking into the building seemed...well, it brought back a lot of memories." She rubbed his back gently. "I'm sorry. I should have thought more about this and tried to prepare you."

203

"Oh, I've talked to my psychologist, Dr. Evans, and she's been helpful. She suggested going to the school the first time wouldn't be easy, but she reminded me to focus on the good memories. And to accept the fact the students may stare when they see me in a wheelchair. It's a natural reaction."

Lindsey nodded. "I'm sure it is. You know, though, when I've run into a few people I know while I'm on campus, they've gone out of their way to make me feel…well, cared about, I guess. They've told me how sorry they are about David. They ask how you're doing, and Amy Chang was thrilled when I told her we'd both be back for the fall semester."

"I couldn't do this without you." Merritt gazed at her, his hazel eyes troubled. "I'm scared, Lindsey. Does that sound really stupid? I don't want people to pity me."

"I honestly don't think that will happen. I believe you'll find they'll go out of their way to be helpful, and they'll welcome you…well, us…back. It will seem strange that none of our classmates will be around." She paused. "No, that's not true. A few will be there because they need to repeat a class or two. People who think earning a music degree is a snap have no idea how difficult some of the classes can be."

She put her arms around him. "I'd offer to protect you, but I don't think you'll need that. Don't forget, you've received a lot of get-well cards from Conservatory students. And not just after the accident, but some sent notes over the summer."

Lindsey had a few anxious moments on the drive to the campus, but once they parked both of them were focused on removing Merritt's wheelchair from the trunk and getting him comfortably situated. Fellow students who spotted them ran over and spoke warmly to both of them. A couple offered to help with Merritt's chair and Lindsey gratefully accepted.

"We're so glad to see you back!" … "Merritt, you look great. So happy you're back at school!" … "So good to see both of you. Please let me know if you need any help with anything."

Merritt began to relax and breathe more easily. "You were right, Lindsey. And you know, it *is* good to be back."

Life goes on, Lindsey thought. The routine became easier with each passing day, and the fact they were only on campus for a short time on Tuesdays and Thursdays helped. On Wednesdays, they were there for most of the afternoon, for one class and each of their voice lessons. Zivah came to the Noble house several times a week to play for both of them.

The final week of September, Ethan arrived at the house to give them the best possible news. "Merritt, the prosthetist you saw at the clinic yesterday tells me your stump is ready to accept a permanent leg," he grinned.

Lindsey did a happy dance around the room. "Already! How terrific is that?"

"It's a process, Lindsey. Merritt has a lot of hard work ahead of him. First, the leg will be built to specification, which requires some time to be measured carefully, and fitted more than once before he can use it. Then the rehab begins, and it's intensive. Those sessions will all take place at the clinic because you'll need even more to use the equipment available there."

"Sounds a little daunting," Merritt observed, running a hand over the back of his neck. "I'm sure glad you're in charge, Ethan. I know I can do it if you're working with me."

"Well, as you know, there'll be a whole team doing that. It's good you only have one class next semester, that's when the toughest work will begin. But you should be able to stand comfortably on the leg within a few weeks." Lindsey plopped into a chair, slightly disheartened.

Ethan placed a hand on her shoulder. "I know what you want to hear. Merritt will definitely be able to walk with you for your December graduation."

Zivah arrived to work with Merritt, and Lindsey took Ethan aside.

"You know how happy you made me. But I want more."

"Don't you always?" He grinned.

"You know Merritt has agreed to do the Alfredo solo in 'Sempre libera.' He said he'd do it offstage." She moved so Merritt couldn't see her face, and kept her voice low. "Here's what I really want: I want to persuade him to sing it from the audience. While he's standing. And then I want him to come up on stage…four steps…and sing 'Parigi, o cara' with me. I want the people in that audience to be as blown away by him as you were when you saw *Hoffmann*. Merritt Noble is back, and there will be no stopping him."

Ethan's eyes widened slightly. "Lady, you're asking a lot. When's your recital?"

Lindsey glanced at Merritt and Zivah studying a score as she played a measure or two to establish the tempo he wanted.

"Let's go in the kitchen." Ethan followed her, and she answered, "November 15, The Friday before Thanksgiving."

"About seven weeks. I can't promise anything."

"First help me get him to agree to sing from the audience." She leaned back against the counter. "I think that may be the biggest hurdle. Everyone at the Conservatory has been great and he's responding to that. I'm afraid he still has this thing…above all, he does not want to be pitied."

"Why would he be?" Ethan crossed his arms over his chest.

"I'm sure he wouldn't, but he'd be putting himself out there, if you know what I mean." She stepped away from the counter. "The voice is certainly there, better than ever, which is great. But...walking up those four steps to the stage. Unassisted. Without stumbling."

Hands together as if in prayer, she rested them under her chin. "He needs to do that, Ethan. Just think what it would do for his self-confidence."

"He can't do it if it isn't safe."

"Yes, I know that. But can we try? I'm going home after we graduate, and I'm not sure when I'll be in Cincinnati again. I'd like to leave feeling he's definitely on his way back."

"Why aren't you coming back? I know you're planning to go to Curtis next fall, but you could start your grad studies with Merritt. Credits from the Conservatory would transfer anywhere."

"My father is going to Sedona, Arizona, for a couple of months to paint. Mom will be with him, and they invited me to come along. I want to go. I think I need to spend some time away from..." she gestured with both hands... "all of this."

"That sounds like a good choice, Lindsey. And you're right, you need to take some time for yourself. You've certainly earned it."

He thought for a minute. "If you can get Merritt to agree to your request, I'll try. But I'll never suggest anything that might be the least bit dangerous for him. And you don't want that either. He's bound to have setbacks, and the last thing you want is to be the cause of one."

She shook her head. "No, I don't want that. Not ever." A glimmer of a smile. "I know I can be insistent sometimes."

Ethan grinned wryly. "I can think of a more accurate word."

"Okay. I can be a pushy broad. I just...I want the world for Merritt."

He studied her closely. "I'm aware of that. I do wonder what you want for Lindsey."

"Right now, I'm not sure," she sighed.

***

"Have you talked to Merritt about what you'd like for him to do?" Zivah stirred a teaspoon of sugar into her black coffee.

"Not yet. I'm waiting for Ethan to give me the green light. But my recital is coming up pretty fast." The women had completed a rehearsal and stopped at a coffee shop at Peebles Corner, not far from either woman's destination. The Margolis home was in East Walnut Hills.

"He's absolutely gorgeous," Zivah commented wistfully, with the unspoken comment hanging in the air: *It's a shame he's gay.*

"Who, Ethan? Definitely a hunk."

"No, Merritt. One of the best-looking men I've ever seen." She sipped the coffee. "You know, I had a huge crush on David when we were in high school. We were in the same class at the arts high school. Watching him play the piano, I did a lot of fantasizing."

Lindsey nodded and smiled. "Watching David play could do that to a person. The way he caressed the keys…on the other hand, he was very forceful when necessary."

"Yes to both." Zivah tipped her head to one side, and the women laughed together. "It must have been interesting, living with a gay couple. How'd that work out?"

"It was great. Oh, you mean…. Well, they were quite considerate most of the time. And I had a portable CD player with a selection of music in my room if needed. Also a good pair of earplugs." More laughter.

"When I was out and they were home, we had a signal worked out. Before I walked through the front door, I did a Beethoven's Fifth on the doorbell."

Zivah almost spit out her coffee. "Did you ever bring a guy home?"

"Not for anything more than a nightcap or a cup of coffee. And that happened very seldom." She grew serious. "Believe it or not, I've never been in an intimate relationship."

An arched eyebrow. "Really? Are you waiting for Mr. Right?"

"That's exactly what Esteban said to me when he was trying to get me to go to bed with him," Lindsey responded.

"That gorgeous Puerto Rican basso? Good heavens, Lindsey. I guess you *are* waiting for 'the one.'"

"I want what my parents have. All these years of marriage and they're still mad for each other. And what Merritt and David had. They were totally devoted. That was supposed to be a relationship for life, Zivah. They understood each other better than most married people do."

"Did you have a serious boyfriend in high school?"

"Nope. I didn't date much. Once in a while, I might go someplace with a group of friends." Lindsey grinned. "I don't think most people knew what to make of me. I was serious about studying opera and focused on that. I wasn't good at gossip or swooning over pop stars. Oh, I had a few friends, mostly fellow music students, and I enjoyed chorus and band. I was even president of chorus, which surprised me because I definitely wasn't considered one of the cool girls." Lindsey played with her napkin, folding it into a tiny square.

"You know…I guess I'm a real romantic, but I think when I meet the man I'm meant to be with I'll know. The thing is, when I was fourteen we were in London, and I saw a performance of the opera *Andrea Chénier*. The baritone who played Gérard I thought was wonderful." She laughed. "That was my teenage crush. While most girls my age were enamored of Prince or Freddie Mercury or Bruce Springsteen, I was in love with a character in an opera." She chuckled. "Am I a weird chick or what?"

The women were silent for a moment, Lindsey recalling the experience that had made such a strong impression on her.

Zivah looked over her cup at Lindsey. "I get that crush thing and waiting for your dream lover to somehow appear. It could be one reason why you were so comfortable living with Merritt and David. But you know...I imagine some people looked at you and wondered about the relationship."

"Oh, definitely. I've been called a 'fag hag.' And a 'fruit fly.' People can be dreadfully unkind, especially because of the AIDS epidemic. It's really caused an escalation of homophobia in this country. I've heard my boys taunted cruelly. It's one reason we didn't go out much."

"Of course, some people have stepped up." Zivah took a final swallow of coffee. "The flip side is the compassion that so many people have shown."

"We need a lot more of that in this country." Lindsey played with her spoon. "Why do people put so much weight on color and sexual orientation, anyway?"

"Don't forget ethnicity. I've experienced my share of crass remarks."

"I'm sorry to hear that, Zivah."

The women were silent for a few moments.

"You need to talk to Merritt about what you'd like for him to do. Don't hit him with it at the last minute."

"Of course, you're right. I'll do that when I get home." She grinned. "And then I'll run up the stairs as fast as I can to my bedroom. Well, Merritt's bedroom that I'm using temporarily."

"That's mean. You know he hasn't even started working on mastering stairs."

"I'm only asking him for four steps. That's all he needs to do. Walk up the four steps to the stage."

***

Kathleen stopped Lindsey as she walked into the house.

"Oh, Ethan called while you were at rehearsal. He left a strange message. He said to tell you he's giving you a green light."

Susan Moore Jordan

Chapter 15

Lindsey's belief that Merritt needed to stand and walk...and climb steps...in front of an audience came as the result of a considerable amount of thought about what made him an outstanding performer and potentially, a stellar opera singer.

The voice was definitely there, thanks to the excellent training from Claudia and an earlier voice teacher. It continued to grow in size and beauty. And perhaps because of his recent challenges, he was singing more expressively than ever. But something that made people sit up and take note of this talented young tenor was his charisma, his ability to engage the audience from the moment he entered the stage in an operatic role. The ease and elegance with which he moved. These were attributes that set him apart, Lindsey believed.

She was convinced Merritt could become a star tenor in the world of opera if that ability were nurtured and grew with more stage experience. She knew he was reluctant at this point to imagine much more than standing carefully in front of an audience. But she also knew Ethan was convinced Merritt could recover what he had lost, and she trusted him to make that happen. What Merritt needed was to have that same conviction.

"This prosthesis is so different," Merritt told her, once the final fitting of his permanent leg took place the last week of October. "It's so much more comfortable. Now I'm going to learn how to really put weight on it instead of hobbling around with that dumb cane."

Trips to the clinic for rehab included many exercises, some of which Lindsey and his family could help him with at home, such as just shifting his weight from one leg to the other. At the clinic he used the parallel bars, the treadmill, and rode a stationary bike.

"He's making remarkable progress, and the best thing is, he's excited about it," Ethan told Lindsey when she called him. "Steps are next. So yes, I think our tenor will be able to do what you're hoping for. Go ahead and see if he's willing to try it."

Her recital was less than three weeks away. With Zivah expected at the Nobles' in less than an hour for a rehearsal, Lindsey tapped on Merritt's door.

"Can I talk to you for a minute?"

He opened the door, and she gasped in surprise. "Wow. Look at you," she said, amazed to see him standing unassisted and with no cane.

Merritt grinned. "Yeah. How about this? I still have to think hard about what I'm doing and I can't move fast…but, you know what? Maybe Ethan's right about me getting back on stage someday."

"That's kind of what I wanted to talk about. Can you come into the living room?"

She stepped back to give him room and watched admiringly as he took a dozen unassisted steps from his door to the sofa, positioned himself, and sat down. *He's walking. He's really walking.*

He sat at the end of the sofa, using his right hand on the arm as he positioned his prosthetic right leg to bear most of his weight, then used his left knee to smoothly lower himself to a sitting position.

"That was incredible. Really."

Another broad grin. "I'm getting there."

"I see that, which brings up something I've been wanting to discuss with you."

Lindsey joined him, picking up a throw pillow and clutching it. "You know we agreed you would sing the Alfredo music from the wings…." She paused. "But I wonder if you'd consider something a little different."

She took a quick breath and said, "I think the people in the audience would absolutely love to see you when you sing so I had an idea of you sitting in an aisle seat about halfway down, and then you could stand up and step into the aisle when you sing instead."

She gulped and continued before he could respond, "Ethan could be sitting right next to you because I will mark those seats off as reserved so no one else could use them."

Merritt's grin became a laugh. "How long did it take you to memorize that speech?"

"I did kind of practice it in my head a few times." She smiled. "Oh, good, you didn't say no."

Merritt removed the throw pillow she'd been clutching nervously and took both her hands. "How could I tell you no, Linds?"

He pulled her close and hugged her. "You've done so much for me these past months. Why do I have this feeling you've already checked with Ethan before you asked?"

She blushed. "Well…yes, of course, I did. I'd never ask you to do anything that might be even the slightest bit dangerous."

"I'll do it." Another embrace.

"Really?" Lindsey took a long breath and smiled.

"Sure. I think it'll be fine. I take it 'Sempre libera' will be the final selection on your program?"

"Yes. And I've got this all figured out. I'll sing the German songs first, then the Fauré selections, and end the first half of my recital with the aria from *Elijah*. We'll take enough of a break during intermission so you can go to Claudia's studio and warm up. The English songs are short, I'll start the second part with those, and the aria will be the final piece. So, you won't have much of a wait before you can uncork your high C."

She leaned forward. "Um, and Merritt…?"

"There's more?"

"You may turn this one down. After I finish the aria…it would make me so happy if you'd come up on stage and sing the final act duet from *La Traviata* with me."

Merritt lifted an eyebrow. "Going up steps?" He shook his head. "I'm not there yet, Linds. I can't imagine…." He paused for a moment. "But I'll think about it…it depends on how much progress I make. We were scheduled to do a duet on your original recital program, and I'm complimented you're asking me to sing this one."

"Well, we've sung it together quite a bit, and I know you probably still have it from memory. And we have over two weeks until the recital. I won't put the last duet on the printed program. But again…I think the audience would love to hear more from you. And I would so love to sing it once again with you."

"I take it Claudia is in on this," Merritt smiled wryly. "Ethan, the staff at the clinic, Claudia, and no doubt Zivah. Your team is ganging up on me."

"I wouldn't exactly call it that." She shrugged, pressing her lips together.

"What would you call it?"

"I'd call it *your* team encouraging you to take a step forward into performing again. Literally."

Merritt thought it over. "Okay, I'll definitely sing from the audience during your aria. But as for the onstage duet, I'll need to have Ethan's guidance about the steps. I don't want to do it using a cane."

"I knew you wouldn't want that," she responded. "But he tells me you're making wonderful progress and thinks this could work."

"Does he, now?" Merritt shook his head, looking anything but upset. "Lots of plotting behind my back."

"I'm so happy. You have no idea how much I wanted you to say yes." *Because who knows when—or even if—I might ever sing with you again?*

Merritt brushed the tears from her face, kissing her forehead.

***

Considering the attributes which made Merritt a strong candidate for a career as a professional opera singer prompted Lindsey to take stock of her own. Good tenors were a rarity; good sopranos could be found in abundance. That was simply a fact in Opera World. She felt she had an edge because of the extent of her range.

She knew she had an appealing appearance. In all honesty, she believed she needed to concentrate more on her acting. She'd done her best work as Antonia in *Tales of Hoffmann*, and Lindsey thought it was partly because of what an exceptional Hoffmann Merritt had been and partly because of her personal hostility toward Esteban as Dr. Miracle, which gave that scene some added drama.

Me having a career in opera will require a lot of luck, Lindsey thought. *But music is my life; what other choices would I have if luck should fail me at some point?*

She shook off the thought. *Come on, Lindsey Cameron, you can't push Merritt toward his destiny and have negative thoughts about your path at the same time. You certainly won't make it without the conviction that you can succeed.*

Lindsey felt honored to have been accepted at the prestigious Curtis Institute of Music for graduate study and was grateful they had deferred her admission for a year. *I'll work hard to become a better actress while in school there. And I'll never give up on myself.*

***

A final rehearsal for her recital took place in the Recital Hall a few days before the performance. Ethan was there, as was Claudia, and of course Zivah. Kathleen was also there since she was turning pages for Zivah; she'd done that for many rehearsals in their house.

The first part of the program went smoothly. As planned, Claudia took Merritt to her studio to vocalize. Since her studio was on an upper floor, Ethan went with them. Merritt had his cane with him.

As they waited, Zivah played through the accompaniment for "Sempre libera" as Lindsey paced around the stage.

"Relax, Linds," Zivah said. "This is going to be great. Merritt will blow everybody out of the water and nobody will even notice that you just sang your guts out."

Lindsey leaned against the piano as she burst out laughing. "Zivah, I can always count on you to tell it like it is."

"I've been told that before," Zivah remarked. "No doubt you've noticed I don't have many friends. I'm so obnoxious most people can't stand me."

Smiling, Merritt returned with his "team." He and Ethan took their assigned seats in the auditorium, and Lindsey gave a

218

brief explanation of the Milne song settings, then sang through the five she had selected. She exited the stage for a drink of water and when she returned, took her position to sing "Sempre libera."

She reached the section in the music where Violetta is interrupted by the voice of Alfredo, the man she has just met who professed his undying love and devotion. Lindsey watched as Merritt stood and stepped gracefully into the aisle and began to sing. Enthralled, she heard the golden shimmer in the sustained high C he sang before finishing his solo. He returned to his seat and Lindsey continued with the aria. Near the end, Alfredo had two brief solo interjections. They had agreed Merritt would sing these while seated, and after the aria, he would stand again as Lindsey acknowledged him to the audience.

Then came the moment Lindsey had been waiting for: Merritt walking down the aisle, over to the side of the stage, and up the four steps to the stage floor. She held her breath as she watched her boy stride down the aisle and easily take the steps before standing beside her. She clung to him as she burst into tears.

Merritt patted her shoulders and held her. "You can't do that on Friday," he mumbled, not sure what else to say.

Lindsey lifted her head, laughing through the tears. "I won't. I promise. Oh, just to watch how you moved right now...it was incredible. The most wonderful thing that's happened in a long time."

Merritt glanced at his friends. "Holy shit, she's got all of you crying. All I did was walk down the aisle and come up four steps. Get a grip, gang."

Lindsey and Merritt, their arms around each other, sang through the love duet, "Parigi, o cara," to end the rehearsal.

219

Ethan walked down to the front of the stage. "Don't linger too long onstage after the duet, Lindsey. You're in control. Merritt's wheelchair will be in the wings. I'd prefer he use that to greet people in the lobby, and I'll wheel him out there."

"I can stand," Merritt protested. "But I guess having the chair out there isn't a bad idea."

"You're still not accustomed to standing unaided for long stretches, Merritt. And after walking down the aisle and up the stairs, you and Lindsey will stand for the duet and for bows for maybe fifteen minutes. Don't push it."

***

Howard drove them to the campus on Friday, Lindsey and Merritt holding hands in the back seat, both of them thinking of David. Ethan met them at the entrance to the building and went inside with them as Howard wheeled Merritt into the lobby. A room near the backstage area, the "green room," provided performers with some privacy and a place to relax before they went onstage.

Lindsey went upstairs to Claudia's studio to warm up. She returned to the green room and sat close to Merritt, trying to read his expression.

"You okay?"

"I'm fine. I'm just remembering…lot of things, I guess. My recital last February. Our rehearsal the day of the accident." Lindsey started to speak, but he put a finger to her lips. "It's okay, Lindsey. I've learned to separate the bad memories from the good memories. That rehearsal is a wonderful memory. I wish David could be here tonight." He paused. "But you know, I think he is here."

Lindsey placed a hand on his heart, and the other on her own. "He's right here."

They heard the audience gathering. Lindsey's eyes widened. "It sounds like a lot of people, doesn't it?" She took a quick breath, then several deep breaths to quiet her nerves.

"You're going to be wonderful," Ethan told her, placing a warm hand on her shoulder. "You both are."

"Merritt...if the audience starts to applaud after your solo in the aria, I'll let them. I'll just look down, and they'll know I won't sing again until I look up."

"I don't know if you should do that. It's your recital."

"It's for all of us...you, me, and David. It's what I want."

The auditorium darkened as Lindsey, Zivah, and Kathleen stood in the wings. Lindsey knew Ethan and Merritt had taken their seats earlier. Her family was all there—parents, grandparents, and M.J. had flown in from Philadelphia. A nice surprise, her Uncle Jean flew down from Montreal. David's parents were sitting with them, and with the Noble family right behind, they filled two entire rows in the center section.

Lindsey took several deep breaths again as she closed her eyes and concentrated on quieting her mind and preparing herself. The three women entered the stage and Lindsey was stunned by the wave of sound that hit them. The auditorium was full. She hadn't expected that.

The first part of the program went smoothly, though Lindsey wasn't thrilled with her performance of the Mendelssohn aria from *Elijah*. She felt she over-sang some sections, caught up in the emotion of the music. But the audience applauded heartily.

Back in the green room, Lindsey took a long drink of water and tried to relax. Kathleen had gone with Merritt and Ethan to hear her brother warm up and came back into the room beaming as she wiped tears from her face.

"He sounds just incredible, doesn't he? I'm so happy for him."

Once again, the audience quieted as Lindsey came back onstage for the Milne songs by Fraser-Simson. She explained briefly to the audience why she had wanted to sing these pieces and spoke of her love of Milne's beloved character Winnie-the-Pooh, which elicited chuckles from many in the audience.

Merritt's name was in the printed program, so the audience wasn't surprised to hear him singing during the *La Traviata* aria. They were surprised when they realized he was standing in the aisle, singing better than ever—including an especially glorious high C.

Lindsey looked down when he finished, and as she had thought would happen, Merritt was enthusiastically applauded.

After Lindsey completed the aria, she acknowledged Merritt and he stood again, to more vigorous applause. Then the audience emitted a collective gasp, applauding even louder as he strode down the aisle and up the steps to join her for the duet.

Lindsey had to collect herself and get her emotions under control before they began. Holding Merritt, seeing the light in his eyes, she knew she was ready. Feeling and hearing their voices join, blend, and soar created a sense of joy beyond anything she had experienced before. *We're truly making music,* she thought, *this is the way it should be.* She felt it was the best she had ever sung. And Merritt was glorious.

They concluded the duet, gazing into each other's eyes for a long moment. Lindsey was sure Merritt felt the connection between them as strongly as she did. It was a moment to be cherished, and the stillness in the room indicated the audience was aware of it as well.

Slowly the room filled with hearty applause and cheers, and Lindsey was presented with not one, but three, bouquets, and gave flowers from each to Zivah, Merritt, and Kathleen.

***

Audience members surrounded them in the lobby for more than half an hour after the concert. Ethan introduced his music therapist friend, Michelle Detweiler, reminding Lindsey he had mentioned Michelle to her before.

"Those songs you performed, the settings of the A.A. Milne poems," Michelle said, her eyes shining. "I have group therapy sessions on Mondays with pediatric patients at the Cincinnati Children's Hospital Medical Center. They'd love to hear those songs. Is there any possibility I might persuade you to come over sometime and sing them for the kids?"

"I would love to do that," Lindsey said. "This would be part of the therapy you do for the children?"

"Yes, it would. Why don't you give me a call over the weekend? If you're free, maybe you could visit the hospital next Monday and see exactly what it is I do with my patients. Music means so much to them. They're in the hospital for long-term care for several reasons, and bringing music into their lives is one of the most important things we can do to help them."

Intrigued, Lindsey replied, "What time do you see them, and for how long?"

"Ten-thirty in the morning, for about a half-hour, maybe a little longer. Here's my card. Call me and we can arrange where to meet. I should warn you, though—being with these kids will tug at your heartstrings."

Howard and Grace had invited all the family members, as well as Ethan, Claudia, and Zivah, back to their house for refreshments. It was a pleasant, mellow reunion on this happier occasion than when they had last seen each other at David's grave. Lindsey was toasted; Lindsey and Merritt were toasted.

Zivah was introduced and was soon deep in conversation with Leah and Arthur Rosenthal. Lindsey smiled when she recalled Zivah speaking about her schoolgirl crush on David. *Oh, good. She may be a big help to them.* A thought flashed through her mind of an ethereal David bringing lives together.

Arthur Rosenthal hugged Merritt and Lindsey and whispered, "I heard you sing that duet more than once with my son playing for you. He would have been so proud."

Jake, who had been talking with Zivah, walked over and spoke to the two of them as well. "Such a lovely evening of music, Lindsey. And what a nice bonus to have Merritt on stage with you. I'm sure that was something you worked hard to achieve, Merritt. Congratulations to you both."

"Thank you so much for coming, Monsieur Couvreur," Merritt said. "Your encouragement was a big part of my being able to sing with Lindsey tonight."

"Please—it's Uncle Jean. I've told you, we're family."

Lindsey caught M.J. eyeing her but couldn't read his expression. "I know it's an old cliché, but penny for your thoughts, baby brother."

"You've changed, Lindsey. You've turned into a thoughtful and caring woman. It even shows in your singing."

Taken aback and moved by his comment, Lindsey had to catch her breath for a moment. "It's been…quite a year, M.J. I guess maybe I have done some growing up."

Knowing Merritt had to be tired, those in attendance kept the after-party brief. Lindsey grabbed her coat to walk Ethan to his car.

"I've been thinking about the first time I met you, and the talk we had then. You're a miracle worker, sir. It's going to happen. Our tenor is going to make it."

"I believe he will. It's a process…."

224

"Oh, you do like to use that phrase," Lindsey interrupted, her eyes twinkling.

Ethan laughed. "It doesn't happen overnight, or quickly, but is the result of concentrated, prolonged effort. But yes, he's on his way. I don't doubt that for a minute."

He hugged her. "And it all began when you and he listened to the Rachmaninoff third piano concerto. David's music." He gazed at her. "You sang beautifully tonight, Lindsey. The duet was particularly lovely. I'm curious, what was your favorite moment in your recital?"

"I'm sure you know. Watching Merritt come down the aisle and almost run up the steps. It was one of the happiest moments of my life."

***

Lindsey said her goodnights to her family and promised to join them at the Vernon Manor for breakfast the next morning. Returning to the Nobles' living room, she glanced around to see if she could find dishes or napkins that needed to be taken into the kitchen, but everything had been picked up and put away.

Kicking off her shoes, she stretched out on the roomy, comfortable sofa for a few moments before going upstairs to bed, allowing the evening's memories to resonate.

M.J.'s words: *'You've become a thoughtful and caring woman.' It was a beautiful, magical evening. Who would have dreamed watching a friend I absolutely adore walk up four steps would give me such a feeling of joy?* Lindsey had an image of David in her mind, smiling at her with loving approval. *Well done, Lindsey.*

A gentle touch on her face, and she opened her eyes to find Merritt sitting next to her. He kissed her forehead softly and wrapped his arms around her. Neither of them felt the need for words. What they had experienced together that evening said it all.

Chapter 16

Lindsey telephoned Michelle Detweiler Sunday afternoon to get the details for meeting her Monday morning. When she arrived at the medical center Michelle was waiting for her, guitar in one hand, bag slung across her shoulder, and a briefcase in the other hand.

"I'm so delighted you could make it," said a beaming Michelle, whom Lindsey could only think of as "cute" with her dimples, oversized round eyeglasses, and short, curly, dark hair.

"Can I help you with something?" Lindsey offered.

"No, I'm balanced," she said, shifting from one foot to the other to demonstrate. "I do this all the time. But thanks for the offer."

The two women went into a bright, sunny atrium on the third floor, where they were greeted by smiles and waves from a combination of children, parents, and nurses. Lindsey immediately realized how sick the children were. There were only seven of them. Most were in wheelchairs, and those who were not had crutches or walkers nearby. Michelle had told Lindsey they were between ages seven and twelve. Lindsey thought they looked younger in some ways, and many had faces that showed far too much strain and sorrow for such young children.

Michelle quickly put down the briefcase, dropped the bag, and started strumming the guitar. A smiling nurse motioned to Lindsey to sit near her as Michelle began a greeting song, talking and singing as she moved around the room, greeting each child she knew by name, and asking the names of those she didn't know. She sang a simple couplet between each greeting, "I'm very, very glad to see you—And I hope you're happy to see me, too." Some of the children began to sing along. Michelle made a point of speaking for a minute or two with each of them before she moved on.

Next, she introduced "Miss Lindsey" to the kids—who called her "Miss Michelle"—saying, "Miss Lindsey is a singer, and she came to meet you today. We hope she'll come back soon and sing some songs for you that I think you will like."

From her bag, Michelle pulled small percussion instruments: finger cymbals, wood sticks, miniature tambourines, rattles, castanets, egg shakers. One little girl on crutches offered to help distribute them, and Michelle gave them to her one at a time. Continuously engaging the children in dialogue, she and her helper passed the instruments around. Michelle picked up her guitar and played a simple tune many of the kids knew, and she helped the newcomers among them learn it, then they all sang and played their instruments.

Michelle told the children she had a beautiful piece of music for them to hear today and produced a tape player. She explained this music was written by a man who lived many, many years ago and wrote such beautiful music people still liked to play it and listen to it today.

She encouraged the children to get comfortable, lean back in their wheelchairs or a chair, close their eyes, take deep breaths, and relax their muscles.

"Think about your feet, and how it feels when you've been walking in sand. Feel like your feet are full of sand, and the sand slowly starts to fall off them and now they're light and calm."

She then invited them to listen to the music and think about how it made them feel. The lovely sounds of Ravel's "Pavane for a Dead Princess" filled the air. Lindsey closed her eyes as well. *Peaceful*, she thought. *It makes me feel peaceful as few other pieces do.*

Michelle waited for a few moments after the music ended and asked softly, "How did you feel when you listened to that song?"

"Like my mommy was rocking me." …. "Like I was up in the clouds, flying." … "I felt like I could listen to it forever." … "I felt like I was in a big swing with my daddy and he was rocking us." …. "Like I was next to a beautiful lake and there were trees there."

Michelle gave them time to express themselves, then taught them a simple song, four lines of music, instructing them to do the best they could and play their percussion instruments again. She ended the session with a goodbye song similar to her hello song while one of the nurses collected the instruments.

Lindsey looked more closely at the children as she and Michelle said their goodbyes. It tugged at her heart to realize how damaged these kids were. All were there for long-term care. That short visit from Michelle and spending time with music had obviously meant a lot to them. On their way out, she asked, "What are these kids being treated for?"

"Many have cancer, and some are here for a second or even third course of radiation or chemo. Some have chronic conditions that may be life-threatening. One of those kiddos is waiting for a heart transplant. If he doesn't get one soon, his life is over. I had such a healthy childhood, the first time I was with kids like these it was a shock."

"That was exactly my reaction. I've never really thought a lot about what some children experience in their young lives, you know? Do you only see them once a week? It seemed to mean so much to them that you were here."

"Twice a week. I come on Thursday mornings, as well. And I also have individual sessions with three of the children you met this morning—at the request of their families."

Their elevator arrived and they stepped into it. "I definitely want to come back and help you with a session, singing the Pooh songs you enjoyed at my recital," Lindsey said. "Maybe teach them one of the shorter ones? And I was fascinated by their reactions to the recording you played. I know I use something like that on myself when I need to…recharge."

She laughed. "I guess all musicians may do the same—and of course, many other people, too—listen to a piece we particularly love and just let ourselves get lost in it."

Michelle nodded. "I know exactly what you mean. Maybe you'd like to choose the listening piece we use at your session? Since my time is limited, I usually keep it to between five and eight minutes."

"Thank you, I'd like that. I had a couple of thoughts as I was listening to the Ravel."

They had reached the ground floor and started through the lobby toward the exit.

"Well, Thanksgiving is this Thursday," Michelle said. "Maybe we could aim for next Thursday? And get together sometime earlier next week to plan the session?"

"That should work. How about Tuesday afternoon for the planning? I have a class in the morning but my afternoon is free, now that I've presented my recital." Lindsey started to turn but stopped. "Tell me something. Didn't you say you had finished your undergrad degree in music education when you decided you wanted to be a therapist?"

"I did."

"What happened that made you decide that?"

Michelle stopped near a bench and placed her guitar and briefcase on it. "I went to a prison with a friend who was studying music therapy," she said. "Well, actually, a correctional facility for teenage boys. Some of them had a lot of attitude, let me tell you. Those were a little scary. Some seemed defeated and hurt. But when Ben started working his magic, all of them—I mean *all*—responded."

She gazed into the distance. "It was a real eye-opener for me. I was only a couple of months away from graduating, so I finished my degree. But I continued to go back to work with those kids—yes, they were kids, despite what they may have seemed like—and enrolled in a music therapy program the following fall."

Michelle picked up her briefcase and guitar. "I had to do over a year's work of undergrad courses before I could begin my master's degree and become a certified music therapist."

She started to move away but turned back. "Let me tell you this," she beamed at Lindsey, "it was the best decision I've ever made in my life."

***

Lindsey spotted Ethan's car as she returned from her second session with Michelle and the kids at the hospital. She found the men drinking coffee in the kitchen. Merritt smiled as she joined them. "Want a cup of coffee, Linds?"

"I'll get it. I don't want to interrupt, though."

"You aren't," Ethan replied. "This is just a friendly visit. I'm trying to convince our tenor here to go to grad school full-time next fall. In fact, I think he could probably handle another class next semester if he wants to do that."

231

Lindsey joined them at the table. "He must be making good progress, then."

"Molly tells me he's been working a lot on balance at the clinic. And endurance," Ethan responded.

"It's a process," Merritt laughed, taking a swallow of coffee.

"Michelle told me you'd be at the hospital with her this morning," Ethan said. "How did that go?"

"I think it went well. I'm still trying to come up with a word to describe how I felt about what I just did…spending time with those sweet kids who are hurting so much." Lindsey stirred her coffee vigorously as she tried to control the shake in her voice.

Both men gazed at her. "What did you do, exactly?" Merritt asked.

"Well…Michelle and I got together Tuesday afternoon and went through three of the Simson songs I sang for my recital a couple of weeks ago. She improvised guitar accompaniments for them—she's very good, by the way—and we decided I could teach one to the kids. It's the shortest one, 'How Sweet to Be a Cloud.'" She sang: "'How sweet to be a cloud floating in the blue. It makes him very proud to be a little cloud.' And that's repeated. I figured it should work."

"I would think so," Merritt said.

"They loved it, really loved it. And they loved learning it. I went to each child and helped them. Some of those children have such pretty voices. Then we all sang it together a few times." More vigorous stirring and Merritt gently took the spoon from her hand.

"It's okay, Lindsey. They got to you." He handed her a napkin.

Lindsey smiled as she blotted her eyes. "We did some other things, too. Michelle let me select their listening piece

232

and I asked for Rachmaninoff's 'Vocalise' by orchestra. In some ways that listening piece is the best part of their session. They relax and listen, and can say aloud how the music makes them feel."

"What did they say?" Ethan finished his coffee.

"One little boy said it made him wish he could dance. He was in a wheelchair. One of the girls said she felt like she was inside a rainbow and it was beautiful. A couple of them said they felt like they were floating in the moonlight."

Merritt's eyes met Lindsey's, and she knew he was recalling the time they had listened together to the third piano concerto. "They felt as if they were someplace else. Someplace beautiful," he said softly.

"Yes. One of the boys said it made him feel like good things were going to happen." Lindsey blew her nose on the napkin. "Yes, they made me cry. But I held off until I got into the car."

Ethan rested a hand on her shoulder and patted it gently. "So have you come up with a word yet to describe how being with the kids made you feel?"

She thought a moment. "Yes. Gratitude. I was so grateful I'd shared music with them and they had a few minutes of happiness. Freedom from pain and stress, maybe."

"That's one purpose of music therapy," Ethan commented. "Whether adults or children. It's rare that a patient doesn't respond positively—and sometimes strongly—to allowing music to permeate their senses."

"Oh, I know that firsthand," Merritt agreed. "Linds, I've talked to Ethan about how you helped me to get past...well, you know."

She gave him a brilliant smile. "I didn't know you did that, Merritt. Thank you for telling me."

"Well, I figure I can tell Ethan anything," Merritt added. "He needs to know why I throw all the crap at his staff members that I do when they're asking me to do something for the five-hundred-thousandth time." They laughed together.

Ethan checked his wristwatch. "Thanks for the coffee and the conversation. I have another appointment to get to."

Merritt stood as he said, "I'll walk you out."

"I love hearing you say that," Lindsey commented.

He gave her a broad grin. "I love being able to say it."

***

The night before Merritt and Lindsey's graduation, the Camerons hosted a dinner at the Vernon Manor for the Nobles and the Rosenthals and also invited Zivah, Ethan, and Claudia. Zivah and the Rosenthals were the first to arrive. Lindsey knew Zivah had been at Leah and Arthur's often, sometimes playing "David's piano"—a Baldwin concert grand—but also reminiscing with them, sometimes playing chess with Arthur and helping Leah with whatever project she was working on at the moment, whether rearranging a room or organizing a fundraiser for David's scholarship fund. Leah spoke of her fondly as "*meyn kmet tokhter*—my almost daughter." *Helping fill some of that empty space in their hearts*, Lindsey thought.

A special guest joined them, a friend of Andrew and Mary's—Kristina Porter Levin, widow of the exceptional collaborative pianist and teacher at Juilliard, Eli Levin. Andrew had known Krissy when he was a child in Tennessee and they reconnected when Lindsey was a baby, not long before her husband's untimely death of heart failure at the age of forty-one.

She was in Cincinnati to speak the next day to the mid-year graduating class, and Lindsey was eager to hear her.

234

Krissy, as her friends called her, was a graduate of the Conservatory, as her husband Eli had been.

After her husband's death, Krissy continued for a few years as personal assistant to the musical director and impresario for an opera company in New York. More recently she had been organizing and fundraising for scholarships she established in her husband's honor for students of collaborative piano at several music schools across the country.

Lindsey knew Krissy Levin had also earned quite a reputation as an inspirational speaker. A small woman with warm brown eyes and light brown hair in a stylish pageboy, she seemed to be enjoying herself at dinner. It was a festive occasion, this time not constrained by concerns for Merritt— who was moving around the room bantering with friends and family, though Lindsey noticed Ethan was keeping a close eye on him.

Krissy glanced at Lindsey, seated across the table from her. "I'm not sure you'll appreciate my saying this, Lindsey, but you were an adorable baby. You certainly 'grew up nice,' as the saying goes."

"Thank you, Mrs. Levin. I've heard about your visit to my parents' home and that you and your husband enjoyed playing with me. Wouldn't it be wonderful if I could remember that? My friend David often said he wished he could have studied with Mr. Levin."

"I'm told your friend David was a remarkable young man in many ways. I know everyone here is thinking of him tonight."

Untimely deaths for two extraordinary men, Lindsey thought. Krissy seemed to read her thoughts because she commented, "How unfortunate that one thing they have in common is lamentable." She brightened and added, "Yet how

235

grateful we are to have had them in our lives as people we loved and admired."

She still misses her husband, Lindsey thought. *But she does something positive with that, just as Merritt and I are trying to do after losing David.*

The evening became a party as Merritt and Lindsey opened presents, most of which were gag gifts. A toy car for Merritt. A baby doll for Lindsey. Legos for Merritt. A toy tea set for Lindsey. At the end of the evening, they asked that the hotel staff help themselves to any of the toys to take home to their kids. Toasts were made, and after that, guests broke into small groups as they continued to socialize.

Again, Lindsey was aware of Ethan's vigilant eye on Merritt, and at one point Ethan quietly spoke to Merritt, nodding toward a nearby chair. Merritt moved to it and sat down. *I won't have to worry about him one bit,* Lindsey thought.

As people began to leave, Lindsey walked to the lobby with Merritt. They found a secluded spot where they could say their goodbyes because she planned to leave with her family immediately after the graduation ceremony since bad weather was forecast. Andrew and M.J. had already packed the van and Lindsey planned to stay with them at the hotel that night.

"I won't say goodbye," Merritt told her, gazing into her eyes. "How about 'see you when I see you'?"

"That works for me," Lindsey smiled, speaking through the lump in her throat. "I'll come to see you after we get back from Arizona. I know you'll be well taken care of."

"Yeah, I will." He thought for a minute. "You know what Mrs. Levin said to me? She said she thought of everyone who was there, in some ways she could probably understand better than anybody what I was going through. It surprised me when she followed up by saying she knew how much I missed the physical intimacy of my relationship with David."

A sigh. "She told me she went through that herself. It's been some time since she lost her husband, and she said she's never considered having a relationship with someone else because she had over twenty happy years with him. But she encouraged me to not shut off that part of who I am. Can you believe that?"

"I think she's a wise lady and she's right."

"It's kind of hard to imagine anyone would want me." A rueful smile. "I'm damaged goods, Linds."

"Nonsense. You're a beautiful, talented, loving man. It's bound to happen at some point, and I hope it's soon. The last thing David would want is for you to become a monk."

Merritt grinned. "There you go again with that 'the last thing David would want' line."

He pulled her close in a bear hug. "Call me. And I'll call you. What a great evening this was. I loved seeing how the Rosenthals have adopted Zivah, and she's so sweet to them. I never think of Zivah as 'sweet,'" he chuckled, "but she sure is good to David's mom and dad.

"Oh, and I signed up for another class for next semester. Zivah's in that one, and she's agreed to play for my lessons."

"Well, now I know I don't have to worry about you. The whole team is going to be right there with you. Kathleen is under strict instructions to let me know if you step out of line."

He gazed at her with eyes overflowing with love. "There are no words, Lindsey. You own a big chunk of my heart, and you always will."

"That goes both ways, Merritt. Just keep singing." She rested a hand on his shoulder. "I want to sit next to Ethan when you make your Met debut."

"I'd rather have you standing beside me on the Met stage if and when that happens."

"From your lips to the ears of the gods of Opera World."

Another warm embrace and Lindsey kissed his cheek.

"Safe travels, and enjoy the desert," Merritt said. "I'm told Sedona is a special place."

"I'll let you know if I find magic there," she laughed.

***

Since there were only twenty-six graduates from the Conservatory, the ceremony was held in the Recital Hall rather than the main auditorium. A small instrumental ensemble and the Conservatory Chorale were on hand to provide music. Once the graduates entered and were seated, the Chorale performed a moving piece, "The Awakening," a new work by the American composer Joseph Martin.

The choral piece began with a nightmare, the depiction of a bleak, hopeless landscape without music. Then with a joyful burst of sound, the awakening to a world filled with the glory of music. When the Chorale sang the final phrase— "Let music live!"—Lindsey clutched Merritt's hand as she blinked back tears. She felt him shaking and knew he had been equally affected.

They would receive their diplomas following Kristina Porter Levin's address. Krissy stood and thanked the administration and staff for inviting her to address the graduates.

"I well recall my own graduation from this institution in 1959, when the school was situated on a hill in Mt. Auburn," she began, speaking in a pleasant, melodious voice. "The physical location and look of this educational entity have changed, but the spirit remains the same. As Mr. Martin's

238

music so eloquently stated, the aim is now and has always been to 'let music live'—to make music a vital part of the lives of not just musicians, but of all who hear it."

The hall quieted as the audience settled down to hear what this engaging woman had to say.

"There is a line from a poem by Robert Louis Stevenson I have always loved, a poem Ralph Vaughan Williams used in his song cycle, *Songs of Travel*. It's in 'The Roadside Fire': *And this shall be for music*. Those six words express to me what we have been chosen for, what we've been called to do with our lives. If we add a word, it's evident that it's about us: *And this life shall be for music*.

"I know the Conservatory suffered a great loss last spring when David Rosenthal left you. It's difficult to know that where once there was a bright light, there is now shadow. Many of you are hurting; he was part of your world. Part of you. But however brief his life, David's life was for music. And I choose to believe that the music David Rosenthal made during his time with us resonates through all of you who knew him and will never be lost. I also choose to believe that so long as you remember him…and I think you will always remember him…he is part of you, and he is closer than you know.

"I truly believe we do not choose music; rather, music chooses us. We are such a diverse population, we musicians. We come from every possible walk of life, from every corner of the world, from every creed, color, and sexual orientation. None of that separates us; instead, it unites us. Music speaks to us in ways it may not speak to other people, and we do everything we can to open doors and windows for them so they can glimpse what we are privileged to know.

"*And this shall be for music.* What will we do with this glorious gift we've received, this remarkable ability to make music? Music can heal and inspire, calm and incite. It can lighten the dark corners of the mind and soothe the pain of a wounded spirit or a broken heart. It is the most powerful force in the universe, and how we share it can make a difference in the lives of many. Whether performing before an audience of thousands or sharing with one person who needs to hear something meaningful, something beautiful. It's the music that is important, the music that resonates throughout the universe and never fades.

"And this shall be for music. Whatever you choose to do with the gifts you've been given, be true to the music. It will never fail you, and it will never end."

PART TWO

Music gives a soul to the universe,
wings to the mind,
flight to the imagination and life to everything.

– attributed to Plato

Susan Moore Jordan

Chapter 17

The bright Arizona sun lifted higher into the sky. Lindsey adjusted the umbrella to provide more shade, always aware her pale skin wasn't accustomed to such strong sunlight, not even in Pennsylvania's summers. She stood, draping her kaftan around her shoulders for extra protection.

A morning swim had become part of her routine, though Andrew and Mary seldom joined her. Their suite at the Enchantment Resort was spacious, beautifully appointed, and comfortable, with the pool conveniently situated not far from their private entrance.

Christmas in West Chester had been pretty much perfect. Jake and his family were there for nearly a week, and Lindsey and M.J. spent a lot of time with their young cousins, including attending a children's symphony concert in Philadelphia and a visit to the Museum of Art. The entire family drove to the Pocono Mountains and spent a night at the Shawnee Inn, situated on the Delaware River. Some went skiing at Shawnee Mountain.

On New Year's Eve, Merritt called to wish her a happy New Year and discuss his rehab progress. "Molly sometimes has me working on different apparatuses. I don't see much of Ethan these days. He's usually at the clinic, but he's busy with other patients."

"I'm sure he's making the best decisions for your progress. He's always done that."

"Everybody on the staff is great, and I know Ethan keeps an eye on my progress. We've had him at the house for dinner a couple of times."

So that's where we are with this, Lindsey thought. *Ethan is keeping his distance professionally—and I know why. But it's just as well that Merritt doesn't.*

M.J. returned to classes just before his parents and sister left for Arizona. "I'm tempted to ditch my first week and go with you," he said. "You know how crazy the weather can be in Pennsylvania in January and February."

"I know you're just talking, little brother. You have to be the most conscientious student on the Penn campus." She giggled. "Every single glorious day I'll send you a postcard that says 'Wish you were here.'"

"Gee, thanks, sis. Way to rub it in."

While the Camerons had traveled all over the eastern United States and spent time in Canada and Europe, they hadn't been to Arizona. Andrew had received a commission for a large mural in the courtyard of a new art gallery and his first few days were spent making pastel sketches around Sedona of the remarkable red rock formations which made up much of the landscape. Lindsey found them mesmerizing, believing there might be some truth in the theory held by certain people that within this area there were powerful vortexes, centers of energy from the earth itself that were conducive to healing and self-discovery.

The day they arrived, Mary and Lindsey went into a music store to browse. Mary discovered a CD called "Sedona Suite," an album by Tom Barabas, and bought it on the spot. Lindsey had her portable CD player with her, and the women listened frequently during their stay to the calming New Age orchestrations, with piano, synthesizer, flute, and guitar. *This music would work well for Michelle's kids*, Lindsey thought. *I wonder if she's heard it?*

Andrew, excited by the unique beauty of the red rocks and buttes, made sketches at all times of day. "Do you see how different they look with every light change?" He asked the women in his life who followed him around, holding sketch pads and all the accoutrements he would need. He shouldered his easel and ran ahead to stop, set up the easel, and stare at the incredible landscape.

He was particularly fascinated by the Chapel of the Holy Cross, which seemed to spring from the tall red cliffs where it stood. Lindsey went with him on a moonlit night and held a lantern for him as he sketched. While Andrew was enraptured by his project, Lindsey had a sense of peace, as well as a feeling of renewed energy. *There is magic here*, she thought, recalling her comment to Merritt.

Six weeks was a long stretch for Lindsey to go without singing, and the committee that hired Andrew for the mural provided a way for his daughter to practice while in Sedona. One of the members invited her to use his home and small grand piano any time during the afternoons when no one was home. It felt odd at first to be alone in a strange house, but the piano was excellent and she discovered her kind host had an extensive library of vocal music. A real find, since she had only brought three books with her.

One of those was the Ralph Vaughan Williams *Songs of Travel*, the song cycle Kristina Levin referenced when she spoke to the December graduates. Lindsey had heard them performed on a senior recital by a baritone and thought they were appealing, and even though she knew they had been written for the male voice, she wanted to familiarize herself with them. They were far beyond her ability as a pianist but Lindsey loved the poems and enjoyed singing through them.

The two Cameron women explored the area, driving up Oak Creek Canyon to Flagstaff, up Mingus Mountain to the old mining town of Jerome, and beyond to Prescott, which Lindsey thought seemed like a transplanted eastern town, complete with a Victorian courthouse, in this wild west landscape. Prescott had four seasons, and the day they went it snowed. Fortunately, it wasn't excessively cold, and they had coats and boots which they had worn to the airport when they left home.

They saved the Grand Canyon for a weekend when Andrew took a break, and all three of them stood awestruck on the South Rim. *Another magical place*, thought Lindsey, watching the colors in the canyon change with every shift of light, especially when clouds danced across the sun. While Andrew had painted many landscapes, he hadn't attempted this one. He took many photographs, intending to make this a subject when he returned home.

Once Andrew chose the Sedona sketch he wanted—the magnificent orange-red Cathedral Rock formation against a cerulean blue sky—he painted it with his acrylics on a canvas as his model for the project.

"What do you think, ladies?" Andrew asked his wife and daughter.

"One of the most beautiful landscapes you've ever done," Mary replied.

"I know it's overused slang, Dad, but it's totally awesome," Lindsey replied. "You're totally awesome, in fact. How do you get that onto the wall where it has to appear?"

"With a lot of effort and a lot of help," Andrew laughed.

His next step was to draw it to scale with pencil on the gallery courtyard's large concrete wall, which had been pressure-washed and then primed days earlier by art students from the local high school. Andrew created large amounts of his color mixes in buckets and color-coded them with numbers on the wall—at this point, it became a paint-by-numbers project. He and the students applied the first layer of the painting over an intense weekend, then Andrew worked with only one student assistant for the next two weeks to complete the mural.

Fascinated, Lindsey and her mother watched all this unfold and even joined in the painting for several hours that initial weekend. Under the supervision of the high school's art teacher, the students were to apply a clear varnish to the mural a week or two after the painting was completed, when the acrylic paint would be completely dry.

Andrew's magnificent mural, painted in his signature neo-impressionistic style, was unveiled and pronounced a great success by the large crowd attending the ceremony. Lindsey couldn't have been prouder of her gifted father.

By special invitation, she performed at the unveiling. She was asked to sing "America, the Beautiful," and allowed to choose two additional songs. Lindsey opted for two of the pieces from *Songs of Travel* that she thought suited this occasion well—"The Roadside Fire," the song which contained the phrase "And this shall be for music," and "The Infinite Shining Heavens," which made her think of David.

She had him in her heart when she sang the final stanza of the second song.

Night after night in my sorrow
The stars looked over the sea,
Till lo! I looked in the dusk
And a star had come down to me.

Refreshed and invigorated, the Camerons returned to Pennsylvania at the end of February. Phone calls to Cincinnati told Lindsey that Merritt continued to do well. "I could have taken three classes rather than two. Grad school is so different. But I talked to Ethan and he says I'm doing enough. Zivah is great, she's my bodyguard if I need one."

"I thought you said you didn't see much of Ethan. When did you talk to him?"

"Well, not at the gym so much, but he came here for dinner earlier this week."

Ethan is being very careful, Lindsey thought. *Merritt will have to make the first move if there's to be anything between them.*

Lindsey and Merritt continued to talk at least once a week. Several weeks later he asked, "What are you doing with yourself these days? I know you had a great time in Arizona, and you've spent some time at Penn with your brother, and you've been to the Met to enjoy opera."

"I'm working on a couple of roles that I might perform—Zerlina in *Don Giovanni*, and Fiordiligi in *Cosi fan tutte*."

"It doesn't sound as if you have a lot going on at the moment. Come to Cincinnati for a long weekend, why don't you?"

"Now that sounds like a great idea. If I get a plane ticket for Friday, can somebody in the Noble family pick me up at the airport that afternoon?"

A pause. "Actually, Ethan and I can do that."

Well, that's interesting. Sounds as if there may have been a new development. "That works." She added casually, "How is Ethan, anyway?"

Another pause. "Uh...Linds...I have something I need to tell you."

Oh, dear. "Nothing bad, I hope. Are you okay?"

"No, I'm fine," he hastily assured her. "In fact...I'm better than fine. I'm great." Another pause. "It's like...well, something has happened that makes me very happy, but I'm not sure how you're going to feel about it."

"You and Ethan?" Lindsey did a tiny happy dance. "It's about time."

"How in the world did you guess?"

"Ethan can explain that to you. Oh, Merritt, I'm so, so, so happy for you. For both of you. Ethan is one of the best people I've ever met."

"So you really mean it? You're happy for us?"

"Did you think I wouldn't be?"

"Well…," another pause. "I was afraid you might think it was too soon. After David, I mean."

"David will always own a piece of your heart, and Ethan is well aware of that. And he'll honor your feelings. I can't wait to see you guys."

"You know, Mom and Dad are over the moon. They both adore Ethan."

"Why wouldn't they? He's absolutely the best." She thought for a moment. "Oh, wait. Are you and Ethan living together?"

"We're looking for a place, but I'm still at home for now. We'll love having you here, and Kathleen will be beside herself. She thinks of you as a sister, you know."

"It's mutual, and I'm looking forward to seeing all of you."

***

Watching Merritt almost run toward her at the airport was a thrill for Lindsey. *Just look at him. Who would ever guess he's got a prosthetic leg?*

Ethan was right behind Merritt, and he picked her up and swung her around. The look of happiness on his face brought tears to Lindsey's eyes

"Didn't I tell you patience is a virtue?" she murmured as he gave her one last squeeze and set her down.

At the clinic the next day they had a chance to talk as Molly worked with Merritt, moving him from one piece of equipment to the next.

"She really puts him through his paces," Ethan laughed. "They get along well."

"Yes, I can see that." Ethan brought her a ginger ale from the vending machine and sat next to her.

"Lindsey, how can I ever thank you for what you did for Merritt? You saved his life. I'm eternally in your debt."

"He's really doing well, isn't he?" Lindsey gazed into the gym where Molly supervised Merritt's weight-bearing exercises. "He's come so far over this past year."

"We went to David's grave on the anniversary of his burial," Ethan told her. "All of us, Merritt's family, the Rosenthals, and Zivah."

"I listened to the Rach Three that night and stared out into the stars. I found it comforting." She placed a hand on Ethan's arm. "I love that you're together. I knew you'd be happy."

"We are. More than I could have imagined."

Lindsey smiled and shook her head. "I don't need details. Merritt is a loving person, and I believe you are as well. And I know you will always take care of him."

Before Lindsey left, she and Merritt looked over the Cincinnati Summer Opera season schedule. "Okay, I want to see *La Bohème*, so I'm coming back here the last week of June. You guys are in charge of getting tickets for us."

***

Lindsey settled back into her plush red chair in the auditorium of Cincinnati's historic Music Hall, one of her favorite places on earth, looking forward to this lovely Puccini opera. She'd heard it most of her life, had learned the role of Musetta, and could sing every note of the entire opera. *It's nice to be so familiar with it,* she thought. *This will be fun.*

The curtain lifted, the lights came up on stage, and her eyes were immediately drawn to the character of Marcello. Standing at an easel, brush in hand, the baritone had the opening line of the opera, which translated roughly into a complaint about his painting of the Red Sea making him even colder than the garret they were in, and ended with a threat to drown a Pharaoh in revenge.

Lindsey sat enthralled. He was the most beautiful man she had ever seen, with the most amazing voice, and what he had just sung sounded to her like a love song. Merritt, seated next to her, poked her in the ribs. *Oh, did I actually say something,* she wondered. *No, but I think I just gasped aloud.* Heart beating rapidly, Lindsey rustled her program, her eyes scanning the cast list for the name of the performer who had completely bedazzled her. *Nathaniel Cohen.*

Who is he? She composed herself as best she could, but for the entire time Marcello remained on stage he might as well have been alone so far as she was concerned. Finally, when he and Rodolfo's other companions exited, Lindsey reminded herself what was going on in this opera and did her best to listen appreciatively to Rodolfo's aria, then Mimi's. In the dark, though, she found the singer's biographies in the program and attempted to read about Nathaniel Cohen, holding the program next to her nose, straining fruitlessly to see the words.

Lindsey knew that in the musical exchange between the two lovers that followed, Marcello would sing offstage. She had a hard time containing herself when she heard that golden voice once again. *Who is this man? Why have I never heard of him before?*

The lights came halfway up for a brief intermission between the first and second acts, and Lindsey hastily read Nathaniel Cohen's bio: undergrad at Ithaca College, graduate study at Eastman, winner of the Met Opera auditions last year, spent a year in the Lindemann Young Artist Program at the Met. Upcoming appearances at summer festivals in the U.S. and Europe, performance dates through the next year mostly in the U.S. She vaguely remembered hearing a baritone had won that audition, but that was during the period just after the accident.

Merritt tapped her shoulder. "I think Mr. Cohen got your attention, Lindsey. He's excellent. It's easy to see why his career is taking off like a rocket."

"Um. Is it? Yes, he's quite…good. A very believable Marcello."

Merritt and Ethan exchanged knowing grins.

The second act began. A festive Christmas Eve in the heart of Paris, and Marcello strode from group to group, all around the stage. *Holy Hannah, can that man move.* Lindsey pressed her hands against her flushed face and lost herself in watching and listening to Nathaniel Cohen. Flash forward to seeing him pick up Musetta near the end of the act and swing her around, and Lindsey was green with envy. *What wouldn't I give to be performing with Nathaniel Cohen.*

A full intermission between the second and third acts and Ethan and Merritt headed for the lobby. "Aren't you coming?" Merritt asked her.

"No, I'm fine. I want to read the program."

Merritt guffawed. "I guess you're planning to memorize Marcello's bio?"

Let's see, he's finished grad school and at least a year beyond that, so he must be…what? Maybe twenty-six? And heading to Europe to perform for the summer, then back to the U.S. I'll bet he'll be at the Met by the time he's thirty.

Ethan handed her a candy bar when they returned. "I thought you looked hungry," he commented, a knowing smile tugging at his lips.

"Oh, please. I've never known you to be crass."

The opera continued, and once again, Marcello entered the stage, costumed as an innkeeper for this act. *It doesn't matter what he wears, he would look fabulous in rags.* Mimi, dying of tuberculosis, entered the stage coughing. Marcello tried to comfort her as Lindsey mentally put herself on stage playing the tormented Mimi.

No, that's not right. I'll never be cast as Mimi. Of course, I could play the saucy Musetta—she's a lyric coloratura—to his Marcello. Lindsey watched as the now-quarreling Musetta and Marcello stomped offstage in opposite directions. *No, I couldn't do that. I'd chase after him and make up.* She giggled at the thought, eliciting another poke from Merritt.

What other opera could we do together? The baritone is never the lover. Well, Don Giovanni, but the Don is a rake. On the other hand, Nathaniel Cohen would be a fantastic Don.

Final act. A poignant duet between Marcello and Rodolfo left Lindsey melting. *What is it about this man's voice that affects me so much?* The dying Mimi was carried on stage, and everybody exited except Mimi and Rodolfo. Lindsey focused on their moving duet, reminding herself there's more to *La Bohème* than Marcello. *Or maybe not. Maybe I've been watching it wrong all these years.*

The opera ended, the applause faded, and the audience began to file out. "Let's go to Meck's," Merritt said, referring to Mecklenburg's Beer Garden, the operagoer's after-party of choice for decades. Ethan and Lindsey agreed.

On the drive to the restaurant, Lindsey remarked, "Heck, if I'd been Mimi I'd have been after Marcello. I mean, an artist tops a writer, correct?"

Both men laughed. "I take it you were impressed by Mr. Cohen, who has been getting rave reviews wherever he sings," Merritt said.

"Why didn't I know that?" She said. "Yes, he's pretty sensational, for sure."

Pulling herself out of her temporary dream world, Lindsey settled down in the restaurant's outdoor garden and let Ethan do the ordering as she chatted with Merritt about how nice it was to be back in Music Hall and now out with them.

A voice at her side. "Excuse me. You're Lindsey Cameron, aren't you?"

Lindsey nearly fell out of her chair when she looked up to see Nathaniel Cohen gazing down at her. Pulse racing, she did her best to appear composed. *How in the world does he know who I am?*

"Y-yes, I'm her," she stammered. "I'm she. I'm Lindsey Cameron." She stared at him. "But…how did you…?"

"How did I know you? I attended your senior recital last November. I was in town for my audition for this role, and a friend who lives here invited me to come with him."

"Oh." *Brilliant response, Lindsey.*

He nodded to her. "I'm Nate Cohen."

"Yes. I know. You're Marcello. I mean, I just saw your performance as Marcello." *At least tell him you thought he was amazingly wonderful, for heaven's sake.* "I saw Marcello in a whole new light tonight."

Ethan covered his laugh with a cough.

"Please join us, Mr. Cohen. I'll apologize for Lindsey. The fact is, you kind of blew her away."

254

"Nate, please. Thank you, I'd like that." He smiled at Lindsey and took the seat next to her. "And that is a huge compliment."

Lindsey gripped the edge of the table as she felt herself blushing furiously.

Nate continued, "The fact is, I wanted very much to meet you after your recital, but I understood the special circumstances and felt I'd be intruding. I'm so glad to have this opportunity to tell you it was one of the most remarkable musical experiences I've ever had."

Her eyes widened. *Sandy brown hair, gray eyes...or are they blue? No, gray. Smoky. A warm, genuine smile. He's even better looking up close.*

Ethan extended his hand. "Ethan Jagodzinski. Lindsey has no idea what you're referring to because she doesn't realize what she did. Because that's the kind of person she is."

Merritt reached across the table and Nate took his hand. "Great to meet you, Merritt. How good to see you doing so well. I hope I'll perform Marcello to your Rodolfo one of these days. You sure nailed that high C in the 'Sempre libera' solo and the two of you sang the duet as well as I've ever heard it sung. I mean that."

The waiter brought their drinks along with platters of potato pancakes and chicken tenders.
He looked inquiringly at Nate, who pointed to Lindsey's stein. "I'll have what the lady is having."

Merritt and Ethan turned to speak to friends who stopped at their table, and Nate leaned closer to Lindsey. "You don't realize what a remarkable thing you did for your friend at your recital, do you? I've never seen any singer honor another in quite that way. As beautifully as you sang, your recital became a tribute to Merritt, and one of the most generous displays I've ever witnessed."

255

"I didn't do anything for Merritt. He did it for me. He walked down the aisle and up the steps, as I had asked him to. It was a high point of my life."

"That was evident." He gave her another warm smile and laid a hand on hers. "I can't tell you how much it means to me to finally meet you. I sure wish I didn't have to leave in the morning. I'd sure like to be able to spend some time with you."

His touch went through her entire body, and the way he spoke her name made her think of the pealing of golden bells. "I'd like that. I should tell you, Ethan was right. You absolutely blew me away tonight. What a joy to witness your performance."

A flash in his eyes made her shiver. "What are your plans for the future?" Nate asked. "Have you started grad school yet?"

"No, this fall. I'll be at Curtis. You have a very full schedule as I understand from your bio in the program."

"A lot of traveling and performing. I'm grateful for the opportunities that have opened up for me, but you're right. I won't have much time to do anything else." He sighed. "Would you consider giving me your address and phone number? I'd like to write and call you sometime, if I may. I think I might be in Philadelphia at some point and I would love to reconnect if we could."

"Yes, of course. Would you do the same for me?" She shivered again. "This is happening so fast."

"I know. I wish now I'd spoken with you last winter, but...well, there was a dark-haired young man who had a possessive arm around you."

"Oh...that's my brother. I know we don't look much alike, especially from a distance."

"So, I made the wrong choice." Nate shook his head. "But it just didn't seem like the right time to approach you."

He gazed into her eyes and she caught a breath, pulse racing. *I've never seen such gorgeous eyes. I feel as if I'm looking right into his heart.*

Nate leaned closer. "The way you looked at me when I came to your table...*colpo di fulmine.*"

"The lightning bolt." A pause. "Do you think this is real, Nate?"

"All I know is, somehow I have to see you again. I don't know when or how that can happen, but I'll sure find a way. I promise you."

He glanced at his watch. "Unfortunately, I have an early flight out, so I'd better get back to the hotel and pack."

"I could drive you to the airport."

A brilliant smile. "Would you really do that? My plane leaves before nine, so I need to be there by eight."

"I'll pick you up at six. Then we can get something to eat at the airport."

***

Lindsey would always remember that drive and the short time they spent together at the airport before Nate's plane left. They crammed into it all the information they could about each other. Nate's family lived in Pittsburgh and were practicing Reform Jews, as were the Rosenthals. Aside from that, his family sounded much like hers. His passion for music matched hers. His dream of a career was unfolding rapidly, though, and hers had not yet begun.

They didn't make any promises, other than Nate would make every effort to see her if he was in or near Philly. She wished him the very best of success with his upcoming performances. He told her again she was a remarkable person.

Just before he boarded the plane, he took her in his arms and kissed her softly.

"Don't forget me, Lindsey Cameron."

"I could never do that, Nathaniel Cohen."

He turned and walked toward his gate. "I'll write. I'll call. We'll see each other again," he called out, taking a large chunk of Lindsey's heart along with him.

Chapter 18

What on earth just happened?

On her way back to Cincinnati from seeing Nate off, Lindsey tried to bring her feet back down to earth and regain some perspective.

Okay, he's a good-looking baritone with a great voice and a ton of charisma. That's no reason to go totally bananas, Lindsey.

Nathaniel Cohen. She had never even heard the name until yesterday, and now he had taken up permanent residence in her head.

He said he'd write. And call. Get a grip, Lindsey. He probably won't have time for any of that. There had been a spark between them, though. *And why would he say it if he didn't mean it? He seems like a super guy.*

Why did this have to happen to me now, when I'm trying to get myself geared up for graduate school? Lindsey thought if Nate had asked her to drop everything and come to Europe with him, she'd have seriously considered it.

She knew she needed to talk to somebody and slide off this rainbow she seemed to be riding. Merritt might be a good person to help her sort things out. Ethan would be even better; he had told Lindsey he went through something similar when he saw Merritt perform the lead in *The Tales of Hoffman*. He said Merritt blew him away.

She knew Ethan's situation was a lot more complicated than hers because he was gay.

Lindsey had no idea whether anyone in Ethan's profession knew—or more important, cared. *I certainly hope not*, she thought. *Ethan is brilliant at what he does and he's helped a lot of people in this community.*

Lindsey asked Ethan at one time about this. "Have you ever been subjected to criticism or discrimination in your work?"

"Not really, but I've been very low-key. My personal life has always been exactly that, extremely personal."

But now he and Merritt were together, and his partner was highly visible in the music community. Word would eventually get around. Ethan had been wise not to approach Merritt about having a relationship with him, no matter how strongly he felt.

For Merritt's part, he told Lindsey he had hoped Ethan would continue to treat him after his discharge from the hospital. "Molly's been great, and I really like her, but all those months I missed Ethan. Then one day at the gym I overheard two other patients talking. One guy said he'd sure like to date Molly, but he understood the rules. She was his therapist and it was *verboten*. The other guy suggested to him he should ask to be transferred to another therapist. He said if he did that and waited a few months he could ask her out, and then it would be up to her."

"So that tipped you off as to one reason Ethan referred you to someone else on the clinic's staff?"

"No, because the policy at the clinic is that Ethan evaluates each patient and then assigns a therapist to work with them. But it did make me think. Ethan had always been completely professional with me; I never had a clue he might be interested in me other than as a patient at the clinic. On the other hand, we had become good friends."

Merritt smiled at the memories as he recalled them. "I'd liked him immediately when he worked with me in the hospital. I liked seeing him whenever he was around. I loved that he came to your voice recital and that he'd kind of become a part of—well, of our circle. I realized he'd become important to me. The next time he came to dinner at the house, I had a minute alone with him and asked him point-blank if he'd ever thought of me as anything other than a patient."

"What did he say?"

"He evaded the question at first, so then I got even more direct and asked him if he found me attractive."

"He didn't deny it?"

"He couldn't. After that, I kept thinking about him. About how much he did for me not just by supervising my treatment, but as a family friend. As *my* friend. And I knew I wanted more. I wanted to be with him."

"So?"

"I got his address and drove to his apartment one night. We had a long talk, and I told him I missed him. And that I needed him."

Merritt smiled at the memory. "We've been together ever since." A pause. "But he can't ever treat me. I can talk to Ethan about problems I may be having physically, but he will always refer me to my therapist…whoever that may be. I understand it has to be that way. Ethan is adamant about maintaining our professional distance."

Lindsey sighed. *It's complicated for them, but hopefully they can make it work. People love who they love.*

***

Lindsey now thought of Merritt and Ethan as "my guys," and for better or worse, they were partners and she was happy for them. She parked in front of the small house they were renting and when she reached the door, rang the bell using the rhythm of "Beethoven's Fifth Symphony"—just as she had when she lived with Merritt and David.

Merritt answered the door promptly, and called out as he let her in, "Hey, Ethan, it's Cinderella."

"Oh, stop," Lindsey said, annoyed.

"Well, wasn't she the girl who fell in love the minute she laid eyes on her prince?"

"I'm so glad you find this entertaining. I'm a mess."

Merritt gave her a bear hug. "I'm sorry, Linds. I think it's great that you fell for the guy. You've needed romance in your life for a long time."

"Some romance." She plopped into the nearest chair. "I just sent him off to Europe for the rest of the summer. And when he gets back, he has singing engagements all over creation. Well, all over North America."

Ethan appeared with a mug of coffee for her. "There's already sugar and cream in it, just the way you like it. Ignore this young whippersnapper, Lindsey. I think you're here to talk seriously." He pulled a chair close to her.

Lindsey gratefully accepted the coffee. "What in the world happened to me last night, Ethan? I didn't even know who I was. I don't act like that."

"I once had a singer affect me pretty much the same way." Ethan smiled sympathetically. "I couldn't take my eyes off him through the entire performance."

"I remember your telling me that," Lindsey sipped her coffee. "But you didn't meet him right after the performance and have him tell you he'd been thinking about you for six months and wanted to meet you."

"No, that didn't happen. That was something, for sure," Ethan admitted.

"So what happened at the airport?" Merritt, lounging on the sofa, asked.

"Don't say anything snarky," Lindsey warned.

"Why do you think I'd do that?"

"Because I know you maybe better than anybody. You were about to ask if Nate declared undying love."

Merritt hooted. "Well, since you mentioned it…did he?"

"This isn't funny. We had a nice talk. He's a great guy, and we have a lot in common besides opera. He's from Pittsburgh. He has an older sister who's married with two kids. He likes being Uncle Nate."

Ethan took the empty cup as he stood. "You're saying he has a lot of qualities you appreciate, other than his looks, voice, and talent. You see him as a possible life partner?"

"I don't see any reason why that couldn't be possible. Except I have no clue when I'll see him again. He says he'll write and call. At least, that's what he says."

"Did he kiss you goodbye?" Merritt asked.

"Well…sort of. He asked me not to forget him." She sighed. "It's all a fairy tale. I don't really expect to ever hear from him again. He won't call. He won't write."

Ethan came back from the kitchen and sat down next to Lindsey, resting a warm hand on hers. "You're wrong. What you don't realize is he was looking at you the same way you looked at him. He's definitely smitten. He'll write and he'll call, and he'll figure out a way to see you again as soon as possible. Mark my words."

"Back up to that he 'sort of' kissed you goodbye," Merritt said.

"You know. He kissed me as if he were…well, I guess a 'chaste kiss' is a good description."

"A wise choice. He didn't want to throw you down on the floor of the lobby and have his way with you right then and there," Merritt said. "He exhibited remarkable self-control."

Lindsey had to laugh despite herself. "Merritt Noble, you are irrepressible. Yes, I really like him, and I hope I see him again. And…I think he's someone I could love."

***

July 6, 1997

Ma cher Lindsey;

I thought a lot about how to address you. 'Dear Lindsey' seemed so ordinary. 'Dearest Lindsey' seemed pretty presumptuous. So, I figured the French would be best. I hope you agree.

It's cliché to say, but I wish you were here. I finally met you after thinking about you for six months, and then I immediately had to take off on this adventure.

I'm enjoying sunny Barcelona right now and rehearsing for the role of Silvio in *I Pagliacci*. I wish you were here singing Nedda. After this gig, I have a couple of auditions and then I go to Italy for a festival performance. More auditions before I head for England for a couple of weeks.

I'll be back in the States by mid-September unless my agent comes up with something else he needs me to do. I'd love to have a letter from you but I'm not sure of the addresses. In the meantime, I'll try to write when I can, to be sure you don't forget me.

I'll need to decompress for a week or so, but then I'm definitely coming to Philadelphia to see you by the end of September. I'll plan on spending a weekend.

I'll call you first, though, to be sure you still want to see me.

Yours,
Nate

***

July 20, 1997

Salut, ma cherie!

I guess since I'm in Switzerland I can be even more French. I wish I'd had a chance to call you, but I've been super busy. *Faust* this time around here in Basel. This is a nice house and the people in the company are very welcoming. I don't know that I'd like to be a regular here, though.

The Alps are definitely spectacular. Everything I've heard about them is true.

I'm spending a lot of time in the air which I'm not crazy about, because I've never been able to sleep on a plane. I catch up on sleep when I can.

I'm not singing as well as I'd like right now, but the company doctor is seeing me tomorrow.

I think of you often. I've never met anyone like you, and I can't wait to see you again. Two more months!

Affectueusement,
Nate

***

"Lindsey? This is Nate Cohen."

"Nate! How are you? And where are you?"

"Made it to England. I have a couple of auditions this week and then a gig in Wales, and then I'm heading for the states after that. Where I may sleep for a week."

"I guess you got this number from my parents."

"Yes, I talked to your mother. She sounds so much like you."

Lindsey settled into the love seat, holding the handset close to her ear. "It's wonderful to hear your voice."

"I can't wait to see you. I think we have a lot to talk about."

"How are you, anyway? This trip seems to be taking a toll on you."

"I'm okay. A couple of nasty colds, but I think it's from all the flying. I'll be fine."

"So I'll be seeing you soon?" She wrapped the cord around her hand, leaning her head against the back of the love seat.

"That's the plan. You haven't forgotten me, have you?"

"I told you when you left...I could never forget you. I think about you all the time and wanted so much to write. In fact...I did write. I kept the letters since I didn't know where to mail them, but I'll give them to you when I see you."

"I will love that. I have a reservation at the Rittenhouse Hotel for the first weekend in October if that works for you."

"That's perfect. And now you have my phone number, so you can call as soon as you get here."

"It won't be much longer. Can you save that whole weekend for me?"

"I will make that happen, Nathaniel. It will be so wonderful to see you."

Lindsey sighed and hugged herself when she hung up the phone. She looked around her small apartment, imagining Nate being there with her. *Who knows what will happen when we see each other again?*

266

Being at the Curtis Institute of Music had been a bigger adjustment than she anticipated. The school, much smaller than the Conservatory, had a campus that was quite different: three nineteenth-century mansions on Locust Street rebuilt to accommodate the needs of a music school, and another more contemporary building, also on Locust, which included housing for part of the student body. The total student body—all of whom were attending on full scholarship—was fewer than two hundred students.

Lindsey had opted to find an apartment in a nearby building rather than apply for housing at the school. She felt the school had a somewhat insular environment and wondered if she would ever feel entirely comfortable there.

The atmosphere was different as well. Lindsey appreciated that her schoolmates were so focused on music. Sometimes she wondered if any of them ever had any fun, though. *Or maybe it's just me who isn't having fun.*

She missed Merritt. She missed David. She missed the delightful times the three of them had together, and how much they had enjoyed everything Cincinnati had to offer. Philadelphia had always been a part of her life and she appreciated the time she spent there, but being at Curtis was not the same.

Something has changed, she thought. *I don't know what or why. Maybe it's me. Maybe I made a mistake coming to school here. I'm not sure I fit.*

Lindsey hadn't made any friends yet, but it was early in the year. It just felt to her that the singers she met were so...driven. Determined to make it in Opera World. *You know...I used to be like that. What happened to me last year somehow changed me. I look at life differently, I think.*

She had a free day the third week of school and called M.J. "I know I promised to come to visit you at Penn. How's

267

tomorrow? It turns out my voice teacher isn't going to be at my school and I don't have any classes."

"Terrific! I'm looking forward to seeing you. and I want you to meet Anita."

"Someone special?"

"Could be. She's a grad student in music therapy at Drexel. Don't even think 'older woman' and don't you dare say it. You'll like her. She was at Temple as a bachelor of music candidate in piano before she got interested in music therapy."

They made arrangements where they would meet for a late lunch. Anita Morrison, dark-eyed, dark-haired, and very pretty, was obviously quite taken with M.J. Lindsey liked her immediately and found her to be sweet, enthusiastic, smart, and charming.

The plan was that Lindsey would hang around and perhaps catch a lecture with M.J. before the three of them got together for dinner off-campus. Anita thought she had a better idea.

"There's a presentation at Drexel University by a music therapist who has done some breakthrough research that I'm excited to hear," she told them. "Why don't you both come with me? It sounds truly fascinating."

Her own brief but decidedly interesting experience with music therapy came to mind, and Lindsey agreed. M.J. considered it but decided he needed to get to his own lecture. Lindsey was happy to have a little time with Anita.

"M.J. tells me you had aspirations for being a concert pianist until you decided to pursue music therapy. Do you mind my asking what prompted your decision?"

"No, not at all, I'm happy to talk about it. I had three years toward my Bachelor of Music at Temple when I realized I didn't really have the chops for a career as a solo pianist and decided to switch to music education. My advisor asked if I'd ever thought about music therapy. Well, I had not, so she arranged for me to meet with a therapist at Children's Hospital and observe the work he was doing there."

Anita smiled at the memory. "I couldn't believe my reaction to being with those kids, and seeing how they responded to that short session. I was full of questions and eager to investigate therapy as a possible future. I completed my B.M. at Temple and applied to Drexel for their graduate program."

"I can certainly relate," Lindsey said. "My two brief exposures to observing and then helping with children in Cincinnati were similar. A very different kind of audience, and the reward is in the smiles on their little faces. As if you've given them this priceless gift."

The presentation was definitely interesting. The presenter was head nurse at a public hospital in San Francisco for mostly indigent patients who had been diagnosed by medical personnel as being in a "persistent vegetative stage" and were therefore not eligible for any resuscitation efforts.

The music therapist insisted she could detect traces of brain activity in these patients, even though their tests did not show that. Determined to learn more, she spoke with relatives of several of the patients and asked what kind of music they liked when they were young.

"I then took my cassette and made tapes of that music, and played them for the comatose patients. In every case, they began to have brain activity which could then be tested and recorded."

There was a stir in the lecture hall and hands shot up everywhere from aspiring music therapists who were excited to learn about this study. *That's just amazing*, Lindsey thought.

At dinner, she discussed this with Anita. "What I learned today about the depth of the impression music makes on our consciousness just makes me feel even more strongly what a powerful force it is," she said as they enjoyed a repast at an excellent Italian restaurant.

"Oh, it was tremendously exciting to learn about that study," Anita enthused. "I agree. I think we're just beginning to understand the profound effect music can have on people. It is without a doubt a healing force."

"Do you remember what Kristina Levin said at my graduation, M.J.?" Lindsey asked. "Something like 'it can heal and inspire, calm and incite.' And she said more, about how music can heal a wounded spirit. It did that for my friend Merritt."

"It did," M.J. agreed. "Well, now that we've agreed music can solve every problem known to man, do you ladies want dessert?"

***

After changing her outfit for the third time—to a powder blue dress with a fitted bodice, flowing skirt, three-quarter length sleeves—Lindsey critically examined herself in the mirror. *I can't believe how nervous I am. It's been over three months since we met. Maybe it was all just a fluke and we won't feel anything at all for each other.*

Her buzzer sounded, and Lindsey felt her heart jump into her throat. "Yes?"

"It's Nate Cohen."

"Come on up."

Her pulse racing, she pressed shaking hands to her face as she waited for what seemed an eternity. Finally, a tap at her door.

Nate stood on the other side, holding roses and candy, grinning at her. She noticed his hands were slightly trembling. *He's as nervous as I am*, Lindsey thought, and relaxed a little.

270

Opening the door wide, she waved him inside. "Oh, I am so, so glad to see you. I was so nervous, but seeing you again is everything I hoped it would be."

He stepped inside, dropped the bouquet and box of candy onto her loveseat, and wrapped his arms around her. They embraced for a long moment. Lindsey wanted to never let go, but she leaned back and gazed at him, and in the next instant, they kissed. This time, a real kiss, a long and satisfying kiss, full of promise.

"Wow," Nate said softly.

Lindsey laughed and disentangled herself, picking up the flowers and candy. "Look what you brought me. Just like in the movies."

"I was pretty nervous," Nate grinned. "I know there was all this...emotion when we first met, but it's been a while."

"I should put these in some water," Lindsey held the bouquet out to examine it.

"Yes, you're right. Just like in the movies. That's exactly what your line is supposed to be."

They both laughed and Nate followed Lindsey to the sink in her kitchenette, where she pulled out a small pitcher. "This is the best I can do."

"Where was my brain? I never thought about what you were going to put roses into. I just knew I wanted to get them for you. That's what a guy does in the movies when he's in love, isn't it?"

Lindsey stopped short and gazed at him. "Are you saying you're in love with me, Nate?"

He smiled and pulled her close again.

Lindsey stepped away and filled the pitcher with water, removed the paper from the bouquet's stems, and shoved them into the pitcher. After several tries, she managed to lean it against the cabinet until it seemed it wouldn't tip over.

"I'll do more with it later. Right now, I just want to sit on the loveseat with you and...."

Nate put his arms around her from behind and walked her across the room, where he turned her to face him and kissed her again before they sank together onto the loveseat for a third kiss.

Lindsey pressed herself close against him, thrilling to the sensations that shot through her entire body, wanting more. Wanting it all. She heard his breathing change and he shifted his position, pulling slightly away from her, and she had a momentary sense of what her desire was doing to him.

"We're supposed to go out to dinner," Nate choked out, his lips against Lindsey's hair.

She sighed and leaned back, caressing his face. "I've dreamed about you. But it's nothing like having you here." Her hand moved up into his hair, down behind an ear, and came to rest in the hollow of his throat.

"I've dreamed about you as well. Sometimes I had a hard time concentrating, I wanted to be with you so badly." His voice was rough.

Lindsey replaced her hand with her lips, moving her mouth slowly up his jaw. Nate took her shoulders gently and tipped her face toward his.

"As much as I want you...and believe me, I do want you...I think maybe we shouldn't rush this. We have lots of time. The last thing I want is for us to do anything you might regret later."

Lindsey nodded. "I should tell you...this is all very new to me. I've never...never been to bed with anyone."

"I wondered about that. You were so open about your feelings when we met. I loved that, but I thought maybe it was because you were inexperienced."

"I was. I still am. I've never felt about anyone the way I feel about you. I think I may be in love with you. But we barely know each other, so I probably shouldn't have told you that— I'm doing this all wrong."

He smiled. "Lindsey Cameron, I've never met anyone like you. I've never been in love, either. Oh, I've had a few girlfriends, but none of them made me feel the way you do." He sat up straight and adjusted his loosened tie. "We have the whole weekend to figure out this relationship. I think the first thing we need to do is get that dinner."

Lindsey sighed again and placed her hand over his. "Yes, dinner is no doubt an excellent idea. But before we go out, I'm sure I need to fix my makeup." She leaned toward him, lifting her face. "And before I do that, would you please kiss me one more time? I never knew kisses could be so delicious."

Chapter 19

As the first rays of sunlight crept into the room, Lindsey opened her eyes and looked to her left, admiring Nate's profile. *He looks so peaceful. And so happy.*

It had been an eventful evening. Dinner at the Italian restaurant in his hotel, during which they had talked for nearly three hours, filling in all the blanks. Nate's childhood had been much like hers. His mother, a singer, performed with a choral group in the Pittsburgh area. His father was a neurosurgeon, and they lived comfortably in the Squirrel Hill neighborhood. Like Lindsey, Nate had grown up hearing classical music. He'd loved to sing as a child, and by the time he was a sophomore in high school began to think of singing as a career.

"Favorite opera?" Nate asked, taking a sip of wine.

"Oh, there are so many. Let me name three—*Otello, Tosca,* and *Don Giovanni.* At least those are my choices tonight."

"Good choices. Three of my favorites as well. Another Verdi I love, *Un Ballo in Maschera.* A dream is to sing Renato. And Scarpia. And Iago." He grinned.

"But my favorite piece of music isn't an opera." Lindsey gazed into her wine glass. "It's the Rachmaninoff Third Piano Concerto."

Nate raised a puzzled eyebrow and she proceeded to give him an abbreviated version of the concerto's connection with

David and what had happened between her and Merritt at the lowest point of his life.

"And the end result was your recital." He leaned back and studied her. "You must know how much I think about you."

A smile that melted her heart. A warm hand resting on her arm. "I know how much I think about you." Lindsey didn't care that her voice quivered.

"I can't make any long-range plans right now. I still have a lot of options to explore. But whatever my future brings, I very much hope you will be part of it."

"I understand completely. I know how this works, Nate. We see each other when we can, and make the most of every minute."

The restaurant had emptied, filled, and emptied again when they stood to leave. "I'll get a cab," Nate said.

Lindsey put a hand on his arm. "I'd like to see your room."

He ran a gentle hand over her forehead, brushing back a stray lock of hair. "Lindsey…are you sure?"

"I've never been so sure of anything in my life." She kissed him softly.

In the dimly lit room, the king-sized bed had the duvet turned down invitingly. Nate reached into his pants pocket but Lindsey stopped him. "I'm on the pill. I have been ever since I met you." She blushed. "Just in case we saw each other again."

"I…haven't been with anyone in months," he said, his voice shaking slightly.

"And I haven't been with anyone ever. We're safe."

"You're sure we're not…I don't want to rush you," Nate said as he removed his jacket and draped it over the back of a chair.

"It seems I'm the one doing the rushing." Lindsey pulled off his tie and began to unbutton his shirt, her hands trembling with excitement. Clothing might have been tossed everywhere, but Nate slowed her, and she soon realized he was right to do so. It became a magical time for Lindsey, experiencing him slowly and carefully removing her clothing as he caressed her, guiding her to do the same for him.

The kisses and caresses became more intense, and Nate's voice in her ear, rough with emotion: "Forgive me, baby. I may have to hurt you."

Lindsey gasped out, "I know. It's all right."

A brief moment of pain, followed by the exquisite feeling of their bodies being fully joined. Lindsey experienced a burst of overwhelming sensations as she clung to Nate, knowing he was right there with her. Their breathing slowed as they relaxed.

"I hope I didn't hurt you too much," Nate murmured, when he could speak.

"You didn't. And oh, was it ever worth it." Lindsey stretched, aware of her body as she had never been before. "I love you." She said softly, running a hand over his chest.

"Not as much as I love you, my angel," he whispered. "The next time will be better, I promise."

He was right, it was. And they came together yet a third time before drifting into a delicious sleep.

Now Lindsey traced Nate's profile carefully with an index finger.

He opened his eyes and smiled at her. "You look happy."

He has such amazing eyes. "I am happy. Happier than I've ever been in my life. You're an incredible man, Nathaniel Cohen."

He stroked her hair back from her face, gazing into her eyes. "You're the best thing that's ever happened to me. I know it won't be easy because of my schedule, but I want you to know I'm deeply committed to you. Asking you to be my girlfriend sounds a little juvenile, but it's used all the time. Sweetheart may be old-fashioned, but that's how I think of you. Or my dearest love. My beloved."

"My beloved Nate. Nate, my beloved." Lindsey murmured. "This is my beloved, Nathaniel Cohen."

Nate lifted an eyebrow. "I'm not too sure how that would fly during an introduction, but I like the way it sounds." He lifted her left hand and kissed her fingers. "One day I'll put a ring here."

"You don't need to do that. Now who's getting ahead of himself? You have a career just underway and don't need distractions."

"That depends," he chuckled. "Spending time with you is definitely a distraction I need to have whenever possible."

"As long as it doesn't interfere with your rehearsals and performances," Lindsey said.

Nate reached for his wristwatch from the night table. "Almost seven. Do you want to get a little more sleep or get our day started?"

"I want to make love with you again. Then we can decide."

Nate complied, willingly.

***

After finishing the breakfast delivered by room service, Nate stopped at the front desk to advise the clerk there would be two in his room for the duration of his stay. They went back to Lindsey's so she could shower and change, and pack an overnight bag for the remainder of the weekend.

"This visit is costing you a fortune. The Rittenhouse is pricey," she told Nate as she worked on arranging the roses at her sink. They had held up well.

"I kind of hoped you might end up in my bed…and I wanted it to be special if that happened."

"'Special' is an understatement." Lindsey admired the roses as she carried them to her bedside table. "They're lovely, aren't they? I think they'll last for a few more days."

They took her bag to the hotel and then strolled through Rittenhouse Square. Lindsey led Nate to Locust Street and showed him the Curtis Institute buildings. "A lot of tradition here," he commented.

It was a perfect autumn day, sunny with just enough of a refreshing breeze. Strolling back through Rittenhouse Square they found an empty bench and claimed it. "Do you think the day will come when we don't have a lot to say to each other?" Nate asked.

"Not likely. I'm a big talker. I'll find something to bore you with."

He laughed and pulled her close. "Do you want to do something special tonight? Go to a movie, maybe?"

"No. I want to make our own movie in that lovely big bed." She leaned back. "But let's pass on the expensive restaurant tonight. We'll find a stand and get cheesesteaks."

"A Philly special." Nate nodded his head in agreement. "You're on."

Lindsey woke during the night, thinking of where she was. So happy to be with Nate, so much in love. But not so happy with the rest of her life. Overwhelmed by her jumble of emotions, Lindsey felt her throat close as tears spilled over. She turned away from Nate, not wanting to wake him, but he pulled her close.

"Talk to me," he said. "You need to know you can tell me anything. Is it something I said or did?"

"No, of course not." She sighed and snuggled into his arms. "You've been perfect. I am so in love with you."

"What, then?"

"I'm completely sure I'm where I should be when I'm with you, but not so sure about the rest of my life. I was excited to come to Curtis. But it's not what I had hoped for."

Another sigh. "Or maybe it's not Curtis at all. Maybe it's me. I miss Merritt. I miss David terribly. I miss what we had in Cincinnati. The three of us, I mean. I can't seem to get into the…well, the rhythm of being at Curtis. I haven't made one friend. I do appreciate my teacher and the acting coach. But the students…well, they're not standoffish, but they aren't any too friendly. Or maybe I'm the one who's not friendly. Maybe I'm even standoffish."

Nate listened patiently, patting her shoulders, holding her close.

"I don't know what's wrong with me," Lindsey finished with a sniffle.

"Lindsey, you told me all about everything that happened after the accident that took David's life and changed Merritt's forever. Think about it. It changed you as well. You went through a traumatic experience from the time you went to the hospital in the middle of that March night a year and a half ago."

He gazed into her eyes, gently stroking her hair back from her face. "You don't just 'get over' something like that. It becomes a part of who you are. Don't be so hard on yourself, angel. You spent so much time focused on Merritt and making sure he was going to be okay, that I think you kind of neglected Lindsey."

She grew quieter, listening.

"Then you decided to continue with the plans you had made before any of that happened, expecting to just pick up where you left off when you decided to come here to Curtis.

Now, you're trying to figure out how to do that. But a lot has happened since you made that decision."

"Yes, that's true. I guess I hadn't really given it much thought. I know I'm not the person I was before the accident." A sigh. "You're right, maybe I'm trying to just go back to that point and pretend nothing happened."

"You say you're happy with your teacher," Nate said.

"Yes, she's excellent. And our acting coach is a dream. I'm learning a lot from him…I think I told you Elliott Jackson was a stage actor. An actor who loves opera. He has lots of ideas as to how we can make our performances better. Bring the roles to life."

"He sounds exciting. So why not start with that? It's why you're here, after all. To continue to develop your talent and hone your skills. It does seem like maybe you need to reach out more to your fellow students."

Lindsey leaned up on an elbow and caressed Nate's face. "I can do that…focus on my studies and try to be friendlier. I think one thing that has held me back was not knowing where I stood with you. I fell hard for you, baritone."

Nate started to speak, but Lindsey put a finger to his lips. "I know what you said the day you left for Europe. But we had barely met each other and didn't have much time together then. Knowing you love me changes everything."

They didn't leave the room the next morning, ordering room service for breakfast. Lindsey went with Nate to the airport that afternoon to see him off to New Orleans, where he would perform Marcello in *La Bohéme* in two weeks. They looked over his schedule, finding possible times they could be together.

"I'm in New York right after Thanksgiving to meet with my agent and spend time with my vocal coach. Think you could get into the city for a couple of days then?"

"I probably could. I'll check the school calendar." Lindsey studied the schedule again, leaning against Nate's shoulder. "Where are you going to be for Christmas?"

"I have a few days, so I'll be with my family. I'd love for you to meet them. And for them to meet the woman I intend to spend the rest of my life with."

"I'd like that. I could probably fly to Pittsburgh for a couple of days. We have an extended break after Christmas. I think until the third week of January."

"Then let's plan on that."

Lindsey laid a hand on Nate's arm. "Oh! Any chance you could come back to West Chester with me for a day or two after I visit you in Pittsburgh? That 'meet the family' thing works both ways."

"Sure. I'll make that happen. It's a little nerve-wracking for a guy, though, especially when I'm the guy who…well, you know."

"De-flowered their precious daughter?" She grinned wickedly. "Somebody had to do it sometime. I certainly never intended to be a nun."

Nate laughed heartily. "Lindsey, you don't mince words, do you?"

"They'll adore you. And you will definitely fall in love with them. You and M.J. will hit it off. He's always been the family member who has kept me honest. He has no trouble reminding me to avoid that pedestal my dad seems to want to put me on."

"Oh, great. Thanks a lot. Even more reason for me to be nervous. Maybe I should get a hotel room when I come."

"No way. You're sleeping with me. In my still very girly room, decorated in blue and white. With stuffed animals on the bed. They will stay on the bed, by the way."

Nate was laughing helplessly by this point. His flight was called and, arms around each other, Lindsey walked with Nate as far as she was allowed.

"Thanksgiving isn't that far away," she said. "And I expect a phone call a week, if at all possible."

"I'll make it happen." One final kiss, and he was gone.

I guess this will be the story of my life from now on. Only even more complicated after I graduate from Curtis and begin my own career.

***

The weekend with Nate made all the difference to Lindsey, who went back to Curtis on Monday with a renewed appreciation for the opportunity she'd won with her acceptance at the school. Her voice teacher, Madame Nadia Dubanowski, a former Polish opera singer, commented, "Lindsey, this is the best lesson you and I have had. Maybe it's the cooler weather?"

"I do appreciate the change of seasons," Lindsey said. *Oh, Madame D., you have no idea what happened to me last weekend.*

Madame tipped her head. "Or perhaps there is romance in the air?"

Lindsey felt herself blush. "I…spent some time with my…sweetheart." *Busted,* Lindsey thought. *This lady is very observant.*

Lindsey worked with Madame's studio pianist on "Come scoglio" from *Così fan tutte* which she would use for her audition for the school's spring opera production. The aria was considered one of the most difficult for soprano.

At her next lesson, Madame took the first section of the aria apart, note by note. "This is not your *fach*, your voice part, Lindsey. In this aria, Fiordiligi is a dramatic coloratura. It's said

283

Mozart disliked the singer who created the role and that's why he made it so damned difficult. All those big jumps, sometimes more than an octave."

"I like the challenge, Madame. I won't blow my vocal cords out, I promise. Help me learn to sing it smart."

"I like your attitude. You'll do best if you remember the opera is a comedy, and look at this aria as satire. Not slapstick, though. Actually, I think you will probably get along with the character Fiordiligi quite well…let us find the humor in this aria."

As she worked at singing the almost impossible jumps from high notes to ridiculously low ones and back up to high notes, Lindsey wondered if auditioning for this role was the best choice for her. *Not just an octave. This is a thirteenth. Maybe Mozart did hate the soprano he wrote this for.*

Merritt called her to see how things were going and told her he had won the role of Pinkerton in the Conservatory's spring production of *Madama Butterfly*. "I was a little nervous about auditioning and getting back on stage, but apparently it's going to happen."

"Congratulations on being cast," Lindsey said.

"You don't sound too convinced I'm ready for it."

"Oh, I have no doubt you'll be fabulous. I'm a little concerned about some of the stage business the role requires. Many directors like to have Pinkerton carry Cio-Cio San offstage after the first act duet. Are you sure you're ready for that? Then when you come onstage at the end of the opera, you may be asked to drop to your knees."

"Molly and I are working on that. She and Ethan both think I can do it. And the director is willing to modify anything necessary. He really wants me for the role."

"Well, then, I'm sure it will be fine. I'm happy for you." Lindsey still wasn't completely convinced, but he sounded so enthusiastic she didn't pursue her concern. "What are the performance dates? Of course, I will be there if it's at all possible."

As he had promised, Nate managed to call at least once a week, sometimes early in the morning, sometimes late at night. The performances of *La Bohème* in New Orleans had been successful and he was heading next for Dallas to perform Valentin in *Faust*. Then he would fly home to spend Thanksgiving with his family before going to New York for a few days, where Lindsey was to meet him.

Seeing this packed schedule actually taking place in Nate's life, Lindsey realized she might very well be doing the same thing after graduating from Curtis. Another option would be to audition for an opera company in central Europe and become part of the theater's ensemble, where she would probably begin with small roles and hope to eventually work up to leads.

Don't get ahead of yourself, Lindsey. Concentrate on working with Madame and Elliott and do exactly what Nate suggested—solidify your vocal technique and hone your acting skills.

Sessions with Elliott were a high point of her week. He worked with the singers on relaxation and concentration, teaching them techniques that could be used by anybody in any profession, but were vital to actors—and at Curtis, singers were considered actors.

Elliott requested that they wear appropriate workout clothing to class, and passed out pieces of blankets for them to lie on. Flat on their backs, they heard Elliott's mellifluous voice telling them to take all the *stuff* in their heads and try to release it. "Take a slow deep breath. Now release it, blow it out slowly and get rid of all the garbage running around in your head. Now another breath, and blow out the last of it. Try to empty your mind."

He strolled around the class as he continued, "Imagine yourself at the shore. It's a warm day, but not hot. Clouds are covering the sun from time to time. Close your eyes. Listen to the surf."

Elliott continued to give them suggestions. "You may hear children nearby…or birds…or a plane far overhead. Feel the touch of a breeze, the warmth of the sun. Breathe deeply."

Lindsey felt her muscles relax even before Elliott continued, "Begin with your feet…relax your muscles. Now your ankles…then up to the knee…keep breathing deeply." By the time he had reached their heads, the entire class was in an almost hypnotic state and the room became completely silent. Elliott brought them back gradually. "Take one more deep breath. Now open your eyes slowly. Very slowly, lean up on one elbow and stretch."

After the exercise, concentrating on character development and movement seemed to flow easily for all of them. Lindsey found herself practicing Elliott's relaxation exercises when lying in bed, her mind churning. It helped to put herself on that beach, and generally she could drop off to sleep within minutes.

***

Nate watched as Lindsey disembarked from her Amtrak train in New York's Penn Station. He took her bag, set it beside him, and gathered her into his arms, holding her for long minutes.

"God, I've missed you," he murmured. "You look absolutely fantastic."

She tipped up her face for a kiss and it lasted for a long time. "I've missed you, too. Especially these delicious kisses."

Nate picked up her bag. "We have a room at the Marriott. I think you'll like it. It's nice."

"Not as expensive as the Rittenhouse, I hope."

He gave her a sidelong glance. "No. But it has a king-sized bed."

"When can we check in?"

Nate stepped out into the street to hail a cab. "I already did." He turned back toward her as he added, "They allowed me early check-in when I sang for them."

Lindsey stared at him as a cab stopped for them, and they jumped in quickly.

"Just kidding, sweetheart," Nate grinned. "They're not full, and the desk clerk was sympathetic when I told her I hadn't seen you in months."

"It's only been eight weeks."

"Feels like eight months."

They made good use of the large, comfortable bed. Lindsey lay in Nate's arms, marveling at everything about him. The little whorls of chest hair. The length of his eyelashes. The muscles across his chest and shoulders. The shape of his hands. The line of his jaw. She ran a hand down his lithe but muscular body, resting it on his hip.

He grinned. "Do I pass inspection?"

"Oh, yes. You're beautiful, Nate. Everything about you." She leaned up on one elbow. "I guess I shouldn't ask you to sing to me, as much as I'd love that."

"I have a voice lesson tomorrow. You're welcome to come."

"That would be intrusive. I can wait," she told Nate. "Sing for me next month when we're together over Christmas. My mother can play anything."

Nate guffawed. "Oh, great. First, I have to sleep in your bed with stuffed animals and now I have to sing for my supper."

287

Lindsey poked him just under his armpit, and his reaction delighted her. He jumped and laughed.

"You're ticklish," she said, reaching to poke again. Nate chuckled, catching her hand and holding it firmly.

"Enough of that. Tell me how things are at Curtis."

"Well, thanks to your good advice, I've been having excellent lessons. And I'm learning so much from Elliott. We've had a couple of private sessions while he helps me try to figure Fiordiligi out. She was so sure of herself, positive that she would never, ever betray Guglielmo. Yet she does exactly that. So, we've agreed 'Come scoglio' is all bravado. She's trying to convince herself how steadfast she is. And that can be humorous, and the aria is less daunting."

"When are auditions?"

"Next week. Wish me luck."

They had tickets for the Met's performance of *Turandot* that night, and Lindsey lost herself in the beauty of the opera, recalling how much she and Merritt had loved being in the ensemble the summer before their senior year.

Lindsey left the following day since Nate had not only a voice lesson but another session with his opera coach as they worked on the role of Mercutio in Gounod's *Romeo et Juliette*, which he was scheduled to sing in Seattle in April. Since that would be after the Curtis opera production in March, Lindsey thought she would be able to fly out to see him. He promised to be at her performance if at all possible, so it would only be a little over two months from the time they'd be together at Christmas. *It's the life of a singer*, she thought.

And Christmas is only a few weeks away. I'm learning to cherish the time we have together and stay busy while we're apart.

Chapter 20

Fiordiligi..............................Lindsey Cameron

Lindsey's heart skipped a beat as she saw the list posted for the cast of *Così fan tutte*. *Well, I wanted this, and now I have it.*

Madame congratulated her. "You will be excellent, Lindsey. And I believe you will enjoy learning and performing this role."

I hope so, Lindsey thought. *I haven't been on stage in an opera in nearly two years.* She had sung very little in public since her senior recital in November of 1996—in Sedona the following February and on a master class at Curtis in October where she performed two songs from Schumann's *Frauenliebe und Leben*, the song cycle she and David had spent so much time on. Working on them again brought back many memories of him, and she had shed a few tears. She recalled Ethan saying that would happen. *I'll miss David for the rest of my life.*

She faced an added challenge with the Mozart opera. "Can I do comedy, do you think?" she asked Elliott at a private acting session. "I've heard it's more difficult than drama."

"Lindsey, you have a wicked sense of humor. Piece of cake."

Winter break started the next week, and Christmas at home with her entire family proved to be a happy time. Jean, Noémi, and their children were staying nearby with her grandparents, and they left soon after Christmas Day to spend a week at Disney World. Lindsey rode with them to the airport, since her flight to Pittsburgh left right after theirs to Orlando.

Nate met her at the airport in Pittsburgh and her heart again skipped a beat. Seeing him, being in the presence of his love for her, gave her a sense of joy. His parents, Lydia and Daniel, immediately made her feel welcome, and the fact that Nate took her bag to his room didn't seem at all awkward. *We're all adults here*, Lindsey thought.

The rest of the Cohen family showed up for dinner: Nate's sister Lisa, her husband Michael Loew, and George and Sarah, ages seven and four. Sarah became Lindsey's little shadow for the rest of the evening, and Lindsey found her charming.

Laughter and music filled the brief visit. Lydia played piano well enough for Nate and Lindsey to sing through the duet from *Don Giovanni*, "Là ci darem la mano." Nate grinned as he pulled out a book of Jerome Kern's music and opened it to "You Are Love" from *Showboat*. "I'm sure you've at least heard this," he said. "Want to give it a shot?"

"You're on." Singing the highly romantic piece with Nate was a thrill, and they ended with a kiss, heartily applauded by their audience.

"I'm so happy to be here," Lindsey told Nate later as she lay in his arms, completely content. "Your family is great. I feel very much at home."

"They loved you even before you walked in the door. I've told them so much about you." He kissed her again. "Sorry the bed is so small."

"It's a double bed, same as mine is. It works fine." She snuggled close to him. "We could manage in a single bed. Or a hammock. Or even a sleeping bag, or…."

"Stop," Nate laughed. "And you worry about performing in a comic opera? Lindsey, you find humor in just about everything. Mr. Mozart gives you a lot of material in *Così*. Wouldn't it be fun for us to perform in it together someday?"

M.J. met Lindsey and Nate at the airport in Philadelphia and drove them to West Chester. The two men liked one another immediately. Andrew and Mary were as welcoming of Nate as his parents had been of Lindsey. Dinner was followed by music, and Nate and Lindsey repeated the duet from *Don Giovanni.*

"My family hears me sing all the time. We have a lot of opera scores here," she said to Nate. "What arias have you worked on that you'd be willing to sing?"

"A bunch. Is there one you'd like to hear?"

"Yes, actually, there is. I'd love to hear you sing Gérard's aria from *Andrea Chénier.* It's my very favorite aria. I'm sure we have a book of baritone arias that includes it."

"Your favorite aria? No pressure," Nate quipped. "Yes, I know it."

Mary and Nate looked over the music and he mentioned specific pauses and tempo changes to her as his potential audience looked on.

"He's everything you said, Linds," M.J. told her. "You done good."

"I absolutely adore the man," Lindsey said softly, her eyes shining.

"There's no question that it's mutual," Andrew told her. "I have to agree with M.J. He's what I had hoped for you."

Mary turned to her family. "Okay, we're ready if you are."

They settled down to listen.

Nate did more than sing the aria, he performed it. Before Lindsey's eyes, Nathaniel Cohen became Carlo Gérard, an official of the French Revolution, who is required to condemn Chénier, a poet who is not guilty of the treason he's been accused of, to the guillotine. Gérard agonizes, wondering how his devotion to the Revolution has caused him to become a person who can do this. In a shift in emotion, Gérard remembers why he became part of the Revolution, the great hopes he had for people to learn to love each other.

The power in Nate's voice, the changes of emotion, sent a thrill through Lindsey. She saw and heard every nuance, musical and dramatic, that the piece required. Enthralled, she was scarcely aware of the tears that crept down her cheeks.

I thought he was splendid as Marcello, and now this. He has the potential for greatness. There's absolutely no question. This is unbelievably magnificent. A few more years, and he'll sing this and all those other roles he loves so much.

Nate finished the aria and there was quiet in the room for a moment. M.J. broke the silence by jumping to his feet and yelling "Bravo!" He pumped Nate's hand. "Good Lord, Nate Cohen. Lindsey said you were great, but she didn't say you were headed for stardom. I've never heard that aria sung better."

Andrew and Mary offered their praise as well. Overcome with emotion, Lindsey pressed her hands to her face. Nate knelt beside her and she put her arms around him.

"Lindsey?"

"I'm overwhelmed. I knew you were wonderful…but I've never heard you sing this. I didn't fully realize what you have. You absolutely bring a character to life, Nate."

"I try." Their eyes met as he smiled.

"Thank you for sharing your exceptional gift with us tonight," Mary hugged him. "We loved you already, Nate, because you've been so good to Lindsey. I agree with M.J. about your talent, it's apparent you have a bright future in Opera World."

"Well, after that, I could do with a glass of wine," M.J. said. "Or champagne? Do we have any?" Andrew and Mary went with him to check, leaving Nate and Lindsey alone.

She gazed into his eyes. "Did you use that aria for your Met audition?"

"I did," he answered with a grin. "The judges liked it."

Lindsey hugged him hard. "Nathaniel Cohen...how did I get so lucky that you should choose me? You truly are my hero. A magnificent singer. An equally admirable human being."

He held her away from him and said earnestly, "Lindsey Cameron, I honestly think we were meant to be together. I've loved you from the first moment I saw you at your senior recital in Cincinnati. I knew I wanted you in my life, even then." He smiled and caressed her face. "I'm so lucky that lightning bolt worked both ways for us."

Andrew reappeared with champagne flutes. "Come into the kitchen. Your mother is fixing a snack for us."

M.J. came down the stairs and joined them. "First toast is mine. To Lindsey and Nate. Talk about a power couple."

Laughter from all, and Andrew offered a toast to Nate. "To Nathaniel Cohen. One day to be an international star on the opera stage."

"My turn," Nate said. "To Lindsey Cameron, the most generous, loving woman I've ever known."

Lindsey caught M.J.'s wry grin. "That's nice to hear," he commented.

Cheese, crackers, fruit, and champagne were consumed until at last, it was time to call it a night. M.J. stood and made a great show of yawning and stretching. "Time to turn in."

As Lindsey led Nate up the stairs she had a moment of apprehension, wondering again how he would react to her "girly" room with all her stuffed animals. Opening the door, they saw lighted candles everywhere and signs on both pillows on her bed: NATE on one, LINDSEY on the other. And not a stuffed animal in sight.

"M.J. at work," Lindsey giggled. Nate stifled a laugh as he sat on the bed and pulled her onto his lap.

"I knew your room would be lovely...like you," he murmured, kissing her.

"And Nate, a warning...tonight I may be making love with Carlo Gérard. The fascinating, tormented revolutionary. I've been in love with him since I was fourteen."

"That's a pretty tall order," Nate chuckled. "I'll give it my best shot."

***

The *Così* cast returned to Curtis early to begin music rehearsals. Lindsey thoroughly enjoyed learning and singing the many ensemble sections of the opera. Kyla Page, a stunningly beautiful African-American mezzo-soprano who had attended Westminster Choir College, was cast as her sister Dorabella, and the two women quickly became friends. Lindsey found Kyla's humor matched hers and their voices were a good fit.

Kyla had moved into Lindsey's apartment building at the end of the first semester, and she found it especially nice to have someone to walk back and forth through Rittenhouse Square with at least twice a day. Lindsey found in Kyla the same kind of companionship she had enjoyed with Zivah, and the two of them shared a lot about themselves and their lives.

"I'm still trying to figure this school out," Lindsey told Kyla during a snowy walk to Curtis. "I had so much fun in Cincinnati with my housemates. But I guess I kind of isolated myself in a lot of ways. Oh, I had some friends, but I didn't really hang out with them much. David and Merritt—especially David—were my best friends for all my time there."

"I get that," Kyla said. "I've had a similar experience. Westminster was all about ensemble singing in many ways, and I hadn't expected the level of competition I found here. I'm still not sure how far I want to pursue this, but being accepted here on a full scholarship convinced me I should at least explore the possibilities. And we have a fabulous teacher. No matter what I end up doing, I will learn a lot during these two years."

"I probably have no business singing the role of Fiordiligi. It honestly surprised me when I saw I was cast. This may be the only time I ever perform it."

"You'll be fine. Remember, we're singing in a relatively small venue. Just don't push for sound. You certainly have the range and the *fioratura* ability. Besides, I like singing with you. We make a good pair of sisters, don't you think?"

Lindsey grinned. "We look exactly alike; people will think we're twins." Laughing, they half ran the rest of the way to the school.

***

Despite rehearsals, lessons, and classes, Lindsey felt a need to fill more of her time, which seemed to pass slowly when she wasn't with Nate. He had at one time described how helpful it was to have some ability to converse in German when in Europe, so Lindsey enrolled in a conversational German class at Penn. She enjoyed being on the campus that one afternoon a week, and generally met M.J. for lunch before her class.

"What do you hear from Nate?" M.J. took a healthy bite of his hamburger.

"He's in Dayton right now to perform the baritone solos in the Brahms Requiem with the Dayton Philharmonic." Lindsey nibbled a french fry.

"He's a busy boy these days," M.J. observed.

"Maybe too busy." She picked up half her grilled ham and cheese sandwich. "From there he flies back to New York and then home to Pittsburgh before he heads for Miami to perform Valentin in *Faust* with the Florida Grand Opera."

"You can see him while he's in New York, can't you?" M.J. helped himself to a fry from Lindsey's plate.

"I don't see how." Lindsey shoveled half her fries onto M.J.'s plate. "He has a voice lesson and several coaching sessions scheduled and he's only going to be there for three days." She sighed. "We tried to figure out a way to see each other, but between his schedule and mine we couldn't see any way to work it out."

"That has to be frustrating."

"I'll say. He's coming to see *Così*, though, and we'll have a couple of days together then. But he has to leave the second week of March to fly across the Pacific for *La Bohéme* at the Hawaii Opera Theatre. Then he goes directly to Seattle from there to do his first performances of Mercutio in *Romeo et Juliette* the first week of April."

"That's a lot of traveling and singing in a short period of time." M.J. stabbed a bunch of fries with his fork. "Is he going to be okay with that?"

"I guess we'll find out. I know last summer when he was all over Europe, he was extremely tired when he came home."

Lindsey had concerns about Nate perhaps doing more than he should. *Nate's just getting started, though*, she thought. *If this is too much for him, I'm sure he'll tell his agent to give him more time between gigs.*

Anita joined them for lunch, her face flushed and eyes shining. She dropped a kiss on M.J.'s cheek and said, "Hi, Lindsey. We just had the most amazing experience."

"I guess we're going to hear about it whether we want to or not," M.J. grinned as he held a chair for her. "What do you want to eat? I'll get it for you."

"What you're having looks great." She turned to Lindsey. "I think you'll appreciate this because I know you really have some idea what can be done with music in a therapeutic setting. We just had an introduction to the Bonny Guided Imagery and Music technique. It's fascinating. It goes far beyond just relaxation and using music to calm and soothe."

"How so?" Lindsey was immediately interested.

"You know that saying, something about music giving flight to the imagination?" Anita smiled at M.J. as he rejoined them.

"Actually, it's part of a quote attributed to Plato," M.J. placed Anita's lunch on the table. "'Music gives a soul to the universe, wings to the mind, flight to the imagination, and life to everything.'"

"Even better," Anita nodded. "This therapy uses specific musical selections to stimulate journeys of the imagination. The therapist uses these to help the patient integrate spiritual, emotional, mental, and physical aspects of well-being."

"Wow, that does sound fascinating," Lindsey remarked.

"You know how Helen Bonny developed her technique, don't you?" M.J. asked Anita. "It was back in the seventies, in conjunction with consciousness-altering LSD studies. Bonny added classical music to enhance the experience, and she discovered almost by accident that pretty much the same effect could be achieved with music alone. And with the plus that the patient could remember everything they experienced."

Anita's eyes widened. "I'm impressed. How do you know all this?"

"I read a lot," M.J. grinned. "It's pretty fascinating. The therapist puts together a playlist, and it isn't all pretty, soothing music that's used. The theory is that more complex, diverse orchestral music opens up new pathways in the brain for the listener. The music usually lasts forty-five minutes to an hour. The patient is brought to a state of deep relaxation…"

"…and then the therapist encourages him to share with her what he's experiencing," Anita added. "Everything he experiences through all the senses. Only the therapist is referred to as the 'guide' and the patient is 'the traveler.' When the session begins, the therapist—the guide—asks the traveler where he thinks he needs to go and helps him establish a starting point. The guide then writes down everything the traveler tells her so when he returns to reality, they can discuss the journey."

"I have a perfect piece in mind," Lindsey smiled. "Rachmaninoff's Third Piano Concerto."

That almost sounds like what happened with Merritt. I didn't know about relaxation exercises, but he had just had a powerful emotional release and was open to what he experienced by listening to that piece. I know it changed his life for the better. And I think it may have changed my life as well.

"I can understand why you're excited, honey," M.J. said to Anita. "That's pretty mind-bending…if you'll excuse the pun."

***

While Lindsey enjoyed her participation in the Curtis opera production, she still didn't feel the same sense of excitement she had while at the Conservatory. *Maybe it's the role*, she thought. *It's a real challenge, but I highly doubt I'll ever sing it again. Or maybe I miss singing with Merritt.*

He called her frequently, full of enthusiasm for his upcoming opera performance. "I think Pinkerton is going to be one of my 'money' roles," he said. "It's a perfect fit. I'm excited for you to see it. Our Butterfly is exceptional. A new grad student, with the perfect voice. And she's tiny…Asian American. Lovely girl."

"Are you comfortable in the staging rehearsals?"

"Yeah, I really am. I can't say I've gotten used to having a prosthetic leg, but I definitely feel more secure all the time. And Linds, being in the support group has helped me a lot. What a great bunch of folks they are. They crack jokes about their condition. And it's amazing what some of them can do, even those that are bilateral amputees. They're planning to buy a block of tickets to come and cheer me on."

"I love that, Merritt. I hope I can meet some of them. I'm so looking forward to seeing your performance. How's Ethan?"

"He's great. And, well, he's a big part of why I feel good about being on stage again. He's constantly encouraging me to try new things. We take a lot of walks and make a point of going up and down steps rapidly wherever we find them. We've even gone jogging a couple of times. I know I don't want to get ahead of myself, but I feel stronger all the time."

Lindsey kept her hand on the phone for a few minutes after they ended their conversation. *I remember how happy it made me to see Merritt stride down the aisle and up the steps during my recital. I can't wait to see him on stage as Pinkerton.*

***

Lindsey Cameron was a lovely and highly satisfactory Fiordiligi. While her voice is lighter than many sopranos who undertake the difficult role, she sang with confidence and ease and had the abundance of high notes and skillful execution of *fioratura* the role requires. Miss Cameron is an exceptional stage performer and her acting was a highlight of the evening.

Well, there's that, Lindsey thought, pleased as she read the newspaper after opening night. *My first Philadelphia review. I've improved my acting, which was a goal when I came here.*

Having her man and "my guys" in town to see her second performance and spend the next day with her was the highlight of her weekend. Nate arrived on a Saturday morning flight and asked her not to meet him at the airport, saying he'd grab a taxi to her apartment. It may have been ten in the morning, but her apartment was decorated with flowers and candles and love was definitely in the air.

"We couldn't have done this if I'd been the one singing tonight." He lay with his head on her shoulder as she caressed him. "However, I've been told lovemaking energizes female singers."

"I guess we'll find out," Lindsey laughed. "All I know is there was no way I could keep my hands off you today. We have lots of time. Merritt and Ethan will check into the Rittenhouse around two, and they invited us to be their guests at the hotel for an early dinner at four."

Nate had been up early to catch a nine o'clock flight, and Lindsey encouraged him to get some sleep. He didn't need urging. She sighed and snuggled close to him, happy beyond words to have him next to her.

"Do you have plans beyond school?" Nate asked Merritt at dinner.

"I'm considering my options. One thing for sure, I'm going to enter the Met National Auditions next year. I'll actually complete my graduate degree this December, so I can

300

focus on preparing for that event as well as the Young Artist Competition."

It pleased Lindsey to see how well her best friend and the man she loved hit it off. *But why wouldn't they? Nate already respected Merritt, and Merritt admires Nate. Maybe someday my favorite baritone and my favorite tenor will share a stage. Oh, and maybe I'll be up there with them.* The thought made her smile.

"Lindsey tells us you have a pretty heavy schedule at the moment," Ethan commented. "How are you holding up?"

"So far, so good." Nate placed a hand on Lindsey's and squeezed it. "My biggest problem is that I haven't been able to spend much time with this lady."

"But we certainly make the most of the time we have together," Lindsey said quickly, causing Merritt and Ethan to chuckle.

"TMI," Merritt commented with a grin. "I'm not touching that."

The theater in which the opera was performed was a relatively small venue, seating less than five hundred. Lindsey had her own cheering section: her parents, grandparents, M.J. and Anita, as well as her dinner companions. Backstage, she warmed up carefully with Kyla. The call for "places" alerted the cast to the beginning of the opera.

The performance went smoothly and was enthusiastically received by the audience. Lindsey felt she had done some of her best singing and thought one reason might have been because there were so many people she loved in the audience— Nate and Merritt in particular.

Lindsey loved singing Mozart's ensembles, and *Così* in particular featured duets, trios, quartets, and even sextets in abundance. The Curtis cast had spent a great deal of time working on them and performed them expertly. There were moments in the ensembles when Lindsey had a strong sense that this cast was serving the music—voices, minds, hearts blending in a realization of what the composer's vision had been. *This is what it's about*, she thought with a thrill. *It's about this wonderful music we're privileged to share.*

Lindsey's parents treated their gang, along with Elliott Jackson and Kyla Page, to a late repast at a nearby restaurant. The Camerons hadn't seen Merritt in quite a while and were overjoyed to see how well he was doing. Kyla and Merritt became instant friends and he told her someday he'd like to play Don José to her Carmen.

They partied until after one o'clock, and the West Chester folks needed to call it a night since they were not staying over in Philadelphia.

Back at Lindsey's apartment, Nate held her in his arms. "Excellent performance from the Curtis cast tonight. And you sang so well. That's a tough role, and you definitely mastered it. You have gorgeous high notes, Lindsey. And you make all that difficult fioratura stuff sound easy. You have a real gift. I knew that when I heard you sing 'Sempre libera.' I really enjoyed being part of the audience."

"That means more than you know, Nate. Opera World is crammed with sopranos, though. It's not an easy journey."

"It's not an easy journey for any of us aspiring opera singers, baby."

"That's true...but if anyone can make it, I believe you can. I can't wait to hear you as Mercutio." She kissed him softly. "I'm going to have very mixed feelings about watching you die on stage. It's just a shame you have to get killed so early in the opera."

Nate laughed through his yawn. "Sorry. It's been a long day."

"It has. How lovely that we have all day tomorrow and part of Monday before you leave." Nate's eyes were closing even as Lindsey kissed him again.

She studied his face as he slept, looking for signs of fatigue. His schedule to this point hadn't been too heavy, but the coming month concerned her. Leaving in a few days for Hawaii to rehearse and perform Marcello, and then, after performing there, immediately flying to Seattle for rehearsals and performances as Mercutio.

I'd like to keep him here, take care of him, and make him happy, she thought. *But singing is what he was meant to do. I'll help him however I can.* She snuggled closer to him.

Without waking, Nate tenderly enveloped Lindsey in his arms.

Chapter 21

Two weeks later Lindsey flew to Cincinnati to see Merritt in *Madama Butterfly*. She found returning to her old "haunts" bittersweet, by turns pleasurable and sad. She stayed with the Nobles again, who seemed to have adopted her as a second daughter.

Being in the Corbett Theater as an audience member rather than on the stage seemed strange. She'd been on that stage every year for four years, and now, two years after Merritt and David's accident, she had come to see her brave friend step onto it without her for the first time.

Ethan held her hand when the curtain rose, and there was Merritt, resplendent in his white Navy uniform, moving around the stage with ease. Lindsey squeezed Ethan's hand hard, tears blurring her vision. He murmured, "I know."

Merritt was an ideal Pinkerton. The music fit his voice perfectly, he looked every inch a dashing American Navy officer from the last century, and the audience loved him. He'd been right in telling Lindsey he felt the role would be a "money role" for him. Even though he wasn't quite twenty-four, his voice showed new weight and maturity. *The perfect Puccini tenor*, Lindsey thought.

The soprano playing Cio-Cio-San—Madame Butterfly—was tiny and lovely, and her voice matched Merritt's perfectly in the lengthy and challenging love duet that ended the first act. Lindsey stiffened in anticipation when Butterfly and Pinkerton prepared to exit the stage. To her relief, they walked off slowly with their arms around each other, gazing into each other's eyes. Aware of her apprehension, Ethan murmured, "Much less risky if they're arm-in-arm. This works fine…and they're both gorgeous."

Pinkerton didn't appear on stage during Act Two, and Lindsey relaxed and relished the performance she was witnessing, imagining Nate singing the role of Sharpless, the American consul. She immersed herself in the luscious music in this act: Butterfly's aria "Un bel di"; the "Flower Duet" between Butterfly and her servant, Suzuki, and the lovely "Humming Chorus" that ends the act.

Merritt returned in Act Three, this time in a dark uniform, to sing an especially moving trio with Sharpless and Suzuki. After a three-year absence from Nagasaki, Pinkerton had returned with his American wife to take the child he fathered with Cio-Cio-San back to America. Heartbroken, Butterfly agreed to give up her son, but then took her own life. Pinkerton ended the opera with two desperate cries of "Butterfly!" as he ran onto the stage to find her dead. Merritt sank to his knees as the curtain closed.

Lindsey glanced at Ethan. "Fortunately, Butterfly is able to help Pinkerton get up for bows," he whispered in her ear. Later he explained to her how they handled the piece of stage business where Merritt sank to his knees. Butterfly's "body" lay downstage, and Merritt entered upstage running down to her. He went down behind her body with most of his weight on his left knee, balancing himself with the right knee. "We think we can figure out how to do just about anything the director needs, as long as they're willing to make small adjustments in staging."

The Nobles took everyone to dinner at La Normandie Restaurant after the performance, and Lindsey noticed an exchange that seemed troubling between Ethan and a man he encountered as they were entering the restaurant. She had a chance to speak with him about it the next day at the clinic while Merritt worked out under Molly's supervision.

"Was that a colleague who spoke to you last night? You seemed a little bothered by what he had to say."

"He's an attorney who does some public defender work. He represented the guy who was charged with David's death. I met him at the sentencing hearing. He was thanking me for attending."

"Did anyone from Merritt's family go? Or the Rosenthals?"

"The Rosenthals were there. Howard and Kathleen went. Merritt and Grace had no interest in going."

"What happened to him? The driver, I mean." Lindsey picked up a letter opener from Ethan's desk and began examining it. *I don't really care what happened to him*, she thought. *Why did I even ask?*

"He pleaded guilty. It's hard to believe, but he was only sentenced to two to eight years for vehicular homicide, and even though there were other charges he was also sentenced for, those sentences will be served concurrently. Chances are he'll be out before the turn of the century."

Lindsey sat silently for a moment, considering this. "He killed David, Merritt's life came close to being over, and now he's in jail for three years? That doesn't seem right at all."

"Well, he'll lose his driver's license for life, if that helps. And he apologized to the Rosenthals and to Howard. I have to say, he seemed genuinely sorry."

"One senseless act with so many consequences," Lindsey said.

"It happens all the time, sad to say. None of us knows when we might be a victim, Lindsey. We can't live in fear, though."

"True. And life goes on…Merritt is proof of that."

***

Nate called from Hawaii just before he departed for Seattle. "You know, I mentioned when I saw you in Philly that I'd like to get a laptop so we can email each other. Everything here in Hawaii is super expensive so I'll go shopping when I get to Seattle."

"That makes sense. We've managed without the luxury of email to this point, we can wait a little longer. But, oh, won't it be great when we can communicate every day?"

"It will be great." He sighed. "I'm not looking forward to this trip. Six and a half hours, and I still haven't learned to sleep on a plane."

"But you'll get there in plenty of time to rest before your first rehearsal, won't you?"

"Fortunately. When can you come to Seattle? You know I'll be there for three weeks."

"Yes, but I would so love to see your debut as Mercutio, so I'd like to come to that first Saturday performance on April 11. And I can stay until Monday. So, I can see the Sunday afternoon performance, too, and we'll have Sunday night together."

"That sounds perfect. When can you get here Saturday?"

"Call me when you get to Seattle and I'll let you know about my plans."

Lindsey was able to book a flight that would put her into Seattle-Tacoma Airport at four-fifteen west coast time and at the hotel by five. It would be cutting it a little close for a seven-thirty curtain, but she felt sure it would work.

On Saturday Lindsey arrived at the airport in plenty of time, boarded the plane, and waited for takeoff. And waited. And waited. Finally, an announcement to the passengers: due to mechanical problems of some kind, they were being put on another plane, and take-off would be delayed for at least another hour.

Lindsey called Nate at his hotel to let him know she'd be delayed in arriving. "It now looks like I won't get to Sea-Tac until after six your time. I know you have to be at the Opera House by six-thirty, right? Why don't I just go to the hotel, change, and head on over to the theater? You can leave my ticket at the box office, and I'll see you after the performance."

"I guess that's what we'll have to do. I'm disappointed, though."

"So am I. But remember, we still have Sunday. And if I can work it out, I'll change my reservation coming back and stay until Tuesday morning. I only have one class on Monday anyway."

"Well, that definitely makes this easier to deal with, baby. I've missed you like crazy."

That settled, Lindsey swallowed her disappointment and people-watched until her flight was called a second time. She noticed a family group nearby, an attractive older woman with a younger couple and their three lively children. The mother of the group resembled the older woman strongly and Lindsey guessed they were mother and daughter.

She found her seat on the plane, an aisle seat, and settled in for the long trip, deciding to attempt to nap if possible. *Maybe if I use Elliott's relaxation exercises, I'll manage that.* Ordinarily, she had the same problem Nate did about sleeping on a flight.

Lindsey had just dozed off when she became aware of a problem several rows ahead of her in the cabin. Two female attendants were standing in the aisle, addressing a passenger who seemed agitated.

The smaller of the attendants, a petite blonde, circulated through the cabin, asking something as she stopped at each row. She reached Lindsey's seat and asked, "Is there anyone here who speaks German?"

"I speak a little German," Lindsey volunteered.

The attendant—her name tag read *Joanne*—bent down. "We have a passenger who speaks no English who has become somewhat agitated. Unfortunately, no one on the crew is able to communicate with her. Would you be willing to try? We're hoping she isn't ill, which would mean an emergency landing, and we'd like to avoid that if at all possible."

I sure wouldn't want that, Lindsey thought. "I'll be happy to try. I don't know how successful I'll be, though. I've just had a few classes of conversational German."

Lindsey unbuckled her seat belt and stood, following Joanne up the aisle. "Can you tell me her name?"

"Frau Bergmann," Joanne replied, turning her head over her shoulder. When they reached the worrisome passenger, Lindsey sat down next to her, and she recognized the elderly woman she had noticed earlier in the terminal.

"Ich heiße Lindsey Cameron, Frau Bergmann. Sprechen Sie Englisch?"

"Nein, nein." A rush of German, and Lindsey picked up a few words: *Tochter, Flugzeug, erschrocken. Something about her daughter, airplane, being afraid.*

"Sprechen Sie langsamer, bitte," she requested, hoping Frau Bergmann would speak more slowly.

Another rush of agitated German, but spoken less rapidly as Lindsey had asked, and she gleaned that a daughter wanted her mother to fly to Seattle, but now she was afraid.

"I think Frau Bergmann may be having a panic attack," Lindsey suggested to the taller, dark-haired flight attendant standing nearby.

"Can you ask her if she's ill?"

"Sind Sie…" *what the heck is the word for "ill"? Oh, I remember. Krank.* "Sind Sie krank?"

Frau Bergmann clutched Lindsey's arm. "Nein, nein. Sind Sie Ärztin?"

Ärztin…doctor. No, I'm no doctor. "Nein, ich bin Opersängerin." *I am an opera singer.*

The frantic Frau Bergmann relaxed her grip on Lindsey's arm and managed a small smile. "Ach ja? Ich liebe die Oper." *I love the opera.*

"Ich auch," Lindsey replied, and Frau Bergmann positively beamed at her.

The flight attendants breathed a small sigh of relief. "She seems calmer now," Joanne remarked. "Can you ask if she's afraid because she's on the plane?"

"Haben Sie Angst vor dem Fliegen?" Lindsey asked.

Frau Bergmann nodded her head vigorously. "Ja, ja. Ich hasse es."

"She says she hates it."

A male attendant joined them, clipboard in hand. "Frau Bergmann is being met in Seattle by her daughter, who had requested we escort her into the terminal because she doesn't speak any English."

"No kidding," the dark-haired attendant said, raising an eyebrow.

Joanne addressed Lindsey. "Miss Cameron, would you be so kind as to change your seat and stay with Frau Bergmann?

311

She seems very comfortable with you, and you are able to converse and reassure her."

"I've pretty much used up most of my German, but certainly, if it will help, I'll be happy to switch seats."

Frau Bergmann seemed delighted when Lindsey settled in next to her. She chattered away in German and Lindsey picked up a few words, apparently something more about the disagreeable *Tochter* who had insisted she fly to Seattle from Philadelphia. But mostly she mentioned names of German composers and even specific songs. Songs Lindsey was familiar with, some she had even performed.

"Könnten Sie 'Frühlingsglaube' von Schubert singen?" Frau Bergmann requested, leaning eagerly toward Lindsey, who glanced at the interested onlookers watching this exchange.

"She'd like me to sing a Schubert song for her. Would that be all right?"

Nods and smiles from those nearest them. "Sure."…"Love to hear it."… "Sounds good to me." … "Thank the Lord you calmed her down."

Lindsey entertained their section of the plane for much of the remainder of the flight, continuing with more Schubert: "An die Musik," "Du bist die Ruh," "Wohin?," and "Der Lindenbaum," grateful she could recall all the words. Much to everyone's delight, Frau Bergmann sometimes sang along.

Just before they landed, another passenger began singing "Vienna, City of My Dreams" in English, and a surprising number of people on the plane joined in, some humming and others singing "la-la-la." They laughed and applauded themselves heartily when they finished the song. *Who would have ever guessed?* Lindsey thought. *Maybe Andre Rieu's orchestra is more popular here than I realized.*

Lindsey made sure Frau Bergmann deplaned safely and found the group waiting for her, much like the one she had left in Philadelphia: father, mother, two children, whose anxious faces transformed into smiles when they saw their mother and grandmother beaming at them. She warmly hugged Lindsey and explained in German to her family who the lovely young woman was that she had become best friends with on the flight.

"How can we ever thank you?" Frau Bergmann's daughter asked. "We were so worried about our mother flying cross-country. It appears that you made it enjoyable for her. You're a miracle worker, young woman."

Lindsey glanced at her watch, and her heart jumped into her throat. It was already half-past six. She couldn't possibly go to the hotel and change and make it to the Seattle Opera House before the curtain went up. She needed to go directly to the theater.

"There is something you could help me with." She quickly explained her dilemma and Frau Bergmann's daughter agreed to take Lindsey's luggage check and arrange to have her bag delivered to the hotel.

Well, talk about being under-dressed for opening night at the opera, Lindsey thought. *It can't be helped, though.* She at least was wearing dress slacks with her blazer, and a turtleneck with a gold pin. The new dress she intended to dazzle Nate with could keep until the next day.

She collected her ticket, asking at the box office if someone could please let Nathaniel Cohen know she had made it to the performance. In the ladies' room, Lindsey refreshed her makeup and ran a comb through her hair, then found her seat—sixth-row center section, almost in the middle. *Well, I'm here, Mercutio. I made it.*

The curtain lifted slowly on the ballroom, with the characters in a freeze. *Good heavens, Nate was born to wear*

313

tights. And boots. She squirmed in her seat, her pulse quickening. Seeing him on stage brought back all the romantic moments they had enjoyed together. As she had when he performed Marcello, Lindsey couldn't take her eyes off Nate through the first act.

Mercutio was quite a different character from Marcello, and as Lindsey had anticipated, Nate immersed himself in the character completely. A genius few opera singers possessed, to use voice, movement, and acting ability to bring a character to life.

Romeo and his friends exited the stage, clearing it for Juliette's aria, "Je veux vivre." Lindsey paid close attention to this, she was currently working on the aria with Madame D. and would be performing it at a student recital next month. The soprano sang beautifully, looked lovely, and acted well. *Another aspiring soprano in Opera World,* Lindsey thought. *And she is so good.*

The guests at the ball reentered, Romeo was revealed to be the son of Juliette's father's bitter rival and Romeo and his friends quickly left as the act ended.

The second act was the balcony scene which the tenor and soprano performed as well as any Lindsey had ever seen. *The Seattle Opera puts good people on its stage. This is an excellent production.*

Act Three, and Romeo and Juliette were married by Friar Laurence in the first scene. Nate as Mercutio would die in a duel with Tybalt in the second scene in the act, after which, as far as Lindsey was concerned, the opera might as well be over. The scene was exciting to watch, and Nate handled the sword with skill. His death scene was convincing and poignant. Mercutio lay dead on stage, and then Romeo killed Tybalt. The curtain fell, and the audience began to file out for an extended intermission.

Lindsey sat perusing her program when she heard her name spoken. "Are you Lindsey Cameron?" She looked up to see an usher leaning toward her. "Nate asked me to bring you backstage." She quickly followed the usher through the lobby, through the cast entrance to backstage where Nate, still wearing stage blood, pulled her inside a dressing room and kissed her hungrily.

She pressed herself close, savoring everything about him; the smell of stage makeup and sweat from the damp costume, the feeling of his strong arms holding her close, his lips moving restlessly over hers. Lindsey's head was swimming and she was tempted to pull him down on the floor, but she took a deep breath and leaned slightly away, gazing into his eyes. *Oh, those eyes. I could drown in them.*

"Does our hotel room have a king-sized bed?" She murmured against his mouth.

He chuckled. "I remember you saying at one time we could make do with anything." He held her away from him and his gaze took in all of her. "God, you are so gorgeous."

"I was supposed to be in this great dress, but that had to wait. I was lucky to get here in time for the curtain."

"You had quite a trip."

"You have no idea. I had an adventure on the plane. I'll tell you about it later."

"Why wait? I can't leave the theater until the opera is over, but once the next act starts, we can relax in the green room. Have you had anything to eat? We have snacks in the fridge." He had a sudden thought. "Unless you want to see the rest of the opera."

"I want to make out with you in the green room. And food sounds wonderful, I haven't eaten since...I can't even remember. A snack on the plane."

315

Nate took off the bloody jacket and hung it outside the door for the wardrobe people, grabbed his shirt from a clothes tree, and put an arm around Lindsey to steer her to the theater's green room. There were only two people there, and when Nate and Lindsey entered, they grinned, gave him a thumbs up, and exited.

"Well, that was interesting. I guess the entire cast knows your girlfriend would be at the performance tonight?"

"Something like that. Nice of them to clear out." He pulled her onto the sofa and kissed her again, causing her breathing to quicken.

"Nate...."

"I know. Food for now. Satisfaction of other hunger put off until we're in that nice big bed."

The refrigerator in the green room proved to be well-stocked with snacks and non-alcoholic beverages, and Nate and Lindsey rummaged and found cheddar and Havarti cheese and olives. On the counter, there were crackers and a stack of small paper plates.

They fixed plates, picked up bottles of water, and returned to the overstuffed sofa. Lindsey was starving and between bites of food described to Nate what had taken place on her cross-country flight.

"So you managed to help a woman overcome an anxiety attack and even enjoy being in the air," he said, studying her thoughtfully. "Lindsey, you seem to have a real knack for this kind of thing—for helping people."

"It made me feel good to see her in better spirits. Her family was certainly appreciative. They were nice, they agreed to arrange to have my suitcase delivered to our hotel so I didn't have to wait to pick it up."

Lindsey blotted her lips and wiped her hands. "Enough about me. How are you? You were dreading the trip from Honolulu to Seattle."

"It was about what I expected. I have to find some way to sleep on a plane if I'm going to continue this kind of schedule. Which I'm beginning to have serious doubts about, frankly. I felt I was off my game the first couple of rehearsals."

"How much do you have scheduled for the rest of this year, and how far ahead do you have engagements?"

"Auditions in Chicago and San Francisco next month, and then solos with the Dallas Symphony in late June. They want musical theater stuff and a couple of arias. Not much in August, thankfully, except two auditions here in the States, the Hartford Symphony and the Santa Fe Opera. I'm singing at the Brevard Music Festival in July—the Fauré *Requiem* and three numbers with the festival orchestra."

"What about in the fall?"

"Nothing past November at this point, and a fairly light schedule beginning in September. No lengthy flights." He swallowed the last of the cheese. "Oh, one more audition next month...the New York City Opera. That's one that I seriously hope I get. I doubt they'll offer me anything for this coming fall...but maybe they'll engage me for next spring."

"Wouldn't it be great if they engage you for the entire spring season? That might lead to also contracting you for next fall."

"Yes, that's my dream. Then I could use New York as my base, and I'd be assured of those two NYCO seasons. I'm not great as a continent-hopper. Of course...if I were invited to sing at La Scala or with the Royal Opera Company, I'd no doubt manage to accept those engagements."

"How about Australia?" Lindsey teased. "Or Japan?"

"Maybe you could work your magic on me and teach me how to relax and sleep on a plane that's flying above open water...which obviously makes me uneasy."

Intermission brought more cast members into the green room, and Lindsey was introduced and included in the light chatter that circled the room.

"I should watch the last scene," Lindsey said to Nate. She smiled at the people in the room and Nate walked her to the door leading into the lobby.

"Meet me here after, and we'll get a cab to the hotel." He kissed her and gave her a brief salute.

She watched the final scene from the back of the auditorium, impressed again with the fine performances of the tenor and soprano. *This is a good gig*, she thought. *But there are so many good singers around...it's hard to know how far either of these people will advance.*

***

At the hotel, they managed to control themselves until they closed the door to their room. Clothing flew everywhere. Nate picked Lindsey up and carried her to the bed, pressing himself hard against her body as he lay beside her.

Lindsey pulled him even closer. "You have a matinee to sing tomorrow," she gasped out as Nate embraced her ardently.

"Two scenes. One short aria," he murmured.

Lindsey's mind slipped sideways. She eagerly joined her body to his, rocketing skyward. He drifted off to sleep almost immediately afterward, which was unusual—Nate liked to talk after making love.

She scrutinized his face as he slept. She'd heard no signs of fatigue in his voice earlier, but she saw a few fine lines around his eyes and mouth. *Stress, maybe. Or maybe he is exhausted. I think this stint of traveling and singing hasn't been easy for him.*

She snuggled closer to Nate, loving everything about him. *Enjoy every minute of this time we have together,* she told herself. *You've had a long day…get some sleep.*

But her mind wouldn't turn off. *What do you want, Lindsey?*

I want to be with this man as much as I can. I want to support his dream however possible. I want to be in the audience listening to his glorious voice, I want him to have success in the world of opera so that many, many people can be awed by his brilliance, moved by his artistry, inspired by his passion.

I want that even more for him than I want it for myself.

Krissy Levin's words drifted into her mind: "Whatever you choose to do with the gifts you've been given, be true to the music—it can heal and inspire, calm and incite. It has the power to lighten the dark corners of the mind and soothe the pain of a wounded spirit or a broken heart."

What a sublime thing is music—whether shared with an audience of thousands or with one person who needs the healing music can provide.

Like Frau Bergmann. Like Michelle's little patients.
Like Merritt.

Susan Moore Jordan

Chapter 22

Once again, Nate's performance as Mercutio was a highlight of *Romeo et Juliette* on Sunday afternoon. And he was correct, when he sang, Lindsey heard no ill effects of their tryst the night before. They had the rest of the afternoon and evening to shut out the world and concentrate on each other. Lindsey cherished this time with her beloved, savoring his touch, memorizing his body, sleeping wrapped in his arms…making the most of their time together as she always did.

"I guess we should eat something," Lindsey said dreamily.

"We'll order room service."

"Nate…I don't want my visit to cost you so much," Lindsey protested. "We could run out and get one of those fish sandwiches Seattle is famous for, don't you think?"

"Our time in this hotel is a gift from my parents," he said. "They're footing the bill for this weekend. After you leave, I'll go back to the housing arrangement provided by the opera company."

"Oh, well, then, room service it is. Please thank your parents for me. This is so nice."

Nate had borrowed a portable CD player from a cast member, and during dinner, they listened to a new recording of *Andrea Chénier* he had brought with him.

"Someday, my love," Lindsey told Nate as they listened to Gérard's aria. "You will be so great in this role. What a thrill it will be to see you. I know I've already told you, but you sang so well today."

"I told you not to worry about that, didn't I?" Eyes twinkling, he pulled her down next to him on the bed.

A late breakfast on Monday was followed by a trip to a tech store in Seattle to purchase a laptop for Nate. They waited as the software was installed, including an email program.

Another customer, a dapper, elderly man, approached them hesitantly. "Excuse me…but aren't you performing at the Seattle Opera presently? In *Romeo and Juliet*?" He used the Shakespearean name rather than the French.

"Yes, I am," Nate smiled.

"You were Mercutio, right? You were outstanding." He extended his hand, and Nate took it. "Why haven't we seen you here in Seattle before?"

"This is my first time performing here. It's a great city, and your opera house is first-rate. The staff is so helpful and pleasant. I'm enjoying my time here."

"Oh, that's so good to hear. I hope you come back. I'd love to see you in a bigger role. In fact, I can see you in the lead in *Don Giovanni*."

"Thank you! That's a great compliment. I hope I'm invited back soon."

Lindsey observed this exchange with interest. Nate was unfailingly gracious when an audience member spoke with him. Of course, that was as it should be, but he always seemed genuinely appreciative.

She remembered his response when she asked him if he sang "Nemico della patria" for his Met audition. He had simply told her the judges liked it. No embellishments, no aggrandizement. And no false modesty. Nate had said more than once he was grateful for any opportunities that opened up for him.

After they returned to the hotel, she took his hands as they sat together on the bed.

"You know…you have a remarkable attitude about all of this." She waved a hand. "I mean, about what you're doing, attempting to get a career underway, and you've had unusually good success so far. But you don't seem…you handle everything easier than some people might."

"It's great when good things happen—like winning the Met audition, but it's not life or death, Lindsey," Nate said. "Maybe it comes from experiencing a crisis that *was* life or death."

"Someone in your family?"

"My mother, for one. She's a cancer survivor." He placed a hand on her shoulder. "She was diagnosed with breast cancer when I was a sophomore in high school."

Lindsey put a hand on the back of his neck and fought to keep from shivering. "Oh, Nate. I can't even imagine. But she's in remission?" *I never expected that. How awful.*

Nate relaxed his hand, but Lindsey realized this wasn't easy for him to talk about. "She's been declared cancer-free. That was the best graduation present I could have possibly received. She was an inspiration through the whole ordeal, and so was my dad. It was a tough few years, but the Cohens are strong."

"I understand. An experience like that helps you keep things in perspective." Lindsey sighed, caressing Nate's face.

"Well, it wasn't the first tough experience we had in the Cohen family." Nate looked away, his face troubled. "We lost my cousin when she was only twelve. She battled cancer for over four years."

Lindsey sat back and gazed at him, attempting to process this new information. "I would think that made your mother's diagnosis even more difficult."

"It did." He gazed into the distance. "The day Sarah died was the saddest of my life. We were the same age and had been playmates all through childhood. We were more like siblings than cousins."

Lindsey wanted to hold Nate in her arms and protect him from all the evils of the world, or wave a magic wand and erase what the Cohens had been forced to deal with. *No wonder he's so strong.*

Lindsey had a sudden thought. "'Sarah.' Your sister named her daughter after the cousin you lost, didn't she?"

"We had a big discussion about that. You can't replace someone, but you can honor them. That's what Lisa wanted to do."

Lindsey wrapped her arms around Nate, holding him close. "You've dealt with a lot."

His lips brushed her forehead. "It's helped me look at life differently than many people do. It kind of makes me sad that so many young singers have this feeling of…well, of entitlement."

He leaned back to gaze at her. "Why can't people just sing for love of the music?"

Lindsey felt a quiver in her stomach. "I'm embarrassed to tell you this, but those singers who seem to feel entitled? If it hadn't been for some people in my life who called me on it, I might have been one of them."

"I never saw that in you."

"Well…from the age of seven, I've wanted to be an opera singer. No, an opera star." She leaned up on one elbow. "By the time I was ten, it became apparent I had a better-than-average voice. I think I told you I started working with a teacher in Philly at that age. At first, I only saw her once a month or so, but by the time I was twelve, it was weekly. I had all those high notes from an early age."

"That's not unusual. Coloraturas often develop earlier."

"Yes, I know." She lay down again, gazing into his face. "But by the time I was in high school, it wasn't just 'I want to sing opera.' I was determined it would happen for me. No matter what."

"Well, it takes more than a little determination."

"That's true, but there's a…I guess there's a fine line. Thanks to M.J., and especially David, I managed to develop some sense of perspective. And of course, the accident made a big difference in my life. I'm doing better with that 'determined Lindsey' thing these days, so you haven't seen that character trait. Or maybe I should say character flaw."

Nate laughed. "Oh, I think I have. Remember, I tried to slow you down when I first came to see you in Philly. But you were impossible to resist, angel. And I was already crazy for you."

Recalling that first weekend, they reached for each other, and that was the end of talking for quite a while.

***

To: nacohen1998@aol.com
From: lindscameron@yahoo.com
Date: April 15, 1998
Subject: Stuff

Dearest Nate,

Now we can write whenever we want! I didn't know what to use on the subject line. How much I love you? How much I loved the weekend we just spent together? I won't say I miss you, even though you know I always do.

325

Being back at school took some adjusting, though. I'm working on the *Faust* aria, even though I'm not sure why Madame has me singing it. I doubt I'll ever perform Marguerite. Even so, I'll attempt to perfect it. I'd like to start working on another role, this time one I might perform somewhere, someday. Maybe Pamina in *The Magic Flute*? I can see myself doing that.

Wishing you all the best for the rest of your run as Mercutio. I'm so happy you agreed to come to Philly the first week of May! And I hope we can find more time in between your auditions in June. What about trying to get away for a long weekend somewhere? Let me know what you think might work.

Love, love, love!
Lindsey

***

To: lindscameron@yahoo.com
From: nacohen1998@aol.com
Date: April 15, 1998
Subject: Long Weekend

Hey Baby,

You're right, being able to communicate other than by phone is pretty nifty. We had a performance tonight and it went well. Nice to feel I've made some new friends and hope I'll be singing with them again somewhere. We have weekend performances and one more

Wednesday night show before I head home for a week or so, and then to Philly.

About that long weekend. I heard from my agent that he's arranged for an audition for the Opera de Montreal the first week of June. You're finished with school by around mid-May, correct? How about we make it a five-day visit to Canada? I know your uncle and his family live there and I'd like to meet more Camerons. Or in this case, Couvreurs. Let me know if June 2-6 would work so I can make reservations.

I can't thank you enough for coming to Seattle last weekend. You have to know how much it means to me to be with you.

All my love,
Nate

***

To: nacohen1998@aol.com
From: lindscameron@yahoo.com
Date: April 16, 1998
Subject: Montreal Trip

Dearest Nate,

I would LOVE to go to Montreal with you in June! And those dates definitely work. At this point, I really don't have any plans for the summer, other than coming to Brevard when you perform there.

Would you mind if I suggest to Merritt and Ethan that they come to Montreal when we are there? I promised Merritt not long after the accident that he and I would visit my Uncle Jean, only I got ahead of myself (I do that sometimes) and said maybe the summer of 1997. Well, no way could that happen, but it's only a year later.

I convinced Madame to let me learn Pamina. I'm excited about this! Papageno is in your repertoire, isn't it? So *The Magic Flute* is an opera we might perform together. And maybe someday I could be Zerlina to your Don Giovanni.

Off to school!

I love you with all my heart,
Lindsey

***

To: lindscameron@yahoo.com
From: nacohen1998@aol.com
Date: April 17, 1998
Subject: Montreal Trip

Hey Babe,

Sure, if you'd like to see if Merritt and Ethan can join us, that's fine. Just as long as it's understood we need time to ourselves, but they're pretty savvy guys and I doubt that even needs to be said. It'd be fun to sightsee with some other people who don't know Montreal the way you do because of your trips to see your uncle and his family.

My family took a trip to Toronto when I was in high school, but this will be my first time in Quebec. I can try out my college French. Or is it true what I've been told, there's a big difference in spoken French in Canada from what we learned in school?

Can't wait to see you in May. Not too far off.

All my love always,
Nate

***

Lindsey was hard at work on the role of Pamina in Mozart's opera *The Magic Flute*, but she couldn't get out of her mind Nate's story about his cousin's long illness and death. It made her think of those long-term pediatric patients she'd worked with in Cincinnati. She asked M.J for Anita's phone number and arranged to meet with her at a café near Rittenhouse Square.

Digging into cheesesteaks and fries, they caught each other up on their college activities and other adventures. Lindsey recounted to Anita the story of her trip to Seattle and how she helped calm Frau Bergmann down by singing German songs to her.

"A nice use of music to help someone, Lindsey," Anita smiled. "Not quite the same as your music therapy sessions with pediatric patients, though."

"No, not music therapy, but I liked the feeling of helping Frau Bergman overcome her anxiety by using music. It reminded me how much I enjoyed the therapy sessions with kids. I'm interested in knowing more about your profession, Anita."

Anita gazed thoughtfully at a french fry. "Don't tell me you might be thinking about not being an opera singer."

"Nothing that dramatic. I'm just curious about what you've had to study for this degree. I would think classes in psychology…but also medical courses?"

"You know I had completed my Bachelor of Music in Piano. That last year I also took guitar lessons, because I knew one requirement to be accepted in the music therapy master's program at either Temple or Drexel—or anywhere, I'm sure—was to perform two songs while accompanying yourself on guitar. As well as the same requirement with piano accompaniment."

Lindsey finished chewing a bite of her cheesesteak and swallowed. "Um. Never thought about that, but of course, a music therapist has to be a troubadour. Have guitar, will travel. I saw that with Michelle, the therapist I helped in Cincinnati."

Anita grinned. "You are thinking about this, aren't you?"

"Well, I don't know about that. But it is something I seem to be drawn to."

"Medical courses…I think they vary from program to program. Mostly psychology, psychotherapy, and counseling courses, though. What you'd expect, I think, from a profession that addresses healing from a mental rather than physical standpoint. Although I believe some programs require anatomy and physiology."

"Well, I guess those requirements make sense, though I have to say I wouldn't be crazy about the last two. Science was never my favorite subject."

Anita took a long drink of her soda. "You told me about singing some A. A. Milne songs for long-term care kids at a hospital in Cincinnati. Would you consider doing that again, this time with me, at Children's Hospital of Philadelphia? I'm there twice a week with kids ages seven to twelve. I need copies of the music so I can figure out a guitar accompaniment."

"You know, I would like to do that," Lindsey wiped her fingers and mouth with her napkin. "What days and what time are you there?"

"Mondays and Thursdays at eleven. That would be great, Linds."

"I'll get copies of the music to you tomorrow. How about next Thursday?" Lindsey stood and pushed her chair in.

"It's a date. I'll request a spot where we can meet early...maybe at ten? I'll buy you lunch after." Anita picked up a satchel, slung her handbag over her shoulder, and the two women headed for the door.

"You don't have to do that, Anita. But let's do have lunch. I may have questions."

Anita smiled warmly. "I'll give you the best answers I can, Lindsey. Welcome aboard."

"I haven't made up my mind about anything yet," Lindsey said as they stepped out onto the sidewalk. "Just doing some exploring."

"Internal or external?"

"Both."

***

There were eight children at the session. Most looked younger than twelve, but Lindsey wondered if that might be because of their illness. Anita had told her a little about them: most had various kinds of cancer. All had been in the hospital for weeks or even months. Most did not have a good prognosis.

As Michelle had, Anita began the session with a welcome song, introducing "Miss Lindsey" first, and Lindsey greeted each child by name after Anita sang to them. They broke her heart, such sweet, anxious faces wearing tentative smiles. She hoped for the next forty-five minutes the anxiety would be eased and the smiles less tentative.

One little girl of about eight or nine, in particular, caught Lindsey's attention. *She reminds me so much of Nate. I wonder if Sarah resembled her cousin.* A few wisps of sandy brown hair, just beginning to grow in after chemo treatments, and wide gray eyes, gazing at her hopefully and trustingly.

Lindsey helped Anita pass out the rhythm instruments, smiling warmly at each child and making a little joke about the instrument. She was rewarded with giggles, which delighted her and gave her the sense she was connecting with these children. At their practice session, Anita had taught Lindsey the simple song she now taught the kids. Lindsey circled the room encouraging them as Anita stood in the center, singing and playing guitar.

Time for relaxation exercises to music on a CD. Anita had allowed Lindsey to select the music, and she chose Fauré's "Après un rêve" performed by a cello ensemble. The warmth of the low strings performing this lovely piece seemed to her a perfect sound to help the children relax.

Anita had asked Lindsey to talk the children back after the relaxation exercise, and she moved slowly around the circle, speaking quietly, watching carefully, asking how hearing the music had made them feel. The anxiety she had seen in their faces had been erased, at least for the moment.

One little girl, Amy—the child who reminded Lindsey of Nate—said, almost in a whisper: "I felt like I was walking through flowers in bare feet." *A lovely image*, thought Lindsey.

Anita was listening closely, and commented, "Amy, that's a wonderful feeling. Did everyone hear what Amy said? That she felt she was walking through flowers in her bare feet?"

Some giggles, and another child, Joey, said, "I felt the same way, Amy."

Ah, remember this is meant to be a sharing time, Lindsey said to herself.

She told them she wanted to sing a song for them and asked how many knew who "Winnie the Pooh" was. All but one hand shot up. Lindsey explained this song had words written by the same man who wrote that book, so it was a poem for children and a song for children.

Anita and Lindsey passed out silk scarves to the group, Anita explaining they could stroke them in time with the music. Accompanied by Anita strumming the guitar, Lindsey sang through 'How Sweet to Be a Cloud' twice, the second time encouraging the kids to join in. They learned the simple song quickly, and eventually, Lindsey, Anita, and all the children sang it, sweetly at first, and then more energetically, and finally, raucously, leaving them all laughing.

Lindsey glanced around at the group, her heart swelling with the joy of watching these children laughing heartily. *We've given them a few minutes of joy this morning*, she thought, *a brief time to forget about what they have to endure daily for many months. Maybe years.*

Anita played a lively piece on the guitar, inviting the kids to again use their rhythm instruments. She next asked the group if they'd like to hear Miss Lindsey sing more, and they enthusiastically urged her to sing for them. She performed two more of the songs from the Milne collection, singing to each child as she circled the room. The smiles were broader now, to Lindsey's great satisfaction.

Finally, Anita and the kids sang their goodbye song, Lindsey joining them. She and Anita watched as the children left the room, some in wheelchairs, some on crutches, all moving with assistance. But they were chattering with each other, and some of the kids turned back to wave, thanking both women for making their day brighter with the gift of music. Several nurses, aides, and parents spoke to them before they left. "God bless you both. We can't thank you enough for what you do for our kids," one said.

Lindsey was quiet at lunch, processing what she'd just experienced.

"You were wonderful with the kids," Anita said. "They fell in love with you. You're a natural, Lindsey." She took a bite of her salad.

"It was quite something to work with them." Lindsey added a spoonful of sugar to her iced tea. "No, I don't think 'work' is the right word. To share music with them, and that's never work, as far as I'm concerned. It's my reason for being on this earth, I believe."

"To be a music maker, you mean."

"Yes, exactly. But I'm definitely learning there are many ways to do that. Performing music is one way, and it's what I've been pursuing much of my life. As much as I admired and appreciated my teachers, teaching is something I never felt drawn to. What we did today was...." she stopped, searching for the right word.

"'Fulfilling' is a good word," Anita said. "Feeling that you've touched a child in a special way with your music. And working with troubled adults provides the same feeling, maybe even more powerful in some cases. So many hurting people in this world, Lindsey, and so few of us to share with them this amazing gift."

Lindsey sighed and gazed into the distance for a moment.

"Thank you for this experience, Anita. It's given me a lot to think about."

Chapter 23

Nate and Lindsey wandered around the suite in the Ritz-Carlton Hotel in Montreal, feeling a little overwhelmed. When she called her Uncle Jean to let him know they would be visiting his city he immediately said, "I'd invite you to stay with us, but I'm sure you and your baritone would be much more comfortable in a hotel, away from delightful but noisy children. I'll make a reservation—and remember, you're there as my guests."

"Wow," Nate said. "Talk about luxury."

"Yes, Uncle Jean doesn't go halfway on anything. This is beyond lovely. This hotel is where he and Noémi were married. And get this, Pierre Trudeau attended the wedding reception."

"Pierre Trudeau?" Nate stared at her. "As in former Prime Minister of Canada Pierre Trudeau?"

"Yes. Him."

Nate's audition was scheduled for the following morning. They had been invited to the Couvreurs' for dinner and took a cab to Jean and Noémi's charming home in Old Montreal. Lindsey's young cousins were fascinated with Lindsey's boyfriend, and she found Nate's response to their attention just right. He spoke to them as equals, and he and André were soon fast friends. After dinner, Nate accepted André's challenge to a game of chess, and Toinette and Marie were avid spectators.

"Your parents told me how much they love Nate, and I can see why," Jake told his niece.

"I feel like the luckiest woman in the world, Uncle Jean. You're sure you didn't arrange for this audition?"

Jake put up his hands. "*Ma fille*, I am on the board of directors of the opera, but our policy is that we never interfere with artistic decisions. No, Nate earned this audition on his own. He's becoming known in the world of opera as an unusually promising talent."

"Well, last month he had auditions in Chicago, San Francisco, and with the New York City Opera—that's the one he's hoping for the most. If they offer him both seasons next year, spring and fall, he feels he could make New York his headquarters. Nate's not a fan of overseas flights, but of course, he wouldn't turn down the right offers."

Back at the hotel, they climbed onto the luxurious California king-sized bed, Lindsey wearing a nightgown, prepared for a chaste sleep the night before a major audition.

"I like your uncle and his family," Nate murmured drowsily. "All the Camerons are good folks."

He put his arms around Lindsey and rested his head on her breast. She held him and stroked his shoulders, neck, and head, as she heard his breathing become slow and rhythmic. She had been tempted to ask if she could attend the audition but knew it wasn't a good idea.

I'd love to hear him sing in an audition. No costume, lights, orchestra, yet he needs to sing so convincingly the artistic directors of this company—or any company—will want him on their stage.

They had breakfast brought to the room, and Nate ate very little. Lindsey observed him. *Not nervous, no...but he's mentally reviewing his music. Focusing on the characters.* He vocalized briefly, picked up his music case, and Lindsey straightened his tie.

"Bocca il lupo, amore," she told him. *In the mouth of the wolf, my love.*

"Crepi," Nate responded, kissing her softly. *May he die.*

He gathered her close for a brief but tight embrace.

So now, I wait.

She went to the hotel lobby and bought a newspaper, went back upstairs, and pretended to read it. Stood by the window and watched life happening in Montreal. Listened to music on her portable CD player. Stared at the wall. Watched housekeeping change the linens and the bed. Went back to the window in time to see Nate getting out of a taxi. Stood in the center of the room, her heart pounding, holding her breath when he strode into the room.

Nate grinned warmly. "It went well." He hugged her.

She leaned back, gazing at him. "That's it? 'It went well.' May I have just a little more information? They complimented you? They offered you a contract on the spot? What?"

"Very nice compliments." Nate loosened and removed his tie. "And they said I would definitely be hearing from them, meaning, of course, they'll be in touch with my agent. I'm hoping for a gig here in the next year or so." He took off his jacket and hung it up.

"You sang how many arias? Two? Which one first?"

"Yes, two…I did 'Nemico della patria' from *Andrea Chénier* first. Then they requested the Count's aria from *Nozze di Figaro*. Terrific pianist, skillful and sensitive." He took off his shirt and unbuckled his belt.

Taking Lindsey's hands, Nate led her to the bed. "Period of abstinence is officially over," he laughed, pulling her down to join him. "Oh, maybe we should put that 'do not disturb' sign on the door."

Lindsey complied, returning quickly as she removed her blouse and stepped out of her shoes. "You know Merritt and Ethan are arriving in a couple of hours. We have plans to go sightseeing this afternoon."

"That's then. This is now." He lifted her onto the bed.

***

Lindsey found Merritt outside seated on a stone wall, staring over the city of Montreal. What had begun as an enjoyable afternoon of sightseeing had fallen apart once they reached the Votive Chapel in St. Joseph's Oratory.

They'd climbed the steps to the Basilica and were enthralled by being atop Mont Royale, the highest point in the city. It meant a lot of walking and climbing, but Merritt declared it wouldn't be a problem for him, and he'd been fine. They admired the interior of the Crypt Church and entered the Chapel, immediately seeing a wall filled with what were called the "ex-votos": discarded crutches, canes, wheelchairs, and other items left by pilgrims who claimed to have been healed miraculously by St. André Bessette. There were hundreds upon hundreds of them, covering several walls.

Lindsey turned to speak to Merritt, but the expression on his face stopped her. A muscle worked in his jaw as he fought back tears. He turned abruptly and left the chapel. She glanced at Nate and Ethan, lifting a hand as she ran after Merritt. "Let me handle this."

She eased down beside him on the wall, not touching him. *I didn't think about how he might react to seeing those items*, she thought. *I should have prepared him.* Lindsey gently touched his shoulder and he didn't shake her off, but angrily brushed away the tears on his face.

338

"I should have asked if you wanted to come here. I am so, so sorry…it was a mistake. I never thought how you might react."

"You mentioned miraculous cures. No artificial limbs on those walls, though, are there?" He stared off into space. "I guess even saints have limitations."

Lindsey moved her hand along his back and rested it on his waist, embracing him. "Talk to me, baby." She could feel the tension in his body.

"Sometimes it's so damn hard, Linds." A hint of bitterness in his voice. "I know everybody tells me how great I am and how great I'm doing. I sure don't always feel that way." A heavy sigh. "I miss my leg. I hate being maimed. I hate knowing I'll have to spend the rest of my life dealing with a prosthesis."

An attempt at a laugh became a sob. "I still dream about my leg sometimes. Dream it's still there, and I'm running around, dancing, jumping, not having to plan every move I make."

"I would never have known any of this if you hadn't told me." She squeezed his waist again. "Do you talk to Ethan? I know he'd be able to help you."

"I try not to say much. He's been so good to me. He's been so good *for* me, he…he makes me feel like I'm a whole man as much as he can." Another deep sigh. "I try to listen to music when I start to get depressed. Sometimes it helps."

Lindsey was aware Ethan and Nate were standing at a distance, watching.

"Tell me how I can help. Would you like it if you and I had some time together so we can talk? I'm sure Ethan and Nate would respect that."

"Yeah, I really would." A slight grin. "They're standing nearby, aren't they? Waiting for a signal from Doctor Lindsey that I'm not going to fall apart."

Lindsey's laugh was as much from relief as from humor. *He's magnificent. I don't know how he does it.* "Something like that." She waved at the two men who moved to join them, Ethan standing close behind Merritt, hands kneading his shoulders.

"My apologies to all of you," Lindsey said. "I wasn't thinking, obviously. Coming to St. Joseph's Oratory is a big part of the standard Montreal tour, but I should have told Merritt what he'd experience and let him make the choice."

"No, it's okay. It's a pretty spectacular place, and the view from up here is incredible. I'm glad we came." Merritt kissed Lindsey's cheek. "You didn't do anything wrong, Linds. You were excited to show us Montreal."

"Why don't we climb down this mountain and find a place to eat?" Nate suggested. They took their time returning to the car, Lindsey and Nate walking a few steps ahead of Merritt and Ethan.

She glanced over her shoulder and spoke in a low voice. "Would you be okay with having dinner with Ethan, and give me a little time with Merritt? He seems to be having a hard time right now. And honestly, how could he not? It's only been a little over two years since the accident."

"Of course, babe. I know how close you've always been. He has to miss seeing you every day. And you've hardly seen him since you started school at Curtis."

In the car, Lindsey addressed her request head-on. "You know, Merritt and I don't get to spend much time together these days. After all those years of being in each other's pockets, it feels strange. Would you two gentlemen mind if maybe we got takeout and Merritt and I can go to your hotel room and…."

"What Lindsey's trying to say is that I need her to remind me life can be good, as only Lindsey can," Merritt interrupted. "She won't sugar coat anything. David taught us well."

"It's okay," Ethan said. "We get it. That best friend thing. Nate can fill me in on life in Opera World."

Once in Merritt and Ethan's hotel room, with orders of Montreal's favorite food, poutine—french fries topped with cheese curds and gravy—unbagged and devoured, Merritt stretched out on the bed and relaxed. Lindsey curled up in a chair beside the bed, kicking off her shoes.

"I don't like to say too much to Ethan, because he works so hard to keep me positive. But I know I have to accept that I'll never be a whole person again. Wearing a prosthesis is something that's now part of who I am." He stared at the ceiling. "Sometimes I get scared. I still want to have a career as an opera singer. Can I really do this?"

"You were fantastic as Pinkerton, Merritt. You had no problems at all creating the character and making him believable." She leaned forward. "I was kind of shocked when you said something about constantly feeling you have to plan every step you take."

He was quiet for a moment, resting an arm across his eyes. "Ethan says it will get easier as time goes on. I sure hope so. And really, after rehearsing the opera thoroughly, I was pretty comfortable during performances. But that was a college production, eight weeks of rehearsals on a familiar stage. What happens when I'm doing what Nate does? A strange stage, two or maybe three weeks to rehearse? Sometimes even less."

Lindsey sat on the edge of the bed. "Merritt, you're one of the strongest people I know. What you're attempting is definitely not easy. But if anyone can make it work, it's you." She lay down beside him. "Have you talked to your psychologist about this?"

"Dr. Evans? I don't see much of her these days."

"Maybe you should."

"You're right, I probably should." Merritt was thoughtful for a moment. "There's something else."

"Oh?"

"I wish I could get rid of the hate I feel for the driver who killed David. That's a negative I can't seem to shake."

"That's something else Dr. Evans might help you with. It's hard. I can't believe the driver is only serving three years, but that's what Ethan told me. I completely understand why you feel the way you do."

Merritt leaned up on an elbow. "The Rosenthals have forgiven him. They're saints. I just can't do it."

"The Rosenthals have forgiven him? They *have* to be saints." Lindsey considered this. "Well…maybe you and I both need to try to resolve our feelings about the driver. Please do talk to Dr. Evans."

She sat up and reached for her handbag, removing her CD player and headphones. "Here's something I can suggest that might help you when you feel stressed."

Merritt grinned at her. "Rachmaninoff Piano Concerto Number Three?"

"Not this time." Lindsey found the music she wanted him to listen to, handing him the headphones. It was the piece she had used with the pediatric patients at CHOP, Children's Hospital of Philadelphia, Fauré's "Après en rêve" with cello ensemble.

"Close your eyes, take some deep breaths. Relax as much as you can. Just let the music take you away. Stay relaxed and imagine you're at the shore."

"Beach." He corrected. "You sound like you're from Jersey, but I guess Philadelphians use that term as well."

"Whatever," Lindsey laughed. "Just listen, please. More deep, slow breaths. In through the nose, and out through the mouth. Now feel the sand under your hands." *I almost said feet. Big mistake.* "Feel the sun on your skin. Feel the breeze that touches your face. Hear the waves lapping on…the sand." Lindsey spoke in a soft, melodious voice.

Merritt began to breathe evenly, almost drifting off to sleep.

"Think of all the good things in your life. First of all, music. The gift you have to make music with that glorious tenor voice. The man who loves you more than life. Your family, who would do anything for you. This friend next to you who will do whatever she can to help you. What it could mean for other people to see you overcoming a handicap. To be an inspiration in so many ways."

They lay quietly until the music drew to a close.

"I get it," Merritt said dreamily, removing the headphones. "When I get anxious, make myself slow down and count my blessings. While listening to great music."

"Something like that." Lindsey slowly sat up. "It just kind of came to me that this could be helpful for you."

"Focus on the positive. Ethan says that often, but he's never tried to hypnotize me into doing it." A smile. "I said earlier I knew I would never feel like a whole man again. That's not completely true. When we make love, Ethan makes me feel like a whole man." He grinned. "Well, a whole man who happens to have one short leg."

Lindsey laughed in surprise. "Merritt!"

Merritt laughed with her. "Something I've learned in our support group. Humor helps. Lots of jokes about 'putting your best foot forward' and 'let's kick up our heels.'"

A light tap on the door and Lindsey went to let in the men who loved them.

Nate had a bottle of white wine in his hand, Ethan a box.

"Sauvignon blanc and cheesecake?" Ethan asked.

"Mais oui," Lindsey responded. "That sounds perfect."

Ethan sat next to Merritt, gently rubbing his arm. "Better?"

"Yes, you bet. Lindsey reminded me how lucky I am to have you, and she's right."

They enjoyed the wine and cheesecake and Lindsey and Nate said their goodnights, taking an elevator to their floor.

"When do you go to the Brevard Music Festival? Next month, right?"

"Yes, I'm there from July eighth through the twelfth. Middle of the month-ish."

"I think I'll take a week later this month and go to Cincinnati. I'd like to see David's parents and spend some time with Merritt. He's dealing with so much."

"Sounds as if he opened up to you." They arrived at their floor and left the elevator.

"He's concerned about his future. He definitely wants to pursue a career, but he sees a lot of obstacles. I know Ethan will do whatever he can to help him, but Merritt's unsure about whether he can handle the challenges. It has to be daunting, Nate."

Nate unlocked the door to their room.

"It does. But in the long run, Merritt has to make the decision about what he can handle, Lindsey." Nate took her in his arms, rocking her gently. "You're right. I don't like traveling much, but Merritt could have some real problems. His best bet might be to find a spot with an opera company in Central Europe—Germany or Austria. Or try for the NYCO, as I am. He may need to limit the engagements he accepts."

"It's pretty amazing what he's able to do. All that walking today, and he seemed fine. Ethan sees to it Merritt stays in great shape. They may both be facing some choices before long, though. Merritt's life would be a lot easier if Ethan were always with him, but of course, Ethan has his orthopedic clinic to consider."

***

The tour of Montreal resumed the next morning with a stroll through Old Montreal and a stop at the Cathedral of Notre Dame. A ride on the metro was obligatory as far as Lindsey was concerned, listening to the rubber tires hum musically each time their train started: a beginning pitch, up a fourth, up a fifth. Dinner that evening for all of them at the Couvreurs'.

Ethan, Lindsey, and Nate played board games with her aunt and cousins after dinner, while Merritt talked at length with Jake and seemed heartened by the conversation. On their way back to the hotel, Lindsey asked Merritt what he and Jake had talked about.

"His fellow patient while he was at Walter Reed—the pianist who lost his sight and whose hand was destroyed in Vietnam. A guy named Matt Geiger. Your uncle has been in touch with him. He's had a good life, despite his handicaps. A great life, in many ways. He's director of a classical music radio station that does a lot more than programming recordings. Because of Matt, that station provides live broadcasts of major concerts, as well as introducing young musicians in recitals. Matt does on-air interviews with a variety of musicians. He's also had a long and happy marriage."

"That must have been helpful for you to hear," Lindsey said, squeezing Merritt's hand.

"It sure was. And your Uncle Jean reminded me how music saved his life…and it was Matt who introduced him to the music he lives for."

Merritt and Ethan left the following day. Lindsey and Nate had a day and a half to themselves before saying *adieu* to Montreal, promising each other they'd come back to this lovely city—hopefully soon.

Nate had lessons and coaching sessions scheduled in New York and then would be heading to Texas for his performance with the Dallas Symphony—a summer concert in a park, where he would sing musical theater pieces as well as arias. Lindsey followed through on her plans to head to Cincinnati for a visit.

The Rosenthals were thrilled to see Lindsey and invited her to join them for dinner, also inviting Zivah. That was a reunion Lindsey particularly appreciated. The talk came around to the Rosenthals acceptance of the man Lindsey still thought of as "David's killer."

"A stupid kid who made a terrible choice," Arthur said. "I go to see him from time to time. He's trying to straighten his life out. That's tough when you're in jail."

"I don't know how you do it. I doubt I could even look at him," Lindsey said.

"I think you might feel differently if you knew more about Emmett," Leah said. "He came from an abusive home and was living on the streets for a couple of years. He didn't even finish high school."

"Yes, but recently he completed his GED," Arthur said. "And he's signed up for a couple of college courses."

"If he was out on the street, what was he doing driving a pickup truck?" Lindsey demanded. "And I wish you hadn't told me his name. I never wanted to know anything about him."

"It wasn't his truck," Arthur said. "He borrowed it from a friend."

"Stole it is more likely," Lindsey said tartly. "A 'friend'? Right."

346

"You're still angry," Leah said. "Don't you know, Lindsey, anger hurts the one who holds onto it much more than the person it's directed at."

"He is trying, Lindsey," Arthur added. "Time will tell whether or not he's able to make a different life for himself. What he needs is help. I don't mean financially, I mean emotionally. Spiritually. Something to help him find a new direction when he gets out of jail."

Leah and Arthur are much kinder people than I am, Lindsey thought. *I wonder if I can ever forgive this man for what he did to my friends. To me.*

***

Back in West Chester after a satisfying visit with her friends in Cincinnati, Lindsey needed to take stock of her life. *I've lost some time recently…I should have been in some kind of summer program this year. I can't lose another summer.*

Lindsey had several brochures at home from Young Artist Programs. Some were for summer programs, and she knew if she wanted to be considered for any of them next year, she needed to apply soon, no later than August.

And I need to find an agent one way or another. I know how Nate got his—winning the Met National Council Audition no doubt meant several agencies pursued him. I don't intend to compete, not this year. I know it's something Merritt is considering and I won't compete against him.

Her life had changed in many ways since *The Accident.* Lindsey always thought of it that way, a title for the moment that shattered three lives, the event that took David's life and changed Merritt's as well as her own forever. But it had been more than two years now, and she needed to focus and concentrate more on the career she wanted in opera. Being in

Nate's life she had witnessed first-hand what it entailed. *Not an easy life*, she thought. *You have to really commit to it.*

Searching through the information she had on hand, Lindsey decided the Glimmerglass Opera in New York appealed most to her. A summer commitment, which meant she also needed to plan something more beyond that. But at Glimmerglass, she might very well find an agent, since the singers who were accepted into these programs were considered singers with promising, marketable futures. *I'm not sure I appreciate being thought of that way, like a good piece of meat,* Lindsey smiled to herself. *But that's the way it is.*

***

Having a window seat on her flight to North Carolina in July meant Lindsey could watch the Blue Ridge Mountains and then the Smokies unfold below her as the plane traveled southwest from Philadelphia. Nate surprised her by greeting her, bouquet in hand, when she deplaned in Asheville.

"These are gorgeous. Is there some special occasion?"

"There sure is." He grinned broadly. "The NYCO has offered me roles for both seasons next year, spring and fall."

Lindsey squealed with joy and threw herself into his arms. "Oh, Nate, that's incredible."

"It's what I'd hoped for. So, I plan to look for an apartment in New York, probably in January, since I'll start rehearsals by February. I figure having a place to live in the city will be a good idea since there's a chance I could become a regular on the City Opera roster. That would be a dream come true."

They chatted happily as he drove her to the cabin the Brevard Music Festival had provided for his appearance there.

"This is very nice. Better than most motels," Lindsey said as she looked around.

"You remembered to bring sneakers, I hope. A lot of the paths aren't paved."

"I did. I also brought jeans."

Lindsey paid close attention to the chorus of high school students at that afternoon's rehearsal, recalling how much she enjoyed choral singing. *Fauré's Requiem is such a beautiful piece, and a joy to sing.* She and Merritt had been in the chorus during their freshman year at the Conservatory. The following year they'd performed the Verdi *Requiem*, more of a challenge and truly thrilling to perform.

Nate sang the baritone solos better than she'd ever heard them. *Or maybe it's just because I love him so much. But since I first heard him as Marcello, he's been my favorite baritone ever. He sings with such love of the music.*

Later that night, they lay close together, blissful in the afterglow of lovemaking. He stroked her hair, touched her face.

"I can't even tell you how much I love you, Lindsey. You've become a part of my life that I never want to lose."

Her breathing grew more rapid. She ran a hand over Nate's shoulders and chest. "You do have the most amazing body."

"As do you, my beautiful sweetheart."

Nate kissed her again, more urgently, and Lindsey responded, thrilled by the strength and warmth of his body against hers.

Susan Moore Jordan

Chapter 24

Since Nate had a free day and the use of a car, he suggested to Lindsey they play tourist and spend some time visiting Asheville. Nate attempted conversation as he drove, but Lindsey's mind was elsewhere. He finally pulled off to the side of the road. "Where are you, Lindsey? Not in North Carolina, I don't believe."

She laughed and kissed his neck. "I'm sorry, my love. Just thinking about all I have to do when I get home. I want to audition for the Glimmerglass summer young artist program, and I need to think about what I should do in the fall. I've been putting this off, for whatever reason, and now I have to scramble to catch up. It's a little scary, Nate."

"Not really." He put an arm around her shoulders and gazed into her eyes. "You have all the tools, baby. An unusually fine voice, for starters. I know you're a quick study and an outstanding musician. You do well with languages. You proved with Fiordiligi that your acting chops are better than good. And it doesn't hurt that you're drop-dead gorgeous."

Lindsey smiled. "Keep talking. You may convince me I'm on the right path."

"Why would you think otherwise? You must believe you have a calling to sing."

"Oh, I do. And it's what I've wanted all my life."

She kissed him again. "Now that we have that settled, why not go on and check out Asheville?"

"Are you saying you don't want to sit here and make out with me?"

"I doubt the North Carolina Highway Patrol would approve," Lindsey smiled ruefully. "I want to see the Vanderbilt estate and find someplace elegant to have lunch. Act like tourists for a little while."

***

Nate's performance the next day with the talented student instrumentalists in the Brevard orchestra was a delight. Mostly musical theater selections by the two soloists and orchestra. "The Impossible Dream" from *Man of La Mancha*, "Soliloquy" from *Carousel*, and "This Nearly Was Mine" from *South Pacific* were Nate's offerings. Lindsey thought they were perfect choices and he performed them splendidly. Apparently, the audience did as well—Nate was not just applauded, but cheered. She stood in the background and watched him interacting with audience members, graciously signing autographs and talking engagingly for over an hour.

He genuinely appreciates them, she thought. *David was like that. He liked people and he was loved by everyone. Nate has that same wonderful character trait.*

A magical walk through the starlit night to their cabin. They turned off the lights and slowly undressed each other, stars glimmering through the window.

"I loved hearing you sing those pieces," Lindsey said softly. "You managed to tell the whole story of the show in each of them. What a gift you have, my love."

"They're great songs. Which was your favorite?" He pulled her close, resting his cheek against her hair.

"The one from *South Pacific*. You broke my heart."

352

"Let me heal it." He lifted her onto the bed, and they savored one final blissful night in the quiet mountains before they had to go their separate ways the next morning.

At the airport, Lindsey's plane left before Nate's.

"It's getting harder and harder to say goodbye to you." He caressed her face as he gazed into her eyes.

"Then let's not. How about 'see you soon' or 'see you next time'?" Lindsey tried to keep it light as she swallowed back tears. "This was extra special, though. And the next time will be even better."

"Promise?"

"Promise. I love you so much, Nate."

A long, lingering kiss and she boarded the plane to Philadelphia.

***

Lindsey continued to learn and memorize the role of Zerlina, with the thought that *Don Giovanni* might someday be an opera she and Nate could appear in together, though the saucy Zerlina sidesteps the Don's amorous advances, which would eliminate onstage kisses. *Maybe a good thing*, Lindsey chuckled to herself. *Although I'd like to think we would be totally professional...well, we would try, anyway.*

She filled out her application for the Glimmerglass Opera Young Artist Program, listing the three arias she had selected. With her mother at the piano, Lindsey spent hours daily polishing each of these and managed to get to Philadelphia twice in August for lessons with Madame.

"Why aren't you considering the Met National Auditions, Lindsey? This is a strong program," Madame asked her.

"I'm not sure I'm ready for that, Madame," Lindsey said, knowing that wasn't entirely true. She had two friends who

353

would be entering, though…Kyla Page was also planning to try for the Met, with hopes she'd be accepted in the Lindemann Young Artist Program even if she didn't win the competition.

Lindsey knew Merritt would continue to work toward his audition. He had told her he didn't intend to audition for the Conservatory opera that next spring but was focusing on learning two complete roles over the coming semester…Rodolfo in *La Bohéme* and Des Grieux in *Manon Lescaut*. *Two more "money" roles for him*, Lindsey thought. But she also suggested he broaden his repertoire beyond Italian opera. He already knew Don José in *Carmen* but he needed another role in French, and something more contemporary.

She took advantage of being in Philadelphia and made a visit to the Academy of Vocal Arts, presenting herself as a potential candidate for study at the school. The people who spoke with her and gave her the tour were encouraging and definitely interested when they learned she was a second-year master's student at Curtis and had applied for the Young Artist Program at Glimmerglass.

Once school started, Madame had a class recital only three weeks into the semester and asked Lindsey to sing Pamina's aria from *The Magic Flute* along with a Schubert song she loved, "Gretchen am Spinnrade"—the dramatic and exquisite song that brought fame to the eighteen-year-old Franz Schubert. It was another song she had learned with David. *I'll never forget our sessions together. His understanding of music had such depth, and he taught me so much.*

She heard from Merritt about the arias he was considering for the Met National Auditions. "I guess I'll probably sing Rodolfo's first act aria from *La Bohéme*. It's got that sustained high C, always a show stopper. I need something in French, so 'The Flower Song' from *Carmen*. Maybe Tamino's aria from *Magic Flute* in German."

"I've never liked competitions, but you seem excited for this one."

"I'm looking forward to it. I think I have a good chance of moving on to Regionals."

"Meaning you think you're probably going to win."

"Well…you never know, but I feel good about the way I'm singing these days."

"How about the rest of you? I'm sure you're still spending time at the clinic."

"That's probably something I'll always do. I have to stay in shape. You know what, though, Linds? I do *not* want my status as an amputee to be a factor in my professional life, beginning with this audition. I guess the local people who run the audition will know about it, but I kind of wish the Met staff member who does the judging wouldn't."

"I doubt that will happen, Merritt. People like to talk."

Merritt sighed. "I know you're right. Well, whenever I'm on stage I'll just have to find a way to make whoever is listening to me forget that I have a fake lower right leg."

"You did that beautifully when you played the role of Pinkerton. You've got this, Merritt."

***

Lindsey kept in close touch with Nate with frequent emails and occasional phone calls. He had reported to the Florida Grand Opera the second week in September to prepare for his performances as Belcore in *L'Elisir d'amore*, a comic role she'd never seen him perform. After finishing there, back to New York and then the first weekend of October, the Brahms Requiem with the Hartford Symphony Orchestra.

When Nate first mentioned this engagement Lindsey thought she might be able to make it there, but then it looked as if it wouldn't work out. However, at the last minute, she was able to rearrange her schedule and booked a flight to Hartford for Friday. Nate had both a matinee and an evening performance, plus a third performance on Saturday night.

To: nacohen1998@aol.com
From: lindscameron@yahoo.com
Date: October 1,1998
Subject: Herr Brahms

My darling Nate,

I had hoped to make this a complete surprise, but it seems I need to let you know I will be in Hartford tomorrow to hear you sing Mr. Brahms' luscious Requiem. My plane gets in fairly early in the afternoon and I know you have a matinee, so I'll just get to the hotel (I reserved a room with a king-sized bed at the Sheraton) and eagerly wait to hear from you. Unfortunately, I wasn't able to get a ticket for tomorrow night's concert, though I did manage to find one for Saturday. Perhaps the orchestra has a few tix put aside for Friday night for a surprise guest of their star baritone soloist?

So, SURPRISE! We will have most of the weekend together!

Love x100!
Lindsey

***

To: lindscameron@yahoo.com

From: nacohen1998@aol.com
Date: Oct, 1, 1998
Subject: Herr Brahms

Hey baby,

Mr. Brahms and I were both super happy to get your email!! I've been missing you like crazy because we talked at one time about your being able to be with me this weekend, but then it didn't work out. How great that I'll see you after the matinee performance tomorrow! I plan to help you make the most of that king-sized bed.

Yes, I checked with the house manager (she's pretty cool) and she's going to put you in a great seat Friday night. Can't wait to see you!

Love x1000,
Nate

***

Room service for a light early dinner consisted of omelets, bacon, biscuits, and fruit. The lovers had healthy appetites after their as-always passionate reunion.

"Don't forget, we have a buffet reception tonight after the concert," Nate reminded Lindsey. "Great people here in Hartford. They couldn't be nicer and more helpful, and the orchestra is quite good. The chorus is exceptional. I know you love this piece."

"My dad's favorite piece of music. He told me more than once how much it meant to him to sing it after he came back from Vietnam. He said it reconnected him with the good in the universe." Lindsey licked honey from the spoon she'd used to drizzle it on her buttered biscuit.

Nate stopped in mid-bite. "You never told me he sang the Brahms Requiem. How did that happen?"

"Well, Dad was completing his undergrad degree in art at West Chester University. Mom had just started on her master's in music. The college choir joined other colleges in performing it with the Philadelphia Orchestra."

"How about that? I'm sure he's a fellow baritone." Nate took another forkful of omelet and bacon.

"He is, as far as I know. I don't recall hearing him sing."

At the theater, the lights dimmed and Lindsey, seated in the fourth-row center, settled into listening to Brahms' ethereal *Ein Deutsches Requiem*, performed tonight in the original German. Her favorite sections included those in which the baritone was featured, but she loved equally the second movement of the work. Rather than using the traditional Roman Catholic mass as his text, Brahms had selected passages from scripture, all of which pointed to the hope of a life beyond this one. It was a work Lindsey had heard all her life.

The final movement ended in total silence for a moment, then the applause began and swelled as the audience stood. Lindsey again had the feeling she'd made a journey to Somewhere Else...somewhere indescribably sublime. *I wish there were some way to share this experience with more people,* she thought. *Knowing how vast and wonderful the universe is— and that it's filled with music.*

They had all day Saturday, another concert Saturday night, and Lindsey's flight didn't leave until after noon on Sunday. Nate would be spending the next two weeks in New York with his coach, memorizing the role of Ping in *Turandot*, and then two weeks of rehearsals in New Orleans plus two weeks of performances.

"Oh, I would so love to see you in *Turandot*. One of my best memories is singing in the chorus of that opera. What a thrill."

"Hopefully I'll sing it again sometime. You're a busy lady these days, I understand."

"I haven't given up yet. I may make it happen."

"That would be great, but I don't want you to go crazy trying to push it."

"You're looking at 'determined Lindsey' right now, Nate. And you know how dangerous she can be."

He chuckled and pulled her close. "You mean the lady I heard about who picked up Merritt's wheelchair with one hand? Ethan told me that story."

"One and the same. See you in New Orleans, if it's at all possible."

"That's my Lindsey," he murmured as he pulled her still closer.

***

Despite Lindsey's best efforts, much to her disappointment there was no way she could work out a weekend trip to see Nate in *Turandot*. He planned to be with her in Philly over Thanksgiving, though, so she was looking forward to that.

Two weeks after Lindsey's trip to Hartford, Madame D. beamed at her when she arrived at the studio for her lesson.

"I have some exciting news. You've been offered a professional engagement. The Philadelphia Orchestra, as you may know, is performing *Hansel and Gretel* in English for special children's concerts during the Christmas holiday, and they've offered you the role of the Sandman. That's quite an honor and I encourage you to accept."

Lindsey nearly dropped the armful of music she was holding as she gasped, feeling a flutter in her chest. "Of course, I'll accept! What a fantastic opportunity, and it certainly is an honor. How much fun will that be!"

They went through the charming solo during Lindsey's lesson and it was clear she was familiar with the music and it wouldn't take much to perfect and polish it. Lindsey was excited, this brief but delightful role would be a new challenge for her as an actress. She immediately made an appointment with Elliott to work on the character with him.

Later that week Lindsey had another gratifying moment when the cast announcement for *The Magic Flute* appeared. She was to share the role of Pamina in the March production. There would be a total of six performances and she would sing half of them. *More Mozart. Maybe I am going to end up being a Mozart soprano. Fun music to sing.*

Lindsey heard from Glimmerglass that she had been accepted for an audition, which was scheduled for New York City in mid-November.

Reading the notice made her stomach tighten. *Ugh. I'm not a fan of auditions, but I guess I have to get used to this. I'll have to do it again for AVA early next year, I think. Well, it's part of my life for the present, so I'd better be ready to sing. All I can do is be well prepared and sing the best I can. And pray I'm in good health that weekend.*

***

How do you behave toward competitors when they are singers probably as good as you are and you've never seen them before in your life? Be gracious, Lindsey.

Smiles…some genuine, some forced…and introductions: "Where are you studying?".… "What roles have you done?".…

360

"Are you doing the Met auditions for this year?".... "Where else have you applied?"

Nowhere, thought Lindsey. *I've only applied to Glimmerglass. For me, it's either this or nothing. Maybe that was a big mistake, not applying to more YAP programs.*

Waiting to be called, Lindsey heard some fine singers. Most were a little older than she was, and some had done summer programs with other opera companies the year before. She struck up a conversation with a tenor who reminded her a little of Merritt. He was a graduate of Juilliard who had been with the Chautauqua Opera the past summer.

"What are you doing now? Are you in a doctoral program somewhere?" Lindsey asked.

"Not really. Pick-up work around the New York area. I'm still studying with my teacher at Juilliard. I have a good church job that pays well, and I've done extra chorus for the New York City Opera. I've been an office temp once or twice. Other stuff so I can pay my rent and eat." He said all this matter-of-factly. "I'll bet a lot of people here have stories very much like mine. We want to sing. And some of us will make it."

Lindsey realized more than ever how fortunate Nate had been. She heard the tenor's audition and was impressed. *Wonder if he's tried the Met auditions yet,* she thought. *But I don't think he's as good as Merritt.*

To her surprise, the audition board requested to hear all three of Lindsey's arias, and she knew from listening outside that the norm was two. *Well, either they like me, or they can't figure me out,* Lindsey thought. She was thanked for auditioning and left to her own devices.

Mary had come to New York with Lindsey but stayed at their hotel while she went for the audition. Lindsey finished earlier than she had thought she might and stayed for a while, listening to more people audition.

She has a lovely voice, she thought of one soprano who sang two of the same arias she had. *But I don't agree with her interpretation. Well, it's a crap shoot. I guess I'll hear something early next year. Why am I doing this, again?* She giggled nervously at the thought.

Lindsey took a cab to their hotel and she and Mary prepared to go to dinner. "Thanks for coming with me, Mom. You being here has definitely made this easier. I haven't been in a competitive audition…well, at least not like this one."

She leaned close to the mirror as she re-applied lipstick. "My audition at the Conservatory was different. And the same with my auditions for graduate school. Neither had the pressure of hearing all my competitors. Is this what they call in show business a 'cattle call'? I'm lucky you're supporting me in this. It definitely eased the stress."

"Lindsey, you know your dad or I will always be here if and when you need us. This was a first. The next one will be easier if you decide to enter a competition again."

Lindsey shrugged into her coat. "I heard a lot of talented sopranos trying to do exactly what I'm hoping to do. We're not all going to make it."

"Yes, but some will…and it could very well be you."

They caught a train back to Philadelphia the next morning, where Mary took a connecting train to West Chester. Lindsey called Nate that evening.

"I really dislike competitions," she told him. "Maybe you don't—you certainly did well with your Met audition. But you went through this when you auditioned for Glimmerglass."

"I liked meeting the people who were there. I knew I'd be working that summer with some of them."

"You were pretty sure they'd hire you."

"I felt good about my audition, yes. And I found the process intriguing. Met some terrific people and as I told you, I had an enjoyable summer with them."

"That's nice for you. I heard a lot of sopranos who were really good. My competition."

"Lindsey, maybe you should try to think of them as colleagues rather than competition. You'll never be the only soprano on the block, so to speak. You might get to like them if you made an effort."

She was quiet for a minute. "I know you're right, Nate. There aren't any one-woman operas that I'm aware of. I had thought I was over myself, but I guess not."

"Remember what a great time you had with Kyla in *Così*? You seem to be doing a lot of Mozart, and in nearly every one of his operas there are two or three female leads."

"Kyla is a mezzo," Lindsey said automatically, and Nate laughed. "Okay, I know you're right. If you and I ever perform *Don Giovanni* together, I'll be one of three sopranos you're entangled with. We might become good buddies if bad Lindsey doesn't get in the way."

"There's no such person as 'bad Lindsey,'" Nate said warmly. "All you have to do is be the woman I know and love."

"I'll try to hang on to that." She walked to the window, looking out onto the city. "The last thing I want is to be considered a prima donna."

"Well, my darling prima donna, I can't tell you how much I'm looking forward to Thanksgiving. I'm sure we'll be with your family for at least part of Thanksgiving Day, but I hope to have you all to myself the rest of the time."

"That's the plan. We'll stay at my apartment and come up for air occasionally. And go to West Chester to stuff ourselves."

They said their goodbyes and Lindsey stretched out on her bed, aware of the faint sounds of traffic below.

And now I wait to hear from Glimmerglass, she thought, hoping it's true that good things come to those who work hard. *If I'm accepted into this program, will it mean I'm on my way to becoming a professional opera singer within the next few years? Or could I end up in the same boat as the tenor I met at the audition...struggling to do whatever is necessary to try to break into the world of opera?*

Chapter 25

In early December Lindsey had a phone call from Anita. "We have a Bonny Method Guided Imagery and Music therapist coming to demonstrate the technique. I could get you in to observe, if you'd like."

Focused on her plans for the future, Lindsey hadn't thought for a while about her experiences and conversations with Anita about music therapy. This call reminded her how intriguing she had found the Bonny Method.

"I'm super busy...but I would really like to be there if I can." Lindsey decided to cut one acting class to see exactly how this technique was used with a patient.

She found it fascinating from the first moment. The practitioner, a man in his forties, talked for a while with his patient, a woman Lindsey guessed to be in her fifties, eventually asking her, "Where would you like to go today?" Lindsey recalled in these sessions the therapist was designated as the "guide" and the patient as "the traveler."

"I need to find a way to reach out to myself as a teenager and let her know to love herself more, and not dwell on a mistake she made," the patient said, offering no further explanation.

Something she still carries with her? I wonder what that could be.

The patient lay comfortably on a cot with blankets and pillows, and the therapist provided music and gently guided her into a different level of consciousness. For the journey, the therapist had selected sections of Edward Elgar's *Enigma Variations*—complex orchestral music which had moments of excitement and moments of calm intertwined. The therapist occasionally asked the patient, "Where are you? What are you seeing?"

In this state of altered consciousness, the patient answered lucidly and in some detail. She was walking through a dense forest, with sunlight sometimes breaking through the trees. In the distance, she could see a white building of Romanesque design.

"What are you feeling? What are you hearing?" The therapist asked.

"The air is cool but pleasant, and there are wonderful fragrances…pine, a hint of flowers. I hear wind in the treetops and feel a gentle breeze along the path."

She came closer to the building, and someone emerged. "I can see myself as a young girl," a voice trembling with emotion.

"How does she appear to you?"

"She looks troubled and sad. She's been crying."

"Have you spoken with her as yet?"

Silence for long moments, then a look of strain on the face of the patient. "I'm talking with her now. We're walking together."

A change of music, this time the second and third movements of Rachmaninoff's second piano concerto.

"We're discussing what happened…and she is finally able to let it go," the patient responded to yet another question by the therapist. "The air seems a bit warmer. I see more flowers along the path. My younger self reaches down and picks a few."

"Are you still talking?" the therapist asked.

"We were, but now she is waving goodbye and I'm moving forward through a clearing. There's a pleasant breeze. I feel the sun on my skin."

Once the music ended, the therapist helped the patient return to a fully conscious state, and they discussed her "journey," using some art tools to help the patient express what she had experienced. They worked together to create a mandala, an intricate circular design that showed elements of the experience the patient had just undergone. She was obviously very much at peace.

Lindsey went to her apartment excited by what she had observed and listened to the music that was the most meaningful to her—Rachmaninoff's third piano concerto.

While it was playing, she did something she'd been meaning to do for a while. An important phone call.

"Merritt, I think you need to let go of your anger toward the young man who injured you."

"Are you talking about the lowlife who killed David? I'm a hell of a lot more than angry at him, Linds. I hate the bastard's guts."

"It could be holding you back. He's not feeling your anger. But you sure are."

"Where's this coming from?"

"We've discussed this before. Anger is a totally negative emotion. You just don't need it in your life, Merritt."

Silence on the other end of the phone. "I don't know how to do this, Linds." A sigh. "I'll talk to Dr. Evans about it."

"That's all I can ask you to do. I wish I could help you. I'm not angry at him anymore. I feel sorry for him. I'll bet the poor slob has never experienced the kind of music you and I love."

"I hear music in the background. You're listening to the Rach Three, aren't you? Thinking about David."

"Yes, and remembering how kind David was. Unfailingly. Except of course to you and me when we got on our high horse."

Merritt had to laugh. "He could really set us straight, couldn't he?" A pause. "I promise you I'll talk to Dr. Evans. That's the best I can do."

"I can't ask for more. I love you."

"I love you too, Lindsey. Go back to Rachmaninoff."

***

Once again, Lindsey's busy schedule meant she was unable to fly to Atlanta to hear Nate sing in Vaughan Williams' Christmas choral/orchestral cantata, *Hodie*—a disappointment for both of them.

Anita called and asked if Lindsey could go with her to spend time before Christmas with some pediatric patients at Children's Hospital of Philadelphia.

"I wish I could, but I have an unusually busy schedule right now. I don't see any way I can manage it. I'm sorry."

"That's fine, I know you have a lot going on. Maybe sometime after Christmas you'll have a little more time."

"Yes, that's possible. I'll call you next month. Have a good Christmas." Lindsey felt a little guilty when she hung up the phone. She had loved the time she spent with Anita's kids. *I wonder how little Amy is doing? The little girl who reminded me so much of Nate.* But she had rehearsals with the Philadelphia Orchestra for *Hansel and Gretel* on top of her already busy schedule.

Nate managed to get to Philadelphia to see a performance of the shortened version of the Humperdinck opera.

"You make a charming Sandman, baby," he told Lindsey, brushing back a lock of hair from her face—a familiar gesture that Lindsey loved.

"I've really enjoyed doing this. So much fun to perform for all those children. And just think, some of them would never hear an opera if the orchestra didn't make this available to them."

"It's an important service to our art form. Audience building. We need all the audience members we can get," Nate laughed.

Nate's visit was brief, but they were able to spend more time together over Christmas and even took a train into New York to see a performance of *The Magic Flute* at the Met. Another production offered with children in mind, performed in English and shortened. Lindsey paid close attention to the performance of the soprano playing the role of Pamina, a role she would perform in just a few weeks. Nate insisted that Lindsey would be just as good, "but prettier."

A night at a New York quality hotel followed their enjoyable afternoon. "You're spending too much money again," Lindsey sighed, her head resting on Nate's chest.

"It's only one night. Besides, you're worth it." He stretched and yawned. "You know I start rehearsals in late January with the NYCO. Can't wait. I want to look for an apartment next month when I'm here for rehearsals and coaching."

Lindsey snuggled against him. "I'm looking forward to seeing my Marcello again."

He leaned up on an elbow. "Did you fall in love with me or Marcello in that performance in Cincinnati?"

"Both." She pulled him down. "I was so envious of Musetta in that performance when you picked her up."

Nate's ardent kiss ended the conversation.

369

***

When Lindsey returned to West Chester from the weekend in New York, she had a phone call from Jake which presented her with a new possible next step in her career.

"*Ma jeune chanteuse*, I'm calling to let you know about something which may interest you. What are your plans beyond graduation from Curtis?'

"I auditioned for the Glimmerglass Opera in Cooperstown, New York, and I should know by mid-January if I am to be on their roster. After that, I'd thought about applying to the Academy of Vocal Arts here in Philadelphia."

"You haven't made a commitment beyond next summer?"

"No. Why, Uncle Jean? What's going on?"

He explained he was a member of a newly formed association which had been planning for more than two years to create a touring opera company. They intended to hire singers looking for performance opportunities following their college training. Target audiences would primarily be school-age children with many performances in schools, though sometimes larger venues would include all ages.

"*L'Opéra Jeunesse de Montréal* will tour throughout Quebec and elsewhere in eastern Canada beginning in the fall of 1999. Applications will be announced next month, and those singers in the States who are selected will audition in either San Francisco or New York. I wanted to let you know. and perhaps you might also like to alert other of your colleagues to this opportunity."

Lindsey managed to keep from squealing and instead asked casually, "Can you tell me a little more about the company? What operas will be performed and how long will the season be?"

"It will be a full company, with singers, stage crew including costume people, two pianists…one of whom will be a conductor for those stops where instrumentalists might be included in the performances. The season will begin in mid-September and there will be a break from mid-December until mid-March. That may be something of a problem for some people, but we will give preference to singers who can commit to the entire season, mid-September through mid-June, and accept the three-month break. We believe it's necessary because of the severe winters we can have in this country."

"I see."

"It *will not* be constant travel, set up, perform, tear down, and on to the next performance. I'm aware that's the routine with some smaller touring companies, and we want to avoid it. We're working on a 'performer-friendly' schedule with reasonable travel time and downtime so we don't exhaust any of the personnel. We'll provide adequate pay and also cover all travel and housing expenses for the company."

"It sounds amazing," Lindsey said, allowing herself to be enthusiastic. "How many operas will be performed?"

"Four total—*Nozze di Figaro, Hansel und Gretel, The Merry Widow* in English, and *The Magic Flute*. All roles will be double cast."

"All to be performed in French?"

"French or English. That's to be determined."

Lindsey could see roles for herself in every opera. "Oh, Uncle Jean, it sounds ideal to me. Exactly the kind of thing I would absolutely love to do."

"I thought you might be interested, *ma fille*," he said. "Be aware, you'll be performing in just about every kind of venue imaginable, often with two pianists, but on occasion with instrumentalists and a few times with a full orchestra. You'll certainly get to know this part of Canada."

"You've never even mentioned this to me before," Lindsey said.

"I didn't mean to be secretive, but until we had all funding and at least some commitments for performances, we agreed better to wait and announce at that time. Now we're ready."

"When can people begin to apply?"

"Applications will be available the first week of March. Auditions will be held in early May, and singers will be notified promptly if they're being offered a position. Within three weeks."

"I think it's perfect for me," Lindsey said. "Oh, I probably shouldn't say that, should I? But yes, yes, yes, I will definitely apply to the company. And hope I win an audition."

Jean laughed. "It's nice to hear you excited about the idea, *ma petite*. I hope we'll have many enthusiastic applicants."

"I can almost guarantee that you will. So many eager singers, so few places to sing. I'll pass this information on to friends."

"About Merritt." Jean paused. "I'm not sure this is something he should undertake, Lindsey, though I would love it if he could join us. It will be a lot of traveling and performing on different stages with very little rehearsal. You might talk to Ethan."

"I'll do that, Uncle Jean, I'll talk to both of them, but I believe you're correct. Merritt will always have to be careful and I think will always need time to feel completely comfortable on a stage."

After they completed their conversation, Lindsey did a happy dance around her apartment, stopping abruptly. *Oh, definitely, that's the program I'd love to be part of. How exciting. But I think I made a mistake by only applying to one summer program…it might be best to go ahead and look into the Academy of Vocal Arts as well as the Canadian company.*

She sighed as she gazed out of her window onto the city street below. *Navigating the opera business is definitely challenging. And as Nate said, 'there are no guarantees.'*

When Lindsey called Merritt to let him know about the new opera company headquartered in Montreal, he'd at first been enthusiastic about what sounded like a great opportunity. But he called her back a couple of days later and expressed reservations about his ability to participate in that kind of situation.

"It's the thing about having no feeling in the foot that isn't there. Not being able to feel the stage floor. It's one thing when I can rehearse numerous times on a stage and go out on that stage before a performance to be sure nothing could impede me from moving around easily. But from what you've told me, this tour might include times when it would mean a quick rehearsal…maybe not even a full rehearsal…just before some performances."

"That's my understanding. I think the directors of the company will be as 'performer-friendly' as they feel they can be, but yes, that could happen. And I understand why you would hesitate to make such a commitment."

"Even with Don José, a role I love and definitely want to attempt again, I have some reservations. A lot of very physical scenes in the opera that would have to be carefully planned and rehearsed."

"But under the right circumstances, and with the right director, I'm sure you'll do that role again, Merritt."

"Sometimes I wonder, Linds. I try to stay positive, but it's not always easy." A pause. "I've done something I needed to do, though. You know how you've been urging me to let go of my anger towards Emmett—the driver who hit David and me?"

"Emmett? I didn't know you even knew his name."

Merritt sighed. "Well, after you talked to me, I had a session with Dr. Evans, then I talked to the Rosenthals. And then I went with Arthur to visit Emmett."

Lindsey gripped the handset. "Oh, Merritt. That couldn't have been easy, baby."

"Not as tough as I had thought, and you were right. He's a guy who has had a dismal life, Linds. He made a horrible mistake and David and I paid the price for that. But I think Emmett is paying even more of a price. He lives with the guilt every day…every minute."

"That's terribly sad."

"It is. He begged me to forgive him…and I was able to." Another pause, and then a brighter tone of voice. "You know what? It was like there was this dark place inside me somewhere that I hadn't even known was there. And now it's gone."

Lindsey's voice shook when she said, "You did a good thing, Merritt. Good for Emmett, but even better for you."

"Yeah…I'm at peace about that now. And I'm focused on my Met district auditions for next week."

To no one's surprise, the following week Merritt placed first in the Metropolitan Opera National Council Auditions district competition in Cincinnati and was scheduled to compete in the regional audition at Indiana University in March. When Lindsey called to congratulate him, Merritt sounded excited and confident.

Well, as Ethan would no doubt say, it's a process. Merritt's disability isn't going to just disappear, it will be a constant struggle throughout his career. I'll do whatever I can whenever I can to help him.

***

The second semester at Curtis didn't begin until near the end of January, but Lindsey was back in Philadelphia to resume lessons and coaching early that month. Much to her delight, she received a nice thick envelope from Glimmerglass Opera the second week of the month offering her a position in the summer Young American Artist Program.

She looked over the list of operas and her assignments with interest. As well as being in the chorus for all four operas being performed, Lindsey would cover—understudy—the role of Zerlina in *Don Giovanni*, and the role of Gilda in *Rigoletto*. Gilda was exciting, a new role. *And I'll bet that's why they had me sing all three arias,* she thought. *Trying to decide if my voice would be heavy enough for the more dramatic role of Gilda. That's quite a compliment...and an affirmation of what I believe I can do.*

The accompanying material explained housing assignments and responsibilities, including sharing a recital with another member of the company during the season. That pleased her as well. *Wonder what kind of music?* She noticed some company members would also appear in a cabaret at some point. *Well, I'll have a busy summer!*

Rehearsals began for *The Magic Flute* at Curtis, and Lindsey and Madame D. began finalizing the program for her graduate recital. Lindsey wanted to include at least some of the songs she and David had worked on for her undergraduate recital at Cincinnati. Madame agreed to the Robert Schumann song cycle *Frauenliebe und Leben* and a selection of Rachmaninoff songs in English, and Duparc songs in French.

For a graduate recital, Madame D. required her students to include a baroque piece for soprano and instruments. Lindsey found one she liked, "Con che soavità" by Monteverdi. She relished the opportunity to work with string players and found she enjoyed performing the music.

All that remained was selecting an aria, and after considerable thought and discussion Lindsey and Madame settled on "Je veux vivre" from *Roméo et Juliette*. She scheduled her recital for the third week of April, after the performances of *The Magic Flute* in mid-March.

Lindsey filled out her application for L'Opéra Jeunesse de Montréal and mailed it off early in March. By then, Nate had begun rehearsing at the New York City Opera. He called her with his own news.

"Hey, babe, I'm pretty excited about this. I'm going to be covering the Count in *Nozze di Figaro* here this season. So, there's a chance I'll get to perform it."

"That I would love to see. Is everything still going well for you there?"

"It sure is. This is a terrific place to work. The man who runs the operation here is absolutely a prince—Paul Kellogg. He's very hands-on and he knows every person who works here, no matter what their job is. He's truly a nice guy."

"That's so great to hear. He also runs Glimmerglass. In fact, he did that before the NYCO picked him up...did you know that? Seems like you're in a good place, and I believe I will be this summer as well."

"Anyway...I'm definitely going to get to Philly to see you perform Pamina in a couple of weeks. Can't wait. It's nice that New York and Philly aren't that far apart."

"Well...they may not be that far apart, but far enough that we don't see much of each other because we have these crazy schedules. But you could come down here for a day, couldn't you? Say this Sunday? I'm the one with an apartment. You're still sharing one, right?"

"I'm hopeful they'll extend my contract beyond next fall and then I'll find an apartment of my own. But you know what? I think I will jump on a train and come down there

Sunday. I could come back to the city early Monday morning."

That quick visit was followed a couple of weeks later by Lindsey's performances in *The Magic Flute,* an opera she had grown to love. She was warmly applauded by the audience and received a glowing review the following day. Lindsey believed Pamina was a role that fit her well, and she looked forward to performing it again.

She had written herself a character study for Pamina and found it helpful as she prepared the role. The music suited her voice perfectly; Lindsey realized once more that being a "Mozart soprano" might be her strength. The opera, ostensibly a fairy tale of good versus evil, had a deeper meaning. Because of that, Lindsey was intrigued that Mozart wrote it in 1791, the year of his death. Pamina, the daughter of the Queen of the Night, comes to know what she had thought was right and good is actually evil. She goes through a series of trials as does her intended, Tamino. Mozart's brilliant music paints all of this in sound.

Lindsey in particular loved the aria, "Ach, ich fühl's." Not knowing Tamino has taken a vow of silence in order to win her, Pamina feels his silence instead means the end of her happiness, and despairs, wishing only for death.

Kyla was in the cast as one of the Queen of the Night's Three Ladies and again joined Lindsey's family for a dinner after their opening night. She was floating on air; she had won the district Met Auditions and would soon compete in the regional audition. While rejoicing with her, Lindsey had the thought, *Another big step forward for a friend and colleague.*

Nate stayed at Lindsey's apartment that night. "One of these days, baby, you and I are going to be singing together in an opera. Somewhere, someday. A dream of mine."

"Mine as well. And I'm going to bet it will be Mozart."

"Um. Who knows? *Don Giovanni* might be a good guess." Nate pulled her closer.

Lindsey pulled back and gazed at him. "You know it's one of the operas at Glimmerglass this summer, and I'm covering Zerlina."

He smiled and kissed her as he murmured, "Yes, I remember. Enough talk, my Zerlina."

Two weeks later, Lindsey boarded a train to New York to watch Nate perform as Marcello *in La Bohème* at his NYCO debut. Her parents joined her, and of course, the Cohens were there en masse.

Watching Nate as Marcello brought back warm memories of seeing him for the first time. *He's even better than he was then,* she marveled, totally immersed in his performance. Nate was warmly received by the audience, and it was apparent he had made a highly successful New York debut.

Lying in his arms that night in her hotel room, Lindsey allowed herself to think about the life she was leading and would be for some time to come. *What Nate and I have these days are little snatches of time together. Will that change or become even more true as we both advance in our careers?*

She moved slightly away from him. *Well, his career is moving forward. I'm still far down the totem pole among hopefuls, and there sure are a lot of us.*

Lindsey had received word from the Montreal company that she had been selected to audition in May. *And if I'm hired by that company, there is no way I'll be able to see Nate for probably three months next fall, unless by some miracle he can come to Canada for a few days.*

Is this really what I want? Nate's doing what he needs to do, what I believe he was intended to do.

I'm not entirely sure that's true for me.

378

***

Lindsey's time at Curtis was winding down. All that remained was completing her course work and presenting her recital, and she appreciated having less stress in her life for a while.

Anita called again asking if she might be able to meet with some of the pediatric patients at Children's Hospital of Philadelphia. "A new bunch of kids, and they haven't heard the Milne songs you do so well. Any chance we can figure out a time? You seemed to enjoy your experience with the kids last year."

"I did, and I'm so sorry I've been unable to get back over there. You caught me at a good time. Absolutely, let's make a definite date."

They agreed to get together later that week at Lindsey's apartment to make plans for her visit with the CHOP patients. Anita arrived with Thai takeout and Lindsey provided sauvignon blanc.

They sat together on Lindsey's loveseat, opening and enjoying their food.

Anita sipped her wine. "I'm so excited to tell you this. I've decided to become a Guided Imagery and Music therapist and I've taken my first steps toward making that happen. The idea of using music even more intensely as a healing power is what I really want to do."

"That is exciting news, Anita," Lindsey was intrigued. "What do you need to do to achieve that goal?"

"First, I have to complete my master's in music therapy. Beyond that, special training under the supervision of certified GIM therapists for at least three years. It's a complex procedure, not the least of which is becoming familiar with the extensive catalog of suggested musical selections."

"How wonderful to be able to help someone resolve some long-held difficulty they may not even be aware of."

"Yes, that's why I want to pursue this." Anita took another sip of wine and shook her head as she continued, "But I'm here to talk about you working with my kids," Anita said. "What we did last year worked so well, you basically ran the session with my help. Are you comfortable repeating that?"

"Yes, of course. I'm happy to do that." Lindsey leaned forward. "There was one little girl in the group last year who enchanted me. I think her name is Amy. Do you still see her?"

"She was a delightful little girl."

"Was? Did she die?" Lindsey felt her stomach clench as she thought of Nate's cousin Sarah, who had died of cancer at the age of twelve. *I think Amy was about that age.*

"Sadly, yes. A little over two months ago. I was actually with her when she died. Her parents had requested private sessions during the last weeks of her life."

Anita gazed off into the distance and added softly, "Those sessions seemed to ease her pain and give her comfort."

Lindsey needed a moment, saddened to hear this. "How wonderful you were able to help her, Anita. She was a sweet child."

Chapter 26

The words to a children's song echoed in Lindsey's mind as she slowly drifted out of her dream. *The wheels on the bus….* She glanced at her wristwatch and noted it was three a.m. She hadn't minded these long stretches of bus travel in eastern Canada; in fact, she enjoyed them. It was the first time in many weeks she had been able to sit quietly and review the past several months.

It seemed that her life shifted into high gear in May. First, her recital, which was well-attended and quite successful. She'd loved singing it and hoped she might find a way to repeat that exact program at some time, strings and all. And the next week she'd been in New York auditioning for L'Opera Jeunesse de Montreal. That same week Nate was with her when they sat together in the Metropolitan Opera House at Lincoln Center to hear the final contestants in the Met National Auditions.

Included in those finals were Merritt Noble and Kyla Page. Lindsey was thrilled for both of them that they had made it so far. Merritt and Ethan were staying at the Marriott and Lindsey and Nate joined them for dinner the night before the auditions.

"Am I nervous? I'm…I guess I have to be, don't I? This is kind of surreal, though. I'm still trying to convince myself I'm actually here and will stand on the stage of the Met and sing tomorrow night." Merritt grinned as he nervously moved food around on his plate.

"You'll be brilliant. And you had a rehearsal today on that stage. Standing there and being accompanied by that extraordinary orchestra had to be a thrill." Lindsey took a sip of wine and dabbed her lips with her napkin.

They made it an early evening, and Merritt took Lindsey aside as they were leaving. "Keep holding me in your heart, Linds. If I do anything at all with this…have any kind of career as an opera singer…it will be because of you."

"No, Merritt. You're the one who had to do all the hard work to get here." Lindsey placed her hands on his shoulders and gazed into his eyes. "I can't even begin to tell you how proud I am. At the very least, you'll pick up an agent, and very likely you'll receive some offers. All the major opera houses have staff on hand to hear this group of singers. Pretty heady company."

"All I know is that a little over three years ago I didn't even want to live. Until you helped me find my way back. I'll be singing for you tomorrow night." They held each other close for a long moment.

As the winners were announced, Lindsey clutched Nate's hand. The third-place winner was announced. Second place, the excitement of hearing Kyla's name, warmly received by the audience. The tension grew almost unbearable.

"First place winner of the Metropolitan Opera National Council Auditions for 1999…tenor Merritt Noble, Cincinnati, Ohio."

It was a hugely popular choice; the large auditorium erupted in applause and cheers, Lindsey laughing and crying at the same time as she repeatedly called out "bravo."

Nate hugged her close. "He did it, baby. He did you proud."

***

Lindsey glanced at Amy Chang, sleeping peacefully next to her on the bus. *I didn't have much time with Nate, since I had to get back to Philadelphia for graduation and then start packing for Glimmerglass. And somewhere in between those events I vaguely remember watching M.J. receive his Bachelor of Science degree from Penn.*

As she was preparing to leave for Glimmerglass, Lindsey received a phone call from the Montreal company inviting her to join them. She was elated, but it meant she would have to be in Montreal by the first of September. *I'm barely going to have time to catch my breath for the next six months or so*, she thought.

Lindsey received her contract and rehearsal materials for the L'Opera Jeunesse tour two days before she left West Chester. Each opera had been shortened because they would primarily be performing for school students, often younger children, and they would have to learn their roles in two languages, French and English. Lindsey's assigned roles were Susanna in *Nozze di Figaro*, The Sandman and Dew Fairy in *Hansel and Gretel*, Pamina in *The Magic Flute*, and Valencienne in *The Merry Widow*.

A big assignment, but she was told all roles would be shared by two singers in the company. She had performed Pamina, of course, but Valencienne was a whole new role for her. Any free time she might have at Glimmerglass would be needed to get these roles learned and memorized. The schedule, thankfully, included a three-week rehearsal period in Montreal.

As for the two roles she was covering at Glimmerglass, Lindsey was comfortable with Zerlina in *Don Giovanni* and had begun learning Gilda in *Rigoletto* as soon as she knew she was assigned to understudy it. But she didn't feel she was at all ready to step onto a stage and perform it, which made her apprehensive.

She shared her concerns with Nate during a phone conversation. "Have you had to do this? I'm fine with Zerlina and would love to sing that role. I don't feel at all ready to cover Gilda, and I have to be there in less than two weeks. Oh, I know the notes and the words but I sure wouldn't want to step on a stage and attempt to sing this role."

"Glimmerglass has a good three-week rehearsal period, maybe longer. You tell me Montreal is the same, and both places I'm sure will have pianists you can work with. You'll be fine."

"You didn't answer my question, Nathaniel."

"Did I have to cover a role I didn't know very well? How about a role that I didn't even know about until I got there? Yes, that actually happened. For some reason no one let me know I was expected to cover Slim in Floyd's *Of Mice and Men*. I learned it in a hurry, let me tell you, and when I had to perform it with basically no rehearsal, I felt like a fish out of water. Thanks to some great colleagues, it went okay. But I get what you're feeling."

"You may sing *Of Mice and Men* at the NYCO…I know they promote contemporary operas."

"They do, and they also program Baroque works, stuff I'd enjoy singing. Mainly, I want to do all the singing I can, and I also like the idea of feeling I'm grounded somewhere. I'm happy I'll be based in New York for at least the next couple of years."

"I can understand that. I'm wondering what I've gotten myself into for this coming year. Three months at Glimmerglass and then three in Quebec. Then a break, and then back to Montreal for the following spring. I guess I'll learn a lot about myself."

"I think it's called 'trial by fire,' baby. You're young, strong, and healthy. You'll be fine, but I'll miss seeing you. I'll catch up with you in Canada whenever possible."

"Do you realize you told me two times in this conversation that I'll be fine?" Lindsey laughed. "Who are you trying to convince, me or you?"

***

Lindsey pressed her face against her pillow and squirmed around in the bus seat, trying to get more comfortable.

Glimmerglass this summer was a lot of fun, that's for sure. I wouldn't mind doing it again, but not as a YAP. The day she arrived she ran into both Amy Chang, the lyric coloratura from her Cincinnati Conservatory days, and Peter Boudreaux, the tenor she had spoken with at the audition in New York. Very quickly the three of them learned they would all be together both at Glimmerglass and in Montreal, where Peter would use his French-Canadian name, Pierre.

They were among the YAPs—Young Artist Performers— who were staying at a charming old home not far from the Alice Busch Opera Theater, an imposing open-air building on Otsego Lake, near Cooperstown, New York, where the season had been performed since the mid-1980s. While massive, the building had a homey feel, bearing some resemblance to a barn. The Glimmerglass folks liked to say it was the only opera house in America built on a turkey farm.

As a member of the Glimmerglass crew, Lindsey felt the same sense of camaraderie that she had loved when she was at the Conservatory. She made a point of getting to know all her fellow performers and everyone else—musical, tech, stage, and costume staff, and the custodial staff. She knew that without all of them this endeavor could not succeed.

She worked long hours to polish Gilda with one of the staff pianists, a talented and personable Black girl named Alice Washington, a recent graduate of Juilliard who wanted to someday conduct opera. Lindsey believed Alice's dream could come true, she was that good.

Days were long, busy, and productive. Lindsey had a rehearsal for Zerlina with the principals in the cast, who inspired her. They were so focused, so talented. *This is going to be a great show*, she thought. The setting and time were updated to small-town America in the first decade of the twentieth century, and the "Don" was portrayed as a sexy snake-oil salesman. The duel between the Don and Donna Anna's father was fought not with swords, but with pistols. The duet Zerlina and the Don sang was performed pretty much horizontally with a sudden blackout, leaving the audience wondering: did they, or didn't they?

Paul Kellogg, who was general and artistic director for both Glimmerglass and the New York City Opera, liked trying fresh, new ideas with old operas as much as he liked presenting new operas—American operas in particular. Lindsey understood Nate's enthusiasm about Mr. Kellogg, who had boundless energy and enthusiasm and seemed to be everywhere at once. Lindsey realized it was Kellogg who set the tone for this opera house. He was a retired high school French teacher when he was invited to help move the festival forward, and his vision kept it going and growing. And he'd been invited to head up the NYCO because of the wonders he had worked at Glimmerglass.

Whenever Lindsey and Alice both had spare time, Alice worked with her on the two roles she needed to learn before she went to Montreal. She only had to review Susanna's music, but Valencienne was a totally new role. Fortunately, since *The Merry Widow* is actually an operetta and they would be doing

386

a shortened version, she was able to learn it quickly. She had one aria and one duet, plus music in some ensembles that wasn't nearly as complicated as the ensemble work in Mozart's operas.

The first part of the season flew by. Nate managed to get away for a weekend and drove to Cooperstown in a rented car to spend a weekend and see *Don Giovanni*.

The audiences received this updated version of the popular Mozart opera enthusiastically. Nate found this production intriguing, the Don Giovanni-Zerlina duet in particular. *And we had a couple of memorable nights together. We staged our own horizontal "duets" under our blankets,* Lindsey thought with a grin.

After sharing this brief time with Lindsey, Nate left reluctantly to head to Europe where he had three festivals to perform. He promised he would try to get to Montreal sometime in September, depending on his schedule at the NYCO.

Lindsey's joint recital with Pierre was definitely a crowd-pleaser, and she relished the opportunity to perform with him. It reminded her of the many times she and Merritt had sung together.

Following the recital, Lindsey and Pierre were both approached by an agent who wanted to represent them. After a thorough discussion, both of them signed contracts with his agency in New York, and Lindsey was relieved to have achieved this necessary step in her pursuit of a career.

She left Glimmerglass with warm feelings and happy memories. Taking a final stroll around the grounds with Amy and Pierre the night before they disbanded, she savored the ambience of the unique atmosphere. *Glimmerglass Opera is definitely special*, Lindsey thought. *I hope I'll be back here someday.*

***

Lindsey had very little time to do laundry and re-pack before she left for Montreal. Upon their arrival, the company was housed in a small, cozy residential hotel. They would spend the first three weeks in rehearsal before premiering their season over the course of a week, performing in the Théâtre Denise-Pelletier, an eight-hundred-seat venue in downtown Montreal. For this special event, a small chamber orchestra would accompany them, and the audiences over that week would be school children from all over the city.

Jean Couvreur held a meeting with the singers of his opera company.

"I want to thank each and every one of you who are bravely stepping out with us in this endeavor. At the moment, we have no plans beyond this season, and it's important for us...and by that, I mean me...to have your input throughout this time. If you have any problems at all, you have my ear. I hope to get to know each of you during our first three weeks together."

He paused. "I'm sure some of you are aware that Lindsey Cameron is my niece. I want all of you to know she underwent the exact process each of you did, applying and auditioning, with none of the three judges aware of our relationship so there would be no hint of nepotism. She's here strictly on her own merit, as you all are."

He glanced around the room and seemed satisfied he'd headed off any potential problems in that area. "Our purpose is two-fold with this company. First, to provide each of you an opportunity to perform as a professional opera singer, and secondly, to make it possible for as many children as we can reach to be introduced to our favorite art form."

He grinned. "Quite frankly, this is an experiment, but I believe you are aware of that. We're not going to fold midway through our season. Whether we continue this project will be determined after we end our tour next spring. So, have a great time, reach out to your audience members during the social time after each show, and together let's grow the love of opera throughout this part of North America. And remember...I'm here for you."

Lindsey thought it an excellent speech and appreciated that he'd cleared the air up front. Their relationship never became an issue, and all the members of the company thought Jean Couvreur was a great guy. During rehearsals, it pleased Lindsey to see one singer or another deep in conversation with him.

***

The bus slowed and then came to a stop, and the sleeping singers stirred. Amy yawned and sat up. "What's going on?"

"I have no idea," Lindsey replied. "I'll see what I can find out."

She stepped into the aisle and moved toward the front of the bus, noticing the driver standing in the open door with red lights flashing outside. One of the men in the company stood on the stairs with his head out of the bus, listening to a conversation.

He turned and grinned at Lindsey. "Moose, apparently. The RCMP is on it." He looked again. "No, wait. New Brunswick Highway Patrol in this province. Well, how about that? We learn something new every day."

The highway patrol successfully shooed away the moose and soon the opera company was en route again, driving through the pre-dawn darkness. They still had a few hours before crossing the border as they returned to Quebec.

Lindsey went back to her seat and saw Amy already back in slumberland. She fluffed her pillow as best she could and returned to her reverie.

***

The thirty singers had all worked hard and arrived well-prepared. Despite Lindsey's concerns, she found she knew Valencienne better than she had realized. *Nate was right, I'll be fine.*

Sets were minimal, but all of the singers were particularly pleased with their unusually attractive costumes, carefully constructed of quality materials. The cast members learned they had been a generous gift from a donor. The company felt ready for its well-publicized premiere performances and began to feel a little like celebrities.

Nate managed to get to Montreal in late September and saw Lindsey in two of the L'Opera Jeunesse productions, *The Magic Flute* and *The Marriage of Figaro*. For these first performances for children, they performed in English.

Lindsey spent as much time with Nate as she could, staying for three nights with him at an uptown hotel with a king-sized bed. She knew it would be almost Christmas before they could be together again, but she tried not to let that affect their time together. She shared with Nate her disappointment at missing some of his NYCO debut performances.

"I would have so loved to see you as Valentin in *Faust*."

"So you could watch me die on stage again?" Nate teased.

Lindsey tried to stifle the sigh. "It's…we won't see each other again until sometime in December."

"I know, baby. It seems a long way off, but in the grand scheme of things, it really isn't."

"What exactly is that, Nate? That 'grand scheme of things?' I'm beginning to feel I may have made a mistake by jumping right into this tour after spending an entire summer at Glimmerglass."

She shook her head. "Well, too late now. I guess I'll just try to continue that 'onward and upward' attitude. But I will miss you terribly. Is this how it's going to be from now on?"

"I think you're tired, my angel. You had a busy summer at Glimmerglass and you haven't had a chance to stop and catch your breath. But your tour schedule for the next few weeks looks pretty light. Three shows a week for the next three weeks isn't bad."

"That's true. And then we have some nice long bus trips, going to New Brunswick and Nova Scotia. And when we get back to Montreal, we only have about four shows before our winter break. I'll be home before the middle of December." Another sigh. "I'll be okay. I'm looking forward to those bus trips, actually. I like riding on a bus."

Still, Lindsey had a difficult time telling Nate goodbye.

"Don't say goodbye." Nate brushed a lock of hair back from her face. "I remember you telling me that one time. Let's just say we'll see each other before we know it." He held her in a tight embrace at the airport.

Lindsey couldn't hold back her tears as she watched his plane take off.

***

Amy was sleeping soundly, even though the sky had begun to lighten. Lindsey slipped out of the seat and moved farther back in the bus, settling beside Michael Hartman, who smiled pleasantly when she joined him.

Michael, an exceptional collaborative pianist and a fine conductor, had caught Lindsey's attention as soon as rehearsals began. She made a point of sitting near him during breaks and striking up a conversation. He reminded her of David in many ways, and she told him about her dearest friend who had died far too young.

Michael's physical appearance prompted Lindsey to comment, "I think he'd probably have looked a lot like you when he got older...if he had lived." Medium height, thin, slightly unruly salt and pepper hair, and thick glasses. But most of all, a warm and engaging smile that was so much like David's.

The man was a wealth of information about the landscape of opera in North America, the United States in particular. Born in 1941, just before the Second World War began, he entered music school at the Conservatory of Music in 1958. Michael had great stories about the Cincinnati Summer Opera from that era right up through the nineteen-seventies. He'd been a rehearsal accompanist often and played for some famous singers.

"In the middle of the twentieth century, there were only a handful of established opera companies," he told her at dinner one night. "There was the Met—which was more a social club for the very wealthy than anything else. San Francisco and the Chicago Lyric Opera engaged European artists along with American singers. Three smaller companies—Cincinnati, Pittsburgh, and Central City, Colorado. That was pretty much it. Oh, there would be an occasional performance here or there, and sometimes an attempt at starting a company, but nothing seemed to last."

"I guess that started to change when the New York City Opera was established right after the war?" Lindsey sipped her tea.

"Yes, thanks to Mayor LaGuardia who wanted 'opera for the people.' It was basically a repertory company in the model of opera houses in Europe. A roster of singers who would sing leads in some operas, and supporting roles in others. And do it for very little pay, but they were hungry to sing."

Lindsey chuckled. "Aspiring opera singers are always hungry to sing."

"What really began to change the climate, though, was the establishment of the National Endowment for the Arts in 1965. All of a sudden, some federal money became available. It made quite a difference. If an ambitious and savvy opera lover could generate the necessary interest, there was seed money there." He paused to take a final bite of his dessert. "And then corporations and foundations—as well as wealthy individuals—could be persuaded to contribute."

"And here we are today in the United States with dozens of companies, some with pretty nifty ongoing programs."

"Yes, where you spent your summer is definitely one such program."

Michael was tremendously helpful to Lindsey as she polished her assigned roles for the season, and they spent quite a bit of time together. She noticed how much he enjoyed watching the singers interact with the children after a performance. *Creating new audience members...and who knows? Maybe a future industrialist who'll make a generous donation a few years down the road.*

For Lindsey, those "meet and greet" sessions were one of the best parts of the company's mission. She loved playing at First Nations venues and watching the somber little faces light up when the cast members talked with them. *This is an excellent thing we're doing*, she thought.

Her Uncle Jean was present whenever he could get away from CBC Radio 2. He'd developed a strong rapport with his young singers, who soon learned their mentor was revered and respected by the First Nations people.

This is fun. The thought often crossed Lindsey's mind, even during a performance. By the time they left for New Brunswick, all four operas had become second nature to the singers, and they were having a good time. There were moments when Lindsey had to remind herself which opera they were performing and what role she was singing, which would make her giggle. The music was in their muscles and minds, as well as their voices, and they could concentrate on sharing the operas with their audiences.

Their first long bus ride to St. John's, New Brunswick, meant a nine-hour trip that would take them through the northern part of Maine, and necessitate stopping at border crossings twice. Lindsey sat with Michael during that drive and they traded stories for hours. She told him more about David and Merritt and the unique relationship the three of them enjoyed.

"You say you were housemates?"

"Yes. And yes, I had some negative response to that…but not from the people who mattered. My family and close friends all loved my boys."

Eventually, Michael confided in Lindsey that he was ill. Very ill.

"I have HIV, Lindsey," he said, in a low voice. "I was diagnosed about ten years ago. So far it's controlled, but I know eventually it will kill me, one way or another."

Lindsey stared into his eyes in dismay, but she saw no anger or desperation.

394

"It's okay. With the help of a remarkable music therapist, I've been able to accept my fate. I plan to do everything I can for as long as I can. I can't say I'm prepared to die, but I believe with her help I'll be able to leave this life in relative peace."

"She's a Bonny Guided Imagery and Music practitioner, isn't she?" Lindsey felt a sudden lift of her spirits. Finally, an actual patient who could tell her more about this fascinating subject.

"Yes, she is." Michael arched an eyebrow. "I'm surprised you're aware of GIM therapy. Most people have never heard of it."

"My brother's girlfriend has her master's in music therapy and is in training for GIM certification. I've assisted her with some general music therapy sessions for pediatric patients in long-term care. And Anita invited me to observe a GIM session last year." *Is that when it was? Just a year ago? I'm losing track of time.*

Lindsey shifted in her seat to face Michael more directly. "Music therapy fascinates me. I think in a way I practice it on myself. I listen to certain pieces of music when I'm troubled. It can calm me, or invigorate me, or just help me see things in better perspective."

Michael told her more about his GIM sessions. "It is definitely a state of altered consciousness. You're somewhere else. Everything is different. The air feels different, sounds are sharper. Colors are more vivid. All your senses are keener. You feel yourself moving, even though you know you're lying prone. It's a beautiful and remarkable experience."

Lindsey nodded. "You know…I'd like to have a session sometime. Right now, I'm struggling with being separated from Nate for so long. I have trouble sleeping. I know it's silly, but there it is."

"It isn't silly, Lindsey. And a session might be a help to you." He was thoughtful. "Have you asked yourself why these separations are troubling you so much? You know he loves you."

"He says he does." Lindsey stared off into space. "It all happened so fast, and we've been apart so much more than we've been together. Maybe in some way, I'm afraid our relationship is more physical than anything else. I don't want to believe that, but...."

"First things first. Have you discussed this with Nate?"

"No, I haven't. And I need to do that. We'll be together in December."

L'Opera Jeunesse de Montreal, now a close-knit group of friends and colleagues, presented four more performances in and around their home base before the company disbanded until mid-March.

Lindsey hugged Michael tight when she left. "I'll miss you. Please keep in touch, will you?"

Chapter 27

After an early Christmas celebration with her family, Lindsey flew to Basel, Switzerland, to see Nate's final performance as Count Almaviva in *Le Nozze di Figaro*. She felt a little anxious as she waited to disembark—it had been more than two months since they'd been together.

But there he was, those piercing gray eyes scanning the deplaning passengers as they entered the terminal, lighting up when he spotted her. Seeing him created the same sense of excitement as it always did, and she moved easily into his arms, enjoying the warmth of his embrace.

"I don't dare kiss you until I get you to my hotel," he chuckled. "God, I've missed you. You look wonderful."

"I look tired. You're sweet," Lindsey snuggled against him briefly. They collected her luggage quickly and soon were at the hotel, where wine and snacks awaited them in his room. Nate led her to the loveseat and poured them each a glass of wine.

"We leave in two days for Vienna. We can explore the city, and do whatever you want. I'm so happy you're here." He stroked her hair as he gazed into her eyes.

"Maybe we shouldn't make love until after you sing tomorrow night?" Lindsey said, nibbling on a small piece of cheese. "Almaviva is a big role."

Nate smiled. "I have plenty of time to recover. It's not even noon. Unless you're too tired from your trip."

She ran her lips up to his jaw. "You know me better than that."

They took their time, discovering each other all over again, then drifting off to sleep as they lay close.

Lindsey woke to the lovely sensation of resting in Nate's arms. She turned toward him carefully, not wanting to rouse him, to see his beautiful eyes gazing at her.

"I didn't mean to wake you." She caressed his chest and kissed his throat.

"You didn't. You can't imagine how happy I am to have you here." He kissed her softly. "I want this trip to be one you'll never forget. I know you've been incredibly busy, so I want most of all for you to relax and completely enjoy yourself during these days we have together."

"That sounds delicious. My life has been a little frantic. When I said I know I look tired, I meant that. As much as I've enjoyed the last six months, I do feel drained."

Nate eased out of her arms and sat up. "Let's order some food, why don't we? How about a late brunch?"

Over omelets and fruit, Nate encouraged Lindsey to talk about her new life as an opera singer. "All that bus travel in eastern Canada must have been tough."

"Not really. It was kind of the first time I could catch my breath. I don't mind bus trips and I can usually sleep when riding one. Ours were roomy and comfortable."

Lindsey stretched. "Oh, it's lovely to not even have to think about anything for a while. I have some time after I get home before I need to go back to Montreal. I plan to get in some lessons with Madame, but I haven't planned a thing beyond that."

Nate didn't comment, and Lindsey asked, "Or should I be doing something for those few weeks? Looking for auditions? What?" She stood and moved to the window.

"No, that's not at all what I was thinking." He wrapped his arms around her from behind and they both gazed out onto the street below. "I'm getting a bigger apartment in the city since I now know I'll be there for at least two years. While you're waiting for your Montreal commitment to resume, why not come and stay with me in New York for a few weeks?"

Lindsey whirled to face him, throwing her arms around his neck. "Do you mean that? Oh, that would be...." She leaned back and stared at Nate, searching for words.

He laughed. "Well, this is something new. Lindsey Cameron, speechless. Yes, I mean it. I know it hasn't been easy, the few days here and there we manage to arrange so we can spend little pockets of time together. It's like we have to get re-acquainted nearly every time we see each other. We've never been together long enough to learn what we might do that's going to be annoying to the other person."

Lindsey joined in his laugh before she kissed him. "Nathaniel Cohen, I accept your offer. I would love to play house with you for a few weeks. That sounds incredibly wonderful."

"Well, I have some nice news to share," Nate said. "Engagements in Chicago, Houston, and San Francisco during the next two seasons. I'm excited about those dates."

"Definitely impressive. You're moving up," she commented.

"Kinda seems that way, doesn't it? Oh, and Montreal as well, and then back to Seattle. I think you know I have a good gig in Santa Fe this coming summer? *Don Giovanni*, end of July through most of August. If you're free, maybe you could go with me for that." He ran a hand over the back of his neck. "But as I said, the others are spread out over the next couple of years. I'm okay with travel when it's not constant. I also like staying on one continent."

399

They went for a brisk walk late in the afternoon before dinner. Lindsey caressed Nate's back and shoulders as he drifted off to sleep.

The thought of the two of them living together for a few weeks gave Lindsey a sense of satisfaction that surprised her. *This is something I want. I want us to be together. I hope eventually, we can be married. I love the idea of always being there with him, being there for him. Well...maybe not all the time, our careers won't allow for that, but at least if we're married it could be most of the time. I have to believe he wants that as well.*

Another brisk walk in the morning for Lindsey while Nate went to work out at a gym recommended by some of the singers at the Basel opera house. An early light supper followed, and Nate wanted to get to the theater early and warm up.

Theater Basel served as home to both the opera company and the ballet, and other events took place there as well. Lindsey found the fairly new building of contemporary design intriguing. Nate said the acoustics were good and he was enjoying this production.

As had become the practice in many European houses, the director had chosen to set the opera in more recent times rather than the late eighteenth century. Costuming was generally less expensive and easier for such productions, and updating *Le Nozze di Figaro* gave it an added layer of intrigue.

Lindsey knew this opera at least as well as she knew *La Bohéme*, having now performed the role of Susanna. It was her favorite Mozart opera because she saw Susanna as the female lead. The character, personal maid to Countess Almaviva, is engaged to Count Almaviva's manservant, Figaro. In the original plot, the Count intended to observe his *droit du seigneur* and bed his wife's servant before the marriage. Moving the story to a contemporary period and culture meant the character of the Count took on a more complex, darker aspect.

And that was what Lindsey saw and heard as she watched the opera. She found Nate's performance a notch above the rest of the cast, though sharing the stage with him she thought probably upped their game. He was truly remarkable. His voice sounded to her richer than ever—sonorous, smooth, silky.

At the beginning of the second act, she paid particular attention to the duet between the Count and Susanna. The soprano playing Susanna was excellent, but Lindsey found herself more intrigued with what Nate was doing with the character at this point in the opera. The Count's big aria followed the flirtatious duet, and in the two pieces, Nate displayed a wide range of emotions, ending with steely anger that didn't bode well for Susanna and Figaro. After the aria the audience gave Nate a resounding ovation. He was applauded even more strongly during the final bows at the end of the performance. This had been his show.

Lindsey made love with Count Almaviva that night. Afterward, Nate slept peacefully as she gazed at him.

I'll never be as good as he is. That's just a fact. He has to be doing what he's doing, he was born for this. Nate's path is clear for him and obvious to everyone who sees him perform. I'm not so sure, so positive, about me…about my path. She snuggled closer. *I may never have the opportunity to perform a duet with Nate on stage…but how lucky I am to be able to sleep in his arms.*

They checked into the Hilton Plaza in Vienna two days later, an especially lovely Art Deco hotel where they enjoyed a great view of the Ringstrasse grand boulevard and the luxury of a large room that almost equaled a suite. The hotel's Christmas decorations for their guests' rooms included a small tree, and Lindsey and Nate placed their gifts for each other under it when they checked in. Christmas morning, they enjoyed an especially delicious brunch as they opened their gifts.

Lindsey presented Nate with a new wristwatch, warm but soft doeskin gloves, an ivory cashmere scarf, and a small framed photo of the two of them taken at her parents' home the Christmas after they met. Her gifts from Nate included a string of seed pearls, a powder blue woolen beret and matching scarf, and a gold bangle bracelet.

"There's one more," he said, a little nervously. "It's to wear on your right hand because I don't think now is the right time for me to put this on your left hand." He produced a small box and showed her the ring: a simply set, square-cut emerald—her birthstone.

Lindsey, her eyes brimming with tears, allowed Nate to work the ring onto the fourth finger of her right hand. "Let's call it a commitment ring, shall we? A token of the deep love I feel for you, my beautiful Lindsey." A long embrace and they made love in the glow of the lights on the Christmas tree.

It was exciting to be in Vienna during this holiday season which saw the change of the millennium. They "did" the city for the next ten days, visiting all the landmarks Lindsey was eager to see, including Schönbrunn Palace and the Spanish Riding School, attending musical performances, exploring museums, and enjoying Viennese cuisine. Nate had managed to get tickets for the Vienna Philharmonic's traditional New Year's Day concert, a special recognition of the year 2000.

But they agreed the highlight of their tour of Vienna was the annual New Year's Eve performance of *Die Fledermaus* at the Vienna State Opera, where the operetta first premiered in 1874. Nate and Lindsey imagined themselves as the characters Falke and Adele, appearing together on that magnificent stage one day. Back in their hotel room, they toasted each other with champagne at midnight, looking forward to the new year and a new century.

***

Before moving in with Nate in New York near the end of January, Lindsey managed to work in two voice lessons with Madame. The first time she went to Philadelphia she connected with Anita for a late lunch. Even though her relationship with M.J. had become a friendly one rather than romantic, Anita made a point of seeing him occasionally.

"We pick each other's brains about what makes people tick," Anita laughed. "Your brother is brilliant, compassionate, and something of a philosopher, Lindsey. He'll zip through grad school and go on to bigger things is my prediction. I don't know that being a practicing psychologist is in his future, but you never know. He'd be a phenomenal teacher."

"I can see him doing that, Anita. M.J. loves to learn, and he loves to share what he's learned. Isn't that a perfect description of a good teacher?"

They smiled at each other as Anita sipped her coffee. "Your life has certainly become exciting," she said. "First a Young Artist at Glimmerglass, and now you're on break during an opera tour. That has to be fascinating."

"It has been. Also a little frantic at times. And at this point, I'm not sure where I will be next." Lindsey gazed off into the distance.

"M.J. says you signed with an agent."

"Yes, I did. An important part of the process of building a career, apparently. I haven't heard anything yet about possible performance dates, though. It's a crowded field. Lots and lots of talented and ambitious sopranos in the world of opera."

Anita glanced at her thoughtfully. "I sense something…maybe some uncertainty about your chosen career?"

"I have to admit…I go back and forth. I love to sing, and I enjoy performing. But…," she stirred her coffee. "Here's something I've discovered about myself. If I didn't have a career as a performer, I wouldn't be brokenhearted. Does that sound awful? I always believed it was exactly what I wanted to do, the only thing I ever wanted to do."

"So what changed? Does being with Nate have something to do with it?"

"Well…I discovered something else about myself in Europe. I absolutely love watching Nate perform. He has a brilliant future ahead of him, barring some horrible unforeseen circumstance. It's as if he was born to do what he's doing."

"He does it because he loves it."

"Yes, but it's more than that." Lindsey lifted a forkful of carrot cake. "I know how hard he works and how he's always staying one step ahead, learning new music, and working with his coach. But there's a certain ease to the way he handles…well, everything. Nothing is really hard for him if you get what I mean." She tasted the cake, savoring the tangy flavor.

"I think so," Anita replied. "But you seem to have that same ability."

"I've always enjoyed performing, but I'm not as single-mindedly focused on it as I used to be…or as Nate is. I've learned there are other ways people can share the music in their lives. What you're doing, for example. GIM therapy seems to be a remarkable experience for the patients. I met a man named Michael who's part of the staff on our opera tour whom it has helped immensely. And the therapists I've met seem also to find great satisfaction in providing that help."

Anita took a spoonful of crème brûlée. "I'm certainly finding that to be true. Another thing about you, though…is it possible your relationship with Nate is more important than you had thought? Not that you'd step away from a career because you'd rather be with him, but that being with him perhaps means more than you realized?"

Lindsey finished her carrot cake and blotted her lips with her napkin. "I always believed I'd find a loving partner—my parents' relationship is such a great example of that. But you're right, I had no idea a relationship could reach this level of importance to me."

She sighed. "Thanks for letting me talk about this, Anita. I'm still trying to figure out what exactly I want to do with my life. What I want to be when I grow up."

***

Nate had found an apartment in Brooklyn in an area favored by performing artists, mainly musicians and actors. It was a friendly, pleasant area, with almost a small-town feeling. Lindsey liked it. The two-bedroom apartment, while not spacious, was comfortable, and it began to feel like home during the six weeks she spent there.

Nate was in rehearsals by February for the spring season at the New York City Opera, where he would sing George in Carlisle Floyd's *Of Mice and Men* and Lescaut in Puccini's *Manon Lescaut*—an opera he was excited about performing. An auspicious season for him. He also had a *Don Giovanni* production in Houston late in the spring.

Lindsey's agent contacted her with offers for the coming fall. Opera North in Lebanon, New Hampshire, offered her a Pamina in *The Magic Flute* and covers for Musetta in *La Bohème*, and he was negotiating for a performance of *Le Nozze*

405

di Figaro with the Taconic Opera House in upstate New York for the following spring.

She loved living in New York. Nate was busy with coaching and rehearsing, and Lindsey took the time to explore the city as she never had before. She found Brooklyn a comfortable place to live, and it was easy to get into Manhattan. She enjoyed wandering around the Lincoln Center area, and Nate invited her to a rehearsal of *Manon Lescaut* since she wouldn't be able to see him perform it.

Paul Kellogg spotted her as she sat waiting for the rehearsal to begin, and sat down next to her. "Lindsey, isn't it? I recognized you from last summer at Glimmerglass. You and that tenor gave a terrific recital. If I remember right, you two were also signed up for a tour based in Montreal, right?"

Immensely complimented that the artistic director of both Glimmerglass Opera and the New York City Opera remembered so much about her, Lindsey replied, "Yes, we're on a mid-winter break from the tour at present, Mr. Kellogg. I have to leave March tenth to go back to Montreal to complete it."

"You're here to see Nate rehearse, I would imagine. I recall the two of you were together last summer."

Lindsey blushed. "Yes, I am. I won't get to see a performance this spring. I hope it's okay that I'm here."

"Of course, it is. Enjoy. Nate Cohen is quite an artist. I hope we can keep him here for a bit longer, but word on the street is he's about to get some pretty exciting offers." He patted the back of her seat and moved away to speak to another person seated in the auditorium.

Exciting offers? I wonder if Nate is aware of that? And what could they be? San Francisco and Chicago are pretty great. Could Kellogg know something about the Met being interested in Nate?

Even though what Lindsey saw was a piano rehearsal—no set, props, or costumes—she found Nate's performance exciting. *What a great role for him*, she thought. She found the music for this opera by Puccini particularly appealing as well and enjoyed the opportunity to watch it. It made her sad to realize she wouldn't see him in this role in the complete production of *Manon Lescaut*, though. *Well, hopefully, another time in the not-too-distant future.*

Another regret was realizing she would miss the picnics and barbeques their nice neighbors in the four-apartment building held outside when the weather allowed. She liked the neighbors and enjoyed feeling part of a community of artists.

In the apartment next to theirs were two dancers appearing currently in *Beauty and the Beast* on Broadway. One floor below that one resided members of the orchestra contracted by the State Theater to play for the NYCO and the New York City Ballet—one a violinist, the other a flutist. Below Nate's apartment lived two members of the Met Opera chorus. Occasionally the residents would find time to have a drink together in one apartment or another, and the impromptu parties were always a good time.

But even better were those carefree times with Nate when there were no outside pressures or demands on him. A lazy Sunday fixing breakfast together and binge-watching a TV series or a couple of movies rented from Blockbuster. The snowy evenings when they would stroll through the neighborhood, return to the apartment, fix hot chocolate and make love. Playing tourist and going to the top of the World Trade Center or visiting the Statue of Liberty, or just taking the ferry to Staten Island. Visiting the Museum of Modern Art and admiring paintings by Andrew Cameron on display in one of the galleries. Attending a service at St. Thomas Church to hear the fabled boy choir. Attending a performance of *I Pagliacci* at the Metropolitan Opera, where Lindsey could picture Nate in the role of Silvio.

Lindsey kept herself busy when Nate wasn't around. He owned a good keyboard, not quite piano-sized but large enough and with a piano action and a decent tone, and she reviewed her tour music thoroughly. She also began studying a new role, Adele in Johann Strauss' delightful operetta *Die Fledermaus*—the operetta she and Nate had seen in Vienna and dreamed they might appear in together in the future.

Lindsey had an especially difficult time saying goodbye to Nate when she left in March. The six weeks they'd been together living as a couple had been one of the happiest times of her life, and she wondered when they might have that again.

It seemed to her that Nate found it difficult as well. He held her tight for long moments before she boarded the plane, taking her right hand and kissing the ring he'd given her.

"Call me whenever you can," he told her. "Write lots of letters. Email and snail mail."

"I will. I'll give my new laptop a workout. Please take good care of yourself."

"I promise. I'll hold you in my heart, my dearest love. I hope you know how very much I love you." He kissed her, his lips lingering on hers and then against her hair.

Reluctantly, she pulled back gently, pressed her hand to his heart, and turned to enter the gate.

Chapter 28

Lindsey vividly remembered returning to the Conservatory campus after Christmas break her freshman year and greeting all her new friends. Her return to Montreal, while not exactly the same, did have much of that excitement of reconnecting with her fellow musicians—people who shared a goal.

Amy extended her left hand to display a wedding band, and Pierre did the same. Amy giggled at Lindsey's gasp of surprise.

"When on earth did this happen?"

"You must have noticed Pierre and I were getting close," Amy said.

"Well, sure, but I guess I didn't know *how* close," Lindsey replied. *Lots of make-out sessions on those long drives, especially at night.*

"Amy stayed with my family over the break and we kind of discovered how much we cared for each other." Pierre's grin threatened to split his face open, it was so broad.

"Well, congratulations!" Lindsey hugged each of them and they moved into a three-way embrace, laughing.

She was happy to see Michael when they entered the studio to do brush-up rehearsals of each opera. Lindsey studied him carefully and was pleased to see he looked much the same. She'd been worried he might begin to show signs of advancing disease.

They'd emailed each other several times during the break and Michael had assured her he was doing okay and expected to complete the tour. Still, seeing him was reassuring.

"So glad to see you." She hugged him tightly.

"Likewise." He gazed at her. "You're glowing. Some good together time with Nate?"

"The best. I spent six weeks sharing his apartment in New York. I've never been so happy."

"Did you have that talk we discussed?"

Lindsey wiggled the fingers of her right hand. "It wasn't necessary. This was a Christmas present."

Michael examined the emerald ring. "Very nice. A pre-engagement ring?"

"Nate called it a 'commitment ring,' but yes, it's the same thing. I have absolutely no doubt he truly loves me. Even with all my quirks."

"I wasn't aware you had any," Michael smiled warmly. "You're a pretty straightforward lady."

"I try to be. And I think Nate knows me well."

For this part of their tour, the company traveled north, first to Quebec City, the capital of the province. Only about a hundred and fifty miles from Montreal, the old city also sits on the St. Lawrence River and includes "Old Quebec," the birthplace of French Canada, a favorite tourist destination filled with historic treasures, cobblestone streets, and fortifications, some dating from the time of its founding in the first decade of the seventeenth century.

L'Opera Jeunesse de Montreal toured in and around the area for nearly two weeks. Andrew and Mary Cameron made the trip to Quebec City where they were joined by Jean and Noémi Couvreur, and Lindsey spent time with her family members whenever she could during the three days they were there.

It thrilled her to know her parents were in the audience for her performance as Susanna in *Le Mariage de Figaro*, performed in French for these audiences. Her family took her out for a late supper and praised her performance highly.

"What a shame Nate couldn't join us," Mary said. "He would have so loved seeing you in this role. You were outstanding, Lindsey."

"Maybe an opera you'll perform together one day, sweetheart?" Andrew asked.

"That would be a real treat. Nate is a fabulous Count Almaviva," Lindsey replied.

"Yet one can never predict the future in the performing arts," Noémi said softly. Lindsey's eyes met hers.

"No. The future is definitely unknown," Lindsey said. *My perceptive aunt has an idea of what's going on with me,* she thought.

When she told her family goodbye the next day, Noémi gave her a warm embrace. "If you ever need to talk, I am here," she murmured to Lindsey.

"*Oui, je sais,*" Lindsey responded. "*Merci.*"

L'Opera Jeunesse continued north to Saguenay, a city that had grown from several settlements established and supported by the lumber industry, in particular, pulp and paper. It was the northernmost point of their tour and they spent a week in April performing for as many children as possible in and near the city.

After returning to Montreal to have their costumes refreshed and take a few days off, they visited several other cities not far from their home base, including Victoriaville, Sherbrooke, and Saint-Jean-sur-Richelieu, until the end of April. The company completed its tour in early May by performing in Ottawa, the Canadian capital, and the picturesque and historic city of Kingston, Ontario. In Ottawa, the company was treated to a private tour of the Parliament building and grounds. For these audiences, the company performed in English.

While it had been a busy time, it seemed less stressful to Lindsey than the fall tour. She knew her colleagues well by now, and all of them were comfortable performing the four operas, joking at times they should shuffle roles around for fun because all of them knew every note of every opera.

Lindsey missed Nate and called him whenever possible and wrote and emailed frequently, but there was never a time when he was able to fly to Canada to see her. After the NYCO season ended in April, he had dates in Houston and Los Angeles until nearly the middle of May.

She had known that would likely be the case, which eased her disappointment, and she focused on being at her best both on and offstage. She enjoyed spending time with the friends she had made, but for Lindsey, some of the favorite moments of this tour continued to be talking with the children after each performance.

Michael concerned her, though. She felt after they left Saguenay he seemed not as energetic, and she saw dark circles under his eyes. He managed to complete the tour, but she felt if it had lasted another week, he wouldn't have made it.

Amy and Pierre took her out to dinner in Old Montreal the night before she left to go back to New York.

"Big news," Pierre told her. "We've both been offered contracts as *comprimarios* for Opéra de Montréal next season."

"And we're thrilled about it, even though they'll be supporting roles," Amy added. "We'll be together, and our agents in the States can still look for performances for us with smaller regional companies there. We've let them know when we're available."

"The Montreal opera doesn't have a full season, and performances are pretty spread out. But it's still a good gig for us." Pierre lifted his glass. "Will you join us in a toast?"

Lindsey lifted her glass as well, "Toi, toi, toi, *mes amis*. To a happy season of opera in Montreal."

They clanked glasses. "There's more," Pierre added, after taking a gulp of water. "My family owns a small house here in Old Montreal that they rent to tourists. They're going to take it off the market for next year and have invited us to use it, rent-free. So we can even start saving money."

Amy laughed. "You probably think we're a little crazy."

"Not at all. You both sound happy and excited." She paused. "I do wonder…what's the climate in Montreal as far as people of Asian descent are concerned? I know you told me you had some bad experiences in the Atlanta area, where your family lives."

"I did. I don't think it's too bad here. It can't be worse than Atlanta," Amy said with a grin. "But just wait until people read their program and see that Amy Boudreaux is playing the role of Annina or Flora in *La Traviata* tonight, and she turns out to be this Chinese chick."

"Why can't the rest of society catch up with the arts community as far as inclusiveness is concerned? Talent tops everything," Pierre said.

After enjoying a delicious meal of foods particular to Quebec, the three of them said their goodbyes.

"One thing I wish you would do for me," Lindsey said. "Can you check on Michael from time to time and let me know how he's doing? I know he will just keep telling me he's fine, but…," she hesitated, wondering if she was saying too much.

"We know about his illness, Lindsey," Pierre told her. "Amy and I both thought he looked pretty drawn by the end of our season. We would check on him in any event, Michael is special. We'll keep you posted."

"Oh good. That's such a relief. I am concerned about him."

***

Lindsey flew home to West Chester with her three suitcases, primarily to get the winter outfits to the dry cleaners and discard a few items from her warm-weather clothing. Nate wouldn't be back in New York until near the end of May, so she took advantage of the chance to spend more time with her family and work in two lessons with Madame.

Reverting to childhood, she stretched out on pillows on the carpet in Andrew's studio as she listened to music and watched him paint. She had many happy memories of spending a great deal of time in this room as a child, sometimes sitting at a table and coloring or drawing under her father's casual supervision. She still felt safe and happy being in this room and knew she always would. *Maybe someday I'll have a child who can visit here and enjoy this as much as I do,*

It struck Lindsey that having children wasn't something she'd ever given much thought to, for whatever reason, and it had never been a topic of conversation with Nate. *Maybe because of the profession I've been pursuing most of my life, though I know that even some famous female opera singers have children.*

Lindsey knew that Renee Fleming had two daughters and was enjoying a spectacular career. And Joan Sutherland had at least one child. *Superstars who had it all*, thought Lindsey. *Would I be able to handle that? It's tough enough to keep a long-distance relationship going, without the added complication of a family.*

414

She had often been told how important her birth was to both her parents, her father in particular. Andrew longed for a child and saw Lindsey as an answered prayer. Her mother said they didn't start their family until after he was treated for PTSD caused by early childhood trauma, his Vietnam War experience, and the disappearance of Jake.

Lindsey leaned up on one elbow to watch her father, so focused on his work. Andrew painted on a large canvas with bold strokes, using his back and shoulders as he moved the palette knife through vivid colors. She recognized Montmorency Falls near Quebec City; not as large as Niagara but taller. Andrew and Mary took numerous photos when they visited, and now she watched as her father created a stunning landscape of the scene as he listened to, of all things, Rachmaninoff's tone poem *The Isle of the Dead. Well, in a way, that makes sense. It has to do with water.*

"Daddy, are you hoping to someday have a grandchild? I mean for me or M.J. to have children?" Lindsey surprised both of them with her sudden question.

Andrew laughed as he rested the knife on his palette. "What prompted that, Lindsey? Hearing *The Isle of Dead* or looking at the waterfall?"

She sat up and hugged her knees. "Neither, actually. I was just thinking about how few female opera singers have children. It has to be difficult, with the schedules we have."

He played in the paint for a moment with the palette knife. "If you or your brother have children, I certainly would joyfully welcome them into my heart. But that's a choice for each of you to make."

He gazed at her. "I think there's more to that question, though. Something you'd like to talk about?"

"Not...really. I'm just sorting through my experiences of the past year and thinking hard about what my choices are at this point in my life. And…one choice is to not pursue a career in opera." She exhaled audibly. "I haven't said anything about this to Nate yet."

"That's definitely not what I expected to hear. You've wanted to be an opera star…"

"…since I was seven. I know. When I was seven, I had no clue what it takes to do this. Even when I was at the Conservatory, I was only vaguely aware of the hoops a singer has to jump through. I watch Nate, and he handles it all so easily. He's not just good, though. He's on his way to greatness. On the other hand, I honestly don't see myself at that level."

The CD player changed the recording to Debussy's *La Mer*. Andrew placed his palette on a table and eased down to sit on the floor beside his daughter as he listened.

"But if I do decide this isn't the life that will be most fulfilling for me, then what do I do? I know my life has to include music—it's what I love most. I'm meant to use my music in some way. I don't really see myself as a teacher."

"Is music therapy something you've considered? I know you've had several experiences with children. What happened with Merritt after his accident…that was music therapy, in a sense. And I know you stay in touch with Anita, who is following what I find a fascinating path with GIM therapy."

"You know me well, Dad. I haven't made any decisions. I'm just thinking. I have to say, my agent hasn't actually overwhelmed me with performance opportunities, and that tells me something. Sopranos have a tougher road than any other singer. There are far too many of us."

"Yes, but you know that old saying—somebody's going to make it. And it might very well be you."

He was thoughtful for a moment. "Maybe you should discuss this with Nate when you get back to New York, sweetheart. It's obvious you feel you may be at something of a crossroads."

"Oh, I will. I need to do some more thinking first, though. And whatever I decide, it will be because I honestly believe that's the path I'm meant to follow."

She stood and examined his painting. "This is fabulous, Daddy. The way you see things is fascinating."

"Not at all the kind of painting I did when I first started. I cranked out a lot of dreamy impressionistic stuff for a long time."

He stood and picked up the palette, wiping the knife on a rag. "We can change as we grow, Lindsey. And you're now considering you may want to use your music differently than you once did."

"It's possible. I never want to stop singing, though. I have a lot to figure out."

"Just know your mother and I will support you—and be proud of you—no matter what path you choose. You are a remarkable young woman, Lindsey Cameron."

***

Nate met her at the airport, his eyes shining, and held Lindsey for so long that she began to feel slightly uncomfortable.

Finally, she gently pulled back. "I guess you're glad to see me."

"You could say that. It's lovely that we have another nice stretch of time together." He took her luggage check as they went to claim her suitcases. "That is unless you have some commitments I haven't heard about."

"No, nothing at all. Not until fall when I have that Pamina in Nowheresville, New Hampshire." They watched the luggage carousel turn.

417

"Don't be so dismissive, Lindsey. It's still a paying job."

"Oh, I don't mean to be, Nate. Not really. I appreciate that my agent has found me a few gigs." She pointed at the carousel. "There are my bags."

Lindsey strolled through Nate's apartment. "You know what? I feel like this is home," she said, as she turned to take him in her arms.

"Now that you're here, I agree—it's home," Nate told her. He carried her to the bed and they lost themselves in each other completely.

Lindsey opened her eyes the next morning to find a smiling Nate beside her, mug of coffee in hand. "Here you go, Sleeping Beauty."

She sat up and accepted the mug, sipping it gratefully. "What's on the docket for today, my prince?"

"Not much," he laughed, sitting beside her on the bed. "We can make love again whenever we want. I've cleared my calendar for two weeks."

"Oh, that is lovely. Do we still have the same neighbors? I'd like to get together with them at some point."

"We sure do. And your wish is granted, princess. Barbecue tonight, outside. In your honor, as a matter of fact."

Lindsey was delighted to see her neighbors again, and an outdoor barbecue provided exactly the right atmosphere. The couple from the Met chorus were her favorites, mostly because they were fellow singers and a soprano and baritone. Their pride in being part of that exceptional ensemble was evident and Lindsey enjoyed their "war stories."

The dancers, who had recently married, appreciated their musical neighbors and provided their own tales, entertaining them with stories of people's surprise that a heterosexual couple even existed in the world of ballet. The instrumentalists, the Black violinist and White flutist, had been partners for years and reminded Lindsey in some ways of "my boys."

The barbecue was a great success and the neighbors lingered outside until close to midnight, enjoying the warm night and the special sense of being with friends and colleagues they had come to appreciate. More neighborly social events followed, some impromptu, some organized. Lindsey felt more than ever that this apartment had become the place she considered home.

Merritt and Ethan arrived in New York in May, when Merritt had several auditions scheduled. One, at the NYCO, was more a formality. He had already been offered a contract with the company for the fall of 2001 and spring of 2002. Other auditions were with representatives of several major opera houses in Europe. Nate had a number of those same auditions, and he and Merritt enjoyed comparing notes.

Lindsey and Nate cooked dinner for their friends, something they had begun to do together. She never spent a lot of time in the kitchen if she could avoid it, but Nate made it an adventure, and they tried a variety of dishes. They felt most successful with Italian food, lasagna in particular, so they proudly sat down with Merritt and Ethan for an Italian repast.

Little was said at first because all four of them were busy eating, but eventually, they leaned back, satisfied. Merritt eyed the empty lasagna dish. "I guess there's not another one stashed away somewhere, is there?"

Laughter from all. "Sorry, Merritt. Next time we'll double the recipe and then you can even take home leftovers," Nate said.

"This has been a productive trip," Ethan said, helping Lindsey serve dessert, tiramisu cheesecake purchased from a local bakery. "We're probably going to be moving here next spring or summer."

"It sounds as if that might be a good choice. But what about your clinic?" Lindsey tasted the cheesecake, closing her eyes as she savored the lovely blends of flavor.

"I think my co-owners will buy out my share, and I can invest that money. We won't need it to live on, I'm sure I can establish myself as a physical therapist here in the New York area. Or maybe join the staff of a hospital or clinic somewhere in the city."

Merritt gazed at his partner. "I can't believe what a lucky man I am to have Ethan in my life. He wants to be sure I'll always be okay when I'm on stage. As comfortable as I've become using a prosthesis, there's always the off chance of a misstep. Maybe someday a prosthetic leg will be invented with sensors in the sole of the foot. That would definitely solve the problem."

"I believe that may happen sometime in the future," Ethan said. "Hopefully while Merritt is still performing."

He grinned at Lindsey. "And you must be happy about the fact Nate and Merritt will be performing together next fall for the NYCO season. *La Bohéme* and Massenet's *Manon*. Pretty great."

She sighed. "Absolutely. A dream come true. Actually, when the three of us first met Nate at Mecklenburg's after that *Bohéme* in Music Hall, he even said something to that effect, if you recall."

Merritt leaned forward. "When I think back to those awful days after the accident, it's hard to believe we're sitting here now talking about the future…which looks pretty bright."

He reached across the table, covering Lindsey's hand with his own. "I would never be here if it weren't for you, and everything you did for me." He pressed her hand. "I didn't even want to live. But you refused to let me stay in that dark place, Linds. You brought me back to life."

Lindsey's eyes blurred with tears. "I tried to help, Merritt. But you were the one who had to do the hard work. I've told you that often."

"The point is…without your love and your belief in me, I might never have climbed out of that hole." He gazed at her, his voice shaking slightly as he added, "You used the music that meant so much to me—to us—to get me out. David's music."

The room grew quiet. Merritt took a deep breath and continued, "You remember what Kristina Levin said at our graduation? 'And this life shall be for music.' She quoted 'The Roadside Fire': 'And this shall be for music when no one else is near. The fine song for singing, the rare song to hear.' Remember?"

"Yes, I remember," Lindsey replied, smiling at him.

Merritt stood and moved behind her, resting his hands on her shoulders as he bent down and pressed his cheek against her head. "That's what you did for me, Lindsey. Helped me hear and love music again. And that's what you do for everyone you care for—open up their souls to the music in the universe, let them hear it with their hearts." He embraced her warmly.

Nate cleared his throat and Lindsey noticed him running a hand over his face. "A story with the happiest possible ending," he said, his voice cracking slightly. "My lady is indeed remarkable."

Merritt and Ethan shooed their hosts away from the table. "We do cleanup detail after that fabulous meal," Ethan told them.

Nate led Lindsey out onto their small balcony into a starry night with a full moon, where he held her close.

"I meant that, my dearest love. You are a remarkable woman. Your musical gifts seem to reach beyond singing and performing. Being aware of what you did for Merritt was the beginning of my love for you."

Is this some kind of sign? Lindsey wondered. *Am I getting a message from the universe that I need to step away from being on stage, and learn how to use music to heal?*

Nate was especially tender with her that night.

***

Two days later, Amy called. "Michael has developed an aggressive cancer—multiple myeloma—as a result of his HIV…well, no. It's now full-blown AIDS. It's hard to say how long he has, but not long. He's in hospice now. Michael doesn't know I'm calling you, but if you can possibly get away and come up here for a few days, I think you should."

"I need to do that. I'll let you know what I can work out."

Lindsey turned to Nate after she hung up the phone. "That was Amy Boudreaux. I told you about Michael Hartman. She tells me he's become very ill, and he may not have long to live. Amy didn't tell Michael she planned to call me, but I had asked her to let me know."

"You want to go see him." He sat beside her on the sofa and put an arm around her.

"Yes, I really do. He doesn't have any family, Nate. His parents are both dead. He thinks of close friends as family, and I'm one of them. I don't have to stay long, but I'd like to spend a couple of days with him. He's been so honest with me about his life and his disease. It's a great compliment that he confided in me."

Nate thought for a moment. "Do you want me to come with you?"

Lindsey shook her head. "I don't think you need to. Amy and Pierre are right there and I can stay with them. Or with the

Couvreurs. You don't know Michael. I just want to see him and let him know I care."

"Then you should go." Nate put his arms around her. "I have plenty I can do that I was putting off for a bit, and this is obviously important to you. And even more, to your friend Michael."

Lindsey kissed him. "Do you know how much I love you? Thank you for understanding. I'll try to get a flight today or tomorrow and I'll be back by the weekend, at the latest. I just want to spend some time with him and tell him how much I appreciate everything he did for me, and let him know how much he's loved."

Susan Moore Jordan

Chapter 29

Upon arriving at Michael's apartment in Montreal, Lindsey found his condition concerning. He was quite weak. She helped him to eat and use the bedpan. She washed his face and hands gently, being careful not to cause him more pain. Yet he was at peace, urging her to not be sorry that his life was nearing its end.

"Everybody dies, Lindsey. But few people die as I will, ready to accept moving beyond this life to what I know awaits me."

Michael told her Sophia, his therapist, had agreed to have a session with her. "I think it's the best way for you to understand what I've been experiencing…to experience it yourself. You need to be open to it, though. I believe you can be, even more than most people. You've told me how your family has always turned to music to help them cope with difficult life events."

"I would love to do that, Michael."

"Please keep in mind this is just one Guided Imagery and Music session, so I believe you will have the most positive experience if you focus on one particular incident in your life you'd like clarity on. In most cases—certainly in mine—the therapy covers numerous sessions in order to achieve the peace and acceptance I now enjoy."

"I understand. Have you arranged a time?"

"Tomorrow morning, at ten."

***

Sophia Archambeau talked with me as we began the session. An attractive woman in her mid-fifties, Sophia immediately struck me as kind and serene.

Michael had shared with Sophia that I was uncertain about my relationship with Nate, and had told her about David and Merritt and The Accident. I gave her more details and also said I was experiencing uncertainty about what my future should be. I found it easy to trust this generous, compassionate therapist. *What a gift she has for helping and healing*, I thought.

"Here's something that I can't seem to get past," I said. "I so regret never making the time to let David know just how much he meant to me. He gave me so much in so many ways, and I hope he knew I appreciated it. With Merritt, I had such a wonderful opportunity to help him with all the difficulties he was dealing with. Part of me wishes I could go back in time and really talk to David, tell him everything that I've had in my heart." I leaned back against the comfortable chaise where I was reclining.

"I observed a session in which the patient—the traveler— needed to try to resolve confusion from her past, something that happened in her youth," I told Sophia. "While she was on her journey, she encountered herself as a young girl. It was fascinating to hear her talk about what was happening as she experienced it. After the session, when she reviewed her journey with her therapist, it was apparent she had achieved peace."

"Yes, that is a hoped-for outcome frequently…to revisit a time in our past in order to resolve emotions that are blocking our forward progress."

Sophia shifted her position and continued to make notes. "Is that what you would like to accomplish on this journey, Lindsey? To find some way to reach out to David?"

"Yes, that would mean so much to me. And the reason I requested Rachmaninoff's third concerto for this session is that David introduced me to that music and we listened to it together often, and I sometimes listened as he practiced it." I knew the request was unusual, since the GIM therapist generally selects music from a catalog of works, and I appreciated that Sophia had agreed.

She nodded. "Is there a place you and David spent time together...perhaps a park...that was meaningful for both of you?"

"Yes, Cincinnati's beautiful Eden Park. The three of us often walked through the park and visited different arts establishments there."

"Then let's see if we can begin our journey there."

I lay back and relaxed, my eyes closed, as Sophia started the music. For this part of the session, she selected the soothing sounds of the Adagio from the Rachmaninoff second piano concerto. Under her guidance, I easily slipped into a different level of consciousness. Not hypnosis, more like a serene sense of anticipation for what was about to unfold. All I could see was restful darkness.

After a time, the darkness began to lift and I found myself in Eden Park on a sunny, pleasantly cool day, and I told Sophia, "I'm here, I'm in Eden Park."

Now I heard the beautiful, inspiring opening notes of Rachmaninoff's third concerto as I strolled across an open area, admiring the flowers and carefully groomed lawn, and walked toward the Overlook above the Ohio River.

Except it seemed I was floating more than walking. The music surrounded me, I felt I could almost reach out and touch it. A gentle fragrance caressed my skin. I talked constantly to Sophia, describing every experience as it unfolded to me.

"I'm crossing a lawn in the park in full sunlight. Everything here is so wonderful it makes my heart ache. Colors are amazingly vivid. I'm approaching the Overlook—I can see the Ohio River and the towns of Northern Kentucky on the far shore. There is someone seated on a bench. A man. He stands and moves toward me."

I gasped. "It's David! Only…it's more than David. He glows with life and love."

"My Lindsey." He embraced me as he spoke.

"He has his arms around me. How wonderful to feel his embrace."

"Where are we, David?"

"Someplace we had imagined might exist, the place we always knew this glorious music would take us, only we never understood how much more beautiful it could be in every way, more than we could ever dream."

Then we were inside the performance Pavilion and David was seated at the piano, playing the first movement cadenza. He played as he always had, with elegance and passion, every note perfect. Yet his playing seemed at an even higher level and I could almost see the sounds pour from his fingertips. I allowed myself to become completely immersed in the music.

"Now we're outside again, and I'm looking up," I told Sophia, "And the pastel clouds are opening. I think I can see straight into heaven. I can't find words to describe what I'm seeing right now."

"Is there anything you would like to share with David?" Her voice seemed to come from far away.

"David, I miss you so much. But sometimes I feel you are close to me."

"I am," he said. "Whenever you think of me, I'm right there."

"My dearest David. I never told you how much I loved you, how much you meant to me, what an important part of my life you were. You made me a better person. I never thanked you for that."

"But you did, Lindsey. When you smiled at me. When we performed together. I knew it all the time because you felt it so strongly. I felt it whenever you hugged me. When you sat beside me and turned pages. When you and Merritt and I listened to this music together. We had a bond death could never break."

I felt tears on my face. "Your death made us so sad, though."

"I know. And I wish you hadn't been made to suffer. But you both became strong, and I witnessed that and rejoiced."

The second movement began and we lay on the grass and looked up at the heavens. We could see stars pulsing, a sliver of the moon. The sky darkened, then lightened. The air became still yet it caressed us.

We walked hand in hand across the open lawn, admiring the flowers, more vividly exquisite than I had ever seen them.

"It's perfect here," I told Sophia.

The third movement began, and David and I ran and danced through moonbeams and starlight. Sometimes our feet left the ground and we floated. The echoes of Russian church bells I had always heard in this movement were stronger, more pronounced. I felt myself deep inside the soul of the Russia that had once been.

"Never forget this," David told me. "Never forget where I am now. Always know my love is endless and that I am with you whenever you think of me. Be happy, Lindsey. Tell Merritt I love him always, and I'm happy for him that he has Ethan now to care for him."

"And Nate? Is he the right person for me?"

"Only you can know that, my sweet girl. All in time will be made clear."

A final burst of brilliant music and rainbows and stars were everywhere.

The music drew to a close, and my vision…if that's what it had been…began to fade. Sophia spoke gently and helped me return to reality.

It took me a few minutes to reorient myself. Sophia handed me a glass of water as we spent some time discussing my experience. "That was…I can't even describe it. It seemed so *real*."

"After that journey, what are you feeling right now?"

"Excited. Elated. To see David…to feel his arms around me…to hear his voice…to feel his love…it was *everything* I hoped for. I know David is with us, even while somewhere wonderful and beyond beautiful, and he's happy, and his life is filled with music. No…more than that. He has become music, in some mysterious way."

We continued to talk, and then Sophia guided me to use colored chalk as we filled in a circular mandala. I picked up a piece of chalk and examined it. It seemed so pale compared to the vivid colors I had just seen.

"He answered all my questions except one. Where does Nate fit into my life?"

Sophia blended colors in the mandala. "He said that is for you to learn, did he not? That could be considered in another session at some time."

"I can't wait to tell Merritt about this experience. I think it will give him so much peace…as it has me."

***

After her session, Lindsey and Michael talked at length. "I don't know what I actually expected. Something very pleasant, I think, and soothing. It wasn't that at all. It was...I experienced so many different emotions. Wonder. Love. Joy. Peace. And, fleetingly, fear, distress, sadness...but those moments were always quickly resolved."

"Yes, everything we've ever experienced in real life...but amplified many times over, and in a good session, the emotions we want overcome those we don't want."

Lindsey took his hand and held it gently. "It's going to take me a while to process this."

"Oh, yes. But now you understand what I've so poorly tried to explain to you."

"Amazing what the human mind is capable of, isn't it?"

They sat quietly for a few moments, and Lindsey sat beside Michael and gently took him into her arms. "I'm so glad I came. Do you want me to stay a little longer?"

"There's no need for that. You have to get back to your life."

Lindsey sighed. "Being here and experiencing a GIM session has given me...well, I think it's changed me, Michael. How incredible it must be to open people's hearts to how powerfully music can affect us. No wonder Sophia seems so serene. She's helping people change the way they deal with challenges. With life."

When she had a chance to speak with Sophia again, Lindsey was full of questions. "One thing in particular I thought about, are most people who become your patients musicians? I mean, grounded in classical music?"

"Many are, that's true. A background in Western classical music means a patient may be more responsive to what they hear. But if a patient has a strong preference for another genre of music, we can accommodate them."

"I've thought from time to time about the circumstances that led to The Accident...if I'd gone to the movies with my boys that night, perhaps it wouldn't have happened," Lindsey mused. "Or perhaps when we got out of the car to go for that drink, I'd have somehow been able to save them. But I knew those aren't helpful thoughts because we never know what fate has in store for us. And if I'd been with them, I might have been killed or severely injured also. And Merritt needed me."

Sophia leaned forward. "So, your primary purpose was your strong wish to have a moment with David, and you achieved that."

"Oh, I certainly did...as I said, more than I ever thought possible." Another pause. "I know I can tell Merritt about it, but would anyone else understand? Would Nate be able to appreciate what just happened to me? In some ways, he's...well, pragmatic, I guess. Very focused on his career. And on my career—and that concerns me."

"You aren't sure a career on stage is what you really want for yourself?"

Lindsey walked to the window and looked outside as if the answer might be written somewhere in the sky or on the trees. "No...I'm not sure. Not at all. And I don't know if Nate will understand that." She returned to her chair.

"How much longer does Michael have, do you know?" she asked Sophia.

"Not long. A few weeks at best is what his primary physician tells me."

"I hate to leave, but he's told me I should. I have a reservation for tomorrow. But I may come back if Amy tells me the end is near."

"Only you can make that choice, Lindsey. Michael is at peace, you've seen that."

"Will you be with him when he dies?"

432

"Possibly, but chances are he'll be in hospital. So I would be there as his friend, not his therapist."

***

Nate overwhelmed Lindsey when she stepped off the plane at JFK, kissing her urgently. They went directly to the apartment where the kisses intensified and clothing went flying.

Nate lay beside her, breathing heavily. Lindsey pulled him close as her own breathing became even, stroking his shoulders. "I guess you missed me," she said. *What on earth was that about? I was only gone three days.*

"I have a surprise for you. We have reservations at Skytop Lodge in the Poconos for four days starting tomorrow."

Lindsey leaned up on an elbow. "Oh, Nate, that's lovely. Thank you."

"I know I don't show you how much you mean to me nearly enough. We'll just concentrate on us for a while and not even think about anything else." He traced her features gently with an index feature. "My lovely Lindsey. You mean the world to me, you know."

Nate had rented a car and they made the drive through northern New Jersey, a scenic part of the state with high hills, verdant valleys, and picturesque small towns. Lindsey had been to the Poconos but never to Skytop, and she found it charming and elegant. As Nate had promised, no talk of musical engagements, no guilt about not practicing. It was Lindsey and Nate as lovers that took precedence.

She still wasn't sure what had prompted this and was reluctant to even mention Michael or the experience she'd had in her session with Sophia. *Was he jealous because I wanted to visit a dying friend? That's just not like Nate.*

433

After they returned to New York, Lindsey called Merritt and told him about her experience. "I'm sure it must sound strange. I'm still processing what actually happened, but it was so real. It honestly felt as if I was there with him, and it was an experience I'll treasure always."

"It reminds me of what you and I experienced…only much deeper. And with David actually there. But we felt he was with us then."

He paused for a moment. "Do you remember Ethan's friend Michelle? She offers sessions in GIM therapy. I may contact her. It sounds as if it might be something that would be helpful to me, too."

"Are you having problems?"

"Not physically…but I have a lot of self-doubts even though I've enjoyed some success being on stage again. I'm hesitant to accept everything I'm offered."

"Well, that's not a bad thing, is it? You do have to be careful about how much you do."

"Ethan thinks I'm overly cautious. And maybe I am, but I have a fear of tripping and falling on stage. It's one thing if it happens elsewhere, but on stage, an actor needs to maintain an illusion. You know that."

"Yes, it's true. I never thought of it quite that way."

"Thanks for telling me about what happened in your GIM session, Linds. I'll talk to Ethan, and I think I'll get in touch with Michelle."

It seems so few people are aware of GIM therapy, Lindsey mused. *I think all creative people would find these sessions helpful and sometimes maybe even life-changing. At the very least, it's a way to expand an artist's connection to the beauty of the universe.*

***

Nate had less than a week to prepare for his extended stay in Santa Fe once they returned to New York. *Don Giovanni* rehearsals would begin immediately, and performances were scheduled from the last week of July through August.

The day before he was to leave, he paused in his packing and poured them each a glass of wine. "Since you don't have anything pressing, why don't you come with me, at least for part of the time? Santa Fe is unique, as is all of New Mexico. We can rent a car and you can explore to your heart's content."

"Why don't I come out for your opening show and then stay for a while? Your rehearsals will be finished, and we can do the exploring together. I could stay for a couple of weeks. I need to do some studying, though, and go to Philly for a lesson with Madame."

"Well…that's a plan, I guess. It makes sense." He set his wine glass on the counter and walked to the window. "Sometimes I wish…."

"What?" Lindsey stood behind him and wrapped her arms around him.

"Oh, nothing. It's not important." He turned to face her with a grin. "I need a shower. How would you feel about washing my back?"

"Hmm. That would mean I'd be in the shower with you."

"That was kind of the idea." He kissed her.

Later, she gazed at his face as he slept, wondering what had prompted the strange mood he'd been in since she came back from Montreal. *Is he wishing we could be together all the time? But I know he wants me to pursue my career.*

The next morning, Lindsey reserved her plane ticket to Santa Fe. Within minutes the phone rang, an unexpected call from her agent, who sounded excited. "How well do you know Fiordiligi? I know you performed *Così fan tutte* last year at Curtis. Think you could get it back in shape pretty quickly?"

"Why? What's going on?"

"Wolf Trap's soprano broke her leg water skiing, and they didn't have the role covered, for some reason. So, they're looking frantically for a replacement. You have to leave by Monday to get there. Then a week of rehearsal and three performances the following week. It's a good gig and the pay is decent."

It means my trip to Santa Fe will have to be put off, but I can't turn this down. "I'll do it. I think I can get the role back in my voice fairly quickly, and that week of rehearsal is golden."

Nate had come into the room and heard just the end of the conversation, and Lindsey told him what had happened. "I guess there's one reason I learned that role. Not a lot of sopranos have it in their repertory."

He didn't say anything, but she caught a flicker of disappointment in his eyes.

"It just means I'll have to wait a bit to join you in New Mexico, Nate. I'll still be there for your final week."

"Yes...of course, you will. It's a great opportunity, Lindsey. Wolf Trap is a good gig—I'm happy for you. I just wish I could come to see you in it, baby."

Lindsey saw him off and turned her attention to Fiordiligi. It pleased her to realize she had retained the role well and it wouldn't require a lot of work to have it up to performance level. Now she was excited, looking forward to this chance to reprise the role.

The next afternoon as she was packing, she had another call, this time from Sophia. She feared the worst.

"Michael was admitted to hospital this morning. He has perhaps three days at most. He's remarkable, not asking for an increase in his pain medication and awaiting death peacefully. The staff doesn't quite know what to make of this."

"I want to be with him when he dies. Does that sound morbid? I want to know that he actually achieves the peaceful death he anticipates."

"I know he would welcome your presence, Lindsey. He sees you as family."

Wolf Trap! She took a deep breath. *This is a huge step, Lindsey. You cancel this Wolf Trap job now and you might as well say goodbye to any chance of a career as a singer.*

A sense of calm, of clarity, enveloped her. *No, this is my friend...and this is truly what I want. I want to be a healer. I honestly believe that is what I'm meant to do with this sublime gift of music I've been blessed with.*

Her agent confirmed what she had anticipated: this meant he couldn't continue to represent her. Her next phone call was even more difficult, much more difficult.

"You're canceling Wolf Trap so you can watch Michael die? What in God's name has gotten into you?" Nate sputtered.

Lindsey, trembling, clutched the handset. "You knew I was fascinated with GIM therapy," she said.

"Not like this. Not to this extent. I don't even know who you are," his voice shook with emotion. "Lindsey, we shared a dream. The same dream...a future together...in music...in opera. Do you have any idea how this sounds, what this means?"

"I know what this means to my career." A deep breath. "But Nate, this is really what I want to do. Please try to understand...it's the way I need to use the music in my life. It's what I was meant to do."

"I'll never understand, Lindsey." He hung up abruptly, slamming down the phone.

Lindsey stared at the handset, stunned, trying to comprehend what had just happened. *Why was he so angry?*

He's been in some kind of mood lately...but I never expected that reaction.

She pressed her hands to her face and sobbed for long moments. Finally, she released a long, shuddering sigh.

So...goodbye to my career as a singer...and to my love.

*** .

After having cried herself to sleep, Lindsey sent Nate an email the next morning before she left for Montreal. She'd hoped he would call her back so they could discuss her decision, but that hadn't happened.

> Please try to understand. This is important to me. I wish you would call so we can talk about it. We can still have a beautiful life together.

***

Michael smiled when she entered his hospital room. She stayed with him, holding his hand at times, watching always. He slept most of the time, his breathing shallow. The medical staff reluctantly respected his wishes and gave him no food or water. Sophia came several times to sit with them, as did Amy.

Just as dawn broke, Lindsey roused herself and gazed at Michael. His eyes were wide open, reflecting the rising sun. A smile spread over his features as he took a final few breaths, then slipped away peacefully.

He saw what he believed he would see, Lindsey thought, awed by what she had witnessed. *What lies ahead is beyond our imagination.*

***

On her flight back to New York, Lindsey's thoughts returned to Nate. He had never called, nor did he respond to her emails. *I can't believe it's over. I can't believe he would be so...dismissive of me without even letting me explain.*

Back in Brooklyn, Merritt and Ethan helped her pack up all her belongings in preparation to driving her to West Chester. They asked very few questions, and Lindsey was uncharacteristically quiet.

"You seem so sure of your decision," Merritt said. "You're giving up so much."

"I'm not, really. I'm about to gain a whole new world. I know what I'm doing. In fact, I think for the first time in my adult life I feel completely sure of myself. And grateful that I've come to understand this step I'm taking. I know there are so many hurting people in this world, and I also know the time will come when I can help some of them."

Ethan seemed to better understand why she had done this. "This doesn't really surprise me. I remember that sweet young woman who wanted so much to give her beloved friend some comfort, some way to deal with his terrible bereavement and pain."

Merritt agreed, "I'll never forget that. Nate will come around, Lindsey. I know he loves you."

Her voice quivered. "Right now, I don't believe he does. But maybe someday he'll understand."

Lindsey asked for a moment alone and Merritt and Ethan left Nate's apartment. One last time she walked through the home she and Nate had shared, collecting memories. In the bedroom, she placed her keys on the bedside table before slowly removing from her finger the emerald ring Nate had given her at Christmas. Placing it next to the keys, Lindsey thought briefly of leaving a note but decided against it. *What's the point?* She softly closed the door and joined Merritt and Ethan.

***

Two months later, after a visit with Dr. Meredith Logan, Jamie Logan's wife and Chair of the Department of Psychology at Montclair State, and her application and acceptance into the Master of Music Therapy program on that campus, Lindsey became a student again, eager to learn everything she could to eventually achieve her GIM certification.

No looking back.

Chapter 30

Over the next few months, Lindsey found herself busier than ever. In addition to beginning her studies in music therapy, she had some "catch-up" classes to take: psychology and anatomy for this first semester, and later physiology and behavioral neuroscience. She would also need to learn to play the guitar, a skill she was looking forward to acquiring.

For the first time in seven years, Lindsey wasn't focused on an intensive study of vocal technique and opera with other students equally driven by the same goal. Instead, the students in this program came from a broader cross-section of society: people whose interest was in psychology or psychiatry and who saw their love of music as a way to enhance the treatment of patients who needed their help. Many had more limited musical ability than Lindsey. *We all bring our own skills to the table,* she thought.

The atmosphere on campus was warm and welcoming, and Lindsey quickly and easily made friends within her new community. Issi Pittchlyn, a student from Mississippi of Choctaw heritage, became a special friend and confidant early on. Issi had earned her undergraduate degree in music therapy at Belmont College in Nashville, Tennessee, where four years of study required six years of her life due to having to take "gap" semesters to earn tuition money. Lindsey admired her friend's dedication.

She immersed herself in her work but found time to also participate in some campus activities—one of which was auditioning for and becoming a member of the Montclair State University Chorale. Continuing to sing was important to Lindsey and it gave a boost to her morale to think she could always find a choral group to sing with, perhaps even on a professional level.

Since campus housing was filled by the time she applied, the Logans generously invited her to stay with them at least until something opened up. She accepted gratefully and before long began to feel like one of the family. While their virtuoso violinist daughter Laura lived in the New York area with her equally virtuosic pianist husband, Leon Weiss, the Logans didn't see as much of them as they would like and enjoyed spoiling Lindsey.

She learned some of the Logan family history which she found fascinating and pertinent to her own situation. Both Jamie and Meredith had been married previously, and the two of them met while singing opposite each other in a production of *La Bohéme* on their college campus. Meredith's first marriage ended within months. "While it's true the best partnership means you are best friends as well as lovers, there are times when first being best friends with someone doesn't necessarily translate into a strong marriage," was all she would say about that.

Even more interesting to Lindsey, though, was Meredith's decision to pursue a degree in psychology after already earning both undergraduate and graduate music degrees. "My parents were both in the field. When I took a hard look at the possibility of pursuing a career as a professional singer, I accepted that my chances were not great."

"I encouraged Meri to try for a career," Jamie commented. "But she convinced me she was certain working as a

442

psychologist would provide a more fulfilling life for her. I couldn't argue that she had a gift for it, since she'd helped me so much over the years." Meredith had eventually earned her doctorate and the position she now held.

Lindsey pursued the subject later with Meredith. "Jamie said you'd helped him over the years. But you couldn't have treated him, right?"

"Not professionally, no. We always talked about everything, though, and my magnificent husband has a remarkable perspective and balance in his life." She smiled. "Our children, on the other hand, were dealing with their own difficulties and we found professionals to help them when it became necessary."

Meredith gazed thoughtfully at Lindsey. "I think with your background and life experience, you will be a therapist who can be of great help to performing artists and other creatives."

"Why couldn't Nate give me a chance to talk to him and explain myself...and make him see we could still have a life together?"

"Give him some more time, Lindsey. Obviously, you shocked him with the sudden change of career path, even though you may have felt he was aware you'd been considering it. You've told me you never had a specific conversation with him about the possibility."

Lindsey sighed. "There just never seemed to be a good time for that, and now I know it was a huge mistake. Merritt and Ethan see Nate regularly, and they tell me he's doing fine. Well...at least that's how it appears. He's busy, and he's happy with the opportunities that continue to open up for him."

She missed Nate more than she liked admitting, even to herself. She especially tried not to think about him late at night, when somehow the sadness and tears were always close to the surface. *We became lovers so quickly—maybe too quickly,* she thought. Lindsey had responded to Nate's lovemaking as she had to his singing, with her whole being. *He said one time he believed we were meant to be together,* she thought more than once. *How could that have changed so abruptly?*

Sometimes she thought of Pamina in *The Magic Flute,* who agonized over Tamino's apparent unwillingness to talk to her. But in that story, Tamino had taken a vow of silence in order to win Pamina as his love. *I don't think that's what's going on with Nate, though,* she smiled ruefully to herself. *At least Merritt and Nate seem to be on good terms, but Merritt tells me Nate has made clear that I am off-limits as a topic of conversation.*

Christmas in West Chester proved to be bittersweet. She loved having Jake and Noémi and their children around for more than a week, but she had some sad, quiet moments alone, remembering the Christmas she and Nate had spent only a year earlier when their love had seemed to grow and intensify.

Her parents' hearts ached for Lindsey. They were as mystified by Nate's behavior as she was, not able to reconcile his actions with the impressive young man they had believed loved their daughter as much as they did.

"Please don't blame Nate entirely for our breakup," Lindsey told them. "I never talked to him the way I did to you, Dad. I know he felt my decision just came out of the blue."

Mary spoke to her daughter privately. "Is there any chance something else may be going on with Nate? Your dad and I went through a very rough patch just before his PTSD diagnosis. I know Nate hasn't been in a war…but there might be something else."

Andrew and Mary tried to keep her occupied as much as possible with the trappings and traditions of the season. Lindsey turned to M.J., but while he was genuinely sympathetic, he reminded her he could only talk to her as her brother and not a therapist, even though he would have loved to. "You know the rules, sis. We don't treat our family members."

Jake, concerned for his beloved niece, managed to find time to talk with her when the rest of the family went to visit a neighbor. "I know you're hurting," he began. "Nate was your first love and you thought your only love. But that's not necessarily the case, Lindsey."

"You sound as if you're speaking from experience, Uncle Jean. Are you? I know you didn't meet Noémi until you were nearly thirty, and she is quite a bit younger."

"Yes, eight years. And there were women I loved earlier in my life. They were deep and sincere loves as well and were remarkable women. But they were not meant to be my partner for life, as I knew Noémi was almost from the moment I met her. She knew me only as Jean Couvreur, and it was important that I tell her my entire story before I could ask her to join her life to mine."

"So you're saying I may find someone who is better suited for me? Especially since the focus of my life has changed?"

"I'm saying don't discount the possibility. I don't like to see you hurting as you pine for Nate."

***

Ethan had secured a position with an orthopedic clinic near Mount Sinai Hospital in Manhattan, and he and Merritt were now living in a small but comfortable apartment in the Murray Hill neighborhood. They welcomed Lindsey fairly often as a dinner guest or even an overnight visitor when the three of them took in an opera at the Met, a concert at Carnegie Hall, or a Broadway show. She began to think of herself as a New Yorker—*whatever that might be.*

"How's Nate?" Lindsey tried hard to sound casual.

"Well, he just landed a recording contract as Mercutio in *Roméo et Juliette*. Quite a nice accomplishment. Otherwise, he's about the same. If what you mean is, 'is he seeing anybody,' the answer to that is definitely not," Merritt responded.

He stared hard at Lindsey. "And don't look so relieved. Why don't you just call him? Honest to God, you people are both unbelievably stubborn."

Rehearsals began for the spring season at New York City Opera. Lindsey knew Nate would be singing in two operas and debated going to see him, but decided against it. She'd seen him as Mercutio. *I would like to see him in 'Of Mice and Men' someday, though. And when the fall season rolls around, I have to see him and Merritt onstage together in 'Manon.' And then Nate's debut as Gérard. That I cannot miss.*

As Lindsey's second semester drew to a close, one requirement for the next step in her studies was to begin her practicum that coming fall in one of the New York hospitals. The one that appealed to her most was Mount Sinai, and on an especially pleasant day in late May, she had an appointment at the hospital to learn more about her responsibilities and when she would begin her work.

Merritt had invited her for dinner at their apartment, and since she had plenty of time after her appointment, she decided to grab a subway to Lincoln Center and pick up a Metropolitan Opera schedule. *Then I think I might walk to Merritt's apartment. It's unusually nice for late May, more like early spring.*

For Lindsey, being in the Met's vast foyer with its magnificent murals by French painter Marc Chagall was always a treat. She lingered for a bit, admiring the paintings. Schedule in hand, she finally left the opera house and stopped for a moment by the nearby fountain to tuck the schedule into her bag. Somehow, she managed instead to spill everything onto the pavement, watching in dismay as several items started to blow away.

On her knees, frantically grasping for the wayward items—one of which was the opera schedule—she became aware of a helpful passerby collecting them for her.

"Oh, thank you so much! I'm not usually so clumsy. I can't believe I just did that." She glanced at her Sir Galahad as he knelt beside her.

It was Nate.

The two of them gazed at each other for long moments, Nate clutching the schedule he had grabbed.

"Lindsey." He offered her his hand and helped her to her feet, and his touch affected her as it had the first time they met.

I'll never stop loving you, Nate.

He continued to hold her gaze. "It's...good to see you again," he managed to stammer.

And you still love me. The thought ran through her like a clear, sparkling stream breaking through a mossy bank. *You still love me...say something, Lindsey. Don't mess this up.*

"I hear good things are happening for you, Nate. I'm so glad."

"You mean the recording contract. And you...," Nate reddened, making Lindsey think of a wayward child caught with its hand in the cookie jar. "Merritt keeps me posted on how you are as well," he added, finally.

"I'm happy to see you, Nate. You look wonderful."

He reached for her face, the familiar gesture of brushing back a lock of her hair, but caught himself and stopped. "Lindsey...do you think we could see each other? Maybe have dinner?"

"I'd like that very much." With a smile, she couldn't resist adding, "Merritt can tell you how to contact me."

Nate returned the smile. "You know…I think of you often." His reluctance to part from her was apparent.

"As I do of you."

"I'll call you soon. Tomorrow." He continued to gaze at her. "Well…I'm on my way to a rehearsal, so I'd better go."

"I'll look forward to seeing you again," she told him. He moved away, glancing back twice as if he weren't sure they had actually met and talked.

***

They agreed to meet at Raymond's, Lindsey's favorite restaurant in Montclair. She arrived about five minutes early to find Nate waiting. His eyes lit up when he saw her, and he gently took her elbow as they went inside.

Orders placed, Lindsey waited for Nate to speak first. After a moment of silence she finally said, "I think we have a lot to talk about, Nate."

He took a long drink of water. "I know I owe you an apology."

Lindsey gazed at him, waiting.

"I can't even begin to tell you how sorry I am about our last phone conversation. I regretted it the minute I hung up, but…."

"It was partly my fault. I thought I had prepared you better for the possibility I might step away from pursuing a performing career."

"It still doesn't excuse my awful behavior, Lindsey. You did catch me totally off guard, though, I have to admit. At that moment it felt like a rejection of our dream, of us."

The server arrived with drinks and salads and they waited until they were alone again.

Lindsey folded her napkin into a tiny square, taking careful breaths to keep her voice from trembling. "You never called or even emailed, Nate. That hurt."

He shifted his gaze away from her as he sighed. "I thought…I hoped you'd be in the apartment when I got back from Santa Fe, so we could talk in person. And instead, I discovered you'd left. Without a word."

She saw a muscle tighten in Nate's jaw as his eyes darkened. "And you left your ring. That felt pretty final." He picked up his napkin, but rather than shaking it out, clutched it in his fist.

Startled, Lindsey considered how deeply this had affected him. She covered his fist with both her hands. "I never intended to hurt you, Nate. I honestly believed you wanted me gone. Out of your life."

Nate moved his free hand to cover both of hers and they sat silently for a time as Lindsey gazed at their hands, feeling the connection, feeling his love. His fist relaxed and she glanced at his face to see a rueful grin twisting his lips. "What we may have here is a failure to communicate."

Lindsey laughed nervously. "Merritt says we're both unbelievably stubborn. Maybe he's right." She picked up her napkin and shook it out, laying it across her lap, her hands still tingling from his touch.

Nate joined the laugh and visibly relaxed. "I knew you were intrigued with music therapy. And…," another long drink of water, "…and I was going through kind of a bad period there for a while. Wondering if I was really going to be able to do this…this career in opera."

She rested a hand on his wrist. "Oh, Nate. I should have picked up on that."

"Why would you? I didn't say anything, and I should have." Another gulp of water, and he gazed at her directly, his gray eyes troubled. "My insecurities, the rough patch I was going through, made me realize how much I needed you with me. To the point of almost asking you to give up your career. And that would have been so wrong because it would seem like I didn't think…well, I'm not sure exactly. Maybe that I thought your career wasn't as important as mine."

He leaned toward her. "Then when you suddenly told me you had found something more fulfilling to you than a career in opera, I saw it as a rejection of me, too—of our future together. I felt like the world was crashing around me, like nothing I believed had been real."

Their food was served, and they ate in silence for a few minutes. Lindsey said thoughtfully, "You're right. A failure to communicate. I should have shared with you everything I'd been considering. I kept telling myself you were busy—you had enough on your plate. I hadn't made any decision. Why should I bother you with that? And then I had to make a decision so quickly…without speaking with you first."

Nate leaned close. "Well, we're talking now. I think it's time for us to be completely honest with each other, and I'll go first."

Lindsey gazed at him. *We can fix this*, she thought. *I really believe we can. Just say it, Lindsey.* "No, let me. I miss you so much I can't even tell you. Do you think we can get past this and find a way to start over?"

A smile lit up his face. "God, I sure hope so. I've never wanted anything so badly in my life. Even more than singing Scarpia."

That prompted a laugh from both of them. Lindsey raised her wine glass. "What shall we drink to?"

"The future." He clinked his glass to hers.

They took their time reconnecting, meeting next in Central Park for a long walk as the discussion continued. They agreed they'd been lovers before becoming friends, and then they both were so busy that learning more about each other seemed to constantly be put on the back burner.

"You always seemed so sure of yourself," Lindsey said. "You had such a handle on…well, everything."

"I think I come across as more confident than I actually am sometimes. Everybody has moments when they wonder what the hell they're doing."

"I never, ever saw you that way. I felt uncertain ever since I started school at Curtis. I think you knew that, though." She found an empty park bench and sank down on it, and he joined her, an arm across the back.

"I know you told me that the second night we were together. We discussed it at length, I think."

"At first, we talked more. I mean, really talked. But then there was so much going on. It was like we forgot how important it was to share our thoughts, ourselves. Never again."

Nate gazed at her. "You're a gifted singer, Lindsey. Even though I understand now this pull you feel toward healing—and I truly respect it—I'm concerned that you won't be using that gift."

"I'll never stop singing, Nate," Lindsey said emphatically. "I love it too much. But I'll use it differently. I've always loved choral singing, and I'm sure there will be many and varied opportunities for me to be part of a choir. And who knows? There may be other opportunities as well."

Nate nodded. "I can appreciate that."

She took his hand in both of hers. "From now on, we share everything we're feeling. Even if it seems inconsequential."

"Well, this is definitely not inconsequential. I have to talk about it right this minute."

Lindsey stared at him, her eyes wide. *What on earth?*

He grinned at her. "I'm absolutely starving. Let's get a hot dog, shall we?"

Lindsey smacked his arm as they both laughed.

She phoned her parents to let them know she and Nate were spending time together. "It's good," she told them. "We're taking it slow, and we're really talking. Nate wants to call you and apologize."

"Yes, I'd like to hear from Nate," Andrew said curtly.

"Be nice, Daddy. Remember, I told you both of us made mistakes."

Another dinner, this time in Manhattan. Talk flowed easily, and Lindsey described in detail her Montreal GIM session to Nate, who listened attentively. "Why didn't you tell me all this at the time?"

"I wish I had. For some reason I wasn't sure you'd understand...or appreciate... my experience. I don't know why I felt that way, but there it is. You always seemed...well, so practical. Kind of pragmatic."

"Yet we both accepted that we felt this uncanny connection with each other when we first met." He leaned toward her and gently touched her face. "I know sometimes things happen in this life that can't logically be explained."

Nate was silent for a moment. "We both know this, though we haven't talked about it much. Your therapy session was all about how the music we love can transport us. I've had experiences where I felt...well, I call them 'transcendent moments.' Like being in Avery Fisher Hall for a performance of the Verdi Requiem my first year at Ithaca. You know that amazing section that builds up to the 'Tuba Mirum'? It's totally quiet and then there's this kind of plaintive sound of a single trumpet. And more and more trumpets are added until suddenly, the full orchestra and chorus flood the hall with sound."

Lindsey nodded. "One of my favorite moments in that piece."

"Well…there were extra trumpets for that performance, and they were everywhere. I mean positioned so that they surrounded the audience." He took her hand and squeezed it. "It was one of the most exciting things I ever experienced. I know I was sitting in a seat in that room but I would swear I was floating a foot above it."

Lindsey gazed into Nate's shining eyes. "What a wonderful memory."

"And I'm not sure you realized how thrilled it made me when you responded the way you did to me singing 'Nemico della patria' in your family's living room. It's why I jump through all those hoops to do what I do…being given a gift to make music, to share it and help other people experience the sense of being in a beautiful place for a while."

Lindsey laid a hand on his wrist. "We really have the same goal…to bring music into people's lives. I believe we can trust each other to make the right choices for ourselves. And I think we can support each other and build a life together."

Nate nodded. "Yes, we need to trust that we can make each other better, and make what's between us stronger than ever."

She leaned forward and kissed him. A lover's kiss. "Take me home, Nate."

Once in his apartment, they took their time, a memory of the first night they made love and Nate was so caring. Lindsey sobbed in a breath when Nate joined his body to hers, and the powerful release was accompanied by his tears. Lindsey held him close, kissing his forehead as he wept in her arms.

"Never leave me. I need you. You're my life." Nate reached into the drawer of the bedside table and withdrew a box. He opened it and removed an emerald ring, the stone surrounded by diamond chips.

Lindsey gasped as he held it up. *It's my ring...but it's different.* "Is it...?"

Nate smiled warmly. "It's the same stone. I had it reset after we saw each other at Lincoln Center. And this time, it goes on your left hand." A soft kiss. "Marry me, Lindsey Cameron."

Lindsey watched as he carefully placed it on her finger. Happiness rose from the depths of her soul as she gazed at the ring.

"Yes, I'll marry you, Nathaniel Cohen. I love you with all my being." Another kiss and she added almost shyly, "I always wanted a Christmas wedding."

"Then a Christmas wedding is what you shall have, my bride. My wife."

She kissed the ring, she kissed her husband-to-be, and they lost themselves in each other once again. Afterward, Lindsey gazed at Nate as he slept peacefully. She wanted to kiss the faint red splotches under his eyes but didn't want to wake him.

He shared himself with me tonight as he never had before, she thought. *I love him with everything I am...and I know he returns that love.*

***

They had several blissful weeks together in June and July while Lindsey was on break. When she returned to school at Montclair in the fall, the Brooklyn apartment would become a problem, much as they loved it. The commute from Brooklyn to Montclair was lengthy and required both bus and train travel. She needed to be close enough to commute easily when school resumed in September.

Sometimes people get an unexpected break in this life, Lindsey thought when they learned an apartment had opened up in Merritt and Ethan's building in Manhattan. A little more expensive than Brooklyn, but Nate was comfortable with the rent increase. They were able to move in on August first. Lindsey would miss their neighbors in Brooklyn but they promised to get together from time to time. With Merritt and Ethan's help, they packed up and moved to their new home.

Lindsey's summer break had been magical, but she was eager to return to her studies, and particularly looked forward to being at Mount Sinai on Tuesday mornings. She met with her supervisor who promised to give her as much responsibility as was allowed when working with patients.

The New York City Opera's fall season was scheduled to begin on Tuesday, September 11, with a performance of Wagner's *Der Fliegende Holländer*. Neither Nate nor Merritt were in the cast, but both were looking forward to attending as part of the NYCO "family."

Out of the blue, Nate had an opportunity to audition for Seiji Ozawa, music director of the Boston Symphony Orchestra, for a performance the following year of Vaughan Williams' Christmas oratorio *Hodie*. The audition was scheduled for late Monday afternoon, and Nate would return Tuesday, flying out of Logan Airport.

Lindsey had a seven a.m. report time at Mount Sinai on Tuesday. Her parents and M.J. arrived on Monday afternoon for a brief visit; Andrew had a meeting on Tuesday morning at the World Trade Center to discuss a possible mural in the lobby of Tower Two. Mary and M.J. planned to do some shopping that morning, and then take Lindsey and Nate to dinner before the opera performance.

Tuesday dawned bright and clear, the air crisp with the snap of fall.

Susan Moore Jordan

Chapter 31

After about a half-hour planning session, my partner for the day, Issi, and I headed for our nine-fifteen a.m. session with pediatric patients. We laughed and chatted on the rapid elevator ride to the fourteenth floor, where a large, airy room with ten kids awaited us.

It surprised me to see Ethan standing outside the door. *What's he doing here?* I wondered. I saw him occasionally around the hospital when he had patients, but he seemed to be looking for someone. *Me, is he looking for me? Something's wrong.*

As Ethan hurried toward me, I noticed from the corner of my eye several nurses and orderlies clustered around a window, looking up into the sky.

"Lindsey, don't panic, but something has happened. Can your friend run this therapy session by herself?"

Nate. Something's happened to Nate. Fear clutching my gut, I stared at Issi as she nodded to Ethan. "Yes, I can handle this. Lindsey, give me your stuff. I'll put it in our MT room before I leave."

My hands felt numb as I wordlessly handed her my backpack and guitar, keeping my shoulder bag. Ethan started to lead me toward a bench. I shook him off, feeling my blood turn to ice.

"No! Tell me what's going on. You're scaring me, Ethan."

"I knew you were in a meeting with Issi to prepare for your session, so you couldn't have heard about this." A deep breath and his voice shook slightly. "Two planes flew into the Twin Towers of the World Trade Center a short time ago. The first plane hit the North Tower about a quarter of nine, and the other plane flew into the South Tower about fifteen minutes later."

Planes…into the…Dad's down there! Suddenly lightheaded, my vision swimming, I felt strong arms under my elbows.

"Deep breaths, Lindsey." Ethan eased me down onto the bench.

Breathing deeply helped and my vision cleared. My heart still pounding, I clutched at Ethan. "Ethan…my dad is in the South Tower. He had a nine o'clock appointment."

"Yes, I know. That's why I came to find you. Where are Mary and M.J.?"

"They planned to go with him…to do some sightseeing and then meet him after he'd finished." I heard my voice trembling and took more deep breaths. *Steady, Lindsey. Don't fall apart. Think.*

"You said two planes? That can't have been an accident."

"No. I agree. Some kind of attack…possibly the same terrorists who bombed the North Tower eight years ago, but nobody knows at this point."

I jumped up abruptly. "I have to find my dad."

"Lindsey, it's total chaos. Both buildings are on fire. The FDNY must have dozens of trucks there. Who knows what else is going on? There may be further attacks, there or somewhere else."

"I don't care." It was hard to keep from screaming. "I have to go down there and find my father." I stared at Ethan.

"If he's injured, he may be brought here. All hospitals are on alert to treat victims. Your family knows you're here, you should just stay. I'm sure they'll find you as soon as they can."

An orderly ran into the hall. "Come up on the roof," he called out. "We can see the smoke." We watched the quick exodus into elevators.

This can't be happening. It's a perfect fall day in our city. This has to be the worst possible nightmare ever.

If so, it's a collective nightmare. I clutched my shoulder bag, pulling at it as I started toward the elevators. "I have to get a cab and head down there."

Ethan stayed right beside me. "If you're determined, I'm going with you."

It was surreal to walk past the room where Issi was providing music therapy and hear children singing.

Issi has no idea what's happening. I wish I didn't either. I swallowed back tears. *Be strong, Lindsey.*

New York sidewalks are always filled with pedestrians moving at a brisk pace, yet when Ethan and I stepped outside, it seemed as though there were more than usual, many milling about rather than in transit, some crying and clutching each other, almost all staring at the sky. Traffic was nearly at a standstill. I spotted a cab, the driver leaning on the horn, starting a cascade of noise that increased the anxiety I struggled to control.

"We'll walk," I screeched, and began to shove my way through a group of people to get to the outside of the sidewalk.

Ethan grabbed my arm, turning me to face him. "That will take about two hours, Lindsey, and your family might be here looking for you while you're making that trek."

"I can't just stay here and wait, Ethan. I *can't*." I noticed how much my voice shook. "Maybe we can find a cab on Fifth Avenue."

He nodded, and we pushed through another clutch of pedestrians, managing to work our way to Fifth Avenue. Bits and snatches of shocked and incredulous conversations reached us:

"Dear God! A plane just hit the Pentagon!" ... "It's the beginning of World War Three." ... "You realize what's happened, don't you? New York is being attacked. What's next?"

Traffic was crawling but at least moving. Looking down Fifth Avenue, we could see the smoke rising from the World Trade Center. Sirens sounded and soon three fire trucks passed us, moving as quickly as they could through the congestion.

It startled me to see people jogging in Central Park. *They can't possibly have any idea what's happening right now in this city.* Ethan spotted a cab and ran to it, dragging me with him. He yanked open the door and we both slid in. "World Trade Center."

The driver glanced back at us. "No way in hell. First of all, why would you want to go down there? Second of all, I doubt I could even get you close."

"You can get us closer than we are now, don't you think?" Shaking, I gritted my teeth to keep from shrieking at him. "My family is down there. I have to find them."

Ethan rested a hand on my back, trying to help me regain control. *I will never be able to thank him enough for sticking with me through this.*

The cab driver gave me a sympathetic glance. "I'll do the best I can." He had a portable radio with him and turned it up. "I just heard the FAA has sealed off airspace in the entire country. No planes flying anywhere as of right now."

"What about those that are already in flight?" Ethan asked.

"They're being directed to land as quickly as they can at the nearest airport."

I clutched Ethan's arm. "Nate was in Boston for an audition last night. He's supposed to fly into JFK…I think at about noon."

"Not today, he ain't," the cab driver said.

From our vantage point in the cab, with no skyscrapers obstructing the view toward lower Manhattan, the smoke was more clearly visible. *How can firefighters possibly put that out? Don't those buildings have…aren't they supposed to be fireproof?*

Sitting in the crawling cab was almost unbearable, but at least we were inching down the island. More and more pedestrians seemed to be gathering in clumps, some staring into store windows. *I'll bet they're watching TV. There has to be coverage.*

"Jesus," our cab driver barked out. He turned up the radio and we listened to the announcer describing the scene at the World Trade Center. "Firemen continue to steadily enter the buildings. We're nearby on the sixteenth floor of our building here. I can make out people on the roof of the Trade Center, above the fires. There are people at the windows on those floors where the fires are burning." This seasoned reporter next let out a muffled sound—a groan? His voice shook as he continued, "It appears some of those people are jumping from the windows.…"

"Dear God," I gasped, closing my eyes. *They've given up hope.*

"It's jet fuel that started those fires. They have to be like the flames of hell," the cab driver said in a raspy voice. All three of us sat, stunned, considering the desperation of people who had made the choice to leap from the building rather than burn to death.

How can this be happening? I wish it was nine-thirty, none of this is real, and Issi and I are having a great session with

461

our kids. I abruptly recalled once before I'd experienced the feeling of being in a horrible nightmare…in March of 1996. My heart in my throat, I grabbed Ethan's shoulder. "Where's Merritt?'

"He's at home, and he's okay. Or he will be. He's having a hard time with this." He gazed at me. "I thought the same thing and managed to get a call through to him after the second plane hit."

Now distraught about Merritt as well as my family, I wanted to jump out of my skin. The cab had managed to crawl to Forty-Second Street, where Bryant Park stood on our right and our apartment building was nearby to our left. I had a thought.

"Ethan, we should get out here. Go to your apartment to check on Merritt…and he may have heard something from my family. They might even be there." It seemed an impossible hope, but I needed to hope. And I needed to be reassured about Merritt's state of mind. *Ethan said he's okay, but I have to see him.*

Ethan hastily thrust money at our driver, who wished us luck, and we walked as quickly as possible toward our building.

Before we reached it, an eerie darkness spread over the city. My heart began thudding in my ears. *This is very bad.* Ethan stopped, took my arm, and we took a few steps back toward Fifth Avenue. As we looked south a strange cloud moved toward us. It rolled closer and passed over us, causing my eyes to sting and both of us to cough.

I glanced at my wristwatch—ten o'clock. We had left Mount Sinai about 30 minutes earlier.

"What was that…that cloud?" I coughed out, seeing the grim expression on Ethan's face.

"Let's not even try to guess what that might be, Lindsey."

Fear so intense I felt physically ill. "No! Not another attack?" I screamed at him, shaking him. He grabbed me and wrapped me tightly in his arms.

"Let's get home. I'm sure Merritt's been watching TV. He can tell us more."

"I don't know how much more I can take," I choked out, but I allowed Ethan to lead me toward our brownstone.

To my enormous relief, when we reached our building, we saw Merritt standing outside with my mother and M.J. We fell into each other's arms crying and laughing, all of us close to hysteria.

"We don't know where dad is," M.J. said. "We had breakfast in Greenwich Village before he headed down to the Trade Center for his meeting, and Mom and I walked over to Washington Square Park. It's such a beautiful day." He stopped and swallowed hard. "I mean, it was...."

"His meeting was scheduled for nine o'clock." My mother looked as if she were on the verge of total collapse. "We're hoping he wasn't inside when the planes hit."

M.J. put his arms around her and she clung to him. "We tried to get to the World Trade Center but the police kept pushing everybody back so the fire engines could come through. We got close enough to see the fires, though." He stopped, taking several deep breaths.

"There were probably hundreds of people milling around, and we figured we'd never find Dad. So we decided maybe it would be best if we came here. He'd know where to find us. We just got here and I guess Merritt spotted us and came outside."

Merritt looked from one of us to the other, an expression on his face I couldn't read. But I knew it was bad. I stared at him. "Just say it. That cloud that just rolled through."

Merritt went to my mother and took her in his arms. "That cloud...." he struggled to say the words..."the South Tower collapsed."

As I heard his words, my knees buckled and I sank to the ground, Ethan catching me and kneeling beside me. I heard sounds and realized I was making them. The same sounds I'd once heard from Merritt when he allowed himself to grieve for David. Wails coming from deep inside me, ripping my throat.

"You don't know what's happened to him, Lindsey." Ethan rocked me comfortingly. "Don't give up yet. It's likely he was outside the tower. Maybe he didn't get there until after the planes hit. He wouldn't have been allowed to go inside."

Numb, we filed inside Merritt and Ethan's apartment, finding places to sit and watch television, while from outside more and more sounds of sirens—fire trucks from all over the city, police cars from everywhere. First responders rushing to deal with a situation the likes of which none of them could have ever imagined.

I motioned to Merritt to join me in the kitchen, where I took his shoulders and gazed into his face. "Are you all right? I know you thought about the same thing I did, The Accident."

"I did, but this is so much worse. So many people are part of what's happened this morning...I'm trying to keep it in perspective." He hugged me hard. "Honestly, Lindsey, I'm okay. This is surreal. I keep thinking it can't be happening...but it is."

I'm not sure how long we sat there, numbly staring at the screen and attempting to make sense of what we saw and heard. We watched in horror as the North Tower collapsed, throwing up another vast cloud of dust and ash. It looked more like a special effect for a horror movie than something that actually happened. What was in the cloud? Dust, ash, particles of everything that had been in the building. Maybe even parts of the plane that had hit it. And even worse...much worse.

I thought about people on the street, breathing in that poisonous mixture. Would they survive? So many questions went through my mind: *Was Dad in the buildings when they were hit? Did he make it out before they collapsed? Could he be dead? My remarkable father, who had survived so much, to die in this way. And how many people were in those buildings? How many fathers? How many mothers? How many souls? So many families shattered by this moment. So much suffering. So much senseless pain. How could this be happening?*

I didn't even hear the tap on the door, but Ethan opened it and loudly cried out, "*Andrew!*" Our unflappable Ethan grabbed my father and sobbed. In seconds the rest of us surrounded him, touching him, weeping with relief and joy. My mother claimed the love of her life, and they held each other as if they would never let go.

Ethan helped him off with his jacket, wadding it up in a bundle, and ran for towels to clean his face and head. Mom pulled him to the sofa and sat close beside him.

"I was about a block away from the towers when I heard the sound of a low-flying jet, and I stopped and looked up, knowing how odd that was." He had to stop and cough. Ethan handed him a wet hand towel and Dad gratefully wiped his face. "Seconds later the jet hit the North Tower. The ground shook from the explosion and seeing the flames and smoke was...well... indescribable."

"We saw it from Washington Square Park, Dad," M.J. commented. He pressed our father's shoulder. "It must have taken you back for a minute."

"You mean to Vietnam? Damn right it did. Right back to my first day there, when our base was attacked." More coughing.

We were all silent for a moment as Dad continued to cough vigorously.

What was in that cloud? I thought. *How long was he walking around in it?*

"But it wasn't a flashback." He set his jaw. "This was different. There were a lot of people outside the buildings on the plaza, and we just stared up at the building and at each other, not knowing what to do. Some guy yelled out, 'I hope to God that was an accident,' and it couldn't have been ten minutes later that the second plane hit."

I was kneeling at Dad's feet, and I reached for his hand and held it tight. Mom took the towel from Ethan and wiped Dad's head, cleaning off more of the debris.

"They had already cleared the lobby, so there was a crowd standing around outside. Some of us…I'll bet most were veterans…started yelling about going inside to help, but the cops pushed us back so the firefighters weren't blocked." He made a sound somewhere between a groan and a sigh.

"I don't think I've ever felt so helpless. More and more trucks arrived, and another guy said, 'How in hell are they going to put those fires out? That's jet fuel.' The firefighters knew that. They were there to save as many lives as they could."

There was a pause as we all considered the gallantry of the members of the NYFD.

"I think we hung around because we hoped to find some way to help." A shaky breath. "This may have been the worst. Those fires were ferociously hot. People were trapped on upper floors. Some opted to…." he couldn't continue.

"We heard about that," Ethan said. "What a choice to have to make. And you witnessed it firsthand."

"I can't talk about it. Maybe someday. Not now." I felt bile rise in my throat. *He saw some of the jumpers...or what was left of them.*

"The police kept pushing us back, trying to open up more space so people running from the buildings could get out more easily. That was one positive, knowing people on the lower floors were getting out. But watching those firemen going in, determined to save more lives...it's one of the most courageous things I've ever seen in my life."

Mom hugged him hard.

Dad continued, "It finally dawned on me you must be frantic with worry, and I decided the best...well, maybe the only thing I could do that made any sense was to try to get to Lindsey's." He gazed at Mom. "I figured you and M.J. might eventually go there as well, so that's when I started to try to get through the crowd and head uptown."

Dad said he had been walking for only about fifteen minutes when he again felt the ground shake and heard the roar behind him. "I knew this couldn't be good, so I quick ducked inside a pharmacy. Thank God I did, because if I'd been outside...."

"That's when the first tower fell," Merritt murmured. "I sure hope you were still inside when the second tower came down."

Dad nodded, and we were all quiet for a moment. "It was about a half hour later, but I thought it was possible the second tower would fall, so I stayed put. When it seemed safe, I went out and saw police and paramedics helping people who'd been caught in the fallout." He took a moment. "They were...covered in a thick layer of ash and...whatever else was in the cloud. The first responders were cleaning out their noses and throats, trying to get the worst of the dust off of their clothing." He took a deep breath, followed by a paroxysm of coughing. My mother rubbed his back, and he was finally able to resume.

"There was…it looked like confetti was floating everywhere, like a tickertape parade. I'm guessing it was paper from the buildings, shredded into bits in the explosion. It added to the surreal scene."

Another ragged breath. "I asked a cop who was helping people if I could do anything. He took a good look at me, thanked me, and said the best thing people could do now was to get out of the area. When I told him I wanted to go to my daughter's apartment in Murray Hill, he flagged down a police car heading uptown and asked the officer to drop me off."

Mom pressed her hands to his face and spoke for all of us. "Thank God you're here. Thank God you're safe." I thought, *he's our miracle.* I knew we all felt the same.

Ethan stood. "Andrew, who knows what was in that toxic brew you were in? I suggest you shower, wash your hair three times, and get into fresh clothes. You and Merritt are pretty much the same size."

Merritt and I prepared food from both our kitchens. Mom offered to help but we urged her to just sit with Dad on the sofa after his shower. They clung to each other, and I had an idea of what was going on in their minds. They'd survived another calamity, this may be the worst of all.

"Nate. I'm sure he's sick with worry," I said to Merritt. "I have to get word to him that we're okay. Are the phones working? Nate has a cell phone."

Merritt put his arms around me and held me tight. "There's no phone service at all. We've learned that the city is virtually sealed off. It's almost impossible to get in or out. Phone service could be restored tomorrow. He should be able to get home then."

How strong he's become, I thought. *He's comforting me as I once comforted him, trying to help me deal with this incomprehensible situation.*

We picked at our food, remaining in front of the television set. We learned three planes had been hijacked, two from Boston's Logan Airport—that sent a fresh chill down my spine, because Nate was in Boston. I took a deep, shuddering breath. *No, he said he'd be back in the afternoon. I can't...cannot even think about the possibility he took an earlier plane. Fate couldn't be that cruel.*

The first two planes had flown into the Twin Towers of the World Trade Center. The third plane originated at Dulles Airport in D.C. and crashed into the Pentagon. Later we learned from TV reports that a fourth plane, from Newark Airport, had been hijacked and crashed somewhere in Pennsylvania. It was thought it had intended to head for the Capitol Building or the White House. There were early reports brave passengers on that flight might have thwarted the hijackers, and it cost them their lives. But everyone in the first three planes had died, too. Did the passengers on the fourth plane know that and choose to die heroes, we wondered?

Eventually, Ethan persuaded my parents to use their extra bedroom, rather than try to go back to their hotel, and they retired to get some sleep. The rest of us continued to watch television late into the night, Ethan stretched out in an armchair. M.J., a throw pillow under his head, sprawled on the carpeted floor. Merritt sat next to me on the sofa, holding me close.

In silence, we watched the floodlights at the wrecked towers, the rescue dogs, the determined firemen continuing to search through bizarre and grotesque piles of smoking rubble. All under the pall created by the cloud, which still hung in the air. Over the hours it became apparent there were few survivors—if any. Thousands of lives erased in a matter of mere moments. *But not Nate,* I thought. *Nate will come back to me.*

Resting my head on Merritt's shoulder, exhaustion overtook me and I slept.

Chapter 32

I fell asleep thinking of Nate, longing to feel him safe in my arms, but I dreamed of David.

"I don't think I can do this," I told him. "The world has been changed forever. Nothing will ever be the same."

"People will need you more than ever, Lindsey. And one thing will never change, you know that."

"Music, you mean?"

"It's gotten you through crises before. And it always will."

A frantic rapping on the door woke us. I opened my eyes to find my beautiful Nate, unshaven and with dark circles under his eyes, kneeling beside the sofa, his arms around me, trembling and barely able to speak. "Thank God you're here. Thank God you're safe. All day I couldn't get through to you on the phone or email, and when you weren't in our apartment, I thought you might...."

"We're all here, and we're all safe." I burrowed deeper into his arms. "Oh, Nate, I'm so glad you're here; it's been a nightmare. I tried reaching you, too, but the phones and computers were dead. And then we heard the first two planes came from Boston, and I thought...oh, thank God you're safe. How did you to New York? What time is it?"

"It's three a.m." Nate stood and gently helped me to my feet. "I had a helluva time getting here." He glanced around the room. "Where are your parents?"

"In our guest room, sleeping," Ethan answered quietly, a finger to his lips. "Why don't you two go to your apartment? We can talk tomorrow. It's good you're here, Nate."

Inside our apartment, Nate and I clung to each other. Being in his arms had never felt so good.

"God, I was so scared for you." His voice shook and he held me even tighter. "We weren't sure how bad things were here at first. And when we saw the fighter jets...."

I pulled back. "Fighter jets? When was that?"

"I'm not sure. Sometime late morning, I think."

"We must have been...my dad was missing and we were terrified. We went crazy when he showed up. I don't know that we'd have even heard them since we were in Merritt and Ethan's apartment with the TV blaring."

"I have to get some water," he said. "I don't think I've ever been so thirsty in my life."

We went into the kitchen and he drained a tall glass of water and filled it again.

"Stress can cause that, but slow down. Just sip this one," I cautioned.

He nodded, sipped the water, and set the glass down. "I felt panicky all day. So much stress and anxiety."

"Just try to breathe, Nate. Let's go to bed and try to get some sleep."

"In a minute." Nate caressed my face as he gazed at me. "I knew your dad was supposed to be at the World Trade Center this morning...no, that was yesterday morning. I remembered you had a therapy session planned, but I thought you might have rearranged things so you could be with him."

I could feel Nate's heart racing as I held him. I kissed him softly. "I'm right here, my love. And I'm fine, now that I'm in your arms."

472

I led him into the bedroom, and we undressed as we talked. "How did you manage to get here? I had no idea when I'd see you." I pulled out hangers for both of us.

"When I found out Logan Airport had shut down, I checked about a bus and learned Port Authority was closed." Nate removed his shoes. "One of the desk clerks at the hotel was fantastic. It took nearly the whole day but she finally found a rental car for me. Then the people at the rental office were terrific, they marked a map for me."

He continued as he hung up his clothing, "One guy was from Westchester County and knew all the ways to get from there into the city. They figured the closer I got, I might find law enforcement everywhere."

"I wouldn't be surprised. On the news, they were certainly visible, and we were informed the city had pretty much been sealed off." I turned down the covers for us.

"It was definitely slow going, and sure enough, when I got close to Manhattan the New York Highway Patrol was checking every car headed into the city. Most people had to turn around." Nate climbed into the bed and reached for me.

With a sigh, I snuggled close to him. "But here you are." I marveled at his tenacity, though it didn't surprise me.

"Yes, I lucked out." He caressed my face, gazing at me as if he wasn't sure I was real. "It turned out one of the cops was an opera lover and he'd seen me perform last fall, so he knew I was legit."

"That's quite a journey you had." I leaned up on an elbow. "And I'm so sorry you were worried about me. I would never have wanted that."

"I thought I might have lost you…forever." His voice cracked.

"So many people lost someone they loved yesterday. We are so, so lucky." I kissed him and again held him close. "We should try to get some sleep, my dearest love. You have to be exhausted."

"I'm...I just can't seem to relax."

"Maybe music will help," I suggested. *What would be good for helping us cope with the end of the world?* When David was killed, the Brahms Requiem had helped me, and then the Rach Three. But neither of those seemed right for this occasion. *Strings, I think.* Rachmaninoff's "Vocalise" for cello ensemble, paired with Ravel's "Pavane for a Dead Princess." The soothing music and my gentle caressing of his shoulders and chest helped my beloved to relax, and finally, to sleep.

I lay awake for a few minutes longer. The CD player was set for repeat, and I let the music take me with it as I listened again, thinking of my dream and my dear, sweet David.

Music, the constant in our lives, no matter what happens. It will never fail us.

***

I had expected the sun to wake us, but that day and for several more, sunrise was subdued. The cloud from the fallen towers continued to hang over Manhattan. We were showered and dressed when a tap at the door revealed Ethan bearing gifts: omelets, and fruit for breakfast.

"I'm going up to the hospital to see if there's anything I can do there," he said as he handed me the plates.

"I should go with you." *I hadn't even thought of that. What kind of helper am I?*

"No, you don't need to. There were very few survivors, and the hospital received only a handful of patients." We were both silent for a moment. "And you have a patient right here you can treat. Andrew needs to cough as much of that toxic brew out of his lungs as he can. I advised Mary to pound on his back, and Merritt's vaporizer is running now. Steam helps."

I nodded and hugged him, went back into my apartment, and saw Nate had coffee brewing. We sat together on the sofa, sharing the food. "I wonder how long it will take us to process what happened yesterday? I mean this entire country. And we have to wonder what the future will bring."

He sighed. "I haven't given it much thought, but our company was supposed to open its fall season last night. I guess that's not going to happen for a while. Maybe it shouldn't. We're at war, one way or another."

"No, Nate, don't say that," I took his hand. "The opera season has to take place. And it will, I'm sure of it."

"It just seems…well, frivolous. When I was trying so hard to get home, I saw television coverage everywhere. What happened here…I kept seeing the firemen, the first responders, head toward the Trade Center. Then when the towers came down.…" He swallowed hard. "All those brave people, heading toward unimaginable danger. Yet willing to give their lives to save others. Those are noble people, Lindsey."

"Yes, they are. They will be honored." We were silent for a few minutes. My voice was unsteady when I added, "There are so many families that have been destroyed by this."

Nate stood and took our plates into the kitchen, staring out of the window when he returned. "It almost makes me want to…I don't know. Enlist in the military, maybe. Do something meaningful with my life…like you're doing, Lindsey."

It shocked me to hear him say that, to speculate he had somehow wasted his life. I put my hands on his shoulders and turned him to look directly at me.

"Nathaniel Cohen, listen carefully. When all else fails, what is there? Some people would say love, and that's true. But isn't one of the strongest manifestations of the love in the universe its great works of music?"

The sadness I perceived in his eyes broke my heart. "Nate...performers like you bring music to life. Music can help restore some sense of order in the world."

He glanced away, and I gently turned his face toward me. "Without artists...including performing artists...the beauty we receive from the universe can't be shared. Can't...*heal*. People will want to see operas, visit museums, and read books. Because without them, life makes no sense."

I didn't even know where that speech came from, but as Nate listened to me, I saw a light in his eyes that hadn't been there before. "My Lindsey. My dearest love. You are a treasure."

He leaned forward and kissed me, a sweet, lingering kiss. "Let's get married, as soon as possible. I don't want to wait until Christmas." I knew what he was thinking: *who knows where we'll be or what will be happening in the world in the next months?*

I nodded, smiling at him but feeling the threat of tears. Something I thought all of us would feel for a long time to come.

"Yes, we should get married. As soon as we can make arrangements. They can be as simple as possible, but...I do want music. There must be music at our wedding."

***

As we walked through the gray cityscape later that morning, two things struck me. The wind was blowing up our island from the south, and an acrid stench permeated the air. A biting odor that reminded me of burning plastic, smelling of death and destruction, stinging our eyes.

476

The other was the posters. Homemade posters, with photographs taped or glued to them. Missing people. People who probably died when the towers fell, and their families frantically looking for something, anything, to give them hope. Nate pulled me close and murmured, "These will multiply a hundred-fold over the next few days." I knew he was right.

People gathered in groups to cheer as FDNY trucks drove by, showing their love and appreciation for first responders. Both my dad and Nate had referred to them as heroes, and they were. And many of their numbers had died in the towers. *Not everyone is called to this service, though*, I thought. *I think I said the right thing to my love, that there are all kinds of heroes.*

Mom and Dad were the first we told about our decision to marry now.

"Your daughter is the most important thing in my life," Nate said. "I want to confirm my complete commitment to her in this way, and I promise you I will spend the rest of my life honoring that commitment."

Hearing him say that erased any lingering doubts I could possibly have had about his love for me, and from the look that passed between my father and my fiancé I knew my dad shared my thoughts.

"I feel the same," I said. "We don't know what the future holds, but we know our lives are meant to be bound together, whatever may come."

Mom nodded in agreement, tears in her eyes, and Dad said, "I think this would be a wonderful affirmation of life and love and hope in this time of destruction and despair." They hugged me for the longest time.

Not all New York state offices were open, but we were able to get our marriage license, thanks to an attorney my dad knew. The chaplain at Mount Sinai agreed to perform the ceremony, and even arranged for us to use one of the chapels.

Nate and I wanted to sing "Du bist die Ruh" to each other. My mom agreed to play for us and be my matron of honor. M.J. would stand as best man for Nate.

While Nate was on the phone with his parents to ask if they would try to get to New York by Friday afternoon, I went to Merritt's apartment to let him know about our plans. "Will you sing for us, Schubert's 'An die Musk'? I know it's a song you love."

He hugged me. "You know I will. Wouldn't it be perfect if David were here to play?"

"You dreamed about him too, didn't you?" We gazed at each other as I felt a thrill run through my body.

"'There are more things in heaven and earth....'" He smiled broadly as he quoted Shakespeare.

Nate reported that his parents promised to move heaven and earth, if necessary, to be there. Both our families would be with us as we joined our lives.

Despite all the horror, a light shone for Nate and me. A hasty shopping trip with my mother provided an ice-blue, tea-length gown. The florist at my parents' hotel was more than happy for the distraction of creating a bridal bouquet and a tiara for me, corsages for our mothers, and boutonnieres for the men. Unknown to me, Nate already had our rings…he had bought them as a surprise for me when he had the emerald reset for my engagement ring.

On Friday, three days after the towers fell, at four in the afternoon, Lindsey Antonia Cameron and Nathaniel Asher Cohen stood with our family and a few close friends and became husband and wife.

Merritt sang, more beautifully than I thought I had ever heard him, Schubert's lovely ode in praise of music, lifting our hearts. Nate and I faced each other, our voices strong and sure as we pledged our love with Schubert's exquisite setting of a poem by Friedrich Rückert, singing of the peace and love we had found in each other in the midst of life's turmoil.

You are repose
And gentle peace,
You are longing
And what stills it.
I pledge to you
Through joy and pain
To be a dwelling for you
In my eyes and heart.

Come in to me,
And softly close
The gate behind you.
Drive other pain
From this breast.
Let my heart be filled
With your joy.
This temple of my eyes
Is lit by your radiance alone.
O fill it utterly.

***

The following afternoon I sat with Ethan as the New York City Opera presented its opening performance in the State Theater at Lincoln Center. Merritt and Nate would be on the stage with the rest of the NYCO family for comments by impresario Paul Kellogg and would join the people they loved before the curtain was raised on the opera.

As Nate had predicted, some people opposed this, thinking an opera performance was frivolous so soon after the attack.

And others were still afraid to go to public places. The theater was only half full and it was apparent that there were those in the audience who were uneasy. I saw more than one glance nervously at the ceiling as if expecting yet another plane to descend on a New York landmark.

The lights in the auditorium darkened, and the restlessness in the audience died down. A new emotion filled the hall when the curtain was lifted to the sight of a large American flag hanging above the stage, and standing together, all the members of the NYCO, performers and staff alike. Stage technicians dressed for work. The cast of *Die Fliegende Höllander* in costumes. Other singers in the company were in civilian dress, as was the administrative staff. The orchestra in the pit, in formal dress. All of them were there for this occasion.

At the center of the stage, Paul Kellogg lifted a hand to be sure he had everyone's attention. Overwhelmed with emotion, I gripped Ethan's hand.

Mr. Kellogg explained that at the request of Mayor Giuliani, the New York City Opera would present its season as planned. In a quivering voice, he then told us: "The performing arts have many functions. Catharsis, consolation, shared experience, reaffirmation of civilized values—distraction." A pause, and he added, "So—we're back."

The orchestra played a brief introduction recognized immediately by the audience, who stood, and everyone in the building joined in singing the National Anthem.

The curtain was lowered, the lights brought up halfway in the house, and my husband joined me, linking his arm through mine. I rested my head on his shoulder and felt his lips press against my forehead.

When I had dreamed of David, I told him the world as we knew it was forever changed. But he reminded me one thing never changed, and that was confirmed when the overture to

Der Fliegende Höllander began. This turbulent, powerful music by Richard Wagner suited the occasion perfectly. A brilliant burst of sound in the high strings followed by a strong theme in a minor key played by the low brass seemed to echo what we'd experienced over the past days.

Wagner quieted the music, the theme repeated softly in low brass and woodwinds before it began to build again to full orchestra. *He might have written such a piece for this time we're living through*, I thought as I gripped Nate's arm. Next a calmer, brighter section. The original theme was repeated, and just before the conclusion, a gentle, peaceful moment for woodwinds and harp.

This performance marks the beginning of the healing of this broken city, I reflected.

All of us are healers, all of us in the music world. I recalled Krissy Levin's words: *"Music can heal and inspire, calm and incite. It has the power to lighten the dark corners of the mind and soothe the pain of a wounded spirit or a broken heart."*

I thought back over my life for the past five years, from the night of The Accident through this horrific disaster we'd all just experienced. We never have any idea what life has in store for us. We hope for all good things, but sometimes, we're faced with the unimaginable. And we have to find some way to pick up the shattered pieces of our lives and move forward.

Even in the darkest hours, music can give us hope.

Bonny Guided Imagery and Music

Researching music therapy for this novel introduced me to the Bonny Method of Guided Imagery and Music (GIM): mental and psychological healing achieved by utilizing guided psychotherapy to expand self-awareness through inner imagery, stimulated by listening to selected classical music.

Dr. Helen Bonny first developed this form of music therapy in the 1970s. Since then, other therapists have explored guided imagery in differing ways. Using any of these methods requires many years of study and application, and there are relatively few qualified GIM therapists in this country.

My heartfelt thanks to Dr. Brian Abrams, Coordinator of Graduate Music Therapy at Montclair State University, for responding to my numerous questions, generously providing me with in-depth, invaluable information which has helped me gain a better understanding of the field of GIM therapy.

The scene in the book in which Lindsey experiences a GIM therapy session is the product of my imagination, based on the research I've done, including reading numerous case histories which are available on the internet, and on my own transcendent experiences when reacting to certain musical compositions. Dr. Abrams generously read and approved this scene.

Acknowledgments

Music has given me a lifetime of beauty and love. I've always found healing during troubled times through the music that is part of me, and the difficult days in which we live now are no exception. Writing has been a great help also, as I immerse myself in a story and its characters for long stretches of time.

I began writing this book almost four years ago, but as sometimes happens, it wasn't saying what I wanted it to say so I put it aside and came back to it recently, when music has become more vital to me than ever before.

We first met Lindsey Cameron in *Memories of Jake,* as the longed-for child of Andrew and Mary Cameron. In *Man with No Yesterdays*, we learned she had shown promise as a classical singer and was preparing to audition for the Conservatory of Music in Cincinnati in 1992. Lindsey was a young woman with spirit as well as talent, and I became curious to learn if she had been successful in her desire to sing opera. Or would her talents take her in another direction, and for what reason?

Lindsey's journey proved to be a fascinating one which took me into areas of research which, as a "music-centric" writer, I had never considered before.

I have many people to thank for their help, first and foremost my more-than-editor, Ashleigh Evans. As always, she helped me work my way through this intricate story, assisting with research, double-checking facts about exactly what happened in New York on September, 11, 2001, as well as controlling my occasional wayward impulses. And most of all, she cheered me on when I became overwhelmed with the task I had set myself with this book, wondering if I could actually write this story.

While a wealth of material on amputations and the care of amputees is available on the internet, I also read first-person articles and books which were extremely informative. Preparing a home for a disabled person I had witnessed firsthand when my friends Ken and Mary Ellen Van Camp's son Michael suffered a severe traumatic brain injury and they were eventually able to care for him at home. Happily, over the years Mike has made a remarkable recovery and is living and working on his own.

Opera World has undergone many changes since the middle of the twentieth century and it was my good fortune to have contacts in the profession who were immensely helpful. Former voice students and friends Stephen Paynter, Caryn Kerstetter Reeves, and Thomas Lehman were more than helpful and generous sharing their knowledge and time.

Stephen is a long-time (over twenty years) member of the prestigious Metropolitan Opera Chorus and currently serves as Assistant Chorus Manager. Caryn is an arts administrator, on the staff of the Glimmerglass Summer Opera Festival, where she serves as Director of Development. Tom has been performing with the Deutsche Oper Berlin for the past seven years and has also performed extensively throughout Europe.

All of them gave me a great deal of insight into what is required of an aspiring opera singer in this day and age, Tom in particular because he is living the life. In his position, Stephen certainly has his finger on the pulse of the world of opera. Caryn put me in touch with Peter Russell, a highly respected leader in the opera industry, who kindly provided more insight into the New York City Opera.

While I had some general understanding of music therapy, Michelle Handy-Fitzgerald, a Board-Certified Music Therapist, answered my many questions about her profession and particularly about music therapy with pediatric patients.

Francine Silvoy Galuska, whom I've known since her high school days locally, has her degree in music therapy and was also helpful. Francine put me in touch with the highly respected Dr. Brian Abrams of Montclair State University who answered my many questions about Bonny Guided Music and Imagery therapy thoughtfully and thoroughly.

Local friends who are exemplary musicians, Bob Riday and Scott Besser, also read sections of the book and gave me extremely helpful feedback. My great-nephew, Elliott Jacobson, was kind enough to help me with the German Lindsey needed when she encountered Frau Bergmann on her flight to Seattle. Thanks also to musical friends Reese Revak and Kyla Page Williams for answering questions about the Curtis Institute of Music and Westminster Choir College.

Thanks to remarkable book cover artist Wesley Goulart, who managed to take my vague meanderings about the design and produce the stunning image that appears on the book.

Many thanks as always to my kind and patient beta readers for their valuable input: Michaele Benedict, Audrey Duffield Henry, Marti Lantz, Eric Mark, Nathaniel Taylor, and Ken Van Camp. Michaele has been my mentor since day one of my venture into writing novels and her input is always invaluable.

And thanks also to my friends and colleagues in the Lady Writers of the Poconos—Sahar Abdulaziz, Belinda Gordon, Evelyn Infante, Kelly Jensen, Mary Ann Moore—for reading and commenting on sections of the book, and for their encouragement.

A word about Rachmaninoff's Piano Concerto Number Three: it's a work I've come to love above all others for many reasons, and listening to it frequently as I wrote the book was a constant source of joy. What a wonderful happenstance that the Van Cliburn Piano Competition winner for 2022 was an 18-year-old genius from South Korea, Yunchan Lim, whose rapturous award-winning performance showed me even more beauty in the work.

As I write these acknowledgments, the country is remembering once again the events of 9-11. Because I've so recently relived that experience, I found the memorials especially poignant. Even more than remembering that date, though, I recall the remarkable sense of unity which we wrapped ourselves in beginning the next day.

It's my sincere hope this country can somehow find healing from the divisiveness we are currently experiencing. And perhaps that will begin, in some way yet unknown, with music.

Susan Moore Jordan
September, 2022
Pocono Mountains of Pennsylvania

NOTE: Numerous performances of the Rachmaninoff concerto can be found on YouTube, including that of Mr. Lim's award-winning concert at the end of June, 2022. If you take the time to listen, I promise you'll find it remarkable and inspiring.

Joseph Martin's uplifting anthem, "The Awakening," is also well-represented on YouTube with many fine performances.

Videography

Since there are numerous operas mentioned in the book, I've chosen instead to focus on those arias/duets which have special significance to the characters.

Sempre libera (*La Traviata*, Verdi)
Renee Fleming, *soprano*, Royal Opera House
Joseph Calleja, *tenor* (singing offstage)

Parigi, o cara (*La Traviata*, Verdi)
Renee Fleming, *soprano*, Joseph Calleja, *tenor*
Royal Opera House

La ci darem la mano (*Don Giovanni*, Mozart)
Bryn Terfel, *baritone*, Hei-Kyung Hong, *soprano*
Metropolitan Opera, 2000

Nemico della patria (*Andrea Chénier*, Giordano)
Giorgio Zancanaro, *baritone*
Royal Opera House

Come scoglio (*Così fan tutte,* Mozart)
Daniela Dessi, *soprano*
Teatro alla Scala, 1989

Hai già vinta la causa (*Le nozze di Figaro*, Mozart)
Dmitri Hvorostovsky, *baritone*
Salzburg Festival, 1995

Ach, ich fühls (*The Magic Flute*, Mozart)
Edith Mathis, *soprano*
Hamburg State Philharmonic Orchestra, 1971

Recurring Characters

Andrew and Jake Cameron began life as Andrew and Jacob Martin in my first novel, *How I Grew Up*. Their mother, Toni, divorced Allan Martin after he shot and killed both her parents, an event which was witnessed by the boys, ages eight and six.

In *Memories of Jake*, Toni married Max Cameron and he adopted the boys. Max gave his new wife and sons the stability they had never known and a strong family life.

All of the Camerons appeared in *Memories of Jake* and *Man with No Yesterdays*. Both books recounted the effect serving in the war in Vietnam had on Andrew and Jake and their family.

Jamie Logan was also part of *How I Grew Up* as the young tenor who played opposite Andrew and Jacob's aunt Melanie in a high school production of the musical *Carousel*. Jamie's story, and that of his wife, Meredith, is found in *You Are My Song*. A sequel, *Jamie's Children*, followed the troubles and triumphs of their children Laura and Niall. Jamie and Meredith were seen briefly in *Memories of Jake*.

Krissy Porter was a close friend of Andrew and Jacob's aunt Melanie in *How I Grew Up*. She became Kristina Porter Levin in *Eli's Heart*, and appeared in *You Are My Song* and *Jamie's Children*. She also appeared in *Memories of Jake*.

About the Author

After a lifetime as a musician, Susan Moore Jordan wrote and published her first novel in 2013 at the age of seventy-five, and she hasn't stopped since.

In her first four novels, the author drew from her life experiences as a voice teacher and stage director. These were followed by a two-book series, "The Cameron Saga," which details the struggles of two brothers whose lives were irrevocably changed by their service in the Vietnam War. *Memories of Jake* received a Red Ribbon Award from the 2017 Wishing Shelf Awards. In 2019, *Man with No Yesterdays* was a semi-finalist in the Kindle Awards and a finalist in the Wishing Shelf Awards.

In more recent years, Jordan embarked on a "cozy mystery" series, "The Augusta McKee Mysteries." Two of the eight books in the series were finalists in the Wishing Shelf Book Awards.

Articles by Jordan appeared in *Musical America* and *The Guardian*. In July of 2019, she was featured on "The Today Show, Hour Three," as a Super Senior, in recognition of someone over eighty years of age writing and self-publishing ten books in six years.

All of Jordan's books are "music-centric" and many readers comment on the strength of the element of music included in her work.

For more information, please visit her website at www.susanmoorejordan.com and her Amazon author page at http://ow.ly/XCjYX

If you have enjoyed

And This Shall Be for Music

please consider leaving a review

and rating at your

place of purchase.

These are extremely helpful

in letting other readers know

about the book, which is

important for indie authors!